FATAL DECREE

ALSO BY H. TERRELL GRIFFIN

Matt Royal Mysteries

Collateral Damage
Bitter Legacy
Wyatt's Revenge
Blood Island
Murder Key
Longboat Blues

Thrillers: 100 Must-Reads: Joseph Conrad, Heart of Darkness
(contributing essayist)

FATAL DECREE

A Matt Royal Mystery

H. Terrell Griffin

Oceanview Publishing
Longboat Key, Florida

This book is a work of fiction. Names, characters, businesses, organizations, places, and incidents either are the products of the author's imagination or are used fictitiously. Any resemblance to actual events, businesses, locales, or persons, living or dead, is entirely coincidental.

ISBN: 978-1-60809-070-9

Published in the United States of America by Oceanview Publishing, Longboat Key, Florida
www.oceanviewpub.com

2 4 6 8 10 9 7 5 3

PRINTED IN THE UNITED STATES OF AMERICA

For Jean,

Forever

ACKNOWLEDGMENTS

Some say that writing is a lonely business. I haven't found it so. I have too many friends involved in the process of writing and publishing to ever get lonely. I cannot thank them all, but there are a few who were particularly helpful in the project that became this book. To each of you, I send my deep gratitude for your advice, support, and friendship.

Bob and Pat Gussin, publishers who really care about their authors as people, not just profit centers. It is because of your vision and hard work that Oceanview Publishing has become a leader in its field. And to Susan Hayes, my proficient and invaluable editor.

Lieutenant James Forrest of the Sarasota County Sheriff's Office, a dedicated public servant, outstanding mystery writer, friend, and collaborator. I loved your jail.

Peggy Kendall and David Beals who have been patient and supportive in reading this book as it was written, and offering invaluable advice and editing. Peggy's gentle harping and butt kicking when I got lazy and slacked off writing impelled me to the finish. I hope she's happy with the product.

The ghosts of Miles Leavitt and John Allred, who hover closely when the story is building. The memories of their wit and good humor, their friendship, and their support serve as my muses.

My readers. I know that your time is valuable, and the knowledge that you spend part of it with my stories humbles me and makes me strive to never let you down. I love hearing from you. Your thoughts, ideas, and kind words sustain me.

The people of that earthly paradise known as Longboat Key, Florida, for sharing their stories and being my friends.

The baristas at the Starbucks in Maitland, Florida, who graciously juiced me with caffeine and smiles during the many months that I sat in a corner of their shop and keystroked this story into existence. Every establishment should have such friendly employees.

Finally, and foremost, Jean Higgins, the girl from Macon, Georgia, who became Jean Griffin when, despite all warnings, she married me while I was still a college student. She is a loving wife, mother, and grandmother, the family rock who supports us all with her eternal optimism. She is my closest buddy, the friend who understands me completely, and overlooks most of it. She edits my books, provides me with ideas for plot and character development, and listens as I run off at the mouth with story ideas that she says, with a grin, leak regularly from my sick mind. She makes even sunless days shine brightly.

FATAL DECREE

CHAPTER ONE

The corpse was floating at the edge of the channel that runs between Sister Key and its larger neighbor, Longboat Key. Only the back was visible above the surface, the body bent over as if tying a shoe, the head and feet submerged. It was moving north, its pace languid, matching that of the outgoing tidal current.

Carl Motes was out early that Saturday morning, cruising at first light toward the Coast Guard station in Cortez. He was commander of the U.S. Coast Guard Auxiliary Flotilla based on Longboat Key, a small island off the southwest coast of Florida. He planned to meet his crew, have breakfast in the station mess, and head out for a safety patrol on Sarasota Bay.

It was the first Saturday of fall, as it was measured in the temperate climes of Southwest Florida. Every year, between mid-October and early November, people wake up one morning and realize the humidity has dropped to the point that they don't break into a sweat simply by walking outside. Autumn has finally come to the peninsula, several weeks after the calendar suggested that summer had ended. The temperature will drop some more in the coming weeks, into the sixties and seventies. Occasionally, the cold fronts will move down from Canada and bring a chill to the subtropical air. But for the most part, the weather will be mild until the middle of May, when the humidity rises to levels that chase the less hardy back north.

Motes knew that the local boaters would be out in force on such a Saturday, rafting up on the sandbar just inside Longboat Pass or nosed onto Beer Can Island or fishing the offshore reefs in twenty feet of water or the back bay flats or tanking up at one of the local bars that provided docks for their boats. It was Motes's job to keep them safe, remind them to wear

their life jackets, and not drink too much. It was a fine day to be an auxiliaryman, and Carl was looking forward to his tour of duty.

Motes spent his weekdays as a law professor, but his weekends were
dedicated to his boat. He'd once been a fierce prosecutor, so was not un-
accustomed to death or even to murder. But that was far from his mind as
he steered his boat north along the narrow channel. The sun was hanging
low on the eastern horizon, the water calm. A commercial mullet fisherman
steered his boat across the flats separating the main channel from Longboat Key, his outboard emitting a high whine as he skimmed across the
surface of the water.

Carl's first view of the body was from the periphery of his right eye, a
quick impression of something out of the ordinary in the shallow water at
the edge of the Intracoastal channel. He had been scanning the water off
his bow, alert for any floating obstruction. The sight of the body registered
on his brain after his eyes had moved on toward the middle of the channel. His head jerked back to the right, and he pulled the throttles into neu-
tral. The boat, a thirty-foot center console with twin outboards, came off
plane and settled into the water.

The manatees were migrating into the bay, searching out warmer water
in which to spend the winter. They would travel south to the more temperate lagoon provided by the outfall of a power plant on the banks of the
Caloosahatchee River. Sometimes they didn't make it. They became victims of boat propellers or waited too long in the cold waters of the Gulf of
Mexico and died from injuries or pneumonia.

Motes sighed and eased his boat toward the carcass, saddened by another death of a gentle creature threatened with extinction. He'd get a line
on the body to secure it in place and call the dispatcher at the Cortez Coast
Guard station to deal with removing it.

Carl watched his depth sounder as he moved toward the body, careful of the bottom rising as he neared the edge of the channel. The carcass
was coming into focus. It was small for a manatee. Probably a baby, Carl
decided.

He was about ten feet from the body when a commercial fishing boat
lumbered down the channel behind him. Carl felt his boat rise as the wake
crossed under it, and watched as the wave continued, rolling over the body

and turning it so that a face emerged briefly from the water. This was no manatee. It was the body of a human. A woman, probably.

Carl knew better than to disturb what might be a crime scene. He picked up the microphone of his marine radio, hailed the Coast Guard station at Cortez and described what he was seeing. The Coast Guard radioman—actually a young woman on that quiet fall morning—advised that she would contact the Longboat Key police, since the body was within their jurisdiction. Motes said he would stand by.

"Don't disturb the body," said the voice on the radio.

"Roger that," answered Motes.

A few minutes passed. A twenty-foot boat with four men aboard, their fishing hats pulled tight on their heads, rods and reels in their holders, passed by, slowed, noticed the uniform Carl was wearing, and heeded his signal to move on. They pulled off the channel near the southern end of Sister Key and waited, curious about the man in the uniform standing guard over something in the water.

It was quiet on the bay. A slight breeze picked up, blowing from the north, rippling the surface of the lagoon that separated Longboat Key from Sister Key. The sun was moving higher in the sky, painting the scudding clouds with orange and gold. A siren whooped in the distance, the sound coming from the south. Birds rose suddenly from their nests in the mangroves, startled by the shrill discord. Motes watched as a police boat came toward him at top speed, its bow cutting angrily through the green water of the bay, blue lights flashing. The picture of urgency.

The police boat came off plane as it approached, the officer at the helm gently easing his vessel next to Motes. "Morning, Carl."

"Morning, Dennis. This looks bad."

"It sure does. I'll get the detective and a crime-scene unit out here. Can you stick around and help keep the gawkers out of the way?"

"No problem," said Motes. "I'll get another auxiliary boat out here to help."

CHAPTER TWO

Detective Jennifer Diane Duncan rolled over in her bed and snuggled down a little farther under the light blanket. The sound of a powerboat on the bay floated gently through the morning air, reminding her that she lived in a paradise. Daylight was seeping through the window blinds, but she didn't have to get up. It was her day off, and she planned nothing more adventuresome than a trip to the Publix Market on Avenue of the Flowers at mid-key. She'd invited Matt Royal and Jock Algren for dinner that evening and she had to feed them something other than wine and beer. She yawned and settled a little deeper into her blanket, the air-conditioning cooling the room to a comfortable sleeping temperature.

The sharp wail of a siren brought her upright in the bed. It was a police siren, a different tone than that of the paramedics and firefighters. The sound was coming from the bay just outside her windows. Either the Coast Guard or one of the police agencies. Some sort of emergency on the water.

She got out of bed and padded to the sunporch of her condo overlooking Sarasota Bay. She grabbed the binoculars from a table and scanned to the south. She saw the blue lights flashing on a boat coming at speed, running north on the Intracoastal. As the vessel got closer, she recognized it as the Longboat Key police boat. She watched as it came off plane and moved toward another boat that was dead in the water. What was going on?

She moved the glasses a bit, searching the area around the boats. Nothing. Then she spotted something in the water. She was too far away to make it out. A dead manatee, perhaps, or a dolphin. But why the siren, the urgency? That only came when a human being was involved. She raised the binoculars to look at the island across the lagoon from where she lived, scanning, trying to see if anything was there, her cop instincts, honed by fifteen years in the business, telling her that something was wrong out on the water. She could see the object floating near the boat, but nothing more. Still, the siren and the police boat added an ominous feel to the scene, and her internal alarm bells were clanging loudly.

J.D. put down the binoculars, rubbed her eyes, and went to the bathroom. She shucked the T-shirt she had slept in and stepped into the shower. She knew from experience that she wouldn't be going to Publix that day.

She was stepping out of the shower when her phone rang. The expected call. She answered. It was Deputy Chief of Police Martin Sharkey. He'd been running the night crew of late, going on patrol, enjoying himself. It beat the paper pushing that had come with the rank.

"J.D., you up?"

"Yes."

"There's a body in the water off Sister Key."

"Yeah. I saw it."

"You saw it?"

"Yes. From my sunporch. Anything suspicious about it?"

"Yeah. Dennis says there's a bullet hole in the back of her head."

"Her?"

"Definitely a woman. The body's nude. When you're ready, call Dennis on his cell, and he'll run over and pick you up at your dock."

"I'll meet him there in ten minutes. Can you call him while I get dressed?"

"Sure."

"And, Martin, put a total blackout on this one. At least until we can talk. I don't want a bunch of gawkers."

CHAPTER THREE

I slept in that morning. Jock Algren and I had made a night of it at Tiny's, the neighborhood bar, and we hadn't left until owner Susie Vaught shooed us out. I was a bit hungover, but it had been a fun evening. Jock had arrived from Houston in the late afternoon. He hadn't visited the island in several weeks and wanted to catch up on the gossip. He had a lot of friends on Longboat Key, and everybody wanted to buy him a drink. By the end of the evening, he was floating on a sea of O'Doul's, the nonalcoholic beer he fancied, and I had pretty much finished off Susie's stock of Miller Lite.

I was puttering around in the kitchen, brewing coffee and getting some breakfast pastries. I heard Jock's shower running and knew he'd be joining me in a few minutes. If he doesn't get his coffee right away, he gets a bit testy.

My name is Matt Royal. I live on Longboat Key, an island off the southwest coast of Florida, south of Tampa Bay, about halfway down the peninsula. My key is ten miles long and no more than a half-mile wide at its broadest point. If you leave the island on the south end, you cross a couple of bridges, wind your way around St. Armands Circle, one of the best dining and shopping venues in Florida, cross another couple of bridges and find yourself in Sarasota. On the north end you cross the Longboat Pass Bridge to Anna Maria Island, drive into the beach town of Bradenton Beach, turn right, cross the Cortez Bridge, and end up in the aging fishing village of Cortez.

I was a soldier once, an officer in the U.S. Army Special Forces, the storied Green Berets. I saw some action, came home, and went to law school. I had been a trial lawyer in Orlando for a number of years until I tired of the rat race, lost my wife to divorce, said the hell with it, sold everything I had, and moved to paradise. I wasn't wealthy, but if I lived carefully, I wouldn't have to work for the rest of my life.

I'm six feet tall, and weigh the same 180 pounds I did when I got out of the army. I have dark hair and a slightly off-center nose. I run four miles on the beach most days and work out weekly with a martial arts instructor. I find that I have to push myself a bit or I'll succumb to the indolence that seems to be a part of island living.

Longbeach Village is the official name of my neighborhood, but everybody just calls it "the village." It takes up the far north end of Longboat Key and is the oldest inhabited part of the island. Not counting the Indians, of course, who had lived there for hundreds of years before the Europeans showed up. There are no condos in the village, and most of the houses are small and quaint, owned by a lot of people just like me who could never have afforded the expensive mansions and condos that took up most of our island. I owned a cottage that backed up to Sarasota Bay, giving me a view out my sliding glass doors that made me glad to be a Floridian. I never tired of watching the seabirds that nested on nearby Jewfish Key and the myriad boats that plied the Intracoastal Waterway.

My doorbell rang. I looked at my watch. Ten o'clock. I was wearing cargo shorts, a T-shirt with the logo of an island restaurant long out of business, and boat shoes. I opened the door to find a beautiful woman standing on the stoop. She was about five feet seven, and this morning her shoulder-length dark hair was fashioned in a ponytail. She was slender, her body honed by years of regular workouts. Her face was a bit pale, her green eyes troubled, and tension lines were etched around her mouth. She was the Longboat Key police department's only detective, and she was my friend. She wore a pair of jeans, a golf shirt, and running shoes. "Come in, J.D.," I said. "Are you okay?"

She came through the door, looked at me, and said one word. "Coffee."

"Coming up. Sit down. I'll be right back."

Jennifer Diane Duncan, known as J.D., had come to our key a year before. Her mom had lived among us for the last several years of her life, and when she died, J.D. inherited her condo.

J.D. was in her late thirties and had joined the Miami-Dade Police Department after receiving a degree in Criminal Justice from Florida International University. She'd risen quickly through the ranks, and after a couple of years as a patrol officer, became the youngest detective on the force. She worked in the fraud division for a while and then moved to homicide where she eventually became the assistant commander of the unit.

When her mom died, J.D. saw an opportunity to leave the stress and danger of the big city and move to Longboat Key. Bill Lester, the chief of police on the key, had jumped at the chance to hire her as Longboat's only detective. She had moved into her mom's condo and quickly became a part of our island community and my good friend. So far, our relationship hadn't moved beyond the friendship stage, and maybe it never would. But, a guy can hope, can't he?

I returned from the kitchen with two mugs of black coffee and handed one to her. I didn't say anything. She was obviously troubled, and I knew her well enough to know she would tell me what she thought I needed to know. I took a seat next to her on the sofa. I waited.

J.D. sat quietly for a few moments, sipping her coffee. "Did you ever see a ghost, Matt?"

"No."

"I did. This morning."

"Want to talk about it?"

"Twelve years ago, when I first made detective in Miami, I worked three murders that had taken place in about a six-week period. We called them the whale tail murders. Or at least, the press did. You know how they like to sensationalize everything. The cops picked it up."

"Each of the women was middle aged or older, and they were found naked and bound to trees with ropes. Shot in the back of the head by the same twenty-two-caliber pistol. They were always found near water, once a lake, another time on the Miami River, and the third time in the Everglades in the western part of the county. We were dealing with a serial killer with big-time issues, and we put a lot of effort into finding the guy."

"Did you get him?"

"No. The killings stopped. There were only those three women. The killer was very careful. He didn't leave any evidence behind, and we even had a hard time identifying the women. Turned out that one was a maid at a high-rise office building, another was a prostitute, and the third was the wife of an accountant who lived in Miami Lakes. We never found any connection between the women. Except that they all had a similar appearance. Caucasian, fairly tall, between forty and fifty-five, shoulder-length hair dyed blonde."

"Why the name, whale tail?"

"That was very strange. The killer pinned an identical small silver whale tail earring through the lobe of his victims' left ears. The medical examiner said they were all done postmortem. We never figured out if the killer was trying to tell us something or if the whale tail had some deep meaning for him. Even the profilers couldn't come up with anything that made any sense."

"And the press got hold of that little detail?"

"Yeah. One of the reporters interviewed the husband of the first victim. He mentioned that she did not own any jewelry that looked like a whale tail."

"Maybe the killer moved on. Started all over in another town."

"We checked periodically and our murders were described in detail in a federal database so that if any similar murders cropped up, the investigators could get hold of us. There was never a similar murder. Anywhere."

"What does this have to do with the ghost you saw this morning?"

"It was another woman about the same age and appearance and she had a whale tail earring in her left earlobe."

"Copycat?"

"No. There was one item we never released to the press and didn't put on the federal database. The killer had carved initials into the back of the neck of each of the victims. Again, postmortem. They were covered by the women's hair and were picked up by the Miami-Dade medical examiner on the first autopsy. The same initials on all three women. KKK."

"The Ku Klux Klan?" I asked.

"We didn't think so. All the women were white and of European descent. No reason to think the guy was a Klansman."

"What did the profiler think?"

"She didn't have a clue. Thought it might just be something to distract us."

"And you found the same initials on the woman this morning."

"Yes. It was the first thing I looked for."

"Where was the body?" I asked.

"Floating just off the channel that runs on the west side of Sister Key."

"Didn't you say that the whale tail killer tied them to a tree near the water?"

"Yes, and apparently he did this one that way. We found a rope tied around her torso. The end was frayed, so we assumed she had been tied up at some point, and the rope broke. It wasn't cut. Maybe the tide came up and tugged her into the water, putting a strain on the line."

"Has she been identified yet?" I asked.

"Not yet. The M.E. will take her fingerprints and we'll see what they come up with. I'll go through the missing person reports for Sarasota and Manatee counties and see if anything's there. Sooner or later, we'll know something."

"Any thoughts?"

"She may have been a Longboater. She was nude, but she had recently had a manicure and a pedicure and she wore a diamond-encrusted wedding band on her ring finger. We don't have any idea where she was killed or where her body was put in the water. The tide was going out this morning, so she could have been swept along from farther up the bay."

"I doubt that," I said.

"Doubt what?"

"That she was dumped farther up the bay. She would probably have caught on one of the shoals that are just south of the channel down where it turns east. That tidal current moves slowly. If she'd been put in the water farther out in the bay, say up around marker seventeen, the deep water would have kept her moving, but she would have probably been pushed into the shallows on the east side of Sister Key."

"You know this water a lot better than I do. Where do you think she went in?"

"Probably no farther south than Emerald Harbor." I was talking about an upscale subdivision that fronted on Sarasota Bay a couple of miles south of the village. "Did you check the tables to see when the tide turned this morning?"

"No. I'll do that when I get back to the station."

"I'll check online," I said.

Jock came into the room dressed in a Hawaiian shirt and pressed beige shorts, sandals on his feet. He stands six feet tall and has the wiry build of a distance runner. His mostly bald head is fringed with dark hair, a vestige of his youth. His skin is as tan as a beach bum's, the result of the many hours he spends in tropical climes doing the work of his employer, a U.S government intelligence agency that is so secret it doesn't even have a name. He smelled of expensive aftershave.

Jock Algren and I had met when we were children, growing up in a small town in the middle of the Florida peninsula. We'd become best friends, and over the many years since we'd graduated from high school, we'd maintained a close relationship. Our friendship had survived the years and the miles of separation, and we were closer than brothers. J.D. stood and hugged him.

"That's what I came for," said Jock. "How're you doing, J.D.?"

"Not good." She filled Jock in on what she'd told me.

"J.D.," I said, "the tide crested this morning at three a.m. I can't do the math, but I'd think that would have given the body time to drift from the area of Emerald Harbor. The flats in front of your condo would have been covered with plenty of water at high tide so that she wouldn't have gotten snagged on the shoals. But I don't think she could have been put in the water much farther south. She wouldn't have drifted this far north in the amount of time after the tide started out."

"That's helpful," she said. "I'll have some people start canvassing Emerald Harbor to see if anybody knows anything."

"I guess dinner is off for tonight," I said.

"Do you mind?"

I shook my head. I knew she'd be busy. The first few hours of a murder investigation were crucial. J.D. would work through the day and evening, running down any leads she could find. The medical examiner would put this one at the head of the line, and evidence would trickle into the detective's office. By nightfall, she would hopefully have the beginnings of a solution, or at least the outlines of one.

"I'll make it up to you guys," she said. "Soon."

"Anything we can do to help?" I asked.

J.D. smiled, shook her head, drank down the last of her coffee, and left.

CHAPTER FOUR

I poured more coffee, and Jock and I moved out to the patio. It was quiet at mid-morning as we sat and sipped and watched the pelicans dive for breakfast in the bay.

Jock grinned. "You're not getting any closer to her, are you, podna?"

"We're just friends."

"And you're okay with that?"

"It's not like I have a choice. But, yeah, I'm okay with it."

"I thought you had put everything out on the table for her."

"I did. Sort of. We had a conversation one night at Mar Vista, but it was kind of vague. I think she has some feelings for me, but not like I do for her. She's never brought it up again, and, frankly, I'm afraid to mention it. I don't want to scare her off."

"Are we going fishing?" he asked.

"Finish your coffee and let's go."

A T-dock jutted from my backyard into the bay. My boat, *Recess*, a twenty-eight-foot Grady-White walk-around fishing machine with a small cabin and twin 250-horsepower Yamaha outboard engines, rested against the pilings at the end of the pier.

We loaded the gear on *Recess* and pulled away from the dock. We went to Annie's at the foot of the Cortez Bridge, bought bait and beer, and headed for a man-made reef about seven miles off shore. The seas were flat and we made good time. We fished for a couple of hours and didn't catch anything worth keeping. We gave up and ran back to the Mar Vista Pub for lunch.

We decided to try fishing the bay in the afternoon, but were no more successful than we'd been in the morning. We were about to give it up for the day when my cell phone sounded the first few bars of *The Girl from Ipanema,* the special ringtone I'd assigned to J.D.

"Isn't Gene Alexander a friend of yours?" she asked.

"Sure is. Why?"

"The lady we found this morning was his wife, Nell."

"Shit."

"It looks as if your tidal calculations might be right. He lives in Emerald Harbor, but he's not at home. Any idea where he might be?"

"He and Les Fulcher went to Alaska on a fishing trip last week. I think they're due in tonight."

"Thanks, Matt. I guess I'll have to wait to notify him."

"I've got his cell phone number if you want it."

"I'll wait. That's not the kind of news you give somebody over the phone. Besides, if he's already on his way home, he's probably on a plane. I'll meet him at the airport tonight."

"Any other developments?" I asked.

"Nothing much. The cause of death was a gunshot to the back of the head. Small caliber. The slug was still in her brain. She never knew what hit her."

"That's the good news, I guess."

"I guess. We'll see if ballistics can match this slug to any other murders in the state. The lab is working on that now."

"You want some dinner?" I asked.

"Afraid not. I've got a lot of work to do tonight."

"You've got to eat sometime."

"What did you have in mind?"

"Meet us at Moore's. We're in Palma Sola Bay, fishing. It's almost five now. We can be there by six."

"Okay. A quick grouper sandwich and I'm back to work."

Moore's Stone Crab Restaurant has clung to the edge of Sarasota Bay for more than forty years, serving up large helpings of seafood, much of it caught earlier that day by the restaurant's own boats. The stone crabs had just come into season, and the place was packed. Jock and I took seats at the U-shaped bar that was separated by a wall from the restaurant proper.

A large stuffed tarpon dominated the west wall of the bar, a bottle of Jack Daniel's Black Label stuck spout first into its mouth. The north wall was mirrored and TV sets perched in their brackets in each corner, both tuned to a sports channel. Large windows were set into the south wall, giving a view twelve miles down the bay to the city of Sarasota.

My friend Debbie no longer worked there, and I missed her every time I came into the place. She'd gotten married at the end of the summer to a man who owned a small chain of movie theaters in the Midwest.

They'd moved to Lakewood Ranch out east of I-75, and Debbie was managing a high-end restaurant in the small village that catered to the wealthy retirees who had bought the homes that bordered the golf courses. I'd had dinner with the happy couple the week before and kept up with her through regular e-mails.

Barbara had taken Debbie's place behind the bar and was fast making friends of all the regulars. She put a Miller Lite in front of me, and I introduced her to Jock. He ordered and she went for his O'Doul's.

"I gathered from your phone call with J.D. that you knew the lady they found in the bay," Jock said.

"I've only met her a time or two, but I know her husband, Gene Alexander. He's a friend of Les Fulcher."

"Shit." Jock pulled his cell phone from his pants pocket and punched a button, waited, then, "Dave, did Gene Alexander retire to Longboat Key, Florida?" Silence. "Yeah. I think his wife's been killed. I'll call you back when I know more." He hung up.

"What is it, Jock?" I asked.

"Alexander was one of ours."

"He worked for your agency?"

"Yes. Can't be two Gene Alexanders on this island. Does the guy you know have just one leg?"

"Yeah. He lost a battle with a land mine in Vietnam. He wears a prosthesis though, and if he has on long pants, you'd never know it."

"Gene was one of our analysts. A damn good one, too. Worked for us for thirty years and retired. I heard that he'd moved here last year. I was planning to look him up for a beer this trip."

"Did you know his wife?" I asked.

"I've known her for years, but it was more of an office wife sort of thing. We never socialized. It just wasn't the kind of thing you do in an agency like ours. I worked a lot with Gene. He had an eye for the unusual blips in all the intel that came across his desk. He saved my ass more than once by keeping me a step ahead of the opposition. Did you say Gene was in Alaska?"

"Yeah. He and Les Fulcher went out there on a fly-fishing trip. Due back this evening."

"Some homecoming. I wonder if J.D. would let me go with her to notify Gene."

"Ask her."

J.D. was walking through the door that separated the bar from the restaurant. She looked tired and a little sad. Murder was a rarity in our island world, but she'd seen a lot of it in the years she'd worked homicide for the Miami-Dade Police Department. It wasn't something anybody ever got used to. She took a seat on the stool between us, the one we'd saved for her.

Barb came over with a glass of white wine. "Hey, J.D.," she said. "I heard about the murder over near Sister Key. I guess you've been busy today."

J.D. gave her a sad smile. "Unfortunately, yes. And my day isn't over, so I'll have to make do with this one glass. Can we move over to that table?" She pointed to a four top by the windows.

"Sure."

We took our drinks to the table. J.D. said, "I wanted to talk about today, but I didn't want the whole bar to hear about it. Lord knows, news travels fast enough on this island as it is."

"J.D.," Jock said, "I know Gene Alexander." He explained the relationship to his agency and told her that they'd worked together a number of times over the years. "I'd like to go with you to make the notification."

"I don't see why not," J.D. said. "He and Les are due into Sarasota-Bradenton at ten thirty tonight."

"Do you know any more than you did this morning?" I asked.

"Not much. Other than the identification. The autopsy confirmed that she died from a gunshot to the head. The bullet was still there, a twenty-two-caliber, light load. It was meant to kill, but not exit the body. The ballistics guy called me a few minutes ago. Said the bullet came from the same gun that killed the three women in Miami twelve years ago."

"Are you thinking the same killer?" I asked.

"I don't know. The killings in Miami had a ritual feel to them. This one looks more like a crime of opportunity. Same gun, same signature, but it's the only one in twelve years. It might be a copycat, but I can't explain the initials on the back of Nell's neck."

"What does Miami-Dade think?" I asked.

"Not much. They're stumped. The twelve-year gap is the puzzler. They're going back through cases and trying to see if anybody we looked at then might have been in prison for the past twelve years and just got out. They're also checking on people I put away for other crimes. See if anybody who might hold a grudge is out now."

"But you don't think it's the same guy," I said.

"Who knows? But, this killing fits the pattern of the ones in Miami. The victim's appearance generally matched the whale tail victims. Lots of circular thinking here."

"Maybe you just don't want to see the pattern." I said. "If it's the same murderer, why place a body where you were sure to be involved in the investigation?"

She just looked at me. Like I'd said what she'd been thinking, but didn't want to acknowledge.

"Were you involved in those cases in Miami?" I asked.

"Mostly on the periphery of the investigation. I was a rookie detective and did some of the legwork, but that was all."

Jock said, "Could there be a connection to you?"

"Maybe. We finally found the other end of the rope tied to a tree on Sister Key."

"So the body didn't drift up from Emerald Harbor," I said.

"No. She'd been tied to a tree right across from my condo. If the rope hadn't broken, I would have been able to see the body from my place."

"You worked the case in Miami," said Jock, "even if you were only involved a little. What if Nell's murder was a signal to you? The killer would have known that the ballistics lab would connect the gun to the killings in Miami."

"I guess that's a possibility, but it seems a little far-fetched," she said.

"Even so," said Jock, "if the body today was meant for you for some reason, I'd think the people you ought to be looking at are ones you put away."

"Do you think it's a coincidence that the body was left near your condo?" I asked.

"That'd be one hell of a coincidence," said Jock.

"I agree with Jock," said J.D., "but why now? It's been a long time. I don't think the killer's been asleep for the past dozen years."

"Have you had anything unusual happen in the past few days?" Jock asked.

"Not really. If this was meant for me somehow, the murderer must have gone to some length to find out where I live. Cops aren't listed in your usual databases."

"Matt," Barb called from behind the bar, "do you guys want to eat?"

I nodded and she brought three menus to the table. We gave her our order, and she disappeared into the kitchen.

Jock said, "I've got to make a call," and stepped out onto the lanai that overlooked the bay.

"Where do you go from here?" I asked J.D.

"I'll talk to the victim's husband. See if he knows something that can give us a starting point. We didn't turn up anything at Emerald Harbor."

"Is there anything I can do?"

She smiled. "No. Just be ready to put up with a stressed-out cop."

"Is there any other kind?"

"Some days are worse than others."

"I'm concerned about you being a target of some kind of psychopath."

"I'm probably not. We'll find the connection to the gun, and maybe that'll give us Nell's killer. Stop worrying."

Jock rejoined us. "J.D., I've been on the phone with Dave Kendall, my director. He said that our agency will do whatever we can to help. We're at your disposal."

"I appreciate that, but I don't think this has anything to do with your agency." J.D. said.

"Dave's not convinced of that. Even if it isn't connected to the agency, Gene is one of ours, and Dave wants the son of a bitch who killed his wife."

J.D. smiled. "Jock, I think you might be one of those crazy conspiracy theorists. You're trying to decide whether the killer is after me or your agency. It's probably neither. Just a random crime."

Jock chuckled. "My work tends to bring out the paranoia, but it's saved my butt a bunch of times."

"We'll see," said J.D.

Barb brought our food and took another drink order. J.D. asked for iced tea. Our conversation turned to island gossip, the weather, the Tampa Bay Buccaneers, the beauty of our view down the bay as the lights of downtown Sarasota began to wink on, responding to the gathering darkness. We were trying to empty our minds of dark thoughts of murder and the damage it would do to a good man who would live the rest of his life without the woman he loved.

It was a little past seven when we left the restaurant. The sun was gone and darkness was enveloping our island, moving rapidly from east to west. A slight chill rode the onshore breeze that ruffled the water of the bay. A gull cackled somewhere in the distance, a dog barked in response, and then the quiet of an early evening surrounded us. We stood on the shell parking lot next to J.D.'s unmarked police car. She said, "I'm going home to a hot shower and a change of clothes."

"Do you want me to meet you at your place?" asked Jock.

"No. I'll pick you up at Matt's in about an hour. Maybe I'll have something more from Miami by then."

Her cell phone rang. She looked at the caller ID. "Blocked," she said. "It's probably Sharkey." She answered, was quiet for a moment, and then closed the phone. She had a look on her face, grim determination maybe, or anger. I couldn't tell.

"What?" I asked.

"I think it was the killer."

That brought me up short. "What did he say?"

"He said, 'You're next, bitch. Or maybe not. But later.'"

"Those were his exact words?" Jock asked.

"Exactly." She pulled a notebook from her purse and wrote down the quote.

"J.D.," I said, "this is serious. Take Jock with you tonight. I'll take the boat home."

"Don't, Matt," she said with an edge to her voice. "I'm not some freak-ing meter maid. I'm a cop. I've got a gun. I can shoot. I hope the bastard does come after me. It'll be the last time he tries to kill a woman."

I'd forgotten for a moment how steely she could be. She was a woman making it in what had traditionally been a man's job. She took my com-ment as an insult. "Sorry, Detective," I said. "I know you can take care of yourself. But I still worry about you."

She softened a little, her face relaxing, and a smile beginning to play around her mouth. "Don't," she said. "But I'm glad you do. I'll see you in an hour." She kissed me on the cheek, got in her car, and drove off.

"You're making progress, podna," said Jock. "You'll notice that she didn't kiss me."

"Yeah," I said, "but you're butt ugly."

Still, I had noticed and wondered if the kiss meant anything.

CHAPTER FIVE

Jock and I ran the boat up the lagoon to my cottage. I pulled her into the dock, secured the lines, and washed her down with fresh water while Jock cleaned our fishing gear. I flushed both engines, turned off the dock lights, and we went to the house. I fixed a pot of coffee, thinking we might have a long night. I didn't know what to expect when Jock and J.D. gave Gene the news of his wife's death.

J.D. knocked on the front door and stuck her head inside. I waved her in. She had changed into what she called her detective uniform, navy slacks, white golf shirt with the Longboat Key Police badge embroidered on the pocket, and the belt with her Sig Sauer, pepper spray, cuffs, Taser, and God knows what else hanging off it. "Want some coffee?" I asked.

"Sure. I'll get it."

I heard her rummaging around in the kitchen, and in a few minutes she reappeared with a steaming cup of coffee. "Where's Jock?"

"In the shower."

"I'm glad he's going with me. I hate these notifications. They always change somebody's life. And never in a good way."

"Gene will tough it out. He was a company commander in Vietnam. Had to write a lot of letters to parents telling them that their son had been killed in action. He once told me that was the hardest part of his job. Sometimes the kid had been cowering in a hole, too scared to even fire his weapon, and a grenade or a stray shot or a mortar round took him out. Gene always told the parents that their kid died a hero."

"Maybe," said J.D., "just being there doing his job was heroic."

"I guess so. They were all heroes. Every damn one of them."

"One of whom?" asked Jock, coming into the living room.

"Soldiers," J.D. said.

"Yeah," said Jock. "Yeah."

"Miami-Dade called," said J.D. "They can't find a connection between anybody I put away and the whale tail killer. Most of the ones I arrested early in my career were small-time hoodlums who did a couple of years and came home. The later ones, from when I was in homicide, are either still in prison or dead. One was executed and a couple of others died of natural causes. Probably of sheer meanness. I think that's a disease."

"Were you able to backtrack the number of whoever called you with the threat?" I asked.

"Yeah. It was to a disposable cell phone. A dead end. The phone was bought in Miami a couple of months ago. But the call pinged off a cell tower in Bradenton. So the guy's here."

"Any thoughts on how he got your number?" asked Jock.

"Good question. That number was issued to the Longboat Police Department. The phone isn't supposed to be used except for department business. When I call out on it, the number is blocked on the receiving end's caller ID. I can't figure out how he got the number, but the fact that it was issued to the department got us some quick action from the phone company. Martin Sharkey is going to look into it tomorrow. See if he can figure out how that number got into the hands of this jerk."

Jock looked at his watch. "You ready to roll, J.D.?" He was dressed in his traveling clothes: black silk shirt, black trousers, black socks, and black Italian loafers. All black. Appropriate, I thought.

"Yeah. Let's get this over with."

They left through the front door, leaving me alone with my thoughts. Which were bleak.

CHAPTER SIX

The terminal at Sarasota-Bradenton International Airport was quiet. The hands of the large clock in the gatehouse moved slowly toward ten thirty. The plane coming down from Atlanta was the last of the day, and the concourse was eerily deserted. A cleaning woman pushed her cart from trash can to trash can, making the last pickup of the evening. An airline employee stood at the gatehouse counter stacking papers.

J.D. and Jock had shown their credentials to the TSA agent at the security desk, explained their purpose, and were allowed to wait at the gate for Gene Alexander and Les Fulcher. Their message would change Gene's life forever. He was expecting to be met by his wife, but would run headlong into the worst news he'd ever heard.

It was not J.D.'s first death notification, but they never got easier. She paced the small waiting area, while Jock sat dourly, lost in his thoughts. The plane nosed into the gate, and the passengers began to deplane. They emerged from the jetway, hunched with fatigue, carrying their bags, and hurrying to home or hotel or vacation condo. Jock watched them, remembering the many nights when he had trudged off a plane in some town far from home.

J.D. stood quietly, tense, as if gathering the courage to plow unbidden into a stranger's life and wreak the havoc that she knew her news would bring. She jerked a little as she recognized Les coming into the gatehouse. The man walking with him was stocky with a head full of iron-gray hair and a face burned by the Alaskan sun. He stood about five feet eight, several inches shorter than Les.

She moved toward the line of passengers, Jock following close behind. "Les," she said quietly as she approached.

"J.D.," he said, "what are you doing here this late?"

"I need to talk to Mr. Alexander."

Les was standing still now, his instincts telling him that something was not right. He'd been a firefighter for a long time, and he knew about tragedy. He knew the look on the faces of those who carried bad news. He knew something was terribly wrong. "Gene," he said, "this is Detective J. D. Duncan, Longboat Key Police."

"Hello, Gene," said Jock, moving up beside J.D.

A look of recognition and surprise crossed Alexander's face. "Jock Algren. My God. What brings you here?"

"It's bad, Gene. Les, would you mind checking on the luggage while J.D. and I talk to Gene?"

"No problem. Let me know if you need me."

"Mr. Alexander," said J.D., "let's sit."

They walked to a corner of the gatehouse. Alexander was worried, his face suddenly devoid of color. "What's up, Jock?"

"Sit here, Mr. Alexander," said J.D.

He took a seat. She sat beside him. Jock stood, his arms at his side, almost as if he were at attention.

"Mr. Alexander," J.D. said, "there's no easy way to tell you this. Your wife died last night. I'm so sorry."

"What? Died? How? When?"

"She was murdered, Mr. Alexander. We don't know why or who did it, but we'll find him. I promise."

He looked up at Jock, bewildered, the shock setting in. "Why are you here, Jock? Was this related to the agency in some way?"

"We have no reason to believe that, Gene. I was here visiting a friend when I heard about Nell's death. I talked to the director. He's put the agency at your disposal. I don't think it was related, but we'll do everything in our power to help the police catch the bastard who killed her."

"Son of a bitch," Alexander said quietly. He swiped a hand over his eyes, brushing away tears. "Son of a bitch. Where did you find her? I called her when we changed planes in Seattle and again from Atlanta. She didn't answer. I figured she just left her cell phone somewhere."

"Her body was in the bay near Sister Key," said J.D. "She wasn't killed there, and we don't know where it happened. When was the last time you talked to her?"

"Last night. About six o'clock Sarasota time."

"Did she mention any plans for the evening?"

"She said something about going out to eat, but I didn't get any details."

"Any idea about where she might have gone?"

"Not really. She would probably have stayed on the key, or maybe the Circle, but I don't know for sure."

St. Armands Circle is an upscale shopping and dining area on the next key south of Longboat. The islands are connected by a bridge. If Nell had been to one of the restaurants there or on Longboat, the police could probably figure it out. November was not a big month for tourists or snowbirds, so most of the customers would be locals.

"How did you find her?" asked Alexander.

J.D. told him. About the body in the water, the bullet to the head, the early morning discovery by a Coast Guard auxiliaryman. She didn't tell him about the connection to the Miami killings.

"She didn't suffer, then," said Alexander. More a prayer than a statement.

"We don't think so, Mr. Alexander," J.D. said. "We'll talk some more in the morning. I'd like for our crime-scene investigator to go over your house before you go back in. Would that be all right with you?"

"Why the house? Do you think she was killed there?"

"It's a possibility. We want to be thorough."

"You're welcome to take a look at it."

"Can you spend the night with Les?" J.D. asked. "I'd like to have our crime-scene guy go through the house first thing in the morning."

"I'm sure we can work that out."

"Do you need anything? A ride? Can I call a family member?"

"No. Les left his car in long-term parking, so we'll make do. And there is no family. We never had children. It was just the two of us."

They left the gatehouse and walked the empty concourse past security and went down the escalator to the baggage claim area. "Wait here, Gene," Jock said. "Les and I'll get the car."

Jock told Les about the murder as they walked to the lot. He didn't go into details, nor did he mention the connection to Miami. That would all come in good time. Les said he'd be happy to have Gene as a houseguest for as long as needed.

CHAPTER SEVEN

The next morning was Sunday, and the island slept in. J.D. had dropped Jock off at my cottage shortly after midnight and went home to sleep. She was going to meet us for breakfast at the Blue Dolphin at ten.

As we drove down the key, I spotted two auto carriers parked in stacking lanes on Gulf of Mexico Drive, unloading the cars shipped south by their owners. They were harbingers of the approaching season, serving much the same purpose as the robins of spring in the Midwest, preparing us for the change in weather and putting us on notice that the snowbirds, those northerners who spend every winter on our island, were returning.

The Blue Dolphin was full of locals, many coming from early Mass or getting ready for the morning services at the Protestant churches on the island. Others, like Jock and me, were simply starting another day in the soft sunshine of early November, planning a fishing trip or a beach walk or a round of golf. The murder was the topic of conversation at most of the tables. Both the St. Petersburg and Sarasota papers had put the story on the front page of their Sunday editions, leaving out the details. Murder did not come to our mellow island with any regularity, and the mental image of a body floating in the bay unsettled everyone. The fact that many in the Blue Dolphin that morning knew Nell Alexander made the crime more personal, and thus, more frightening.

Jock and I took an empty table and waited for J.D. She'd called just as we were parking to tell me that she was running a few minutes late. We drank coffee as Jock told me more about his evening at the airport. He planned to call Gene Alexander later in the day to see if there was anything he needed.

J.D. arrived and took a seat. She looked beat, as if she had not slept well. "Sorry to be late," she said. "I've been at the station since eight. The forensics people started at the Alexander home at daybreak. Place was clean. Wherever Nell was killed, it wasn't inside her house."

"That should make things a little easier for Gene," said Jock. "Have you called him?"

"Yes. He's probably home by now. Another thing. There was no sign of her BMW at the house."

A server came to the table with a pot of coffee, filled our cups, and poured one for J.D. "I guess you've been busy, J.D.," the server said. "Nell was a fine lady and one of our regulars."

"We'll find the guy, Jeanine," said J.D. We placed our order and Jeanine left for the kitchen.

"Did the newspapers have Nell's name?" I asked.

"No. Just that an unidentified woman had been found dead near Sister Key. The island grapevine apparently knows about Nell, though."

"News travels fast on the key," I said.

J.D. laughed. "I'm still getting used to that. We may have gotten our first break in the case. We got a call early this morning from a delivery captain in Tampa. He read about the murder in the St. Pete paper."

"Was he any help?" I knew that some people who read stories of murder want to be part of the action and will thrust themselves into it, sometimes making up evidence to enhance their value to law enforcement.

"Actually, he was. He was bringing a yacht up from Naples, heading for Tampa on the Intracoastal. There was no moon and he was moving slowly in the dark, using his spotlight to find the markers. His beam caught a boat pulled into the mangroves near the south end of Sister Key about three o'clock Saturday morning. The same area where we found the body."

I was skeptical. "Why would an experienced captain be on the inside?" I asked. "He could make much better time out in the Gulf."

"I asked him about that," said J.D. "He said there were storms way out that night and the swells were pretty huge. He didn't want to take any chances on damaging the boat, so he came inside at Boca Grande pass."

"That makes sense," I said. "Were there storms in the Gulf Saturday?"

"I checked. He was right about the high seas. We even got a little more erosion up by the North Shore Road beach access."

"Did he have any details about the boat at Sister Key?" Jock asked.

"He said it was a flats boat, probably a twenty footer with a poling platform. There were no lights showing, which made the captain take a closer look. There was a man in the boat with a fishing rod who waved at the captain, so he figured it was just some fool who didn't have enough sense to turn on his anchor light."

"Any description of the man in the boat?" I asked.

"No. Just that he was white. He was wearing a baseball cap, shorts, and a T-shirt. Nothing more definitive."

"That could be our guy," said Jock. "Any chance of finding the boat?"

"Needle in a haystack," said J.D. "A boat generally fitting the description the captain gave me was stolen Friday night from a lift behind a home up on Bimini Bay."

"Where's that?" asked Jock.

"North end of Anna Maria Island," I said. "The killer probably set the boat adrift somewhere when he finished with it. It might turn up."

Jock said, "If the killer stole the boat from Bimini Bay, he would have had to have some way to get there. Assuming he's working alone, he could have left his car somewhere nearby, walked in, stolen the boat, and taken off. But how would he get back to his car? Wouldn't it make sense for him to take the boat back to near where his car was parked?"

"How would he have gotten the body into the boat?" asked J.D.

"Maybe he left the body somewhere near the water where he could bring the boat after he stole it," said Jock. "Load her up and head for Sister Key."

J.D. nodded. "That makes some sense, but where could he have left the body so that nobody would find it while he was stealing the boat? Matt, you know this area better than we do. Any ideas?"

"There're lots of places to put a body for a few hours at night. Most anywhere along the beach, a lot of places on the bay. It'd be impossible to search all of them."

J.D. frowned. "Well, that's a dead end, I guess."

Jeanine brought our breakfast and we ate quietly. I finished my eggs and toast and sat back with a fresh cup of coffee in my hand. "Assuming the boat the delivery captain saw was our bad guy," I said, "we have a pretty definite time for the body being tied to the tree on Sister Key. If we can find out where she had dinner and when she left the restaurant, we'll be able to get a window of time for the murder."

"Yes," said J.D. "We'll have officers canvassing the restaurants on the key and the Circle as soon as they open. Maybe we'll get lucky."

Jock looked toward the door and grinned. "Look who's here. Our man Sammy."

Sam Lastinger was coming through the door, talking to a couple walking with him. I watched as he came inside, wave to a family sitting in one of the booths, and say something to the couple with him. They both laughed and Sam came our way, splitting off from the couple who moved to a table near the front door.

"Jock, you old bastard. When did you get here?"

Jock stood, hugged Sam, and said, "Couple of days ago. How've you been?"

Sam laughed. "Look at me. It doesn't get any better than this."

Sam was the bartender at Pattigeorge's, an upscale restaurant that sat on the bay at mid-key. The bar was always packed with locals and, during the season, snowbirds. Sammy knew them all and introduced the newcomers. His personality made for a friendly bar. He was about forty years old, stood six feet tall, had dark hair, a permanent grin, and an engaging laugh. He was perennially happy.

"Sit down," I said.

He pulled up a chair and motioned for the waitress. She came and took his order. Coffee and a muffin. "I thought you guys might have been in last night. We had a full bar."

"J.D. got busy," I said. "Did you hear about the murder?"

"Terrible thing. Nell was in my bar Friday night. Must have gotten killed right after she left."

J.D.'s coffee cup stopped midway between the table and her mouth. "What time was she there?"

Sam thought for a minute. "I'd say she came in about nine. Had dinner at the bar. Stayed for a couple of drinks. She probably left around eleven."

"Who else was there?" asked J.D.

"The bar was packed. Usual crowd, and Miles Leavitt, of course. He's there every night. Miles closed me up and went with me to the Haye Loft for a drink with Eric."

"Any strangers? Somebody you didn't know?" asked J.D.

"Just a couple of tourists Billy Brugger sent down from the Hilton."

"Did either of them talk to Nell?"

"No. They were at the opposite end of the bar."

"Who was Nell talking to?"

Sam was quiet for a beat. "Miles mostly. He had a load on and you know how that goes. He was explaining world economics to her, I think. Or maybe it was the South American llama trade. After a lot of Scotch, he becomes an expert on all kinds of things."

J.D. laughed. Miles was a favorite character on the island and a good friend.

"Wait a minute," Sam said. "There *was* a guy who sat next to her after Miles moved down the bar to talk to Mike and Cyndi Seamon."

"Did you know him?"

"No. But I introduced myself to him when he came in. He told me his name was Craig. No last name."

"Did he tell you what he was doing on Longboat?"

"No. He wasn't too friendly. He talked to Nell for a few minutes and left. Didn't finish his beer. I figured she blew him off."

"Can you describe him?"

"Pretty standard-issue tourist," Sam said. "Light-colored shorts, tropical patterned shirt, loafers, no socks."

"Tall, short, white, black, hair color?"

"He was white and about my height, sandy hair, a little long, kind of hanging over his ears. And he had some ink on his arms. Looked like an amateur had done it. It was faded, like it'd been there a while."

"Prison tattoos?"

"I don't know what prison tats look like."

"Can you describe them?"

"Not really. They were mostly letters, but they didn't make sense. They weren't words, but I only saw his arms below the elbow. Could have been better work on his upper arms."

"What time did he leave?" J.D. asked.

Sam thought for a moment. "It must have been a little before eleven, because Nell left a few minutes later."

"How did he pay?"

"Cash."

"How about Nell?"

"Credit card. VISA, I think."

"Would that have a time stamp on it?"

Sam smiled. "It sure would. The time would be in the register at the bar."

"Did Nell pay just before she left?"

"She did," said Sam. "As soon as she signed the receipt, she told me goodbye and walked out the door."

"Can we get to the register this morning?"

"Sure."

CHAPTER EIGHT

As it turned out, Sam was off by seventeen minutes. Nell had left the bar at 11:17. We now had a rough timeline. Nell was killed sometime between 11:17 on Friday night and approximately 3:00 on Saturday morning when the delivery captain spotted the flats boat in the mangroves. If that was the boat that carried Nell's body to Sister Key.

"Can I get you guys something to drink?" asked Sam, as he leaned over the polished mahogany bar. We had caravanned to Pattigeorge's, Jock riding with me, J.D. in her personal Camry, and Sammy on his Vespa. The place was quiet, deserted except for us. Sammy had pulled up the information on the computer and given J.D. the printout showing the date and time of Nell's last credit card charge.

"Got some coffee?" I asked.

"I'll make some," said Sam. "Anybody else?"

"Coffee all around," I said.

Sam went to the kitchen. "Any ideas?" I asked.

"That description fits about half the people on the island," said J.D.

"Except for the prison tats, if that was what they were," said Jock.

"There's that," said J.D., just as her cell phone rang. She opened it. "Duncan." She was quiet for a few moments. "Okay. Thanks, Martin."

She closed the phone. "A Manatee County deputy found a car this morning in the Bimini Bay neighborhood about a block from where the boat was stolen on Friday night. One of the neighbors called it in. Said it had been sitting there since yesterday morning when they got out of bed. Turns out, the car was stolen in Tampa on Friday."

"Any prints or anything?" Jock asked.

"They've taken the car to the sheriff's forensics lab. If there's anything there, we'll have it by the end of the day."

"That was Sharkey?" I asked.

"Yes."

"What's the deputy chief doing working on Sunday?"

"Bill Lester's in Spain on vacation and Martin's worried about me."

Bill Lester was the island chief of police.

"When's Bill due back?" I asked.

"He's flying in this afternoon. He'll be in the office in the morning."

Sam returned with a tray with three steaming cups of coffee. He set them on the bar and took a bottle of red wine from the shelf, opened it, and poured himself a glass. I looked at Sam. "Do you have any kind of video surveillance in here or out in the parking lot?"

"No. We've never had any need for that sort of thing on the key."

"Sam," said J.D., "I want you to take a minute and think about the guy talking to Nell. Are you sure you've never seen him before?"

"I think I'd have noticed the tattoos if I had."

"Suppose he was wearing a long-sleeve shirt?"

Sam was quiet for a moment, then shook his head. "No. I don't re-member ever seeing him before last night."

"How long was he talking to Nell?" she asked.

"Not long. He sat down, ordered a beer, took a swallow, said some-thing to her. She talked to him for a few minutes, just being polite, I guess. He got up, threw a ten on the bar, and went out the door. She sat by her-self for a few minutes, asked for her check, paid, and left."

"Did she seem to be in a hurry to leave?"

"No. She signed her credit card receipt, said 'bye,' and left."

"You said she came in about nine o'clock. Did she say where she'd been before she came here?"

"No, but I didn't ask her," said Sam.

"Wouldn't nine seem a little late for her to come in for dinner?"

"Yeah, but I didn't think anything about it. I knew Gene had gone to Alaska with Les, so I assumed she'd been home watching TV or some-thing, got hungry or lonely, and came down here."

"Did she make a point of saying goodbye to anybody at the bar?" asked J.D.

Sam was quiet for a few moments, replaying the evening in his head. "I think she did stop to talk briefly to Susan Phillips. But it was a very short conversation."

"Do you have Susan's phone number?" asked J.D.

"Sure." Sam pulled his cell phone from his pocket, opened it, and scrolled down his phone book, gave it to J.D. "Here it is. Use this if you want to call her."

J.D. took the phone and walked out the front door. She was back in a few minutes. "Susan said that she stopped Nell as she was leaving to make sure she was all right. She looked a little frazzled, and Susan wondered if the stranger she was talking to had upset her. Nell said that he hadn't, but he was asking her if she lived alone and some other personal things. Nell told him to leave and he did. Nell said she was going home. She didn't seem worried at all, so Susan wasn't alarmed."

"I think I need to go see Gene," said Jock.

"Want some company?" I asked.

"No, podna. I think it'd be best if I go by myself. Can I borrow your car?"

"Sure. J.D. can take me home." I looked at her. She nodded. I handed Jock my keys and he left.

I looked at J.D. "What now?"

"I'm going home and calling the chief of detectives in Miami-Dade. I need to light a fire under somebody down there. There has to be a connection to some perp I put away. Otherwise, why would the killer involve me in his madness?"

"Maybe the call was somebody's idea of a joke," I said.

"I don't think so," she said. "I'll call Miami and see if we can come up with any names."

"You realize it's Sunday," I said.

"Yeah, calling the chief at home will add a little urgency to the situation. He and I go way back."

"Matt," Sam said, "you want to go boating this afternoon?"

He had recently bought a forty-six-foot Hatteras motor yacht that had been built forty years before. The boat was in great shape with almost new Detroit diesel engines and a new paint job. The interior had been a shambles, but Sam had put it back together and was living aboard. *Sammy's Hat,* as he'd named her, was moored behind the restaurant.

A couple of months earlier, Sam, Mike Seamon, Logan Hamilton, and I had brought her around from Melbourne on Florida's east coast. It had been a slow cruise down through the Florida Keys with a two-day layover in Key West. By the time we pulled the boat into her new slip behind Pattigeorge's, we were tired, hung over, sunburned, and happy to be home. It was the kind of trip that would add to the store of island legends, and we were not above embellishing our tale with gross exaggerations.

I looked at J.D. "Why don't you come along? You can call from the boat and there's nothing else you're going to accomplish today."

"I don't know, Matt. I feel like there's got to be something I can be working on."

"Look," I said, "we know all we can at this point. When you get the records from Miami, you'll have something that may begin to shed a little light on this. But until that happens, you're just going to be stumbling around in the dark."

"I guess you're right," she said. "The soonest I'm going to get the stuff from Miami is tomorrow morning. Let me call Sharkey. See if he has any thoughts."

She walked out the front door, digging her phone out of her pocket. She was back in a few minutes. "He said for me to take the day off. We can start fresh in the morning."

"Come on, J.D.," said Sam. "Let's run down the bay and have lunch at Marina Jack."

"Okay," she said. "I'll run home and get changed. Matt, do you need anything?"

"Nope. If we decide to go swimming, I'll just skinny dip."

"Oh, please," she said, grinning. "I'll be back in a few minutes."

CHAPTER NINE

The bay was flat, not a ripple on it. The cold front that had moved through the area on Friday night had wiped the sky clean of clouds. Our universe was defined by the turquoise sea and a sky of crystalline blue. Sam was at the helm, keeping our speed at a stately seven knots. The soft breeze generated by our passage was suffused with the briny smell of the bay. J.D. and I sat on a bench seat placed at right angles to the helm. She was dressed in navy-blue shorts, a white T-shirt bearing the logo of The Old Salty Dog restaurant, and flip-flops. Her dark hair was tied in a ponytail, her smile radiant, and her emerald-green eyes a shade or two darker than the water that surrounded us.

A Cigarette-style go-fast boat roared by us on our port side, its unmuffled engines pushing it along at fifty or sixty miles per hour. The captain waved at us and poured on more juice. Two women in bikinis sat next to him, laughing, their hair blowing in the stiff wind over the bow. As if on cue, they both pulled up their bikini tops, flashing the old fogies aboard the ancient Hatteras. Fun in the sun. A Florida tradition. Life never gets much better than this, I thought.

"What did the chief of detectives say?" I asked.

"He's going to get his people moving. He'll send me a list of names of violent men I arrested, along with their pictures and information or whether they're still in prison, on parole, or dead. Maybe one of them was at Pattigeorge's Friday night."

I smiled. "How would you rate the chances of that happening?"

"Probably nil."

"Even if you could identify the killer, it'd take some doing to round him up."

She shrugged. "At least we'd have a starting place."

•   •   •

It was almost two when we pulled into the harbor at Marina Jack. Sam checked in by radio with the dockmaster, and then backed *Sammy's Hat* into a slip next to a floating dock. J.D. and I handled the lines as Sam used the engines to hold the boat against the pier.

The lunch crowd had thinned out, so we didn't have to wait for a table on the patio overlooking the harbor. We ordered drinks and chatted about gossip on the island, forgetting for a moment that a woman had been brutally murdered in this tranquil piece of the world. While we were waiting for our food, J.D.'s phone rang. She looked at the caller ID, said, "Sharkey," and took the call. She listened, said "thanks," and closed the phone. "They found a boat that fits the delivery captain's description of the one he saw at Sister Key yesterday morning."

"Where?" asked Sam.

"Tied up at a dock in a canal in Emerald Harbor, two houses down from the Alexanders' place."

"Somebody's just now noticing it?" I asked.

"The couple who live there have been out of town for a few days," J.D. said. "They got home an hour or so ago and noticed the boat at their dock. They called us. Steve Carey went down there, called in the registration number, and got a hit. It was the one stolen from Bimini Bay Friday night."

"If the guy in my bar that night is the killer, how would he have gotten from Pattigeorge's to Bimini Bay?" Sam asked.

"Were there any cars in your parking lot when you and Miles left on Friday night?" I asked.

"Only Miles's convertible."

"How about in the parking area underneath the Harbour Square building next door?"

"There're always cars there."

"It'd have been pretty simple," I said. "He followed Nell home, popped her before she got into the house, stashed her body somewhere, drove his car to Bimini Bay, stole the boat, ran down the bay to the canal, put the body in the boat, went to Sister Key, left the body, took the boat back to the canal, and drove away in Nell's car."

"One of the neighbors would have heard the shot," said Sam.

"Not necessarily," said J.D. "That little twenty-two doesn't make a lot of noise, and if he'd shot her in the car or inside the house, the noise would have been very limited."

"Did your people take a look at the house to see if she was killed there?" asked Sam.

"Yes. The forensics people went over it with a fine-tooth comb. I don't think she was shot inside the house. Maybe in her car."

"You haven't found her car?" asked Sam.

"Not yet."

"The killer could be anywhere by now," said Sam.

"He could," said J.D. "Maybe we'll get lucky."

Our trip back up the bay was uneventful. I called Jock to let him know that we were on our way back, and he met us on the dock behind Pattigeorge's. J.D. left for the police station to see if she could get an update on the forensic examination of the boat. Jock and I helped Sam wash down *Sammy's Hat* and left for home.

CHAPTER TEN

Jock and I settled into a couple of deck chairs on my patio, he with an O'Doul's and I with a Miller Lite. The sun would be going down soon. I loved watching the sunset from the Gulf side and I often did, usually at the outside bar at the Hilton. But sundown on the eastern side of the island was beautiful as well. In a few minutes, as the sun sank toward the surface of the Gulf, its rays would reflect off the cumulus clouds hanging over the bay, painting them in bright pastels as the turquoise water turned gray in the diminishing light.

"How's Gene doing?" I asked.

"Not well, but he's tough. He'll survive this, but it'll take some time."

"What's he doing about a funeral?"

"He'll bury her here as soon as the medical examiner releases the body."

"Do you think the murder was some sort of revenge against Gene for his involvement with your agency?"

"I don't see how. I don't think anybody could connect him to our group. His cover was as an analyst for the State Department. But I think the murderer is going to be very surprised to find out that he killed one of us."

"What do you mean?"

"He won't like the final result."

"Explain that to me."

"The director told me to take the bastard out."

"You mean kill him," I said.

"Yep."

"Will you?"

"If I get to him before the law does."

"I don't know, Jock. What about J.D.?"

"What she doesn't know won't hurt her."

"You can't do that to her."

Jock sat silently for a few minutes. I let him stew. He found himself in a paradox. J.D. was his friend and yet, so was Gene Alexander. Jock lived in a world where the bad guys were taken out. He killed them to protect all of us, his countrymen. I think he died a little with every one of the enemy he killed, no matter how deserving that person was of death. I was one of the few people in the world outside his agency who knew what he did for a living. He was a sometime assassin, a man sent by his government to kill those who would kill us. And when the deed was done, when he'd carried out his orders, finished his mission, he'd come to Longboat Key and crawl into a bottle of bourbon for a week. His nights were long and arduous, filled with regret and anger and self-loathing. He'd talk about our childhood in the small town in the middle of Florida where we'd grown up, of how he'd ended up in the service of his country, a noble calling, but one filled with duties beyond the understanding of the ordinary American. He hated what he did, but knew he was better qualified than almost anyone in the world to carry out his missions. And he knew that those missions were crucial to the survival of our nation. So he went out into the world and did evil to the evildoers. Was there some balance there? Or was he just another killer, no better than the idiots who killed for their rancid causes?

The answers never came, but by the end of the week, the week we called the cleansing time, he slowed down on the drinking, nursed less severe hangovers, and began running miles each day on the beach, leaching the alcohol and the hatred out of his system. Then he'd go back to the wars, back to the dismal pursuit of his deranged quarry, back to protecting his country.

"I won't betray J.D.," he said.

"What then?"

"She's potentially a target. If I killed the guy and she didn't know about it, she'd continue to feel threatened. I won't do that to her."

"Where does that leave you and the director's order?"

"It wasn't really an order. More like permission."

"Then what'll you do?"

He chuckled. "Play it by ear, I guess. If I can kill the guy without compromising J.D., I'll do it. If not, he belongs to her and the law."

I said, sarcastically, "I know she'll be pleased."

Jock laughed. "We're not going to mention this to her, are we?"

"Not on a bet. She'd pack your ass off to Houston before you could get your gear together."

"She's tough, podna. God, she's tougher than you and me put together."

"And a lot prettier," I said.

My phone began to play the first bars of *The Girl from Ipanema.*

"J.D.," I said as I wrenched the phone from the pocket of my shorts.

"Geez," said Jock, rolling his eyes.

"Good afternoon, Detective," I said.

Jock shook his head, grinning.

"Aren't we formal?" said J.D.

I looked at my watch. It was after six. "You up for some dinner?"

"Sure. What've you got in mind?"

"How about the Lazy Lobster in thirty minutes?"

"I've got to shower and change. Give me an hour."

"Okay, Toots."

"Toots? Have you lost your mind?"

"Sorry, Detective. See you in an hour." I closed the phone.

"Call her 'Toots' again and she'll probably shoot you," said Jock.

"Yeah. I gotta watch my mouth."

We drank another beer, showered, dressed, and left the cottage for the two-mile drive down the island to the Lazy Lobster Restaurant. We didn't know that we were driving straight into the path of a murderer.

CHAPTER ELEVEN

The restaurant was housed in the Centre Shops on Gulf of Mexico Drive. We pulled into the parking lot, a sea of asphalt that was well shaded during the day by trees planted in the medians that bordered the parking spaces. At night, the trees partially blocked the security lights, giving the place a dappled look, one that could be a bit scary in a city, but not on our key. We didn't have much crime and what we had was never violent. An occasional car burglary, but that was about it.

We parked and were standing in the shadows at the end of a row of cars, waiting for J.D. to join us. I saw her Camry turn into the lot. She passed us, waved, and drove toward an open space about halfway down the line of cars. A cream-colored BMW coupe came in behind her and turned down the same parking lane J.D. had taken.

"Shit," said Jock. "That's Nell's car."

"What?" I asked, but Jock was moving like a sprinter coming off the blocks, pulling his ever-present pistol from the rear waistband of his pants, running toward J.D., calling to her. I had been so engrossed in my thoughts that I'd missed the BMW. Jock was several feet in front of me as I began to run after him.

J.D. was getting out of her car as the BMW passed her and stopped a couple of car lengths from where she had pulled in. The BMW did not move, just sat in the driving lane, lights on, engine idling. The door opened and a man stepped out. Even from a distance of fifty feet, I could see the look of alarm on J.D.'s face as she perceived the danger. Her instincts were good. She dropped to the ground and rolled to her right, sheltering behind a parked SUV. I was running after Jock, not sure what was going on.

The man from the BMW was standing beside the car, a pistol in his hand. He fired two shots in rapid succession toward J.D. Missed. He looked in Jock's direction and his pistol barrel started to move toward a new target. He was a half-second slow, and that cost him his life. Jock fired just as the man let loose his second shot at J.D. Had the man fired only once, he might have had a chance. Maybe his concentration on J.D. was so intense he didn't see Jock barreling toward him, pistol coming out, rising to point at him. We'd never know. Jock's shot, made on the run, caught the man just above his right eye. He fell backward from the impact, dead in the instant the bullet hit.

Jock was past J.D., running full out to make sure the man was truly dead. I stopped to check on J.D. She had her pistol out and was positioning herself to join the firefight. I told her it looked like it was over. "I think Jock killed the son of a bitch," I said.

She got up, her pistol in her right hand, pointed toward the asphalt, her phone in her left calling for backup. We moved cautiously toward Jock, who was standing over the dead man. "This could be Craig," she said, "the man Sam told us about. Look at the tattoos on his arms."

The man lay sprawled on his back next to the open door of the BMW, his arms stretched out over his head. The interior light from the car shown weakly on the ugly tattoos that covered his arms below the elbows. He was dressed in a tropical print shirt, cargo shorts, and ancient boat shoes. A foul odor emanated from him, a mélange of unwashed body, day-old booze, and bad breath. Except that he wasn't breathing anymore.

We were only a half mile from the police station and within minutes two cruisers careened into the parking lot, sirens screaming, blue-and-red lights flashing. The first one came to a stop a few feet from us and Officer Steve Carey stepped out, pistol drawn.

"J.D.," he said. "You all right?"

"I'm fine. I don't think there're any more bad guys around."

"Where'd he come from?" he asked, pointing to the dead man.

"He was in that BMW. I think he followed me from my condo."

"Did you call in the tag number on the BMW yet?"

"Sorry," she said, her voice tight. "I've been a little busy."

Steve grinned, reaching for his radio mic. "Yes, ma'am. I'll take care of it."

The cop from the second cruiser walked up. "Should I call the medical examiner?"

"Yeah," said J.D, "and let's get this area cordoned off. We'll need the forensics unit, and somebody better let Sharkey know."

"I've already called him. He's on his way. The chief, too. He just got in from Spain."

A crowd was gathering, but so far no one had gotten too close. The young officer went to his cruiser trunk and pulled out a roll of yellow tape and began to surround the area with it. One of the spectators asked the cop when he could get his car out, pointing to a Mercedes parked next to J.D.'s car. "It may be a while, sir. We're investigating a death."

"I'll be in the bar," the man said.

The crowd was good natured and turned back to the restaurant. I suspected the bar's booze stock would be greatly diminished before the scene was released and the guests could get their cars out.

"J.D.," Carey said, "the BMW is Nell Alexander's car."

"Okay," said J.D. "Nobody touch it until the forensics people have a look at it. Steve, can I borrow your flashlight?"

She shined the light on the dead man's arms. "Those are prison tats if I've ever seen them," she said. She ran her hands over his body, searching for any weapons or anything else he might have on him.

"Matt, help me roll him over. I need to see if he has anything in his back pocket." We checked. "Nothing," she said. "He'll be in the system. As soon as we can run his prints, we'll know who he is."

"J.D.," I said, "how do you know he followed you from home? And why? If he was planning to kill you, wouldn't it have made sense to do it there? Less people."

"That may have been his intention. When I came down the elevator to my car, several of my neighbors were in the parking lot, talking to that cop over there putting up the tape. He recognized me and said there had been an incomplete 911 call from one of the condos, and he'd been sent over to check it out. It turned out to be just a mistake in dialing by the owner. She and a couple of visitors were in the lot talking to the officer. I guess the shooter was spooked by the patrolman."

"That was a lucky break," I said.

She smiled ruefully. "Yeah. When I came out onto Dream Island Road and turned onto Gulf of Mexico, I noticed a car behind me, but didn't think anything about it. No reason to. I guess he followed me here, and took his shot. He probably didn't see you and Jock, or at least didn't think you were any danger to him. Bad mistake. I owe you a big one, Jock."

Jock had been standing quietly next to the BMW. "That's what friends are for," he said.

"How did you know, Jock?" I asked. "You reacted so quickly."

"I'm not sure. Instinct, I guess. There was something wrong about the scene. The BMW was similar to Nell's and it was right behind J.D. As soon as J.D. got out of her car, he got out of his. It just looked like a setup of some kind. Maybe the fact that Nell's car was a BMW was banging around in the back of my brain. And I thought I saw a glint of light reflected off his gun. But that may just have been my imagination. I wouldn't have pulled the trigger though, if he hadn't shot at J.D. first."

Steve Carey came over. "J.D., Sharkey and the chief will be here in about ten minutes. The crime-scene people are sending a wrecker to tow the BMW to the sheriff's forensics garage so they can take a good look at it. The chief said for you to go on into the restaurant and make yourself comfortable until he gets here."

"I can't go in there looking like this," she said.

I noticed for the first time that the slacks she was wearing had a tear at the knee. "Are you hurt?" I asked.

"No. I skinned my knee when I jumped behind that SUV, but nothing serious."

"Let me look at it, J.D.," said Steve Carey. The Longboat cops are all trained emergency medical technicians. He bent down and pointed his flashlight at the area where the slacks were torn. "A little road rash. Let me clean it up and get some antiseptic and a bandage on it. You don't want it to get infected."

By the time Steve had finished with her knee, Sharkey and Chief Bill Lester drove into the parking lot. Martin Sharkey was a tall man who kept in good shape and probably wore the same size clothes he had in high school. His close-cropped dark hair was turning gray at the temples. Lester was shorter, his brown hair thinning a bit on the top. He had a little belly that he needed to be careful of, and a demeanor that told you he was in charge, even when his face was split by his famous grin. Both men were well liked and respected on the key, and they often fished with me aboard *Recess.*

"Well, Jock," said Lester as he walked up, "here you are on my island, and the shit hits the fan. What is it with you?"

"Must be my personality, Bill. How was Spain?"

"Muy bueno."

"Learned some of the lingo?"

"*Sí.*"

"Good for you."

"You just heard my entire vocabulary. But the wine was excellent. Where's Logan? When you two are causing trouble, he's usually in the mix."

Logan Hamilton was my best friend on the island. "He and Marie are spending some quality time down in Key West," I said. "He should be back tomorrow or the next day, assuming the island doesn't run out of Scotch in the meantime."

He turned to J.D. "I understand somebody took a shot at my favorite detective."

"Your only detective," said J.D. "Jock saved my butt."

"Bring me up to date."

"How much do you know about the Alexander murder?"

"Martin called me yesterday about finding the body, but I couldn't get a flight out until this morning. He kept me updated by phone though, so I'm pretty much up to speed. Do you think this guy killed Nell Alexander?"

"Maybe." J.D. told Lester and Sharkey what we'd found out from Sam earlier in the day. "I put it all in a report that's probably on your desk by now. This guy fits the description and the BMW belonged to Mrs. Alexander. I don't think there's much doubt that he's the killer. Maybe the car will give up the evidence we need to be sure."

A Manatee County Sheriff's SUV pulled into the lot, towing a trailer.

"Here come our portable lights," said Lester. "You guys know the drill. We'll have to have detailed statements from all of you. Why don't you go on home, and I'll send somebody by later."

"We can't leave," I said. "Our cars have been impounded."

"I'll get Steve Carey to drop you off."

"We'll be at my house, Bill," I said.

I ordered pizza from Oma's on Anna Maria Island, and the kid in the Jaguar delivered it. He was probably the only pizza dude in the whole country who drove a new Jag. I liked his chutzpa and always gave him a big tip. I opened some cold beer for J.D. and me and an O'Doul's for Jock. We were still a little shaken from the ordeal at the Lazy Lobster.

"What do you make of this, J.D.?" asked Jock.

"I think you got the guy."

"But why was he trying to kill you?"

"I don't know. I guess he was the same one who was on the phone last night."

"Have you gotten anything from Miami yet?"

"No. But the chief of detectives down there promised me something by noon tomorrow. I think it'll be a lot more detailed than anything they've sent us. But I'm pretty sure I've never seen the one from tonight. If I'd put him away, I'd remember."

"If he's the one who killed Nell," I said, "I guess both your jobs are done."

"What do you mean?" asked J.D.

"You got your murderer, and Jock took out the guy who killed Gene's wife."

"I don't know," said J.D. "There's something screwy here."

"What?" I asked.

"I'm not sure. I don't understand why he was trying to kill me. I had no connection to Nell Alexander until she was killed. I worked the cases in Miami, but we never caught the perp. So why would somebody connect me to the murders and want to put me out of commission?"

"Unless," I said, "you might have put the Miami killer in jail on other charges. That would explain why the murders stopped and why the killer is after you."

"This guy tonight wasn't anybody I've ever seen before. And he couldn't be over twenty-five. He was too young to be involved in the Miami murders. Maybe he's just hired muscle, and the real killer is still out there somewhere."

"Let's see what the forensics people find in the car and get an identity on the dead man," said Jock." Maybe we'll know more then."

"J.D.," I said, "why don't you stay here tonight. In the spare bedroom."

"Thanks, Matt. But I think I'd rather sleep in my own bed."

"We've still got to wait for somebody to come take our statements."

"Since it's an officer-involved shooting, it'll be somebody from the Florida Department of Law Enforcement," said J.D. "The agent will probably have to come down from Tampa. I don't think they work this late. I'll call the chief and see what he says."

She stepped into the kitchen to make her call, returning in a few minutes. "Chief said to go to bed. Somebody will come by tomorrow. They'll call first. I'm going home."

"I'll drive you," said Jock.

"Thanks, but a patrol car's coming to get me. I'll see you tomorrow."

"Want another beer?" I asked.

"Not tonight, Bucko. I'm headed for bed."

"I love it when you call me pet names," I said.

She grinned and said quietly, "You're some sicko, Royal. Night, Jock." And she was out the door.

"I think she likes you, Bucko," said Jock, grinning.

I gave him the finger and went for more beer.

CHAPTER TWELVE

Jeff Worthington wore a navy-blue suit with a yellow handkerchief in the breast pocket, white dress shirt, yellow tie with blue polka dots, and cordovan loafers with tassels. He was a small man, perhaps five foot six and 135 pounds. His brown hair was thin and a little long over the ears, and his face bore the scars of the acne he'd suffered as a teenager. He had high cheekbones, a slender straight nose, a weak chin marked by a small dimple, and large teeth that, on the rare occasion when he smiled, looked as if they would jump out of his mouth. In short, he had the look of a predator.

This was a good day. The sun was shining, the humidity was low, and passersby were smiling and greeting each other. Worthington stood for a moment on the landing that fronted the main entrance to the Sarasota County Judicial Center, looking up into a cloudless sky. He watched for a moment as a flock of seagulls wheeled in the currents high above, their harsh cries blasting the morning air. He shrugged and walked down the steps leading to the street, a smile struggling to break through the coarse visage he presented to the world.

Jeff Worthington was a lawyer and had been one for about ten minutes. A harried judge had given him the oath of office, stumbling over some of the words, and shooed him out of chambers with a curt mumble of congratulations. All the documents certifying to his newly acquired profession were in the file folder he carried in his left hand. Today was the first day of what he planned to be a very short career. He had one client, one case, one matter to handle to its conclusion, and when that was completed, when he had won the case and done his client's bidding, he would retire a rich man. The whole thing would be over in days, weeks at the most. Failure was not an option. The wages of failure were death. No appeal, no stay of execution, no clemency; just the agonizing death that he'd been promised as payment for failure.

Worthington was perhaps the only member of the Florida Bar who had never been to law school. He'd gotten his license to practice law the old-fashioned way. He'd stolen it. From a dead man. That had not been easy, but he was a very smart guy, his intelligence quotient immeasurably higher than the half-wits who served as corrections officers in that pigsty they called Glades Correctional Institution. Fifteen hard years he'd been there, his entire fifteen-year stint. The prison executives were more interested in keeping the prisoners calm than rehabilitating them. Not that rehabilitation usually worked. Most of the cons were dumber than the dumbest of the men who guarded them.

Worthington had grown up in public housing in a Tampa neighborhood that the city ignored. The elementary school that served him and his friends was one of those dying places where the teachers had given up and the administrators could not justify spending any more money on facilities. Jeff was bored with sitting day after day listening to the teachers as they tried to teach him things he already knew. He cut classes without anyone noticing, because to notice a truant kid meant paperwork and the teachers and administrators could find no good reason to spend their time on one more useless task. On the rare occasions when his parents weren't drunk, they weren't interested in making sure that the boy went to school.

Jeff was a loner, a boy who wanted nothing to do with the other kids. He scratched around for things to do to occupy his mind, and one day, when he was about twelve, he found himself in the main public library in downtown Tampa. As he ambled idly through the stacks, he pulled random books from the shelves, thumbed through them, and put them back. His curiosity was piqued and he began to read passages from the books he chose so haphazardly. A spark was ignited in his nimble and curious brain and he began to read in-depth books that even his teachers had not read, and perhaps did not know existed.

When he was fifteen, Jeff left the squalid apartment where his parents lived and moved to the streets. He never saw either of his parents again, and as far as is known, they made no effort to find Jeff. He made his living with small crimes, much as he had been doing for most of his life. A little shoplifting, a small-time burglary or two, a smash and grab. It provided all the money he needed to pay his share of the rent on a small house on the edge of downtown that he shared with several other young men whose circumstances mirrored Jeff's own.

Most of his roommates were addicted to one or another drug, but Jeff shied away from the temptations offered. He wanted a better life, somewhere other than public housing projects, and he figured that none of the men he lived with would ever get out of the rut in which they found themselves. Certainly not alive.

When he was eighteen, Jeff was ready to make his move. He had studied the real estate market in the Tampa area and was convinced that he could make a lot of money investing in property. He just needed a stake, some money with which to get into the market and begin building his portfolio. He understood leverage, that you put the minimal amount down and borrowed the rest. He also knew that nobody would lend money to a teenager who lived in what amounted to a drug den. So Jeff set about building himself a new identity. He used the computers at the public library and became adept enough with them to fashion a new and fictitious persona. It hadn't been easy. Computers were still rudimentary devices then, and the Internet was in its infancy. Still, with the help of a very good forger he had become acquainted with on the streets, he was able to turn himself into somebody he very definitely was not.

Jeff's alias was manufactured from whole cloth, but he appeared to be the scion of a wealthy family in Braintree, Massachusetts. The story was that the son dropped out of college the year before and decided to move to Florida and invest in real estate. He was twenty-one years old. Jeff thought the legend he'd built would do fine, but he still needed capital. About twenty thousand dollars for starters, and Jeff knew just where to get it.

An old warehouse on the edge of an industrial area near downtown Tampa had been turned into a club called simply "The Place." It was a large space and drew hundreds of people every night. It stayed open until four in the morning, providing its patrons with booze and food and loud music. There was an underground economy within the club that relied on the retail sale of drugs of every kind. The management knew who the salespeople were and extracted a percentage of their nightly take as the price of doing business.

The best thing about it from Jeff's perspective was that it was an all-cash business. The owner of The Place advertised it as such. His thinking was that there would be a lot of patrons who would not want their credit card statements to show that they had taken part in the offerings of the establishment.

Jeff had worked as a busboy at The Place for several weeks and had come to understand the system the proprietor used to handle the nightly receipts. He was convinced that the owner was skimming the take, sending most of the money to the bank by armored car shortly after closing each morning, but taking a substantial part of the cash for himself, probably from the payoffs provided by the illicit drug entrepreneurs who worked the floor. It was a neat way to cheat the tax man, and even a detailed audit would have shown that the money generated by the sale of food and alcohol was sent to the bank and duly accounted for.

On the night that Jeff decided to stake his real estate empire, he hid in a closet after closing. He heard the armored car pull into the alley behind the club, and listened to the conversation between the owner and the driver. When the driver was gone, Jeff stole out of the closet and walked down the short corridor to the office. His face was completely covered by a Halloween mask that looked like Bill Clinton. He carried the Glock nine millimeter he'd stolen during a burglary two weeks before.

Jeff stopped at the door to the office. There were voices, a low conversation coming from inside. He had not expected anyone else to be there. He stood silently for a beat, then shoved the door open gun in hand, pointing inward.

The owner stood stock-still, an amused look on his face. Another man stood across the room holding a pistol, pointed at Jeff. He was one of the bouncers who stood nightly at the front door. The man fired, hitting Jeff in the left shoulder. Jeff fired at the same time, hitting the bouncer in the heart. A lucky shot? It saved Jeff's life, but put him in jail for fifteen years.

The owner pulled his own gun and stuck it in Jeff's face while he used his cell phone to call the police. Jeff was in too much pain from the bullet in his shoulder to resist.

Jeff was initially charged with first-degree murder, but it turned out that the bouncer had a checkered history and warrants for his arrest were outstanding in three states. The state attorney agreed to a plea to manslaughter with a fifteen-year sentence and no chance of parole. Jeff served every minute of it and had been released from prison on June 1, five months before.

On the day Jeff walked down the steps of the Sarasota County Judicial Center, he had no understanding of any legal doctrine and would be unable to answer even the most rudimentary legal questions. That did not present a problem to him. He had no intention of practicing law, counseling clients, appearing in court, or, heaven forbid, going to a local bar function where as best he could figure, lawyers gathered to drink and brag about the cases they had won.

When he was released from prison, Jeff had a mission. While not absolutely necessary, his being a lawyer would make his tasks easier to accomplish, and he didn't have time to spend seven years at some university. At the beginning of October, he was told of a young man named Ben Flagler who had finished law school and sat for and passed the Florida bar exam. Jeff was assured that Flagler had no family and no friends in the area. He was from North Dakota and had gone to school there. His parents had been killed in a car wreck while he was in his second year of law school. He had no siblings, and if he had cousins or other family, he'd never met them. He decided that sunny Florida was a better place to practice law than the Dakotas, so he applied for the Florida bar exam and took it in August. When the results were posted in late September, the young man from North Dakota was among those who passed.

Flagler rented a furnished apartment in Sarasota, dealing with the real estate agent through the Internet and by e-mail. Jeff was made aware of all these small details by his client, and he marveled, not for the first time, at the client's ability to acquire information. On the day Flagler showed up to move into the apartment, Jeff was waiting for him, sitting on the sofa, a silenced pistol in his hand. Flagler walked in the front door and Jeff shot him in the head. He waited until dark and moved the body into the trunk of his car. He drove east, out Fruitville Road past I-75 to an intersection that held a closed gas station. As instructed, he pulled behind the station and waited. In a few minutes, an old Buick approached, blinked its lights twice, and pulled in next to Jeff.

"You got the package?" asked the man behind the wheel of the Buick.

"In the trunk," said Jeff, and reached over and pushed the button that released the trunk lid.

The other man wrestled the body out of Jeff's trunk and into the Buick's. "That one'll keep the gators' bellies full for a few days," he said.

Jeff got into his car and drove away without answering. He went back to the apartment Flagler had rented and went to bed. The next morning he would present himself to a judge at the courthouse and show the North Dakota driver's license with his picture on it that identified him as Ben Flagler, and be sworn in as an attorney and counselor-at-law, duly licensed to practice law in the state of Florida.

It was this chain of events that brought Jeff Worthington, now known as Ben Flagler, Esquire, to the Sarasota County Judicial Center on a beautiful November day. Not bad, Jeff thought, for a kid from the projects. A small cloud of fear sliced through his brain taking the luster off the day. There had already been a problem, and now he had to report to his client, try to explain the fuckup to the man he knew only as the controller.

CHAPTER THIRTEEN

Monday morning. The village was alive with people leaving for work. One of the things I like best about being a beach bum is that I didn't have to join them. I was drinking coffee on the patio and reading the morning paper when Jock came out, a steaming cup in hand.

"Have you talked to your people yet?" I asked.

"I let the director know we'd gotten the one we think killed Nell, but I want to wait until we hear from forensics and get an ID on the dead guy before I give him a full report."

"You think there's more to this than just the guy you shot?"

"Yes, but I don't know what. We've still got some digging to do."

"Want to go for a run?"

"Sure. What about the statements?"

"I'll take my phone. If we get the call, we'll come back."

We ran on the hard-packed sand of the beach, leaching the lethargy out of our systems. If you weren't careful, the desultory rhythms of the key would overtake you, turn you into a couch potato or worse. When there was no schedule, no plan to your existence, the sheer randomness of life would overwhelm you and turn you into a TV-watching, booze-swilling barfly. Running seemed to give some purpose to my existence, a way to corral the uncertainty of the day, to know that there was at least one thing I had to accomplish each day. Four miles on the beach. A tiring, sweating, balls-to-the-wall run. Then I'd slip back into beach bum mode.

We finished our run at the North Shore Road access ramp and walked back through the village to my home. The peacocks that roamed the area were out in force that morning, pecking at the lawns and shrubs, occasionally letting out one of their raucous cries. They were pretty, but messy, and the village people were a bit schizoid about them. They liked the image of the birds running free in the neighborhood, but hated the mess they made and the god-awful noise. And the birds bred faster than rabbits. Every few years, the flock was thinned, and many of the birds were taken to a farm out in the east end of the county. For a while, a relative peace would fall over the village, but soon enough, the little buggers would start procreating again, and the problems would start all over.

As we were nearing my house, J.D. called. "The forensics people are finished with Nell's BMW. Found some interesting stuff, but it didn't answer many questions. The only fingerprints that didn't belong in the car were the dead guy's. A man named Pete Qualman, twenty-three years old, did time at Glades Correctional. He was released on parole two months ago. Never checked in with his probation officer."

"What was he in for?" I asked.

"Held up a convenience store in Orlando when he was eighteen. Got six years and released in five."

"Any connections to Miami?"

"None that we can find. Guy lived in Orlando his whole life. Dropped out of high school in the tenth grade and mostly worked at fast-food joints and did drugs."

"Anything else in the car?"

"A couple spots of blood that were definitely Nell's. The techs think she was probably shot while she was sitting in the driver's seat. We're thinking that when she came out of Pattigeorge's, the killer was hunched down in the back seat. She probably died right there in the parking lot."

"At least it was quick," I said.

"Yeah. They also found some rope that matched the one Nell was bound with and some boat keys that matched the stolen boat. Another interesting tidbit was the mileage on the car. Nell had her oil changed at the BP station on the south end of the key Friday afternoon. The little sticker they put on the window, you know the one that reminds you when your three thousand miles is up and you need more oil, didn't jibe with the odometer. Somebody put a little over three hundred miles on it after the oil change. I don't think Nell did that after she left the BP."

"Did you check the time of the service?"

"Of course I checked. She paid with her VISA card at five fifteen Friday afternoon. And her neighbor told me that the BMW was in the driveway of Nell's house between six and eight, because the neighbor was sitting on her front porch chatting with her husband during the entire two hours."

"What about the gun that was used to kill Nell?" I asked.

"Nowhere to be found. He must have ditched it somewhere. I ran the ballistics through all the federal databases, and there's no indication that the gun has been used in a shooting anywhere in the country since it was used to kill the Miami victims."

"Any thoughts on how he came into possession of that particular gun?"

"No. And that scares the hell out of me. Where did he go in that BMW after he killed Nell? And where did he get the gun, and what did he do with it? He's too young to have been involved in the Miami murders. Was he just a killer hired by the real Miami murderer? If so, where is the real killer, and why does he want me dead?"

"This isn't doing my indigestion any good. Did you get anything from Miami yet?"

"Not yet. It should be along shortly."

"What about the statements?"

"An FDLE agent's coming down from Tampa. He'll talk to me and then he'll meet with you and Jock. I'll call you when he gets here. Bye."

I related the information to Jock.

"Doesn't sound good, podna. Maybe I shot the wrong man. It's obvious that he's not the killer from Miami."

"It's also pretty obvious that he's the one who killed Nell."

"It could be just a fluke that the pistol ended up in Qualman's hands. Or maybe, the killer from Miami is running this show and wanted to let J.D. know that he's still out there."

"And you want the guy who ordered the hit."

"Damn right. It's an article of faith in the agency that if you take out one of us, you pay the price. You die. And that applies to our families."

"You shot the right man. It just might not be the one you wanted most."

CHAPTER FOURTEEN

J.D.'s call came an hour later. The FDLE agent was at the police station and ready to speak to us about the shooting. He met us in the lobby and identified himself as Don Fielding. He wanted to talk to Jock first, so I spent a few minutes reading an ancient magazine I found in the lobby. Jock came out and said the agent was ready for me.

"That was quick," I said.

"He took one look at my credentials, called the number in Washington, and then talked about Florida State football for a while. He seems a bit obsessed with it."

I laughed. Jock carried credentials identifying him as a special agent of the president of the United States and giving him extraordinary powers. Jock told the agent to call a phone number in Washington, D.C. The number was to an office in the White House and the person who answered told the agent not to question Jock. He also told the agent that the agent's boss in Tallahassee would call him right back. Fielding got the call within a minute, recognized the voice of the director of the Florida Department of Law Enforcement, said yes sir, hung up, and turned the conversation to football.

I didn't have any credentials, so I spent the better part of an hour with Agent Fielding, answering all his questions. He was an astute interviewer, and by the time we finished, he knew exactly what I knew about what happened. We discussed Jock's actions in protecting J.D., and Fielding seemed satisfied that Jock had done the right thing. He told me he would recommend that the FDLE find that the actions of a private citizen, one Jock Algren, who held a concealed weapons permit, were taken to protect the life of a police officer and were fully justified. In short, a righteous shooting. We were finished. We shook hands and Fielding said, "Nice to meet you. Go 'Noles." I left, shaking my head.

It was almost noon, and I was getting hungry. I stuck my head into J.D.'s office and asked if she wanted to go to Mar Vista for lunch. She shook her head. "Sorry, Matt. I'm going through the information Miami-Dade e-mailed me. I'll touch base later. I want Jock to see what we have. So far, I can't make much sense out of it."

Jock and I were pulling into the Mar Vista parking lot when my phone rang. Blocked number. Probably Agent Fielding wanting to talk football. I answered.

"Matt, David Parrish." The deep voice rumbled over the circuits, tempered with the accents inculcated into him during a childhood in Statesboro, Georgia. The many years he had lived in Orlando had not robbed his voice of the richness of the Old South.

"Damn, it's good to hear your voice. It's been too long."

"It has been too long, but I'm afraid I'm calling on business. Do you have time for lunch?"

"Sure. When?"

"How about now?"

"Where are you?"

"Just crossing the Cortez Bridge."

"Come on to the Mar Vista. Jock Algren's with me. We'll meet you there. You know where to go?"

"Sure do. And it'll be good to see Jock again. Be there in about ten minutes."

Jock and I had worked with David in the past, and he knew Jock and his connections to the U.S. government.

The Mar Vista Pub was housed in one of the oldest buildings in the village. It had been there well before any of the homes and condos were built to the south. It sat on a piece of property facing the bay and was a favorite hangout of the locals. I pulled into the shell parking lot and walked through the old bar area to the outside. Jock and I told the hostess that we were waiting for one more person, and she led us to our table. I knew most of the people at the other tables and waved as we passed. We sat under an ancient banyan tree, shaded from the noontime sun by its branches. A slight breeze blew off the bay, carrying a tinge of diesel exhaust that emanated from the large boat maneuvering into the restaurant's dock. The temperature was about seventy degrees, the humidity low. Florida at its best, I thought.

"David must have some interest in our recently departed hit man," said Jock.

"Maybe. But if it's that, he's moving fast. It's a couple of hours drive from Orlando. That means he was brought into this either last night or very early this morning."

"Here he comes," said Jock.

Parrish was a large man with quick movements, like the college linebacker he'd once been. His blond hair had turned mostly gray, and he moved a little more slowly than he had when he roamed the football field, taking down runners, as swift and sure as a lion attacking a gazelle. He walked with a slight swagger, a man confident of his place in the universe and contemptuous of anyone who dared question it. He was courtly in his approach to others, a gentleman of the Old South with a mind as incisive as any I'd ever met. He was wearing a gray suit, white dress shirt, maroon striped tie, and black wingtip shoes. The quintessentially buttoned-down lawyer, decidedly out of place at the Mar Vista.

David and I had been law school classmates and good friends. When I moved to Orlando after graduation and joined an old, established law firm, he came too. He went to work in the office of the state attorney, which in Florida is the chief prosecutor of a judicial circuit, not unlike the district attorney in many states.

He'd enjoyed the work and became a career prosecutor, a man devoted to taking the bad guys off the streets. After a few years as a state prosecutor, he moved to the United States Attorney's office and prosecuted federal crimes. He rose to chief assistant U.S. attorney and, finally, a new arrival in the White House had seen fit to appoint him the United States Attorney for the Middle District of Florida, in effect making him the chief federal law enforcement officer in a district that included Jacksonville, Orlando, Tampa, Ft. Myers, and everything in between. It was a big job, and David Parrish was ultimately suited for it.

David ambled over to our table, shook hands, and sat. "Great to see you guys," he said. "Man, I love this island. I think you won the rat race, Matt."

"Congratulations on your promotion," I said. "How do you like being the big cheese?"

"Thanks. I don't think much has changed except now I'm the one responsible for every screw-up in the district. And I'm too bogged down with administrative crap to get into the courtroom."

"Can't you pawn that off on an assistant?" Jock asked.

David grinned. "I'm in the process. I hired a woman from the state attorney's office who never was much of a lawyer, but is the best administrator I've ever seen. I think she's going to work out fine."

"Okay, David," I said, "I'm glad you're here, but I suspect it's not just to spend a day in the sun with your old buddies."

"Not exactly. Jock managed to kill one of my informants last night."

"Informant?" asked Jock.

"Well, he used to be an informant. He got involved with a bunch of drug dealers when he was about fifteen. The Drug Enforcement Agency caught him selling cocaine near an elementary school in Osceola County and gave him the choice of working with us or being tried as an adult and spending the rest of his life in a federal prison."

"How'd that work out for you?" Jock sounded skeptical.

"Actually, he did a good job. We got several convictions of some of the upper echelon of the group based on information he gave us."

"What happened?" I asked. "How did he end up in state prison?"

"Pussy."

I laughed. "Better explain that one."

"He fell for some little bimbo who turned tricks on South Orange Blossom trail in Orlando. She got into some kind of jam and needed money to get out of it. Our boy Pete decided to knock over a convenience store and got caught by the locals."

"You guys didn't try to work a deal?" asked Jock.

"We talked briefly to the state attorney about it, but it seems that young Pete beat the crap out of the Pakistani guy behind the counter. And he did it with a Glock pistol he'd stolen from an unlocked police car about two weeks before. They might have dealt, but they weren't going to let him walk. We were afraid if we got involved in it, he'd be marked as an informant, and he'd last about two days in prison before somebody put a shank in him."

"He only got out a couple of months ago," I said. "Did you guys put him back to work?"

"We were going to, but he never showed up at the probation office. He completely dropped off the grid."

"Until today," I said.

"Right. I've been in the Tampa office for a couple of days and got a call this morning from a DEA agent who saw something in the St. Pete paper about the shooting in Longboat. Pete Qualman's name was in the story, so the agent called me. I talked to Bill Lester and he told me Jock had shot the little bastard, so here I am. Since you're involved, Jock, I'm wondering if somehow there are any national security issues in this thing."

"We don't think so," said Jock. "Qualman killed a woman who was the wife of an old friend of mine, one of my agency's analysts who retired here last year. We think she was probably just a target of opportunity, not connected to the agency in any way. I just happened to be on the island visiting Matt when it happened. My director asked me to look into it to make sure there were no national security implications."

"Give me your take on this whole thing," David said.

Jock nodded at me, and I spent the next twenty minutes bringing David up to speed on what we knew, what we suspected, and what we were concerned about: that Qualman may have just been a hit man hired by somebody who wants to kill J.D. Jock chimed in when he had a nugget to add, but otherwise sat quietly sipping iced tea. The server had taken our order and brought it to the table. We ate as we talked.

"There's a disconnect here somewhere," said David, when I'd finished the update. "Qualman was never violent, except that one time at the convenience store."

"Prison does a lot of damage to people, especially the young ones," I said.

"Yeah," said David, "but I thought he might be one that would make it out. He had no record of trouble at Glades Correctional. A model prisoner." He shook his head. "I thought he might turn out to be the exception to the rule. I guess not."

"Do you have any information on whom he might have been friends with in prison?" Jock asked.

"None. Why?"

"I'd sure like to know how he got involved with someone who wants to kill J.D. The most logical place for him to meet somebody like that would be in prison."

"Probably," said David. "But he's been out for two months. Maybe he ran into somebody after he was released and the murder was a way to make some quick cash."

"Could he have hooked up with his old girlfriend when he got out?"

"No," said David. "She died of an overdose about two years ago."

"Any of the drug people he used to be involved with?" I asked.

"I doubt it. We rolled up most of them, and the rest are dead. Their life expectancy isn't very good on the streets. There's always somebody who wants the territory and the best way to get rid of competition is to simply kill it off. Literally."

"After Qualman killed Nell Alexander," said Jock, "he apparently drove about three hundred miles in her car before turning up in the parking lot last night. Does that make any sense to you?"

"Not offhand," said David. "There are a lot of places in Florida within a hundred-fifty-mile radius of Longboat Key."

"Other than the Orlando area, can you think of any place Qualman could have gone to ground for a couple of days?" I asked.

"I guess he might have hooked up with someone in prison that would have taken him in. Maybe he went there."

"The gun that killed Nell Alexander also killed the three women in Miami twelve years ago," said Jock. "The gun didn't turn up in Qualman's possession, and I don't think he would have ditched it. The gun may be some sort of an icon. It's been around for at least a dozen years. There's no record in the federal databases that it has been used in all that time in another shooting. That tells me that there is somebody else involved, somebody who pointed Qualman toward J.D., and somebody who now has the pistol that killed Nell and those other women in Miami."

"You're probably right," said David. "But, unless there is some federal connection, I can't get my office involved. I'll be happy to share whatever we have on Qualman or any of his old associates, but I doubt that's going to be much help."

"Are you in a hurry to get back to Tampa?" I asked.

"I've got to be back for a dinner meeting at six this evening."

"I'd like you to meet our Longboat Key detective, J. D. Duncan. She's gotten a file from Miami-Dade PD with information on all the people she put away that might have a grudge against her. I'd like to get her over to my house so we can take a look at it. See if anything jumps out at you."

CHAPTER FIFTEEN

Parrish followed us the couple of blocks to my house. I called J.D. on the way and told her that the U.S. attorney was at my house and would like to talk to her and see her files from Miami.

J.D. arrived about ten minutes after us, and I introduced her to David.

"Nice to meet you, David," she said and pulled a flash drive from her pocket. "Can we use your computer, Matt?"

She plugged in the drive and brought up the file. "I've culled this a great deal. I've made hundreds of arrests over the years and most of them ended up in convictions. Not all of the perps went to prison. Some were sentenced to probation or county jail time. Of the ones who went to prison, most are still locked up, and some died. Any one of those still in prison could theoretically be running the show from there, so I've tried to eliminate the ones that didn't commit violent crimes, the burglars, embezzlers, scam artists, and the like. Some of the ones I put away toward the end of my career with Miami-Dade would have been too young twelve years ago to have been involved in the original murders. And I got rid of anybody who was in jail at the time of the murders in Miami."

"How many did you end up with?" I asked.

"Ten, but none of them seem to have any connection to the murders in Miami. Or at least I can't find any. I'm going to have my old partner take a look at them and see if he can come up with anything. David, maybe some of these guys will ring a bell with you."

We scrolled carefully through the file. There was a synopsis of each of the men, giving his personal information, the crime for which he was convicted, the date of the crime, how much time he served, and in which of the

144 Florida prison facilities he had been incarcerated. Several had spent time in more than one institution.

"Each of these ten guys did some of their sentences at Glades Correctional, which is where Qualman served his entire sentence," said J.D., "and they were there for at least part of the time that Qualman was. They may have known each other. I've got the warden down there scratching through records to see if he turns up anything. Like, were any of them cellmates with Qualman. I'm looking for any connection, no matter how tenuous."

"How about somebody that you put away who has been released?" I asked. "Wouldn't someone like that be a pretty good suspect?"

"I've tried to factor that in. I ignored the ones who were released before Qualman got to prison, but he may have met somebody when he got out or knew them before he went in. I have no way of knowing that. This is just a process of elimination, and I want to rule out these ten before I start beating my head against the wall trying to tie a bunch of old cons to Qualman."

"I can get you a list of the people Qualman dealt with in the drug business," said David. "You might turn up a name there, somebody you arrested who also knew our boy before he knocked over the convenience store. It's a pretty long shot."

"Thanks," said J.D. "Let me dig through this pile first. I'll be in touch if none of this works out. I don't guess you see anybody in this group who jumps out at you."

"No. Sorry," he said.

"Do you guys have any thoughts?" J.D. asked.

We all shook our heads just as the front door opened and Logan Hamilton walked in.

CHAPTER SIXTEEN

The controller sat at his desk staring at Biscayne Bay and the skyline of Miami Beach. He was a careful man who spent his life making money from money. He was an investment advisor and a money launderer. He took the proceeds of drug deals throughout Florida and the Caribbean and laundered them through legitimate stock offerings, bonds, certificates of deposit, and any other kind of financial instrument that he deemed worthy of his time. He always made money on that which he invested, turned a fair profit back to his clients and, most importantly, gave them back clean money to replace the enormous sums they made in the drug trade. The controller kept an agreed percentage and became wealthy in the process.

The dirty little deal he had working now bothered him. The drug dealers were ruthless and would think nothing of killing him if he did not perform up to the standards they expected. But they weren't crazy, or at least most of them weren't. They understood finance, and the controller had helped make them immensely wealthy, so he was pretty much in the position of any other businessman dealing with other people's money. If he bet wrong, he would lose the account. If he hadn't lost too much of his client's money, he'd probably survive, since his clients knew he was doing his best. At least, that's what he told himself, and that gave him some peace of mind.

But, this deal could come off the rails without any reason. A dozen years before, one of his clients had given him ten million dollars to invest. He was told that this would be long term, that there was no reason to hurry the money through the laundering process, because it would be years before the owner of the money needed it. The controller invested the funds and sent the investor regular reports showing how wisely he had grown the money. The reports showed that the controller took his percentage and made the money grow, so that the client was satisfied that in twelve years the ten million had become almost thirty million.

Now it was time to start moving the money out of the account. His instructions had been explicit and had come from the same client who had given him the money, a man named Arturo Fuentes, who was also known as the crazy don. The controller had no illusions about Fuentes. The man ran one of the biggest drug cartels in the region. He was based in Puerto Rico and ran smuggling operations into the mainland United States through Florida and Mexico. He was absolutely ruthless and unforgiving. Men had died terrible deaths because they'd made a small mistake in carrying out the crazy don's orders.

The controller thought Fuentes was probably insane. He seemed to take pride in the fear he induced in his subordinates, and he made a point of regularly killing one of his managers chosen at random. Each of the men who reported to Fuentes knew that he could be next, that he might be the one chosen for execution. But, each of the managers also knew that if he tried to leave the cartel, he would invite not only his own painful death, but the death of his family members out to the second degree.

The controller was, thankfully, not one of the managers. He stood outside the organizational chart, hidden in his Miami office, quietly moving money. He became well known in Miami social circles and had a number of legitimate clients drawn from the moneyed layer of South Florida society who would have pulled their funds and run if there had ever been a hint of scandal attached to the profits they made.

The controller was accustomed to dealing with the insane drug dealers, greedy businessmen, and trust fund babies. He was not used to dealing with the scum the crazy don had now ordered him to support. In his mind, the controller heard the faint tolling of his own funeral bells. Maybe it was time for him to pull the plug and put into operation the escape plan he had so painstakingly built over the past thirty years. Maybe it was time to go.

CHAPTER SEVENTEEN

"When did you get in?" I asked Logan.

"Just now," he said. "Why do we have a federal prosecutor and the local fuzz here? You guys get caught running drugs?"

"Hello, Logan," said David. "I wondered when you'd turn up."

"Just got back on the island," Logan said. "A little down time in Key West with my woman."

"You look a little ragged," said Jock. "Too much partying?"

"There ain't no such thing as too much partying," said Logan. He looked at J.D. "How're you, dollface?"

"That's it," she said. "I'm going to shoot him."

Logan laughed. "Tell me what you all are up to."

David stood. "They can fill you in, Logan. I've got to be getting back to Tampa. Good to see you guys. You too, J.D."

"I'll see you out," I said, and followed him to the street.

"David," I said, as we reached his car, "if you get any hint of anything that might have something to do with this mess, let me know. J.D.'s tough, but somebody's after her. Maybe if we use Jock's resources and yours we can figure out how to stop this."

"Count on it. It'll be off the record, but you'll know everything I know."

We shook hands, and he drove away.

When I got back to the house, Jock and J.D. were bringing Logan up to date on the last few days. He sat quietly, taking it all in. When they finished, he said, "Matt, it's time for a little Scotch."

"Anybody else?" I asked.

J.D. looked at her watch and shook her head. "It's almost four. I've got to get back to the station and catch up on some paperwork. Why don't I meet you guys at Tiny's about five thirty?"

And that's what we did. Logan called his girlfriend, Marie Phillips, and she got to Tiny's just as J.D. pulled into the lot. A quiet evening on the island, a few drinks with friends at Tiny's, a few more at Pattigeorge's, and a finale at the Haye Loft with pizza and beer. Jock ordered the coconut cream pie for dessert, the one he always said was almost as good as sex, and which therefore made it the world's second-best treat.

As I drifted off to sleep, I hoped that the rhythms of the island were reasserting themselves, that maybe we were wrong and the deaths and turmoil of the last few days were over, that the sun would come up on Tuesday morning and our key would resume its lethargic existence, lulling those of us lucky enough to live on its shores into the near somnolence that defined our existence. I would not have slept so well had I known that the sunrise would bring death to an innocent and peril to my friends and change perceptibly the placid view we had of our island sanctuary.

CHAPTER EIGHTEEN

Tuesday morning. The strains of *The Girl from Ipanema* roused me from a deep sleep. The anemic light of a false dawn was seeping through my bedroom windows. I looked at the clock on my bedside table as I reached for the phone: 6:30.

"Morning, J.D.," I said.

"Sorry to wake you, Matt. Sharkey just called. There's another body."

"Where?"

"Leffis Key. I'm on my way there."

"Jock and I'll meet you. Where'll you be?"

"Just come down the path. You can't miss us."

I woke Jock, brushed my teeth, and threw water on my face. We took my car and stopped for coffee to-go at the Village Deli that shared a parking lot with Tiny's. We crossed the Longboat Pass Bridge and turned into the parking lot of the Leffis Key Preserve, nestled on the bayside near the southern tip of Anna Maria Island. A sand path ran from the parking lot toward the bay. A few hundred feet east of the parking lot the path forked, with each trail leading to a boardwalk that wound through stands of dogwood, fig, southern red cedar, green buttonwood, sea grape, and other plants, skirting the water in numerous places.

Longboat Key and Bradenton Beach police cruisers were in the parking lot. I saw J.D.'s Camry nosed in against a sand dune. Jock and I started for the path and were stopped by a cop in a Bradenton Beach uniform.

"Sorry, sir. The key is closed for now. You'll have to go back."

"I'm Matt Royal," I said, "and this is Jock Algren. We're supposed to meet Detective Duncan."

"I'll have to check, sir," he said, and pulled his radio mic from the Velcro tab on his shoulder. The conversation was short. "Go on down the path, Mr. Royal. You'll run into them."

I thanked the officer, and Jock and I followed the path until we came to the fork. A half-dozen uniformed officers from both forces were standing around, eerily quiet, respectful of the dead woman who had brought them to this place. J.D. and a Bradenton Beach police lieutenant were at the edge of the knot of uniforms, talking softly. I could see beyond them to a stunted tree that stood at the apex of the fork in the path. A dead woman was propped against the tree, hands folded demurely in her lap. She was middle aged, possibly older, blonde hair that was two shades too bright to be natural, a thinness bordering on emaciation, tattoos on her arms and shoulders. She was nude and a rope snaked around her torso holding her to the trunk of the tree.

I recognized the three Longboat Key officers as men who would have been on the night shift, their tour coming to an end. Steve Carey was standing alone a couple of yards from the other officers. He nodded as Jock and I came up. "Morning, Steve," I said. "Know anything yet?"

"No. J.D. just got here. We're waiting for the forensic guys."

J.D. saw us and walked over. I handed her the cup of coffee I'd brought, knowing she'd need it. She smiled. "Thanks, Matt."

"Is it the same M.O.?" asked Jock.

"It is," J.D. said. "Shot in the back of the head, small caliber slug, no exit wound."

"And the whale tail earring?"

"Yeah. And the initials in the back of her neck."

"I guess I did shoot the wrong man on Saturday," said Jock. "Qualman was just a hired gun."

J.D. shook her head. "The man you shot was trying to kill me, Jock. But I don't understand your argument. If Qualman didn't kill Nell Alexander, why did he have her BMW?"

"I think he killed Nell," said Jock, "but he was just the messenger. I think whoever is running this show may be after you, and Nell was just a random kill. Something to get your attention, to draw you toward the Miami killings."

Steve Carey had been looking toward the victim as we talked. I wasn't paying any attention until I heard him yell, "Hey."

I looked up in time to see him knocked to the ground, blood pouring from his left shoulder. In the same instant, I heard the crack of a rifle coming from the east, farther down the sand track that formed the southern fork in the path. Everyone hit the ground, a trained response to the sound of gunfire. J.D. was already moving toward Steve, and I had risen to my knee, pistol drawn, beginning to point toward the sound of the rifle, when it cracked again. Anyone who has been in combat, and I have, knows the sound of a round whizzing near your head. That sound took me back to the ground. In the second I was on my knee, I had seen two men in the distance, perhaps a hundred feet away at the point where the southern fork intersected with a boardwalk that ran down to a viewing platform at the water's edge.

J.D. was next to Steve, who had not moved since he hit the ground. "He's breathing," she shouted. "We've got to get that sniper."

Cops were coming alive now, firing from their prone positions. Jock was moving at a crouch through the trees and bushes that bordered the path. Seconds had passed since the first shot and Jock hadn't gotten very far. The rifle fire had stopped, and I could see only one man on the path. He was holding a weapon, bringing it into firing position.

A hail of automatic fire came our way. It was high and I could hear the slugs ripping through the foliage above us. Everybody put their heads down again. No one wanted to be standing if the shooter brought the muzzle lower. He ripped off a fusillade and then disappeared. I stood, as did a couple of the other cops. The man stepped back into the path and fired again, a short burst, high. We went back to the ground. Jock hadn't moved. He was still in the foliage, but only a few feet down the path. The man ducked toward the boardwalk, and seconds later, reappeared and let go another short burst.

The shooter disappeared again, and this time, he stayed gone. Nobody moved for a minute or so. We didn't know if he was coming back. Jock moved a few feet down the path, still in the bushes. Another minute passed, and then I heard the roar of high-powered marine engines coming from the bay to the south of us where a sheltered anchorage lay.

Jock was moving at a run along the path. I got to my feet and followed. J.D. was ordering somebody to call for an ambulance. I wasn't sure the guy with the gun was gone, and I ran on the edge of the sand, ready to jump into the bushes that lined the path if he showed again.

Jock was only two or three yards ahead of me when he reached the intersection. He turned right toward the boardwalk and I followed. We got to the viewing platform in time to watch a go-fast boat receding in the distance, her wake roiling the three sailboats anchored in the cove. The boat cleared the anchorage and turned right into Longboat Pass heading at high speed for the open Gulf of Mexico.

We ran back toward the fork and met some of the officers coming our way. "They're gone," I said. "They were in a blue go-fast boat with white topsides, possibly a Fountain, thirty-five feet in length, center console, headed out Longboat Pass."

One of the officers said, "I've got this," and began speaking into his mic, putting out the word to the Coast Guard and the marine patrols from the various law enforcement agencies. He also asked for a helicopter. I didn't think it would do much good. That boat could run better than seventy miles per hour, and the Gulf had been flat when we crossed the Longboat Pass Bridge a few minutes before. The boat would be into Tampa Bay in a few minutes.

Steve was awake when we got back to the fork. He was in pain, but he only grimaced. "You okay, buddy?" I asked.

"I will be. I think. Matt, lean down here." I did and he whispered something I didn't hear. I shook my head. "Closer," he said. And when I was close enough for him to whisper into my ear, he said, "You take care of J.D. She's not as tough as she thinks she is, and I'm pretty sure that round in my shoulder was meant for her."

CHAPTER NINETEEN

It was nearing midnight, a time when the predators stalk their prey and death comes quickly to the unwary. Jeff Worthington was not pretending to be a lawyer on this dark Monday evening. He was carrying out the orders of the controller. Sort of.

The controller had saddled him with a cretin named Steiffel, a man Jeff had known in prison. If Steiffel had a first name, Jeff had never heard it. Steiffel was big and slow and stupid, but the controller had been told that he was an expert with a sniper rifle, that he'd been trained by the Marines before he ran afoul of the law. Jeff didn't believe it, but there wasn't much he could do about it.

Steiffel had acquired a car earlier in the afternoon by simply taking the airport shuttle bus to Tampa International and stealing a vehicle from the long-term parking lot. He'd driven back to Bradenton and was parked in the parking lot of a bar on Cortez Road waiting for Jeff to call with instructions.

Jeff parked his Mercedes in the lot of a small strip mall in West Bradenton and walked three blocks to an all-night Walmart store's parking lot. He stood in the shadows of the store overhang and watched a Hispanic couple leave an older Nissan in the lot and trudge into the store. In two minutes, Jeff was in the car, hot-wired it, and drove to a dark section of Bradenton that catered to the Mexicans who were employed by the landscape companies that trimmed the yards of rich people.

Jeff found a sad old prostitute whom no one would miss. She worked the street in this bleak part of the world, selling herself to the farm workers, most of whom were illegals, and would not go to the law even if they knew that a crime had been committed. He offered her twenty dollars for a quick trick in the backseat. She willingly got in the car, took the bill from the man's hand, and asked what he wanted.

Jeff pulled a twenty-two pistol from under his seat, hiding it down by his left leg. "I think just a little loving will do me fine," he said. "Uh-oh, is that the law?" He was pointing out the right side of the car with his right hand. The doomed whore turned to look, and Jeff brought the gun up in his left hand and shot her in the back of the head.

He let the body sag onto the floorboard. He threw a blanket over the dead woman and drove to Leffis Key. He pulled into the parking lot and stopped at the entrance path that ran back into the mangroves. He removed the woman's body and placed it near the path, hidden by the undergrowth. He drove across the street and parked in the Coquina Beach parking lot. If the police saw the car, they'd probably find out that it was stolen, but by then Jeff would be long gone.

He used a towel to wipe down the car, cleaning every surface he'd touched. He wasn't worried about cleaning up any blood. The cops could match DNA and determine that the whore had been killed in this car, but there was no way to connect him to the car. He pulled his backpack from the backseat, shrugged it onto his shoulders, and walked across the street and back to the body. He lifted it over his shoulder and walked down the path. He leaned her against the tree at the apex of the fork and placed her hands in her lap. He pulled a large cork and a small plastic case from the backpack. He opened the case and retrieved a large gauge needle attached to a syringe. He put the cork behind the left earlobe of the dead woman and pushed the needle through the flesh. He pulled another small case from the backpack and pulled out a silver whale tail earring and placed it in the hole he'd made in the earlobe. He bent her over at the waist, lifted her hair and used a small knife to carve three initials in the flesh of the back of her neck. He stripped her clothes off and propped her against the tree again, tied her there with rope from the backpack. He stood and surveyed his handiwork. It looked good. He rummaged around in the backpack until he found a high-resolution digital camera.

He was sweating now, but he was about done. He took several pictures of the woman, taking the chance that there was no one about to see the flash. He'd use the photographs later in the privacy of his bedroom to help win the release of the devils that built in him until he'd found another victim. He'd been taught well. He smiled, pulled the phone from his pocket and called Steiffel to come get him. He looked again at the dead woman, smiled, repacked his gear, and walked back to the parking lot that abutted the entrance to Leffis Key.

Steiffel arrived a few minutes later. They drove to the strip mall where Jeff had left his Mercedes. Steiffel followed him back to Longboat Key and to a beachfront condominium complex. Jeff parked his car and the two of them drove to a large house that fronted Anna Maria Sound just south of Palma Sola Bay where a large Fountain go-fast boat perched on a lift. Jeff had watched the place for two days and was pretty sure nobody was home. They parked in the back of the overflow lot of the Seafood Shack, a popular restaurant a few doors south of the house. The car was invisible from the street, hidden in the shadows thrown by the trees that bordered the back of the lot. It was after midnight and the restaurant was closed and dark.

Jeff sat in the car and watched Steiffel walk down the street and around to the back of the house. He powered up the electric lift motor and slowly lowered the boat into the water. When Jeff heard the boat coming toward him, idling, its engines burbling quietly, he walked across the street to the restaurant and out to the dock. The boat eased against the pier and Jeff stepped aboard.

Dawn was two hours away, and they didn't have to be in place until just before sunup. They motored at idle speed to the middle of the bay and let the boat drift as they drank coffee from a thermos and talked of their days in prison.

They had known each other for years but had formed none of the emotional attachments that friends usually do. They were not friends and if anyone had ever asked either of them about other friends, they would have been stumped. They did not understand the concept. There were just people, some weak, some strong, and they usually figured out their place in the pecking order. The strong ruled and the weak followed orders. Jeff figured he was one of the strong ones.

Just before daybreak, they moved the boat at idle speed to the viewing platform in the little cove. They went in slowly and quietly, not wanting to disturb the boats at anchor and call attention to themselves. They shut down the engines and sat without talking, waiting for someone to find the body and summon the police. Jeff knew that the detective bitch would be among the first on the scene.

When they heard the first police siren coming from the direction of the little town of Bradenton Beach, they left the boat and moved to the place they had decided would give them the best shot. They hid in the undergrowth and watched the police gather. The woman detective arrived and was talking to a policeman who seemed to be in charge. There was no clear shot. Then two men in civilian clothes arrived and the woman went to talk to them.

Jeff did not plan to show himself, but he carried an Uzi submachine gun, ready to provide covering fire if needed. Steiffel had a rifle with a scope. He was peering into the scope trying to gauge the shot that would take out the detective. "Now," he whispered and squeezed the trigger. Jeff saw a man in uniform look at them, take a step and yell at the same moment the shot was fired. Then the cop was down. The step he'd taken put him between the detective and the sniper and he'd taken the bullet.

The cops hit the ground and began returning fire. Jeff told Steiffel to get to the boat and then sprayed the crowd with the Uzi. He wasn't trying to kill anybody, just keep them down. He wasn't afraid that Steiffel would leave him, because the man knew his life depended on Jeff getting back to make the calls he had to make. The calls that would make Steiffel very rich.

Jeff sprayed the cops twice and then ran for the boat and clambered aboard. Steiffel was at the helm and immediately pulled away from the little viewing platform and headed for the open sea. They ran west through Longboat Pass, staying within the marked channel, and turned southwest, travelling at eighty miles per hour according to the speedometer in the dash. The depth sounder was reading twenty-five feet when Jeff told Steiffel to come down to idle speed.

The boat was rocking in its own wake as Jeff got out of his seat. "Get the guns," he said. "I want them overboard. Nobody will find them out here."

Steiffel retrieved the two weapons and stood at the gunwale to drop them overboard. Jeff pulled a nine-millimeter pistol from his pocket and shot Steiffel in the back of the head, grabbing him by the belt before he had a chance to fall overboard. The spray from the bullet exiting the front of Steiffel's head went into the Gulf, leaving only a few droplets on the boat.

Jeff let the body fall so that it was half in the boat and half out, the blood from the head wound draining into the water. He'd clean the little that got on the boat as soon as the body was gone. He didn't plan to leave any DNA evidence to be found by the police when they located the boat.

Jeff stripped and took a set of different clothes from a canvas bag, replacing them with what he had worn that morning. He tied the bag securely to the legs of the body hanging over the gunwale, and then secured an anchor to the body with a length of chain he'd brought for this purpose. He used a towel that had been in the clothes bag to wipe down the boat, clearing all fingerprints and the spots of blood on the gunwale. The towel went into the bag and he closed it tightly with its drawstrings. Finally, Jeff lifted the body by the legs and tumbled it into the sea. The anchor took it out of sight within seconds. Jeff shrugged and wiped his hands. "The wages of failure," he said, quietly. "So be it. The bitch is still breathing."

Jeff ran the boat straight toward shore, keeping the speed at about fifty miles per hour, the craft lighter without the dead man. He was pretty far south and did not think the police would have had a chance to get assets in place to find him. He'd only left Leffis Key fifteen minutes before. As he neared the beach, he slowed, used the boat's hydraulics to lift the engines, and drifted the bow onto the sand. He wiped down the steering wheel and throttle controls with the tail of his shirt. He threw an anchor onto the beach, hopped off the boat and secured it. To a casual observer, he was just some guy in a fancy boat coming onto the beach.

He was now dressed in white shorts, a white golf shirt, and white running shoes. He walked across the beach to the boardwalk that crossed the dunes into the condominium property. The building was built on tall pilings with parking underneath on the ground floor. When he was in the garage and could not be seen from any of the condo units, he walked south until the garage ended, crossed onto another property and into the same first floor garage setup. He went to the Mercedes that he'd parked there four hours before, got in, and drove off.

CHAPTER TWENTY

The emergency room of Blake Hospital was full of officers from Longboat Key, some in uniform and the off-duty ones in civilian clothes, a mixture of jeans, shorts, T-shirts, golf shirts, running shoes, flip-flops, and boat shoes. J.D. and I sat with Jock and Chief Bill Lester. We were all waiting for an update on Steve Carey's condition.

In the more than fifty years of the existence of the Town of Longboat Key, no police officer had ever been shot. I wondered if we would make another half century without more bloodshed. The world was changing, coarsening, becoming more violent, and it was only natural that some of that would bleed across the bridges onto our island paradise. Technically, Steve had been shot on Anna Maria Island, not Longboat Key, but the difference was only one of degree. Leffis Key was only a few hundred yards north of the bridge leading to Longboat Key, and Steve Carey was certainly one of us, a Longboater.

A woman in blue scrubs came through the doors that led to the treatment rooms and walked toward us. Bill Lester stood. He was in civilian clothes. He intercepted the woman. "I'm Bill Lester," he said. "Chief of police on Longboat Key. How's Officer Carey?"

"I'm Dr. Montoya," she said. "Where is Officer Carey's family? I need to talk to them."

"We're his family," said Lester. "Talk to me."

She let out a breath, smiled. "Way too much testosterone in here. He's in good shape. The bullet went through his upper arm without hitting anything important. I stitched him up and he'll be sore for a few days, but he'll ultimately be good as new."

I could see the relief written on the faces of all the men and women who had gathered in a tight circle around the chief and the doctor. Steve had been lucky, and each of the officers had spent at least a moment or two contemplating the fact that he or she could have been the one shot. And that the shot might not have missed something vital.

"Can I see him?" asked the chief.

"Sure," said the doctor. "We're going to keep him overnight to make sure an infection doesn't set in. Go on back before we send him upstairs."

"I need these three with me," the chief said, gesturing toward J.D., Jock, and me.

The doctor nodded and led us back to a treatment room.

Carey was sitting up in bed, his arm bandaged and in a sling. He was grinning when we walked in. "Chief, you got to start paying me hazardous-duty pay."

"What did you do to piss off the shooter?" asked Lester.

Steve turned serious. "He wasn't after me, Chief. That shot was meant for J.D."

"Why do you think that?" asked J.D., surprise in her voice.

"I had just moved in front of you, between you and the shooter, when he fired. If he hadn't winged me, I think that round would have gotten you."

J.D. was quiet for a moment. Then, "Were you trying to protect me, Steve?"

"No. I saw the gunman and started moving toward him. I never thought about him shooting at you. Not until afterward, anyway. The shot came so quick after I took that step that he had to have zeroed in on you. You were the target, J.D., not me."

J.D. stood for another moment, mulling that over. "Maybe you're right," she said. "But you saved my butt, Steve, whether you meant to or not. I owe you big-time."

"Bring me a six-pack of Bud and we'll call it even," he said.

That broke the icy tension that had settled over the small room. We laughed for the first time that day. "I'll see what I can do," J.D. said. "You get some rest. I'll check in on you this afternoon."

●   ●   ●

J.D., Jock, and I were in my Explorer headed back to Leffis Key to get J.D.'s car. "Do we know who called this in?" I asked J.D.

"Yeah, a guy named Don Buckler."

"Is he a suspect?"

"No. I met Don last spring. He's from Louisville and comes to visit his daughter. He's an artist and was out birding, planning to sketch some species they don't have in Kentucky. He parked in the lot and walked right into the body. Called 911 and waited for the law to show up."

"Was he able to give you any more information than that he found the body?"

"No. The Bradenton Beach lieutenant took a pretty detailed statement. He told me what Don had to say. I'll get a copy of the recorded statement as soon as it's transcribed."

"Is there going to be a turf war over who gets the lead on the case?" asked Jock.

"No. I told the lieutenant about the murders in Miami and the threats to me here, so he's happy to let Longboat run the show."

"Threats?" I asked. "As in more than one?"

"Well, there was the phone call on Saturday evening when we were leaving Moore's, then the attempt to kill me in the parking lot at the Lazy Lobster."

I shrugged. "I kind of figured those were one and the same. The caller trying to make good on his threat."

"And of course, there was the call I got last night."

I sat up straighter. "You got another threat?"

"Yeah, about midnight."

"Same voice as at Moore's?"

"I don't think so, but I wouldn't swear to it."

"What did he say?"

"I hope you enjoyed today's sunset, bitch. It could be your last."

CHAPTER TWENTY-ONE

"What?" I said, my voice rising. "You went to that crime scene in spite of that threat? Are you crazy?" I didn't like her being a target and I didn't think she was taking the threats seriously enough.

"Calm down, Matt," J.D. said. "I wouldn't have gone if I'd thought somebody would try to shoot me. Last time he waited a couple of days to come after me."

"For some reason," said Jock, "whoever is murdering these women has you in his sights, too. I know our working hypothesis is that the guy running the show is probably someone you put away. But we might be sniffing the wrong trail. If so, when we figure out the reason for wanting you dead, we might be able to find the bastard."

"None of this makes any sense to me," J.D. said. "I was a rookie detective when the killings happened in Miami. I was just a small part of a larger task force, and we never found the killer. But if it's not tied to those murders—and the murder weapon says it is—why is the guy after me?"

"You're pretty sure it's not somebody you arrested later?" Jock asked.

"So far, I can't find anybody who would have been involved in any way with the Miami murders and who had some contact with me."

"What about the other detectives on the task force?" I asked. "Have any of them had any death threats over the years?"

"No. I checked. The chief of detectives talked to everybody on that task force and none of them have been approached. Two of the detectives are dead, but both of them died of natural causes several years ago. My old partner couldn't come up with anyone who we thought could be involved."

"Do you think the guy committing the murders here is just using the dead women as bait to get to you?" I asked.

"That doesn't make any sense. He could get me with a lot less trouble," she said. "I'd be pretty easy pickings on the key most any time."

"Then why the dead ladies on our island?" I asked

"I think they're connected," she said, "but I can't figure out why."

"Maybe," said Jock, "the guy is just as twisted as the one in Miami. Or maybe our murderer is the one from Miami who's just been asleep for twelve years. For whatever reason."

"Two problems with that theory," said J.D. "One, serial killers don't just stop. They get too much of a rush out of the murders. Particularly the ritualistic ones like we have. Secondly, even if the guy was in prison or for some reason just decided to take a twelve-year sabbatical, why would he be after me? I can't see where I fit into this."

"There's a connection there somewhere," I said. "We just don't see it yet."

"Do you want to stay involved in this, Jock?" asked J.D. "I'm pretty sure Nell Alexander was just a random victim. No connection to your agency."

"Intended or not, the bastard took out one of ours. I'm in until we get him. The director said to stay as long as I need to. He's ready to give you whatever help he can from Washington."

J.D. nodded. "I'll keep you in the loop. Tell your director we appreciate his offer."

We pulled into the parking lot at Leffis Key. The crime-scene truck and two Bradenton Beach police cruisers were still there, parked amid several civilian cars. Perhaps twenty people dressed in shorts and casual shirts milled about on the sand parking area. Yellow crime-scene tape was strung across the entrance to the preserve, and a uniformed cop stood behind it, keeping out the curious who gather at every tragedy.

J.D. got out as I pulled to a stop. She stood at the open door and said, "I'm going to the station. I want to get an update on what's going on. Do you guys want to meet for lunch and let me fill you in?"

I looked at my watch. It wasn't quite ten, early for a day that was already long. "Dry Dock?" I asked.

"Sure. Grab a table outside. See you at noon."

CHAPTER TWENTY-TWO

The sun was high and bright, but the lack of humidity and the breeze off the bay made for a pleasant day. Jock and I were led to a table under the roof that had recently been added to the Dry Dock's bayside dining area. The space was open on three sides, giving us a panoramic view of Sarasota Bay and the city beyond. The green water shimmered, the occasional ripple as bright as an emerald. The tables were mostly taken, some locals, a few snowbirds and tourists, all enjoying a peaceful day in the sun. Servers hustled about their business, filling glasses, bringing food, clearing plates.

The great white egret that lived on the property ambled along the sea wall, seemingly oblivious to the funny-looking humans who sat in the shade. I saw J.D. making her way to our table. She was wearing her usual cop attire, dark slacks, white polo shirt, and sensible pumps. She'd left her equipment belt in the car, but I knew she would have her .38 police special in an ankle holster, hidden by the slacks. Her hair hung loosely to her shoulders, and a smile of recognition lit up her elegant face. "She's a beauty," I said under my breath to Jock.

"She's also armed and dangerous," he said, smiling. "Be careful, podna."

I watched her walk toward us, her gait relaxed, the smile radiating good cheer. My heart did that thing it always does when I see her, a little jig of joy at the prospect of spending time with her.

I had been in love only once in my life and I had managed to screw that up. While I was working so hard at being a lawyer, I forgot that a marriage takes a little work, too. My wife Laura gave it her all, but it wasn't enough. Not when she had to deal with a husband who was so intent on climbing the success ladder that he didn't realize that without Laura, nothing else would matter.

She finally gave up, divorced me and left with nothing but her car. She'd found happiness with a widowed doctor in Atlanta and was raising his two daughters as her own when she died. I had never filled the hole left in my life when she moved out, and her death taught me that some things cannot be remedied; that sometimes a hole just gets bigger and bigger until it consumes you.

J.D. had slipped up on me. We had become friends, and one day I realized that the hole in my life was being filled ever so slowly by this lovely cop. I was falling in love, but so far our relationship had remained platonic. I was afraid to push it, as I'd had almost no indication that she had feelings for me that were more than casual. There had been one or two moments when I thought something might break, that we might take that next step and become more than friends. But those moments always slipped away, and our connection had remained that of friends, nothing more.

She reached our table, took a seat, and ordered an iced tea from the server. "We found the boat," she said. "They beached it behind a condo at mid-key. The crime scene techs are working on it now, but it looks clean. No prints at all, nothing."

"Anything on the shooters?" asked Jock.

"A condo owner saw a man beach the boat and walk away. Like he was just strolling the beach. A couple of hours later the boat was still there and was getting some pretty rough treatment. The wind had swung the stern around and the outboards' lower units were banging on the beach. She called us."

"Just one man?" I asked.

"Yes. He might have dropped his partner off someplace else. We've got our guys and some Bradenton Beach cops canvassing all the condos along our beach."

"That'll take forever," said Jock.

"Not many of the snowbirds are here yet," said J.D. "A lot of condos are empty. We're talking to the managers of each complex and asking them to contact the owners who are in residence. That saves a lot of time."

"Was the boat stolen?" I asked.

"The registration numbers said it belonged to some people who live on the bay over in Cortez. Nobody's home, but the boat lift in back of the house was down in the water. A neighbor said the owners are visiting family in Chicago, but he noticed that the boat had been on the lift last night when he took his dog for a walk."

"And," she continued, "there was a car in the lot across the street from The Seafood Shack that was stolen in Tampa yesterday. The techs are going over it now."

"Did we get an ID on the victim?" Jock asked.

"She was a forty-five-year-old drug addict named Audrey McLain who worked as a prostitute to feed her habit. Bradenton P.D. knew her well. She worked the same few blocks for years. She was a confidential informant for one of the detectives, and as long as she provided them with good information on the drug dealers, they left her alone."

"Another random victim," I said.

"Probably," said J.D.

"Did the crime scene folks find anything at Leffis Key?" I asked.

"A lot of shells from an Uzi, some shoe prints, but nothing that'll help us nail the bastards."

"Is there anything about the murdered women that stands out? Similarities? " Jock asked.

"They're all a type," she said. "White, middle aged, blonde, but those were the only similarities. They came from different backgrounds, had different jobs. We couldn't find anything that would have connected the women in Miami to each other. We're following up on that with Nell and Audrey. I doubt we'll find a connection, but we have to cover the bases."

"Anything else?" I asked.

J.D. nodded, her face tightening. "Audrey was killed with the same .22 pistol that killed Nell Alexander and those women in Miami."

CHAPTER TWENTY-THREE

The controller was pissed. His angry voice penetrated Jeff Worthington's eardrum, accompanied by a low, regularly spaced tone from the cell phone he held. His battery was low. He hoped it wouldn't expire before the controller finished his rant. He could be executed for such a breach of protocol.

"What the fuck do you mean, you went on the mission? You dumb ass. Your job is to coordinate the idiots I'm saddled with, not get involved with them. What if you'd gotten caught? I set you up to be our goddamned lawyer, the man who can get into the jails and take care of any of these idiots dumb enough to get arrested. You can't do that if you're in jail yourself."

"I thought it'd be better for me to oversee the operation from close-up. You know, after the first fuckup."

"Qualman did okay," said the controller. "He almost had the bitch detective, but he couldn't have anticipated that a man with a gun would be in the parking lot. Did you ever find out who he was?"

"The local newspaper said two men were involved. One of them is a lawyer on Longboat Key named Matt Royal. The other man was unidentified. That was it."

"I'll see what I can find out about him. In the meantime, if you so much as think about going on another operation, your life will be over. Do you understand that?"

"I thought—"

"Your answer is 'yes, sir' or 'no, sir,' nothing else," the controller shouted. "You don't take initiative, you don't make plans. You do exactly as you're told. Do I make myself clear?"

"Yes, sir."

"I'll be in touch." The phone went dead.

Worthington thought it was a good thing that the controller didn't find out that he'd gone with Qualman, too. He, not Qualman, was the one who took the woman from the house on Longboat Key, killed her, and tied her body to the tree on Sister Key. How was he to know that old rope wouldn't hold her when the tide started moving.

Qualman had set up the meeting, but it was Jeff Worthington who was in charge. The controller had told him where to leave the bodies, but he couldn't have known that he, Worthington, had to do the killing. It was not something he would delegate. His involvement had always been part of the plan. The plan drawn by the master himself.

The only reason he'd told the controller about his involvement in the most recent fiasco was that he was sure the controller would read about the operation in the papers. He'd want to know who the second man was, and Worthington thought it prudent to get ahead of the bad news. It hadn't gone as badly as it could have. The controller would get over being pissed, but Worthington had no intention of bowing out of the operations.

He needed to make the kills. It gave him a godlike power, knowing that the person he killed had no inkling of what was happening. One second they were alive, and the next second they were dead. No warning. No time to get ready. Just life one moment and death the next. And he needed the excitement that came with the kills. He'd first tasted that rush when he killed the bouncer so many years ago at the club called The Place, and he'd dreamed about that moment during the fifteen years he'd spent as a guest of the Florida Department of Corrections. Once, when he was pretty sure he could get away with it, he'd killed a young druggie during his first few days in the system.

Now he was building memories. Later, after the kills, while the bodies were cooling in some medical examiner's morgue, he would stare at the photographs and remember each detail of the kill and feel the power it brought him. A power that most mortals never tasted or even understood. It was as simple as that. He needed to make the kills. But he was good for now. He could wait a few more days before it was time to start hunting. He breathed a sigh of relief and plugged his phone into its charger.

CHAPTER TWENTY-FOUR

We finished lunch, and J.D. headed to Bradenton to the sheriff's forensics lab. She was hoping to get some information on the stolen car found
parked across the street from the Seafood Shack. It was so close to where
the boat had been stolen, that it seemed reasonable to assume that whoever
had taken the boat had also stolen the car.

Jock and I went home and took *Recess* out on a completely unpro-
ductive fishing trip to a man-made reef near the north end of Anna Maria
Island. The sea was flat, the sun warm, and the beer cold. Even without
fish, it was a fine way to spend a November afternoon.

J.D. called to report that the car had been wiped clean. No fingerprints
or anything else that would be of any use to law enforcement. She declined
my dinner invitation, saying she was tired and wanted to go home, fix
something simple for dinner, sip a glass of wine, and get back into the
David Hagberg novel she was reading.

Jock and I called it a day. That evening he got a call from Gene Alexander telling him that the medical examiner had released Nell's body and
the funeral would be the next day, a short graveside service in a cemetery
out near I-75. Eleven o'clock in the morning. Gene was going to ride to the
cemetery with Les Fulcher. Some of the other islanders would be there.

I called J.D. to see if she wanted to join us. She did, and so did Sammy.

We arrived at the cemetery shortly before the services were to begin. Like
much of the developed interior of Florida, the cemetery was a flat expanse
carved out of an old cattle ranch some years before. A stand of pine trees
bordered the property, separating it from the cars passing by on the highway.
The grave markers were those flat plaques that lay on the ground so that the

lawn mowers would clear them. One had probably been ordered for Nell.

It seemed a small ending for a life that had been lived well. But then, that's the way funerals always are. A life stops and all that is left is the corporeal body that needs to be buried or cremated. The dead will be remembered for as long as their loved ones live, but then even the memory is buried. It all seemed so useless in this context, the first step of a child, the striving for success, love, children of their own, success or failure, happiness or despair, all gone in that blink of an eye when life leaves the body. In the end, our entire lives are only a short brushstroke on the cosmic canvas.

Jock, J.D., and Sammy walked toward the little knot of people gathered at the gravesite. I lagged behind and then stopped. I watched J.D. as she moved across the close-cropped grass of the graveyard, her graceful movements so alive in this field of the dead. There is such a fine line between life and death and we never know when we'll have to cross it. I hoped it wouldn't be soon.

"Matt," J.D. said, "are you coming?" She was a few feet in front of me, looking back, wondering, I guess, why I had stopped. Jock and Sammy had moved on.

I wrenched myself back to reality. Only a couple of seconds had elapsed as I stood rooted. I looked at her, thinking that life does go on and as long as we are breathing, happiness is within reach. Maybe she was my happiness. I smiled. "Coming," I said.

The service was short and the crowd dispersed quickly. We paid our condolences to Gene and drove back to the key. J.D. told us that the forensic people had finished examining the go-fast boat that was assumed to be the one used by the Leffis Key killers. It had been wiped clean, but one of the technicians found a single fingerprint on a stern cleat. It looked as if one of the men had touched the cleat while he was securing a line.

"Were you able to match it?" Jock asked.

"Yes. To a man named Barry Steiffel. He was on parole, released a month ago from Glades Correctional."

"The same place where Qualman served time," I said.

"Exactly," said J.D.

"Do we know where Steiffel is now?" asked Jock.

"No," said J.D. "He never checked in with his parole officer in Miami."

"Is that where he's from?" I asked.

"Yeah," said J.D. "He went up for armed robbery in Miami Beach. Did eight years of a ten-year sentence."

"Did you arrest him?" I asked.

"No. Miami Beach is a different jurisdiction. I checked with Miami-Dade, just to be sure I'd never had anything to do with him. As far as we can tell, Steiffel and I never crossed paths."

"The lady who saw the man get off the boat on the beach said he was alone," I said. "There were definitely two leaving Leffis Key on that boat. What happened to the other guy?"

"Good question," said J.D. "Maybe one of them got off farther up the beach."

"Maybe he'll show up," Jock said. "At least we have a name now."

"You want to join us for lunch, J.D.?" I asked.

"Wish I could," she said, "but I've got to finish up some paperwork. That's the worse part of this job."

"Sammy's got to work, but Logan's going with us to Tommy Bahama's restaurant on the Circle tonight. You want to join us?"

"Sorry," she said. "I'll be on the Circle, but I'm meeting an old friend from Miami for dinner and drinks at Lynches Pub."

We dropped her at the police station and took Sammy a little farther south to Pattigeorge's. "I wonder about the friend from Miami," I said as Jock and I drove north toward the village.

"Slow down, podna. I know what you're thinking, and you're probably wrong."

"I hope so," I said.

"We could stop by Lynches for drinks after dinner."

"Yeah. That wouldn't be at all obvious. You're not very good at this, are you?"

"Hey," he said, "I'm not the one in love."

"I don't know whether I am or not. It's confusing."

"Geez. We sound like we're still in high school."

And I guess we did. But if I had known what the night would bring, I would have turned around and taken J.D. home with me. Even if I had to kidnap her to do it.

CHAPTER TWENTY-FIVE

During her early years in Miami, J.D. had become friends with a young prosecutor named Deanna Bichler. While J.D. moved up the ranks of the Miami-Dade Police Department, Deanna had left the state attorney's office and moved into private practice with a Miami law firm. Over the years, her brilliance and penchant for hard work had made her one of the top criminal defense attorneys in the state. She was now almost forty years old, but seemed forever young. She had not aged since her mid-twenties, and, in the parlance of the young men who lusted after her, she was "hot." She was wearing her lawyer uniform, gray suit, white blouse, low-heeled pumps. Her dark hair was fixed in a bun at the nape of her neck, a small diamond stud in each earlobe, a single gold strand necklace around her neck.

J.D. and Deanna had been bridesmaids in each other's weddings, but unlike J.D.'s disastrous stab at matrimony, Deanna's had prospered. She now had three children and a husband who practiced civil law in another large Miami firm. She was happy, but missed the camaraderie she and J.D. had enjoyed over the fifteen years they had known each other. Telephone calls and Facebook just weren't the same as sharing a drink and some laughs in South Beach.

Deanna had spent the day in federal court in Tampa doing battle with the U.S. Attorney's Office on a fraud case. There had been several motions to be heard, and they hadn't finished by the time the judge wanted to call it a day.

Her client was wealthy and had made his money with a sophisticated Medicare scam that milked the taxpayers for millions of dollars. She had called J.D. on Sunday and told her that she would be in Tampa and, if J.D.

had time for dinner, she would drive down and meet her. She had to be back in court early the next day and would drive back to her hotel in Tampa after dinner. They had agreed to meet at Lynches Pub on St. Armands Circle.

J.D. parked in back of the pub, in a large parking lot that accommodated visitors to the shops and restaurants that lined the Circle. She had what the Lynch sisters, Ethna and Chris, who owned the place, called "back-door privileges." It was a perk that was given only to the locals who were friends of "the girls," as they were universally called by the islanders.

She came in through the kitchen, and saw Deanna sitting at a small table in the front of the narrow space that housed the pub. She smiled as she noticed how Deanna was dressed. She felt decidedly unprofessional in white Capri pants, a pale-green blouse, and sandals, her hair in a ponytail. But then, that was the island uniform. They hugged, ordered drinks, and caught up with all the gossip from Miami. "So," J.D. said, "sounds like a big case in Tampa."

"Yeah. My client is guilty as sin, but there's a lot of money involved, so the U.S. Attorney himself is handling it. Big Daddy."

"Big Daddy?"

Deanna smiled. "Yes, that's what he's called. He's pretty much a big teddy bear, but he gives no quarter in the courtroom."

"David Parrish?" asked J.D.

"You know him?"

"A friend of a friend. I actually met him a couple of days ago."

"Small world. How does your friend know him?"

"They were classmates in law school."

Deanna smiled. "So, your friend is a lawyer. Male or female?"

"Most definitely male."

"I see. Might he be more than just a friend?"

"It's complicated," said J.D.

"I thrive on complications. Give it up, old friend. How long have you been sleeping with him?"

"I haven't."

"Hmmmm."

"I told you it was complicated."

Deanna made a "come on" gesture with her fingers.

"Okay," said J.D. "I can't sort it all out. He's the most intriguing man I've ever met. He's a retired trial lawyer who insists his only goal in life is to be a beach bum."

"Ah, an older man."

"Not at all. He retired early. Got disgusted with the practice of law. Says it turned into a business instead of a profession."

"I think he knows whereof he speaks."

J.D. laughed. "Yeah."

"Did he practice here?"

"Orlando."

"What's his name?"

"Matt Royal."

Deanna sat back. "He was big-time."

"You know him?"

"Only by reputation. Never met him. But he was at the top of his game when he just up and quit. Somebody told me he'd moved to an island. I didn't know it was this one."

"Well, he's here, and he's—unsettling, I guess."

"How so?"

"I'm not sure I can explain it. He gives me something I thought I'd never feel again. A sense of comfort and a little tingle every time I think about seeing him."

"Do you see him a lot?"

"It's a small island. I see him almost every day. And he has a way of getting in the middle of some of my cases. And he thinks he needs to protect me. I'm a big girl. I don't need that."

"The male ego," said Deanna. "Those old-boy trial lawyers seem to have some sort of genetic disorder that floods their systems with testosterone. That leads to outsized egos. I don't think they could spend their lives the way they do without it. They're problem solvers by nature and they think they can fix anything; particularly women in need of protection. And in their fevered little brains, all women need protection."

J.D. laughed. "You're a trial lawyer. How do you handle it?"

"I ignore it most of the time. Men like David Parrish are almost courtly.

Sometimes he treats me like I'm his daughter, but when it comes to a case, he's sharp as a spear. And he's aiming it at me, smiling, and treating me with the utmost respect. But I know, and he knows, that he's going to gut me if he can."

"So," asked J.D., "what's your take on the way Matt treats me? All protective."

"I think he sees you in a lot more than a professional light."

"He's told me as much."

"And your response?"

"I told him that he was a very special person to me. We even discussed sleeping together once, but we both decided we weren't ready for that."

"And since?" asked Deanna.

"It's never come up again."

"And how do you feel about that?"

"I don't know. It's a small island and I don't want complications. I've only been on the police force here for a year, and the chief is one of Matt's best friends."

"You're going to have to discuss this with Matt sooner or later."

"I know. I keep putting it off."

"He hasn't brought it up again?"

"No. I think he's too much of a gentleman."

"Or too scared."

"Well," said J.D., chuckling, "there's that."

They changed the subject and spent another hour talking about their lives and those of mutual friends in Miami. J.D. didn't bring up the fact that she had been the target of two murder attempts in the past three days. No sense in putting a wet blanket over the evening.

Deanna looked at her watch. "Good grief," she said. "It's almost eleven and I've got an early morning with Big Daddy. I'd better get on the road."

They said their good-byes and hugged. Deanna left by the front door and J.D. went to the bar and spent a few minutes talking to Jill, the night manager. It was nearing midnight when she took her leave and went through the back door, headed for her car and home. She didn't notice the man hiding in the shadows of the building next door.

CHAPTER TWENTY-SIX

J.D. never knew what it was. Maybe a minuscule change in air pressure brought about by the proximity of another person. Perhaps she heard a footstep on the asphalt of the parking lot or a squeak from a running shoe worn by the man in the shadows. An intake of breath, an exhalation, a grunt as he pulled the large KA-BAR knife from its scabbard. Something. Somehow she knew that danger was close, that her life was about to be snuffed out. Whatever it was, it put her on alert and set off the alarm bells in her mind, the ones that she'd honed during her fifteen years of police work and regular workouts with her martial arts master.

She pivoted on the ball of her left foot, coming to rest facing her assailant, her knees bent, her arms up in the strike position. Only a fraction of a second had elapsed since she felt the alert. It was almost enough.

She saw a big man, maybe six two, 220 pounds, a large knife in his left hand, held at waist height in striking position. As she planted herself on the asphalt, the knife was moving toward her midsection. She dodged to her right, putting her weight on her right foot as she felt the knife slice into her left side. She refused to think about it. Her left foot came up in a power kick, catching her assailant off guard, his momentum from the slashing dive still carrying him forward. Her foot impacted with his left rib cage. J.D. knew that bones were broken.

The big man fell forward and to his right, the blow from J.D.'s foot pushing him off balance, the pain of the broken ribs already flooding his system. J.D. brought her left foot to the ground, shifting her weight onto it as she pivoted again. The man was hitting the ground, his knees bending to catch himself, his arms outstretched to break his fall, the knife skittering across the surface of the parking lot. He was hurt badly, moaning as he landed on his knees. His hands had slid along the rough surface, but his knees held. He was in a position not unlike that of Muslim men praying, his legs slightly splayed. J.D. finished her pivot almost directly behind the man. She aimed her right foot between his legs and delivered a powerful blow to his scrotum.

The man yelled in pain, turned on his side and drew his legs up in a fetal position. J.D. sidestepped and kicked him in the face, just for the hell of it, and because the adrenalin rush was still in full force, giving her more energy than she'd ever felt.

Then, the pain hit her. She felt her side. Her blouse was wet and sticky with blood. She was armed only with a cell phone. She looked down at the man writhing in agony on the pavement. "Look, buddy," she said, "I know you're hurt. I'm calling the medics, but if you move a muscle, I'm going to kick you in the face again. Understand?"

The man on the ground nodded. Blood was running from his nose and mouth, but his hands were still in his crotch, holding onto what he probably considered his most important body part. J.D. dialed 911.

"This is Detective J. D. Duncan, Longboat PD. I'm in the parking lot behind Lynches Pub on St. Armands. I've been attacked, but I have the assailant under control. I need two ambulances and backup ASAP."

"On the way, Detective. Are you hurt?"

"Yes. He got me with a knife."

A couple of minutes after she hung up, she heard a siren and saw the blue lights of a police cruiser rushing into the lot. She wasn't surprised at the quick response. She knew that the Sarasota Police Department always had a unit near the Circle. It allayed the fears of the tourists who sometimes kept the bars open until the wee hours of the morning.

The cop behind the wheel came running, his pistol drawn. He recognized J.D. and said, "Are you okay?"

"I got a knife in the side. I don't know how bad it is, but it's bleeding."

"Let me take a look."

"Secure that asshole first," she said pointing at the man on the ground.

"I don't think he's going anywhere. Did you search him?"

"Not yet." She smiled to let him know she wasn't angry at the question. The Sarasota officer did a quick pat down of the assailant and then pulled his arms behind him and cuffed his wrists. J.D. heard another siren and looked up to see a Sarasota Fire Department ambulance pulling into the parking lot. She thought it was probably from the St. Armands station three blocks away.

A paramedic rushed over. "Who's hurt?" he asked.

"This dirtbag can wait. Check on Detective Duncan first. She's bleeding," said the Sarasota cop.

The sirens had brought Jill and a cook out of Lynches' back door. Jill sat on the pavement next to J.D. and put her arm around J.D.'s shoulders. "She's bleeding pretty badly," Jill told the medic.

"I'm okay, I think," said J.D. "I don't think he got me too bad."

"What'd he get you with?" asked the medic.

"A knife. In the left side. I don't think it's too deep."

"Let me take a look," said the medic. He placed his kit on the pavement and knelt beside J.D. "I'm going to have to cut your blouse."

J.D. nodded that it was okay. The medic pulled a pair of scissors from his kit and began to cut the side of the blouse. The Sarasota cop called over. "Detective Duncan, your department has been notified. Your chief is on his way."

"Thanks," said J.D.

"What do we do with this idiot?" the cop asked the medic.

"Another ambulance is on its way," said the paramedic. "From the Longboat South station, I think. It's the closest one to us. Is he hurt bad?"

"I don't think so. It looks like the detective broke his nose and kicked his nuts up into his chest, but I think he'll live."

"You'll want a statement from me," said J.D.

"Yeah, but we'll wait until your chief gets here."

"Doesn't look too bad," said the medic. "It's just a slash, no puncture, but I think we'd better transport you. You'll probably need some stitches."

J.D. looked down at her side. "There goes the bikini," she said.

The medic smiled. "Maybe they'll be able to use some butterfly bandages and it'll heal without a scar. How's your pain?"

"Not too bad."

"You want something for it?"

"No, thanks. I think I'd better keep my wits about me."

Another ambulance came into the parking lot, its blue-and-red flashers alive. J.D. saw the Longboat Key Fire Rescue logo on its side and felt oddly relieved. It was nice to have the home team there.

The Longboat Key paramedic went to the man who lay groaning on the pavement, squatted down and looked closely at his face. They spoke quietly and then the paramedic stood. "Guy says you kicked him in the face, J.D."

"I sure did. Right after he knifed me."

"You did good," said the Longboat Key medic. "Took out a couple of teeth and broke his nose."

J.D. grinned. "I don't think that's all I broke."

The medic laughed. "He'll be walking gingerly for a while."

The back door of Lynches swung open and a man ran toward J.D. The cop moved forward to intercept him, but J.D. waved him off. "He's okay," she said.

The man knelt beside her, looked at her slit blouse and the bandage on her side. He pulled her toward him and wrapped his arms around her, holding her tightly. "Are you okay?"

"I'm fine. It's just a little cut. Probably won't even leave a scar."

He held her, his cheek to her forehead. "Goddamnit, J.D.," he said. "Goddamnit it."

She reached up and put her hand gently on his cheek, and said quietly, "I'm okay, Matt. I'm okay."

CHAPTER TWENTY-SEVEN

Jock, Logan and I had a couple of drinks at the bar at Tommy Bahama's and then moved to a booth for dinner. From there we walked to Cha Cha Coconuts for a couple more drinks, sitting at one of the sidewalk tables, enjoying the soft air of a November evening. I was into Diet Coke, since I didn't want to run the risk of a DUI, or a hangover, for that matter. Our conversation was not at all memorable, just the idle talk of three people enjoying a pleasant evening on the island.

"Sure you don't want to go across the street to Lynches?" Jock asked at some point in the evening.

"Certain," I said.

"What's wrong with Lynches?" asked Logan. "I thought that was one of your hangouts."

"J.D.'s there with a friend," I said. "I don't want to intrude."

"Matt's afraid it might be a man," Jock said.

"Ah," said Logan, grinning. "Want me to go check him out?"

"Keep your seat," I said, forcing a frown.

"Is that his serious face?" asked Logan.

"I think so," said Jock. "Or maybe he's got to pee."

"Have your sport," I said. "Man or woman, it makes no difference to me."

"Now that's his lying face," Logan said.

"That it is," said Jock.

"I think I'll go take a peek," said Logan.

I looked at my watch. It was almost midnight. "The trollies have stopped running," I said. "That'll be a long walk back to your place."

Logan laughed and raised his glass. "Point taken," he said.

I heard a siren and watched a Sarasota Police cruiser rush down Boulevard of the Presidents and turn left onto Madison Drive. "A little excitement for the cops," said Logan. "Those guys spend the whole night sitting in their cars listening to talk radio. They all hate Circle duty."

"Can't blame them," I said. "I guess it gets pretty boring."

More sirens, and an ambulance roared west on Madison Drive and crossed Boulevard of the Presidents. Just as it disappeared from sight behind the building on the southwest corner of the streets, the siren stopped. Another police car came by, lights flashing, but no siren.

"Looks like the same place the other cops went," said Jock.

"Wonder what that's all about?" asked Logan.

"Probably somebody had a heart attack," I said. "There's a lot of that around here."

"I hope whoever it is, is okay." Logan said.

We went back to our conversation.

Another ambulance came from the north, a Longboat Key ambulance this time. It turned right onto Madison and then cut its siren.

"What's Longboat Key Rescue doing down here?" Jock asked.

"It's the closest firehouse to St. Armands, other than the one around the corner," I said. "They probably only have one ambulance there, so Longboat covers. It's some kind of mutual assistance agreement between the city of Sarasota and the Town of Longboat Key."

"I wonder why they need two ambulances," said Logan.

My cell phone rattled in my pocket. I took it out and looked at the caller ID. "Bill Lester," I said. "What's he calling about this time of night?"

I opened the phone. "Isn't it past your bedtime?" I asked.

"J.D.'s been stabbed. In the parking lot behind Lynches. I'm on my way now."

"How bad?"

"Don't know yet. Paramedics are on the scene. I just got the call."

I hung up and stood abruptly, pushing my chair backward. "J.D.'s hurt," I said as I began to sprint across the street toward Lynches. As I stepped off the curb and into the northbound lane of Boulevard of the Presidents, my peripheral vision picked up a car headed north toward Longboat, coming at high speed. I was committed, too far into it to stop.

I hoped the guy had good brakes. But I don't think he even saw me. If anything, he was picking up speed, coming faster. I sprinted toward the grassy median that separated the lanes. I leapt across the last few feet and landed in the median as the oncoming car brushed past me. I felt the air displaced by its passing against my back. I crossed the median and the southbound lane and into the front door of Lynches. Only one waitress was there, standing behind the bar. "Out back, Matt," she said as I rushed through.

I hit the back door at full gallop. My first visual was of a man lying on the ground curled into a fetal position, J.D. with blood on her side, and a cop moving toward me. Paramedics were at work, one hovering close to J.D., another working on the man. Jill sat on the pavement next to J.D., but was moving away as I came to a stop and kneeled on the pavement. I thought she was dying, until I saw the smile. But that moment or two, when all I saw was blood and J.D. on the ground, would remain seared on my brain like some ugly scar.

I put my arms around her. Appearance be damned. I held her tightly, my cheek was pressed against her forehead. She put her hand on my other cheek, a gesture that seemed so intimate that I wanted to bawl. "I'm okay, Matt," she said quietly. "I'm okay."

I pulled back a little to see her face. "Are you sure?" I asked.

"I'm sure," she said, and kissed me on the lips. She held it for a second or two. It wasn't a passionate kiss, but it sure as hell wasn't just a friendly one either. "Will you ride to the hospital with me?"

"I'm not going to let you out of my sight," I said.

She grinned. "I'll probably have to undress," she said. "You know, it being an emergency room and all."

"I'll just have to suffer through it," I said.

She pulled my head down and hugged me. "I'm glad you're here."

Jock and Logan came through the back door at a run. "Is she okay?" Jock called.

"She's fine," I said.

"Then you can let her go," said Logan. "She might suffocate."

I realized I was still hugging J.D. and I loosened my grip. The Sarasota medics were putting the bad guy into their ambulance. The Longboat Key medics were waiting with a stretcher to load J.D. She stood and climbed aboard the gurney on her own. "Can Matt go with me?" she asked the medic.

"Sure, J.D.," he said.

Another car came into the parking lot, and Bill Lester scrambled out. "Is J.D. okay?" he asked.

"She's fine, chief," said the medic. "We're taking her to Sarasota Memorial for a doc to take a look. She might have to have her side stitched up, but she'll be good as new in a couple of days."

"Good to know," said Bill. "Our workers' comp premiums are already too high." He was already bleeding off the tension, trying a little humor to put us all at ease. He came over and talked for a minute to J.D. He patted her hand and waved to the medics. They loaded her into their ambulance. "Coming, Matt?" one of the medics asked. I nodded, told Bill I'd see him at the hospital, and started toward the ambulance.

"Hey, Matt," Jock said. "I need the keys to your car. We'll head on home. Looks like you've got everything in hand." A grin was plastered on his face.

I threw him the keys, gave him the finger, and climbed aboard the ambulance.

CHAPTER TWENTY-EIGHT

The Sarasota County jail stands six stories tall and sits next to the courthouse in downtown Sarasota. If not for the small windows spaced symmetrically in the façade, one would think it another of the high-rise condos that had sprouted in the downtown area.

The Thursday morning traffic was light as the man known as Ben Flagler crossed the street from the public parking lot. He glanced at his watch. A little after seven. He knew the jail would be busy, the officers trying to get the inmates ready for first appearance before a judge at the judicial center next door. His client would not be among them. He'd been at the hospital for treatment before he had been brought to the jail. He was booked into the system too late for the six a.m. cutoff for first appearances. He would have to wait until the next day for his chance to see a judge.

Ben walked through the glass doors into the anteroom of the jail. There were two deputies sitting on an elevated platform, walls hiding them almost completely. He assumed the officers were sitting at desks, but he couldn't tell. A security station manned by a guard in the uniform of a private company was directly across from the deputies. A dismal-looking waiting area was to his left as he entered, a dozen or more plastic chairs bolted to the floor, a flat-screen television mounted on brackets in a corner near the ceiling. Thankfully, at this time of the morning it was turned off. Visitors were not allowed until later in the day.

Lawyers, however, had twenty-four-hour access to their clients. Flagler handed up his driver's license and Florida Bar identification card to one of the deputies sitting on the platform. "I'd like to see my client, Fred Bagby."

"Yes, sir," said the deputy. "Have a seat and I'll have him brought to an interview room. Won't take but a few minutes."

Flagler took a seat in the waiting area. The plastic chair rocked back at an uncomfortable angle. The county had not spent a lot of money making jail visitors comfortable. He watched as a woman of about twenty came through the entrance. Her clothes were shabby, probably retrieved from a Salvation Army bin, a plaid skirt that fell to mid-shin, a ragged old golf shirt with the logo of a country club that she'd never be invited into, tattoos encircling both ankles, flip-flops on dirty feet. She spoke to no one, but walked quickly to what appeared to be an automated teller machine attached to the wall near the security guard's seat. She put a credit card into the slot, pushed some buttons, withdrew the card, and left the building without a word or even an acknowledgment that she wasn't alone in the reception room.

Curiosity compelled Flagler to examine the machine the woman had used. It wasn't an ATM, but a device that allowed anyone to put money into an inmate's account for use in the jail's canteen. You put in a credit or debit card, punched in the prisoner's number, and the amount was credited to the inmate's account. He or she could buy toothpaste or candy or whatever was available in the canteen.

He thought for a minute and went to the deputies seated on the platform. He got his client's inmate number and returned to the machine. He pulled out a credit card in Ben Flagler's name. He put it in the machine, punched in his client's number, and deposited twenty dollars.

He went back to his seat and waited quietly until a deputy came through the door on the other side of the security station. "Mr. Flagler, your client is in an interview room. I'll have to check your briefcase. If you'd just put it on the desk and step through the metal detector."

Ben set his briefcase on the table and stood to watch the private security guard open it. Security personnel were not allowed to look at any document a lawyer brought into the jail, but they were required to make sure there were no weapons. When the guard closed the briefcase, Flagler walked through the metal detector and retrieved it. The deputy led him into the bowels of the jail.

A holding cell near the entrance was full of men in orange jumpsuits. There were not enough seats for them, so most stood quietly staring at the deputy and the man in the suit. Ben nodded at one small man wearing a full gray beard. He was ignored.

The deputy said, "They're waiting to go over for first appearance. Bagby didn't get checked in soon enough to make it over today. He'll be in the bunch going over tomorrow."

The deputy stopped at an elevator, pushed the button, and waited. They went to the fourth floor and walked down a narrow corridor, the walls painted in drab institutional green. There were doors on the left that appeared to lead to small rooms. Doors on his right were more substantial and led down hallways lined with individual cells.

The deputy stopped at one of the doors on the left, opened it, and allowed Ben to enter. The room was small, just enough space for two straight chairs and a two-by-four-foot table. Bagby sat in one of the chairs, his left arm hanging at his side, the wrist encircled by one end of a handcuff, the other end attached to a ring embedded in the concrete floor. He was wearing the ubiquitous orange jumpsuit, his face haggard, hair unkempt, a day-old beard sprouting on his cheeks. His nose was bandaged and what looked like a small metal splint was visible under the dressing.

"How you doing, Fred?" Ben asked.

"My balls hurt and my nose is killing me. Every time I cough or sneeze my side hurts like a motherfucker. That bitch broke three of my ribs and my nose, knocked out two teeth, and kicked me in the nuts. You didn't tell me she could do all that kung fu shit."

"I didn't know about it. Why the hell did you use a knife? Why didn't you just shoot her?"

"I wanted to see her lights go out. Up close. As I was putting the blade in her gut."

"Geez. You're some piece of work, Bagby. Tell me what happened."

"I followed her from her condo, watched her park in the back of the restaurant, and I waited. I didn't know she was going to take all night. That pissed me off."

"Is that it? You lost your temper and got your ass kicked?"

"No. I waited until she finally came out of the restaurant and went after her. She was quick, and I wasn't expecting her to be some kind of commando chick."

The lawyer just shook his head. He'd gotten a call from the controller the morning before that scared the hell out of him.

"Look," the controller had said, "I'm tired of you fucking up. I want that detective dead. Today. Do you understand?"

"I don't know if we can set it up that quickly," said Flagler.

"It isn't rocket science. Just kill her."

"I've got to find another woman to be a whale tail victim, and—"

"What the hell is wrong with you? That first woman was to get the detective's attention. It did. The second one was to set the trap, but you blew it. We don't need any other women. Just take this one out."

"I never did understand why we needed to make this look like the whale tail murders. Why didn't we just shoot the detective in the first place?"

"Worthington," said the controller, "I take orders just like you do. The difference is that I follow mine. Get this over with, do you understand?"

"I understand. Consider it done."

But he hadn't gotten it done. Bagby blew the assignment, and the controller was going to hold it against him, Worthington.

Bagby interrupted his thoughts. "You going to get me out of here?"

"As soon as we get to the preliminary hearing in the morning. I've greased the judge. Won't be a problem."

Bagby's face twisted into a grimace. "You mean I've got to stay here until tomorrow?"

"Sorry, but that's the best I can do."

"Man, I'm not going to make it." He held up his hands. They were shaking. The sure signs of a drug addict coming off his meds.

"I've got something for you," Ben said, "but you have to save two of these until you go to bed tonight."

"Let me have them."

"I will in a minute, but you have to tell me that you'll save the blue ones for tonight. I can give you another one on the way to court tomorrow morning, but you need to space this out so that you'll sleep tonight. Understand?"

"Yeah. What've you got?"

"Oxy."

"I need it now, man."

Flagler handed him two small white pills. "Okay. Here're two. Take one now and another at lunchtime. They'll hold you through the day. Understand?"

"How many do you have?"

"Four. Take one of the white ones now and another at lunch. I've got some more for you to take at bedtime. Not before. You got that?"

"I got it," Bagby said, an edge in his voice.

Flagler handed him the two white pills and held up a small envelope. "There are two blue pills in this. Take them both when you go to bed. They'll make you sleep and keep you sharp in the morning. If you need more then, I'll have some for you before court."

"Okay. I'll hold them for tonight. I promise."

Ben knew the promise wasn't any good. A junkie will take the drug anytime his body starts screaming for it. But he didn't have a choice in the matter. The white pills were controlled release oxycodone and he thought that would keep Bagby calm until bedtime. He couldn't come back to the jail later in the day. It might raise some questions.

"These might make you drowsy today," Flagler said, "but I don't think you'll be expected to do anything but stay in your cell. Don't forget. You need to wait until lunch to take the second white pill."

Bagby put one white pill in his mouth, swallowed and smiled. "Thanks, man."

"Remember, the blue pills are for tonight. Take both of them when you're ready for bed. They'll hold you through the night. The pills look different, but they've got the same kick as the white ones. They look like capsules for indigestion. If the bulls find them, tell them that's what they are. I don't think they'll make a big deal out of it. If you take them before bedtime, you won't have anything for the rest of the night. If I find you strung out in the morning, I'll be out of here in a New York second. You'll be on your own. Do you understand?"

Bagby grinned. "You won't do that. I'll let the cops know who actually killed that woman you and Qualman put in the mangroves. I've kind of got you by the balls, Counselor."

"You listen to me, Bagby. I can get you out of here if you do what I tell you. If you don't, you'll get a shank in your gut. You don't think I'd let you stay here without some insurance in case you got talkative, do you? You won't live long enough to talk to the cops. Your only chance is me. And with me, you get a lot of money."

"You mean I'm going to get paid, even though I didn't kill that detective?"

"Our deal was that you'd get paid when she's dead. You get out, you go after her again. You kill her, you get paid."

"Okay. I'm good. And I owe that bitch."

"Hide the envelope and take the pills tonight."

"I will."

Ben stood and opened the door. The deputy was standing outside, leaning against the wall. "I'm done, deputy."

"I'll escort you out."

They went back the way they'd come. Ben was confident that Bagby would not be subjected to a search on his way back to his cell. There was too much going on at this time of the morning for the deputies to be as thorough as they would at other times of the day. Besides, lawyers did not bring contraband into the jail. To do so would mean disbarment. That was not a concern of Ben Flagler, who didn't really exist anyway.

He would come back in the morning and get the word from the jailers that his client was dead. The blue pills were instant release oxycodone. The drugs would spread through his system like poison and Bagby would drift off to sleep, never to wake again.

Flagler would be devastated, of course. Hopefully, he would be finished with this mess and gone before any toxicology results came back to the medical examiner. That usually took awhile. The toxicologists would no doubt find the poison, but by then Ben Flagler would just be a memory and Jeff Worthington would be a rich man basking in the sun on some Caribbean island.

CHAPTER TWENTY-NINE

It was early Thursday morning and the controller was on the phone with the only other person in the world, other than the crazy don, who absolutely terrified him, the one he thought of as the puppeteer. "If you don't get your ass in gear," said the voice on the other end of the line, "things are going to get complicated for you. I'm losing my patience."

"I'm sorry," said the controller, "but you didn't exactly set me up with brilliant operatives. I can't be held responsible for their fuckups."

"The one we put in as a lawyer is bright as hell. And he knows what happens if he fails. Maybe he needs a little object lesson."

"What do you mean?" asked the controller.

"Think about it," the puppeteer said, and slammed down the phone.

The controller slowly put the receiver back in its cradle. He let out a long sigh and shook his head. He didn't like being in this position, but what could he do? He'd signed the pact with the devil a long time ago.

Maybe he had assembled the wrong crew. He'd had the man now known as Ben Flagler foisted upon him. He'd argued at the time that he needed a professional to take out the detective. The puppeteer was determined to use Flagler and the men Flagler picked. The argument was that Flagler was a ruthless killer, he was smart, and the puppeteer wanted the detective to suffer before she died. Flagler could make her life difficult, frighten her for even a few hours, and then kill her. A professional would simply take her out. Not much in the way of vengeance if the detective didn't know exactly why she was dying.

He stared out his windows, enjoying the view of Biscayne Bay. Some sort of small boat sailing regatta was taking place just offshore. The blue water of the bay, the bright sails in a variety of colors, and the sun glinting off the fiberglass hulls gave him a sense of well-being. He would take care of this mess and get the puppeteer off his back. He just needed to come up with a plan to impress Flagler with his resolve.

His thoughts moved to taking the puppeteer out. That would solve his immediate problem, but then the crazy don might get wind of the controller's part in any such action, and the consequences for the controller would be too horrible to contemplate. The puppeteer was too close to the don and his vengeance would be swift and brutal. Even a very small chance that the don would find out that the controller had any part in the puppeteer's demise was simply too big a chance for the controller to take. He shrugged off the idea, and moved on, his mind sweeping through many scenarios before he landed on one that just might work and would never cause any blowback to him.

The controller smiled and his mind wandered on to the island where his new life would begin if he had to shuck himself of this one. He just needed a few more days to have everything ready. The money was already in place, hiding in secret bank accounts around the world. New identity papers, done by one of the world's foremost forgers, were in a lockbox in a bank in Orlando, the forger now sleeping with the angels after a well-placed gunshot to the back of his head. The controller had stashed a pickup truck in a parking garage in North Miami, using a fictitious name. Not the one on the papers in the bank in Orlando, but one that would pass the cursory inspection of the people who ran that parking garage. He'd arranged for an illegal Mexican farmworker to drive the truck every other Sunday, keeping it in working order and full of gas. If he had to run, he'd drive to Orlando, retrieve his documents, and park the pickup at the airport. He'd rent a car, using yet another set of papers, drive to New Orleans, and catch a plane to Atlanta. Each leg of his trip would be with false papers, each set different from the others. Even if his pursuers somehow were able to trace him to the pickup and thus to Orlando, the trail would run cold there. Or maybe in New Orleans. He didn't think they'd ever be able to trace him further. From Atlanta, he'd use the master forger's documents and the credit cards that he'd set up with false identities over the past five years. They'd never find him on the island where he'd spend the rest of his life.

It was a good plan, one that he had been putting in place for a long time. He understood that nothing was completely foolproof, but this one was as close as it got. Life was full of gambles, and he only bet on almost-sure things. This plan was as near perfect as he could make it. If it didn't work, then he would die. But he had set up trip wires that would let him know if he was being closed in on. If his discovery was inevitable, he'd simply kill himself. He would maintain control of his destiny and his death would be painless, not the gruesome end orchestrated by the crazy don.

The controller chuckled to himself. No matter how good his plan was, or how long he was able to maintain his secret life, the end result would be his death. With any luck, the Grim Reaper would sneak in and take him during his ninetieth year while he was asleep in a comfortable bed in his island refuge. Maybe with a nubile native girl lying beside him, sated after a night of wild sex. Did ninety-year-old men still have sex? He didn't know, but he smiled at the thought of someday discovering the answer.

CHAPTER THIRTY

I awoke a little after eight the next morning, a Thursday. We had not gotten home from the hospital until almost four a.m. Chief Bill Lester had
stayed in the ER to make sure that J.D. was okay, and then drove us home.
He and I talked J.D. into staying at my cottage for the night, or what was
left of it. I have three bedrooms, each with a private bath. I had the one
overlooking the bay and one was Jock's room, where he left what he called
his island clothes when he went home to Houston. The third bedroom
was my guest room, and that is where J.D. had crashed.

I didn't want her unprotected during the night, and I wasn't sure she
might not need some help with her bandages. She had reluctantly agreed
to stay, but said she would be going home first thing in the morning. She
had to work. Bill told her that if she showed up at the office, he would arrest her. "Take a few days," he said. "This is the third time in four days
somebody's tried to kill you."

"I can handle this, Chief," she said.

"I know you can, J.D., but not with your side split open. You heal a bit
and then get back and take over the case. We need you."

I hadn't slept well for the three hours I lay in the bed. I was worried
about J.D. and the fact that somebody was trying to kill her. But I was also
puzzled by her reactions the previous evening. She had never kissed me on
the lips before, and I didn't know if we had passed some threshold, or if it
was just the circumstances.

I was sitting on the patio sipping coffee and watching the birds when
the sliding glass door to the living room opened. "Matt? Can you help me
with this bandage?"

She was barefoot, wearing the same pants she'd had on the night before and a green shirt from a set of scrubs that had been given to her at the hospital to replace her bloodied and ripped blouse.

I followed her into her bedroom and sat on the bed next to the package of bandages and tape one of the nurses had given her as we left the hospital. She raised her shirt and I pulled the tape off as gently as I could. The cut had not been stitched, but was held together by a number of small butterfly bandages. The laceration wasn't too big, about three inches in length. Her skin had a reddish-orange hue left over from the antiseptic poured over it by the hospital doctor. I rubbed some antibacterial salve from the package onto the puckered skin of the cut. "That's going to start scabbing over soon," I said. "How bad is the pain this morning?"

"Mostly gone. I did feel it when I rolled over on that side during the night, but otherwise, I think it's okay."

"You've got to check in with the doctor tomorrow. Why don't you stay here until then and let me play nurse?"

She smiled. "Pour me a cup of coffee, and let's talk about it."

I finished bandaging the wound, and she followed me to the kitchen. I poured coffee into a mug that had the Army Special Forces logo on it and we sat on the patio. "Jock sleeping in?" she asked.

"No. He was up early. Said he was going to Starbucks and then to spend some time with Gene Alexander. We're supposed to meet him for lunch at the Old Salty Dog."

She was quiet, sipping her coffee, and looking at the bay. "Matt," she said finally, "we need to talk about last night."

"I know. We've got to find the people who're trying to kill you. Maybe the one from last night will tell us something."

"I'm not talking about that."

I let out a breath. "I know."

"You don't want to hash this out?"

"I very much do, J.D., but I don't want whatever we have to blow up in our faces."

"Neither do I."

"We talked about this once before, that night at Mar Vista, back in the summer."

"I know."

"And you've never brought it up again. Like what we said to each other was a mistake."

"You've never mentioned it either."

"I know. I'm scared of you."

She laughed. "Right."

"Maybe I'm just afraid of my feelings."

"And that's exactly why we have to talk."

"You first," I said.

"Chicken. Okay. Here it is. Last night I was scared out of my wits. I'd been stabbed by a maniac in a dark parking lot at midnight. It was the third time in four days that somebody tried to kill me. Jill was there, trying to help hold me together. It wasn't working. Adrenalin was pumping and God knows what other hormones were taking over my system. I was about to break down in front of all those cops and paramedics. Real detectives just don't do that. The word would be out that I was just some silly female. And I didn't care. Screw 'em all. I had almost died and I didn't think I could spend another day with the fear that put in my gut.

"Then I saw you coming through that door, and it was like some kind of calm came over me. It was really weird, but I knew that you'd take care of me. I don't mean like protecting me from the bad guys. It was just that I knew you cared about me, not the detective, just plain old me, warts and all."

"You have warts?"

She smiled. "I'm serious, Matt. My girlfriend Deanna and I had talked about you over dinner. She thinks I'm crazy not to just grab you and hold on for dear life. See where it takes me."

"Deanna? Your buddy from Miami? That's who you had dinner with?"

"Yes. Who did you think I was meeting?"

"I was afraid it was some man."

She laughed, that big laugh that turns me into jelly every time I hear it, the one that makes me want to spend the rest of my life telling her funny stories, trying to jimmy just one more burst of laughter out of her.

"I didn't think it was that funny," I said.

"Ah," she said, "I think I like a little jealousy in you."

"It's an ugly emotion," I said, laughing, despite myself.

"It's sweet."

"So Deanna thinks I'm a catch."

"Well, she didn't actually say that."

"But you think I am."

"I do."

"So, what are we going to do about it?"

"You scare me, Matt."

"Why?"

"Your instinct is to always protect me. That will eventually smother me. If I let myself fall in love with you, I'll end up becoming just an appendage of Matt Royal."

I leaned forward and took her hand, looking her in the face. "J.D., I do try to protect you, but it's not like you think. I'm not hovering over you thinking that the girl needs me. I would expect you to protect me, too. We're a team, and team members look after one another."

"But you want to be the team leader."

"No. It's like Jock and me. I'd do whatever is in my power to do, anything, if he needed it. That includes dying. And I know he feels the same way. Neither one of us leads, but we've taken care of each other since we were twelve."

"And you want to take care of me."

"It's not like that. Look, when I was in the army, I was part of a team of twelve men, all trained to be the best soldiers in the world. I protected each of them and each of them protected me and each other. That's what a team does, covers for each other. It's a joint effort. That's the way I see us."

"I don't know, Matt. I've been on my own for a long time."

"You were married once."

"For about three months. That sure didn't work out very well."

"I won't ever hit you."

She laughed. "That jackass only did it once and I beat him to a pulp and left."

I grinned. "That's a pretty good reason for me to never hit you. Why did you marry a guy like that?"

"I was young and stupid. I didn't see the bad side of him until after the wedding. And it all started off with him trying to control me."

"I'm not that man."

She smiled. "I know you're not. I know the kind of man you are, but I'm still gun-shy."

"You kissed me last night. What was that?"

"That was me feeling a great need for you and being very glad that you were there."

My phone rang. I ignored it. It kept ringing. "You better answer that," said J.D.

"Not now." But I picked it up and looked at the caller ID. "It's Bill Lester," I said.

"Answer it. We'll talk later."

"Matt," the chief said, "I'm just turning onto Broadway. I need to talk to you and J.D."

"Coffee's on. See you in a minute." I closed the phone, looked at J.D. "Bill wants to talk to us. Must be important."

"I'm not exactly dressed for company," she said.

"I'll take you home for some more clothes later, but you're staying here for the next couple of days."

"Is that an order?" Her voice had tightened.

"It's a request," I said. "I need you close. For my sake."

She smiled. "Now that wasn't so hard, was it? I'll stick around."

CHAPTER THIRTY-ONE

Bill's news wasn't good. The guy who had attacked J.D. had lawyered up. "He's not saying a thing. He was hollering for a lawyer before they got him into the patrol car."

"Do we know anything about him?" asked J.D.

"His name is Fred Bagby. He's from Jacksonville, on parole, and recently released from Glades Correctional. Sound familiar?"

"I'll be damned," I said. "All three of them were in Glades. That's got to be the connection."

"And," said J.D., "I bet Bagby didn't check in with his parole officer."

"Bingo," said the chief. "We need to follow up on any connections at Glades."

"We're already working on that," said J.D.

"I know, but we're not getting anywhere. We need to build a fire under the warden down there. It ought to be easy enough to cross-check cell assignments and see if these three guys ever intersected with somebody J.D. has crossed paths with."

"A call from the governor would probably get him moving," I said.

"Do you know the governor?" asked the chief.

"No, but I know somebody who does. David Parrish."

"The U.S. Attorney?" asked Bill.

"He's in court today," said J.D.

"How do you know that?" I asked.

"Deanna Bichler is arguing motions against him today in Tampa."

"I'll call him," I said. "Leave a message on his cell phone. He'll get back to me during a break."

"This is critical," said Bill. "If we can find somebody with a connection to J.D., we'll probably know who's running this show."

I made the call, got David's cell, and left the message. "David, Matt Royal. Please call me ASAP. J.D.'s in a lot of trouble." I left my number.

Parrish called back in ten minutes. "Is J.D. okay?"

"Yes," I said. "For now. Somebody tried to kill her last night. That's three tries in four days."

"How can I help?"

"You're buddies with the governor, aren't you?"

"Yes."

"We know who three of the bad guys are. They all served sentences in Glades Correctional at the same time. None of them have any connection to J.D. that we can see. The warden down there is supposed to be checking any contacts they had with any inmates that might have a grudge against J.D. I think he's dragging his feet. I thought the governor might have a little chat with him. Maybe light a big fire under his ass."

"I'll call the governor now. You should be getting some pretty quick action."

"Thanks, David."

I related David's end of the conversation to the others. "Maybe the governor can break something loose."

"In the meantime," the chief said, "I want J.D. protected."

"I can take care of myself," said J.D., an edge to her voice.

"Yeah, I know," said Bill, "but if I were in your shoes, I'd want somebody covering my butt."

J.D. smiled. "I've got Matt."

"Not enough," Bill said. "You stay here with Matt and Jock, and I'm putting a uniform outside the house."

"Do you really think that's necessary?" asked J.D.

"I do. And I'm still the chief and that makes me your boss."

"He's right, J.D.," I said.

"I know," she said. "I know he's right and you're right, but I don't have to like it."

"Bill," I asked, "would you do this if the cop were a male?"

"Damn straight. Whoever is trying to kill the detective here is real serious about it. And there must be a bunch of them. We've arrested one, killed one, and both the guys on the boat got away. They're still out there. If she gets killed, I'll have to train a new detective, and I sure as hell don't have time for that."

J.D. grinned. "Okay. If you put it that way. I sure wouldn't want you to have to teach somebody else the fine art of detecting car break-ins."

He laughed and pointed his finger at her. "There you go."

Bill waited around until the officer he'd called appeared at the front door. "I'll be in the car, Chief," he said.

Bill Lester took his leave and passed Logan Hamilton coming up the sidewalk. They chatted for a moment and Logan came on into the house. "So, Matt, the chief tells me you're shacking up with this cute little chick."

J.D. said, "As soon as I get my gun, I'm going to shoot him. I'll be in the shower." She strode out of the room with a smile playing on her gorgeous lips.

"You know," I said to Logan, "she just might do that."

"What? Shoot me?"

"Yeah."

"Ah, I think she's sort of got the hots for me and doesn't want you or Marie to know it."

"That's probably it. I'll put it on your tombstone."

"I wanted to see how she was doing. Glad to see she's full of piss and vinegar, as usual."

"It was a close thing, Logan. Have you heard anything about it on the island?"

"Sure. A lot. I had breakfast at the Dolphin this morning."

No surprise there. News travels fast on a small island. I filled him in on everything we'd learned.

"Where's Jock?" he asked.

"He's visiting with Gene Alexander."

"I take it J.D.'s okay," said Logan.

"She's fine. She got her left side sliced up a little, but it's not too bad. She wants to get back to work."

"She staying here?"

"For a couple of days."

"Be careful, Matt."

"I know."

J.D. came out of the bedroom, cell phone in hand. "Matt, a Sarasota detective called and wants to meet with me to take a statement. Can you take me back to my condo? I'll shower there and get into some clean clothes."

"Sure," I said, "and I'm going downtown with you."

She gave me a frown, but didn't argue.

"I've got to go," said Logan. "I just wanted to make sure J.D. was okay. Watch your back, Matt. Hers, too."

"I will," I said.

But as it turned out, I didn't do a very good job of watching anybody's back.

CHAPTER THIRTY-TWO

The Sarasota Police Department is housed in brand-new quarters on Adams Lane a couple of blocks from the judicial center. J.D was wearing fresh clothes and her equipment belt with a nine-millimeter pistol holstered at her side. Her gold badge was pinned to the front of the belt. She looked tough, but I could tell from the small grimaces she made from time to time, her side still hurt.

I left my pistol in the glove box of my Explorer, knowing I couldn't get it through the metal detectors that were sure to be in the police station lobby. An exception was made for fellow cops. J.D. announced herself and we were told to take a seat in the waiting room. Detective Robson would be right with us.

Within minutes, the detective came through the door leading from the reception area to the interior of the building. He was a tall man with gray hair, a prominent nose, sunken cheeks, and sallow complexion. He was wearing a beige suit, a light-blue button-down shirt, and a tie patterned in blues and reds.

"Detective Duncan?" he asked, as he walked up to us. "I'm Harry Robson."

J.D. and I both stood. "I'm J.D.," she said, "and this is Matt Royal, my babysitter."

He looked at me. "I don't understand," he said, shaking my hand.

"My chief wants him to look after me," said J.D. "He's okay, and he's brighter than he looks. Tougher, too."

"I still don't understand," Robson said. His look said that he didn't like being jerked around.

"Sorry, Detective," said J.D. "Matt's a good friend and Chief Lester thought he should stick with me for a few days. The chief also put a uniform outside my house. Matt's house, actually. We left him on the key."

"J.D.'s a little defensive," I said, "but somebody has tried to kill her three times since Sunday. The chief is just being careful."

"You're on the Longboat force?" asked Robson.

"No," I said.

He shook his head. "I still don't get it, but y'all come on back. This shouldn't take long."

We were taken to a small interview room that held a table and four chairs. Nothing else. Robson told us to make ourselves comfortable and left us, saying he'd be right back. J.D. and I sat quietly, my thoughts going back to our unfinished conversation of the morning, wondering if we were both reacting to the events of the past few days, or if there really was a future for us that held more than just friendship.

"He's calling Bill Lester," J.D. said.

"Babysitter?" I asked.

She grinned. "What would you call you?"

"Gallant protector?"

"I can see that. But, you'd be wrong. Grown-up detectives don't need protecting."

"How about companion, then?" I asked.

"I think that implies that we're more than friends."

The door opened before I could reply. Robson came in and took a chair across the table from J.D. "I called Chief Lester," he said.

"I thought you would," said J.D.

"He said that even though Mr. Royal isn't law enforcement, he's family and should be treated as such."

"Thank you, Harry," J.D. said.

"He also said that Royal's the toughest son of a bitch he ever met, with the possible exception of somebody named Jock, who is also family."

J.D. smiled at that. "Did the chief also tell you that Matt's a lawyer?"

"Good Christ," said Robson. "No. He didn't mention that."

"Don't let it bother you, Detective," I said. "I'm a retired lawyer and I'm only here as a babysitter. Nothing official."

He laughed. "Everybody says you island people are strange. You ready, J.D.?"

"Shoot," she said.

J.D. talked into a tape recorder. Robson asked a number of questions, got answers, doubled back to some of the same questions, got the same answers. When he was finished, he sat back and said, "Thanks, J.D. I hope I wasn't too intrusive."

She smiled. "Just doing your job, Harry. I understand that Bagby lawyered up and isn't talking."

"Yeah. He'll have his first appearance in the morning. I don't think the judge is going to set bail. He's already on probation and the attempted murder of a law enforcement officer charge should keep him behind bars forever."

"I don't guess you found out anything about who's behind all this," said J.D.

"We've got nothing. I wish I could give you better news."

CHAPTER THIRTY-THREE

We walked out of the police station into the bright sun of late morning. J.D. was talking about Steve Carey, the young cop who'd been shot at Leffis Key. He was doing well, and the chief was keeping J.D. updated on a daily basis. "He wants to get back to work and the chief is going to let him start coming in tomorrow to do admin stuff. His arm is still hurting, he says, but he can answer phones."

I noticed a car with darkly tinted windows idling at the curb about thirty feet from us. I'm not sure what caught my attention, maybe that it was idling in a no parking zone in front of a police station. It obviously hadn't been there very long or some cop would have been writing a ticket. Three officers in uniform were coming up the sidewalk, apparently heading toward the door we had just come out of.

The car started to move and the right rear window glided down. The muzzle of a shotgun was beginning to poke out of the window as I dove to my left, taking J.D. to the sidewalk. We fell behind a concrete receptacle that held a trash can, giving us some cover. I twisted as I fell, bringing J.D. on top of me to cushion her fall. At the same instant, I heard the explosion of the shotgun and heard buckshot hitting the trash container.

I landed on my side and back, with J.D. on top of me. My head hit the sidewalk. I felt pain shooting through every lobe of my brain. My eyesight dimmed and the buildings within my line of sight seemed to sway. My world slowed down. I heard pistol shots, people running, a crash. A weight lifted off me, my sight sharpened some. I saw J.D. standing next to me, her knees flexed, her hands holding her pistol. More gunshots. The smell of cordite. A yell of pain. Darkness was edging into my consciousness. I pushed it back, tried to sit up. I felt pressure on my chest, somebody holding me down. The darkness receded further. My eyes began to focus. I saw J.D.'s face looking down at me, marked by worry or fear or sadness or, maybe, pain. I couldn't read it. I realized that she was sitting beside me, my head in her lap, her hand resting on my chest. She was saying something I couldn't make out. Her lips were moving and sound was coming out of her mouth, but it was just noise. Nothing made sense.

I heard sirens. They were coming toward us, getting louder. J.D.'s words were becoming clearer, starting to make sense. I tried to get up. "Stay down, Matt, please." It was J.D.

"I have to get up," I said.

"No, Matt. Stay down. You're hurt. The paramedics are on the way."

"Was I shot?"

"No, I don't think so. You hit your head pretty hard. You've probably got a concussion. Just stay still until they get here."

I felt a stickiness through my shirt and reached down to my waist. I was relieved that I couldn't feel any holes in my precious hide. My mind was clearing. Then it hit me. J.D. was bleeding. "You're hit," I said.

"I'm fine. I think you busted up my bandages when you pulled me down. It's just blood from the knife wound."

"Did you get the bad guys?"

"I think I hit one of them. The officers on the street fired at the car. They must have hit the driver, because he crashed into a parked car. Just as I was getting untangled from you, one guy came out of the car's rear door with a pistol in his hand. I think I hit him, but there were other cops firing, so who knows. How're you doing?"

"My head hurts like a son of a bitch."

A paramedic came up with his bag of supplies and squatted down beside me. "You get hit?"

"No," said J.D., before I could form an answer. "But he hit his head when he pushed me out of the line of fire."

The medic snapped on a pair of latex gloves and felt around on the back of my head. "I don't think there are any fractures, but you've got a large bump back there. We better get you to the hospital for x-rays."

"Check her side," I said. "She's bleeding."

J.D. lifted up her blouse. "It's from a knife fight last night. I think I opened up the wound."

"A knife fight?" the paramedic asked.

"Yeah. But you ought to see the other guy," I said.

He smiled and pulled the bandages from J.D.'s laceration. He pulled a spray can out of his kit and doused the area. "A little antiseptic," he said. "I'll get another bandage on this and we'll take you in to the hospital."

"Can we ride in the same ambulance?" J.D. asked.

"Sure," said the medic.

"Can we share a stretcher?" I asked.

"You're going to ruin my reputation, Royal," J.D. said.

The medic laughed. "I'll go get the gurney."

CHAPTER THIRTY-FOUR

I was in the Sarasota Memorial Hospital emergency room for the second time in less than twelve hours. Only this time, I was the patient. They were going to take me upstairs for an MRI to see if my brain had been scrambled. The doc was pretty sure there was no skull fracture, but the imaging would tell him for sure.

J.D. was in the next cubicle having her laceration tended to. When they finished, she came and sat by my bed. "You're going to have to buy a whole new set of blouses, if this keeps up," I said.

"How're you doing?"

"Head still hurts, but they gave me some aspirin or something and it seems to be getting better."

She leaned down and kissed me on the forehead. "Does that help?"

"Yes, but I probably need a few more doses."

She leaned down again and kissed me on the lips, softly and fleetingly. "You're my hero," she said, grinning at me.

"Ah, I'm just the babysitter. Not a very good one, I'm afraid. I almost got the baby killed."

"Your famous quick reflexes saved us both," she said.

"Yeah, but I messed up your side."

"Not a big deal."

"If it scars up, we're finished, you know."

"Just like that?" she asked.

"I like my women unblemished."

"Better stay away from cops, then."

"Let's wait and see how it turns out. The scar and all."

She laughed. It was that big laugh that made me feel good enough to jump up and do the watusi. "How about another kiss?" I asked.

"We better wait. You know, see how the scar turns out."

"My head isn't getting any better," I said.

She leaned in and kissed me again. On the lips. Very quickly. I'm not above using sympathy for my own ends.

"That's better," I said. "Have you heard any more about the bad guys?"

"No, but Bill Lester's here. One of the Sarasota cops said he and their chief are talking out on the ambulance loading dock. He'll be here soon."

"Okay. Tell the nurse that I don't want to go to imaging until I've talked to Bill."

"If they try to take you away, I'll just shoot them."

"You're getting pretty aggressive."

"I'm feeling aggressive. I want the bastards who're behind this. And it's not just about me. There're two dead women whose only connection to me was that somebody was trying to tell me something. Make a statement or scare me. Something that got them killed just because somebody wants me dead."

"That's not your fault."

"I know that. But there will be more innocent women killed if we don't stop these people."

Lester walked into the cubicle. "You okay, J.D.?"

She nodded.

"How about you, Matt?" he asked.

"I'm good, Bill. They're going to run some tests, but everybody seems to think I'm fine. What do you know?"

"The two guys in the car are dead. Apparently one of those Sarasota cops who was on the street when the firing started got a lucky shot and hit the driver in the back of the head. The car crashed into a parked car and some guy crawled out of the backseat with a pistol. He took five or six shots to the chest. I think they're still counting the hits over at the morgue. Sarasota P.D. will need your weapon, J.D."

She pulled the nine-millimeter out of its holster, pointed it toward the floor, dropped the magazine out of the butt, pulled the slide back to clear the chamber, and handed it to the chief. "How did they know we were going to be at the police station?" she asked.

"This may not be the same bunch," Lester said. "One of Sarasota P.D.'s gang detectives was on the scene and he said the tattoos on the guys in the car were Guatemalan gang ink. They've recently moved into the area."

"Still," said J.D., "somehow they knew we were going to be at the police station today. How?"

"That's the sixty-four-dollar question," Lester said. "How did they know you were going to be at Lynches last night?"

"Somebody followed me from home to the Lazy Lobster Sunday night. Maybe they've been following me all along."

"What about a tracking device, Bill?" I said. "Somebody put one of those on my Explorer a couple of years back."

"I remember," said Lester. "I'll have your car and J.D.'s car checked out."

"My car's at the Sarasota police station."

"I figured as much. I've got a patrolman bringing Jock here."

"Why is he coming here?"

"I told him to come armed. I want a little more protection for you two."

I laughed. "You know, Bill, I'm never going to live this one down. Jock will tell everybody we know that he has to protect my fragile ass."

"Obviously, somebody's got to do it."

"Call your guy," I said, "and tell him to take Jock to my car. It's parked on the street about a block south of the station. Jock knows where I hide the spare key. He can bring it here and take us home later. And tell him to bring me the pistol in the glove box."

The MRI showed no damage, but the doctor wanted to keep me overnight for observation. I told him I couldn't do it. I had to get home. He said I'd have to have somebody there to check on me every couple of hours. I told him I had two houseguests, and we'd make do.

Jock arrived while I was in imaging and was sitting and talking quietly with J.D. when they brought me back to the emergency room. "How you doing, podna?" he asked.

"I'm fine, Jock. Don't even have much of a headache any more. I've had worse after a night at Tiny's."

"You ready to go home?"

"They said they've got some paperwork for me to sign. They'll be along soon. How's the side, J.D.?"

"No problem. They gave me a couple of Tylenol for pain."

"I guess they told you that somebody's got to stay with me for the next couple of weeks," I said.

She smiled. "They said a couple of days."

"Well, I knew it was a couple of something," I said. You never know what sympathy will do for you. Sometimes it works, sometimes it doesn't.

A lady in a dress came with a sheaf of papers for me to sign. We left the hospital in the Explorer and Jock drove us back to the key. It was nearing four in the afternoon when we crossed the Ringling Bridge onto Longboat. "Anybody hungry?" I asked.

We stopped at Harry's Corner Store for take-out sandwiches and drove on to the village. A Longboat Key patrol car was parked on the side of the street in front of my cottage. The cop sitting behind the wheel waved at us. I was pretty sure he'd be there all night. I'd keep him supplied with sandwiches and coffee until we turned in for the evening.

The chief called just as we settled into the living room with our lunch. "I'm sending a tech out to go over your car, Matt. If there's a tracking device on it, he'll find it. Tell J.D. he'll need the keys to her car. Is it back at her condo?"

"Yeah," I said. "One of the Sarasota cops drove it back early this morning."

"Okay. If you need anything, call," he said, and hung up.

Logan showed up as we were finishing our food. "Lester called. Said you guys were causing trouble downtown. Everybody okay?"

"Pretty much," I said. "I just can't figure out how the bad guys knew J.D. was going to be at the police station this morning."

"I've been thinking about that," said Logan. "Maybe they weren't after J.D. Maybe they came for you."

"That doesn't make any sense at all, Logan," I said. "Why in the world would a Guatemalan hit squad be after me?"

"I don't know," said Logan. "But you almost got killed by that car in front of Cha Cha's last night."

"I ran in front of him."

"But he didn't even try to stop. He was speeding up, like he was trying to hit you."

"Logan's right," said Jock. "I thought that was a little odd at the time."

"Just some drunk," I said.

"Then he was a Hispanic drunk," said Jock.

"Are you sure, Jock?" asked J.D.

"Pretty sure. It was dark and I only got a glimpse of the driver, but he was looking right at Matt. Like he was aiming the car. And he was picking up speed. I'm pretty sure he was Hispanic. His skin was dark and he had black hair. I wouldn't have thought anything about it except for what Bill had to say about Guatemalans. I figured he just didn't see Matt."

"Why would they be after Matt?" J.D. asked. "He didn't have anything to do with anybody at Glades Correctional."

"Matt's name was in the paper," said Logan. "In the article about Qualman getting killed in the Lazy Lobster parking lot. It didn't name Jock and it wasn't clear as to who fired the shot that killed him."

"Revenge?" asked J.D.

"Why not?" asked Jock. "That's apparently what's motivated the attacks on J.D."

"I'll be damned," I said. "You think he was waiting for me to cross the street? That doesn't make a lot of sense."

Jock shrugged. "Maybe he was waiting for you to leave Cha Cha's, or maybe he was about to do a drive-by and he saw an opportunity to get you with the car."

"I guess that's a reasonable hypothesis," I said.

My cell phone rang. Blocked ID. I answered. It was David Parrish. "The governor called back," he said. "He talked to the superintendent down at Glades. I think you'll get everything he has by first thing in the morning."

"Thanks, David. I hope you didn't have to call in too many favors."

"No. Nothing like that. Glad to help. Tell J.D. hello for me."

"Before you go," I said. "Do you have any information on Guatemalan gangs operating in this area?"

"There's one. A bunch of really bad hombres. Why?"

"Two guys took a shot at J.D. or me or both of us this morning. They had tattoos that the Sarasota P.D. gang unit said are tied to a Guatemalan gang. I understand they probably operate out of Tampa."

"Are they in custody?"

"No. They were killed by some really pissed off Sarasota cops."

"What do you need to know about them?" asked David.

"Do they hire out as killers?"

"They do. If there's a buck in it and it's illegal, they're your go-to guys."

"We're thinking that they may have been hired by whoever is trying to kill J.D."

"I wouldn't be surprised. Let me check in with my people who're monitoring the gangs."

"How'd you do with Deanna Bichler this morning?"

"She kicked my ass. I'll call when I have something."

"Thanks, David."

I looked at J.D. "Your buddy kicked the big man's ass in court this morning."

J.D. laughed. "She thinks Parrish will get her in the end. But she keeps on plugging."

"You two are a lot alike," I said.

"Yeah," she said, grinning. "But she has better taste in men."

I wasn't going to touch that one. I told them that David was looking into the Guatemalan gang based in Tampa and would let me know when he had something.

CHAPTER THIRTY-FIVE

I was on my patio drinking coffee and watching daylight slowly push back the darkness. There was no sun that Friday morning and the bay looked bleak. A chilly wind blew from the north. A weak cold front was moving in and would probably bring some rain.

We had turned in early the night before. Jock drove to J.D.'s condo and retrieved the suitcase of clothes she'd packed that morning. She was tired and went to bed early. Jock and I sat for an hour talking about old friends and times gone by. He went to bed and left me with my thoughts.

J.D. and I hadn't yet finished our conversation about our future, or lack thereof, and somebody was trying to kill her and perhaps me. Not a good way to start a relationship, even if that was what she wanted. I couldn't tell. I gave it up and went to bed. I slept fitfully and was up early.

The somber bay, gray and foreboding under the cloud cover, matched my mood. Even the seabirds that nested nearby were quiet. In deference to the weather, I was wearing socks, boat shoes, jeans, and an old sweat-shirt that read "Longboat Key, a Place in the Sun." Well, most days that was true.

The morning paper was full of bad news, but then that seemed to be the state of things these days. The Bradenton City Council had annexed some land a few months before when the county fathers balked at a developer's plans to turn a beautiful piece of bayside property into another condominium complex. The city then granted permits for the developers to start tearing up more of our limited waterfront property. They were planning a couple hundred condos in five high-rise buildings overlooking the bay near the Manatee Avenue Bridge. It didn't matter that someday when the big hurricane came ashore, the roads would not be able to handle the traffic fleeing to safety. No thought was given to what that many people would do to our beaches or the strain they would put on our water supply. All the councilmen could see was the taxes that would flow from the new residents. More money for them to piss away. The Florida I knew and loved, the one in which I'd grown up and lived in for most of my life, was dying under the onslaught of the omnipresent bulldozer.

Soon the coastal zone would be overrun with people and they would start moving inland. That was already happening north of Orlando, all the way to the Georgia state line. Towns springing up, old Florida villages becoming boom towns fueled by the new retirees' need for sunshine. I supposed the growth would eventually make its way into the cattle ranches and truck farms of the interior of South Florida. What then? What would we do when that last vestige of old Florida filled up with people ignorant of the history of this magical place? Invade Cuba, I guess. Build a bridge across the Florida Straits so the snowbirds could move easily into the Caribbean. Castro wouldn't know what hit him.

My cell phone rang. I looked at my watch, not yet seven. Blocked ID. I answered.

"Matt, Martin Sharkey."

"Good morning."

"I understand our detective is sleeping over with you."

"Well, she's in the guest room."

He laughed. "Sorry about that. Is she up yet?"

"No. She's sleeping in. I can wake her."

"If you don't mind. It's important."

"I'll have her call you back. You at the office?"

"Tell her to call my cell. She has the number. And tell her I'm pulling the cop from your front yard. We'll have somebody there again tonight."

I knocked on the guest room door. "J.D.?"

I heard a sleepy voice say, "What?"

"Sharkey called. He needs to talk to you."

"What time is it?"

"Almost seven. He said to call him on his cell. Said you have the number."

"Okay. I'm awake. I'll call him. What's the weather like?"

"A little chilly. Better put on some clothes."

"I thought I would, you pervert."

I went to the kitchen and put on a fresh pot of coffee and then back to the patio and my paper. The news hadn't gotten any better.

J.D. came out fifteen minutes later. She was wearing jeans, a plain white sweatshirt, and running shoes. Her hair was in a ponytail, still wet from the shower. She had a cup of coffee in her hand. "Good morning, Sunshine," I said.

She smiled and sat down next to me. "Good morning, Matt. Wouldn't you be warmer inside?"

"Are you cold?"

"A bit. Want to go to the Dolphin for breakfast?"

"Sure. I'll wake Jock up."

"He's up. I heard him rattling around in his room."

"Sharkey sounded as if his call was important," I said.

"The superintendent down at Glades Correctional e-mailed a bunch of stuff to Bill Lester during the night. I guess the governor must have chewed on him a bit."

"Anything that'll help?"

"Martin said there was a lot of paper. He wants me to come in and look at it. He said if I showed up without you or Jock, I'd be in trouble."

"You got time for breakfast?"

"Sure. An hour or two isn't going to make a bit of difference."

CHAPTER THIRTY-SIX

Jock stayed at my cottage, saying he had some e-mails to catch up on. He also wanted to talk to his director and bring him up to date on what progress had been made on finding Nell Alexander's killer. Not a whole hell of a lot, I thought.

"Not much to tell," I said.

"Yeah, but I've been thinking about that Guatemalan connection."

"If there is such a thing."

"I've spent a lot of time in Central America," he said. "Maybe they're after me and you just got in the line of fire. Mistaken identity kind of thing."

"That doesn't make a lot of sense. I've got hair and I'm a lot better looking than you."

"In a feminine sort of way," he said.

I gave him the finger, and followed J.D. out the front door. She was shaking her head, and had one of those looks on her face that I can only describe as a frown of dismay.

Breakfast was a quiet affair. She didn't seem in the mood to engage in a lot of small talk, so I held my tongue. Finally, she said, "Do you think the Guatemalans are after you?"

"No."

"What about that car trying to hit you?"

"I think the driver was just a drunk tourist. There's no reason for a Guatemalan gang to be after me."

"You don't think whoever is trying to kill me might hire those guys to do their dirty work?"

"It's possible, but why would they be after me?"

"Other than revenge for the shooting of Qualman, I don't know."

"That's possible, I guess, but if this whale tail bunch is hiring Guatemalan gangbangers, why wouldn't they just hire out the hit on you? Put another layer between you and the people who want you dead."

She shook her head. "I just don't know. Maybe they did. Qualman and Bagby definitely weren't part of the original whale tail murders."

"We'll figure it out sooner or later," I said.

"I hope so."

By the time we reached the police station on Gulf of Mexico Drive, it was raining, a soft cold drizzle that was part of the front enveloping the island. The temperature had dropped while we were having breakfast, bringing a touch of winter to our usually sunny key. By tomorrow, the front would be gone, and we'd have clear skies for a couple of cool days, with the thermometer reaching only into the low sixties. Winter in southwest Florida didn't amount to much.

I followed J.D. through the reception area and into her office. A stack of printouts sat on her desk, the trove from Glades Correctional. Martin Sharkey followed us into the office and shut the door. "J.D." he said, "I've got more bad news. Fred Bagby woke up dead this morning."

J.D. had a puzzled look on her face. "What do you mean?"

"He was dead in his bed when the jailers tried to get him up for chow call."

"How?"

"They don't know. There weren't any obvious signs on the body. Other than the ones you left when you kicked his butt. The medical examiner will do an autopsy today, so maybe we'll know by late this afternoon."

"Could I have killed him?" J.D. asked.

"I doubt it. It may have been a natural death. We'll have to wait for the M.E. Let me know if you find anything in that stuff from Glades." Sharkey left, closing the door behind him.

"Darn," she said. "There goes our best shot at getting information."

"His lawyer wasn't going to let him say anything," I said.

"He might have if we offered him a deal."

"You'd deal with a guy who tried to kill you?"

"If it'd get us to the one pulling the strings."

"The puppet master," I said.

She smiled. "That's a good name for him."

"Or her," I said.

She chewed on that for a moment. "You could be right," she said. "But there are no women prisoners at Glades."

"Maybe Glades isn't the connection."

"It looks good so far. Let me see what's in all this paper. You go on. Nobody's going to take a shot at me in the police station."

"I'll come get you for lunch. You're supposed to be at the hospital at two. We can eat downtown."

"Okay," she said, and gave me a little wave goodbye.

As it turned out, we didn't make it to the hospital that day.

CHAPTER THIRTY-SEVEN

I was buckling myself into the Explorer when my phone rang. Jock.

"You still at the police station?"

"Just leaving."

"Meet me at Gene Alexander's house."

"Sure. What's up?"

"Maybe nothing. I'll see you there in five minutes."

Gene lived in a small ranch house dating to the 1960s in a neighborhood known as Emerald Harbor, about five minutes from the police station. His house was perched beside a wide canal that emptied into Sarasota Bay. The yard was dominated by an ancient gumbo-limbo tree and spotted with beds of flowers that bloom in the fall in Florida. Begonias, impatiens, and geraniums provided splotches of red, pink, and white, less brilliant than usual as they hunkered down under the low clouds that dripped rain. The lawn was slightly overgrown, as if no one had mowed it in a couple of weeks. Jock was pulling up just as I arrived. We met on the sidewalk leading to the front door. "What's up?" I asked. "It's a bit wet out here."

"Gene's not answering his phone. I've been trying to get hold of him for the past two hours."

"Maybe he's sleeping in."

"Maybe. But he always has his phone on. Old habit."

"The battery could be dead."

"So could he."

Jock knocked on the door. No answer. He knocked again. Nothing. "Can you look in the garage?" he asked. "There's a door on the side that has a small window."

I went to the side of the garage and looked in. There were two cars in the garage. That wasn't good. I reported back to Jock, and he tried the door. It wasn't locked. It swung open to reveal a living room that opened to French doors facing south to a patio overlooking the canal. A kitchen with a breakfast bar open to the living room was to my left. A short hall ran to what I assumed to be a door to the garage. A conversation area with a sofa and two club chairs was grouped at the middle of the room, providing a view across the patio to a pool and the wide canal. The floor was a rich wood, probably oak. Expensive-looking Oriental carpets were spread about. A fireplace took up most of the west wall, bordered by a hallway that must have led to the bedrooms. At right angles to the fireplace, a large flat-screen TV sat on a table to my right, against the north wall. Two identical recliners were placed in front of it. One of the recliners was in the open position, footrest even with the seat, the back all the way down. Gene Alexander was lying in the chair, as if he'd fallen asleep watching television. But he wouldn't be getting up.

We were looking at his right side. His temple had a large hole in it, black around the edges. His right hand was in his lap, clutching a pistol that looked like a .45 caliber. Blood and brain matter had splattered the chair to his left.

"Shit," said Jock. "Call it in, Matt."

We didn't move, standing as if we were rooted to a single spot on the hardwood. I took out my phone and dialed 911, identified myself, gave the operator Gene's address, and told her there was an apparent suicide, the body still on the premises. We backed out the way we'd come in, not wanting to contaminate the scene. We waited for the cops on the front stoop. Neither one of us had much confidence that Gene had taken his own life.

"I'm sorry, Jock," I said.

"Thanks, podna. You know Gene didn't kill himself, right?"

"Doesn't look that way."

"Why do you say that?" asked Jock.

"The hand holding the gun was in his lap. That big a pistol will have some kick to it. It would have thrown his arm outward, away from the path of the bullet. It would have been hanging by his side, the pistol on the floor."

Jock was quiet for a moment. "I didn't even think about that, but you're right."

"What were you thinking?"

"Gene isn't the kind of guy to kill himself."

"I don't know, Jock. He just lost the only family he had."

"Yeah, but he's a tough guy. He would've handled it. And if he'd killed himself, he'd have called somebody before he did it. So that we'd know. He wouldn't have left a note. He'd have called."

Sirens came whooping into the street leading to Gulf of Mexico Drive. A patrol car was followed by an ambulance and an unmarked. A uniformed officer, a captain, crawled out of the cruiser. J.D. and Martin Sharkey got out of the unmarked and walked toward us, a fire department paramedic close behind. "What've we got?" asked Sharkey.

"Gene Alexander's in there, dead," said Jock. "Looks like a suicide, but I don't think it was."

"Why?" asked J.D.

"You guys take a look," said Jock. "See what you think."

Sharkey turned to the police captain. "Set this up as a crime scene. I'll get the forensics people out here, but that'll take a while. They've got to come from Bradenton. And get me some more uniforms to keep the gawkers away. Let's take a look, J.D."

They went to the front door and looked in. They didn't enter the room. They stood there for a few minutes, talking quietly. They walked back to Jock and me. "Gun's in the wrong place," said J.D. "It just wouldn't have fallen into his lap, and when he died his fingers would have let go of it. Somebody tried to set this up."

"I agree," said Sharkey. "What do you guys think?"

"Matt thought the same thing you did, J.D.," Jock said. "I agree. I think if Gene was going to kill himself, he'd have called somebody first. Just to let them know. I'll check with my director, see if he called any of his old friends. If he did, they would have called it in. Martin, can you check with the 911 operators, just to be sure?"

Sharkey nodded. "Let's get J.D. under cover. I don't want a repeat of that fiasco at Leffis Key."

"I'm fine, Martin," said J.D. "This is what I do. Investigate murders."

"I know," said Sharkey his voice tense, "and as soon as forensics finishes, I want you on top of it. But for now, just until we have a better handle on the situation, I want Matt to get you the hell out of here."

"But—"

"But nothing, J.D. I'm not going to have you shot while we stand around with our thumbs up our asses. I'll call as soon as the forensics guys have anything."

J.D. was steaming. "Damn it, Martin, what's the chief going to say about this?"

"He'll back me up. He'd say my first job was to keep you safe. He's at some kind of meeting at the sheriff's office over on the mainland. Dispatch called him and he's on his way here."

"Right," J.D. said. "Protect the girl." Her voice had taken on that edge that I recognized as repressed anger.

"Get her out of here, Matt. J.D.," Sharkey said, his voice softening, "you're the toughest cop I know. But you're not invulnerable. I'd send any of my people, man or woman, out of here under the circumstances. I'll call you as soon as we're sure there're no shooters lurking around."

She turned on her heel and walked toward my car. I followed. I thought I could see steam coming out of her ears, but it was probably just my imagination.

CHAPTER THIRTY-EIGHT

I figured I was in for a long morning. Living with a really angry woman can be trying. But J.D. seemed to accept the wisdom of Sharkey's decision to get her out of the line of fire for the time being. She was quiet, pensive, as if she had a lot on her mind. She'd had a tough week and seemed to want some time with her own thoughts. I read the paper and watched the rain and stayed quiet. At some point, she called the hospital and canceled her meeting with the doctor, telling them that she'd reschedule.

Jock stayed at Gene's house, working his phone, talking to his director and who knew who else. It was nearing noon when he called. "I'm leaving in a few minutes. I'll stop for sandwiches on the way to your place. What do you guys want?"

I turned to J.D. "Jock's going to pick up some sandwiches. What do you want?"

"I'd prefer to go out," she said. "What about Moore's?"

I told Jock to meet us there and hung up.

J.D. grinned. "I think I'll be safe with two big brave men babysitting me."

"Sarcasm does not become you," I said.

"Sorry. I don't like being benched."

"I know. But in this game, you're the football."

She frowned. "Football? I think we need a new metaphor."

"Let's go eat," I said.

At Moore's, we took a table by the windows overlooking Sarasota Bay. The rain was still falling and our world seemed small and isolated. Sister Key was barely visible through the mist and the homes that hugged the shoreline of the little lagoon on which the restaurant sat were draped in opacity. The bay was gray, somber under the lowering clouds, its surface ruffled by little whitecaps dancing in the wind. Halyards rattled on the sailboats anchored nearby as they rocked in time with the feeble gusts of the dying front. Springlike weather would come with tomorrow's sun, returning our island to its natural state. Winter was not a welcome visitor, but we would see more of it in the coming months. The fronts, weakened by their passage across the landmass of America, would make their way down the peninsula, bringing cold air and rainy days. Then, as suddenly as they'd come, they would dissipate in the warm currents of air moving north from the tropics and our key would resume its life in the sunshine.

J.D. shivered. "Sometimes, I feel like I'm a long way from Miami."

"Miami doesn't have bad weather occasionally?"

"Yeah, but I'm not really talking about the weather. If we were in Miami, I wouldn't have to have a babysitter."

"Okay," I said, an edge creeping into my voice. "I'm getting kind of tired of this babysitter crap."

She reached out and covered my hand with hers. "I'm sorry, Matt. I don't mean to take it out on you, but this little island is starting to stifle me."

"How so?"

"I can't do anything here that isn't the subject of common gossip within hours. I'm already getting stares from some of our locals who're damn sure I'm not sleeping in the guest room at your house."

"I think you're picking up the wrong signals. I doubt that any of the islanders care if we're sleeping together. In fact, I'd bet if you took a vote, most of them would vote in my favor."

"Your favor?"

"Sure. You know, so that I could enjoy your favors." I was trying to jolly her out of something rarely seen: J.D. in a bad mood.

She smiled and squeezed my hand. "Well, I guess if the island voted for it—" Her voice trailed off.

"What else is bothering you?"

"I'm cramped here. Miami is a big, sprawling city. If somebody was after me down there, I'd still be able to work. I'd get lost in the crowd.

Here, I feel like a sitting duck. If somebody wants me, they don't have to look very far."

"Is this something new or have you been feeling this way for a while?"

"Look, Matt, I love this place, but I was thinking this way before the killings started, if that's what you're asking me."

It was what I was asking. "Are you thinking about leaving? Going back to Miami?"

"I don't know. It's crossed my mind. The chief of detectives down there made it clear he'd take me back. Maybe I made a mistake coming here in the first place. I guess I was looking for a little refuge from the big city. Maybe a new life."

"You found a new life. Aren't you happy with it?"

"I am," she said. "It's not that. Sometimes I feel an overpowering sense of ennui here. Miami always made me feel like I was on steroids."

"Maybe it's just what we call island fever. It hits us all sometimes. We get off the key for a few days and it goes away. We're always glad to get back."

"Maybe that's what it is. I feel like I've been on vacation, and now I'm ready for it to end so that I can get back to work."

"Do I fit into this scenario?"

"You may be the only reason I'm still here."

"Tell me," I said.

"It's not easy to figure out, Matt. I have feelings for you, maybe more than I have a right to, but I've kept you at a distance because I don't want to get trapped on this island if it isn't working out for me."

"How would I trap you?"

"Would you leave here?"

"Probably not."

"So if I fall in love with you, and you won't leave the island, I've either got to stay here or lose you. It's a trap."

"It's a trap for me as well," I said.

"How?"

"If I'm in love with you and you decide to leave, I'll either have to go with you or stay here without you. Either way, I get a broken heart because

I had to make a decision which of my two loves, LBK or J.D., I'd have to give up."

She grinned. "Damn. Everybody says you were a great lawyer."

"Were?"

"Are, I guess. You make a heck of a case."

"But do I get the verdict?"

"Which verdict?"

"The one where you stay here and take up with me."

"Here comes Jock."

"And the verdict?"

She patted my hand, withdrew hers, and smiled. "We'll talk." Her mood seemed to have lifted a bit.

CHAPTER THIRTY-NINE

Jock came in brushing rain off his bald head. "Sorry I'm late," he said. "I stopped by Matt's to get into some dry clothes."

"Did you turn up anything?" I asked.

"Maybe. There were fingerprints on the gun that didn't belong to Gene. Forensics is running them now. We'll see."

"Did the gun belong to Gene?" asked J.D.

"The cops don't think so," said Jock. "The serial number was filed off, but that might just mean that Gene got it from the agency. The director is checking on that."

"Did Gene call anybody before he died?" asked J.D.

"No. He didn't call the director, and if he'd called someone else in the agency, it would have been reported immediately. No 911 calls either. Bill Lester checked."

"Note?" I asked.

"No. And nothing on his computer."

"Did the canvass of the neighborhood turn up anything?" asked J.D. "Strangers in the neighborhood, that sort of thing?"

"No," said Jock. "And only one of the landscape crews showed up today. A lot of the companies take the day off when the weather gets bad."

"Do we know which company had a crew working today?" I asked.

"Not yet, but the cops are working on it. None of the neighbors paid any attention to it."

"Those crews are just part of the landscape," I said. "No pun intended. They're here every day."

"Sharkey said the members of those crews are almost all Mexicans,"

Jock said. "I suppose a Guatemalan could slip in without any of the neighbors noticing."

I shook my head. "Jock, I think you're seeing Guatemalan boogie men under every bush."

Jock sat quietly for a beat. "J.D.," he said, "I'd like to tell you something, but I need to swear you to secrecy."

"Does it have to do with any of these cases?"

"Yes."

"Then I can't do that, Jock. It might be something that I'd have to share with the chief or other law enforcement agencies."

"Fair enough," Jock said.

The waitress came and took our lunch order, commented on the nasty weather, and left.

"Aren't you going to tell me, Jock?"

He shook his head. "Sorry, J.D. I can't. Not without a promise of confidentiality."

We ate our meal in virtual silence and returned to my cottage.

Jock said he had to make some calls and went to his bedroom and shut the door. J.D. paced back and forth across the living room, a look of concentration on her face.

"Matt," she finally said, "I'm not going to stay cooped up here while somebody else is doing my job. I'm the only detective in the department. I'm supposed to be looking for these killers."

"They're certainly looking for you."

"They may be," she said, "but if they want me badly enough, they're going to get me. If those Sarasota goons had been better at what they do, they'd have taken me out and you as well. They aren't too picky about whom they kill."

"I don't know, J.D. If I'd been with you at Lynches, that guy probably wouldn't have come at you with a knife."

"You're probably right. He'd have used a gun and gotten us both."

She had a point, but I didn't like it. "Okay," I said, "but two pairs of eyes can be a plus when you're trying to dodge a killer."

"You don't object to Jock going out by himself, and he thinks there may be somebody after him."

"Jock's the most competent person I've ever met."

She glared at me. "And you don't think I'm competent?"

"That's not my point. I know that you can take care of yourself, but Jock spends every day of his life dodging people who're trying to kill him. You don't. And neither do I. It's just second nature to Jock. He's always on the lookout. Normal people like you and me don't have to worry every day that some killer is going to jump out of the bushes and whack us."

"So, Sir Matthew in his shining armor takes care of the damsel in distress."

"I'm hoping that sarcasm isn't becoming a way of life with you." My voice was tight, perhaps a bit strident. This wasn't the J.D. I knew.

"I'm sorry, Matt. I'm not being fair. I'm just frustrated, and I guess I'm taking it out on you."

"The murders are very real, J.D. And they all seem to be part of a plan to kill you."

"The murders may not be connected," she said.

"I've thought of that. The two whale tail murders certainly were connected, and I think the guy in Lynches' parking lot, Bagby, was connected to them. I'm not sure about the Guatemalans who tried to take us out at the police station, and I can't see how Gene's murder is connected to any of the others."

"If Nell's murder was random, like we think, would the people who killed her have a motive to take out Gene?" she asked.

"I don't see it. Not if Nell was just a random victim. But suppose she wasn't? Suppose her killing is connected to Gene's. Maybe the killers were looking for Gene and Nell got in the way somehow."

"But Nell's murder was definitely connected to the whale tail murders in Miami. And if this was all a plot to get Gene, why would somebody threaten me? And why would Qualman, if he really was the one who killed Nell, come after me?"

"Good questions," I said. "And what was Bagby's connection to any of this?"

"We may never know. I wonder what Jock wanted to tell us at lunch."

I chuckled. "We may never know," I said.

Her cell phone rang. She looked at the caller ID. "It's the chief," she said, excused herself, and walked into the kitchen to take the call. I only heard three words of the conversation, including a word I thought foreign to J.D.'s vocabulary and two others that stunned me. They were loud and angry and profane. "Bullshit," she said, "I quit."

CHAPTER FORTY

I sat on the sofa, dire scenarios dancing across my brain. J.D. had only been on the island for a year, but she had somehow burrowed her way into my psyche. My world would be greatly diminished without her in it. It was damned disconcerting, but I did not have the moral authority to ask her to stay.

J.D. came out of the kitchen, a big smile on her face. "I've got to go," she said, sending my heart down into the pit of my stomach.

"What's up?" I asked.

"I've got a murder case to solve. Cases, I guess."

"You're not leaving the island?"

"Why would I do that?"

"I heard you on the phone. You quit."

"Actually, I threatened to quit if Bill Lester didn't take the leash off me. He agreed that he was being a bit silly, so I'm back to work. Without babysitters or bodyguards."

"Are you sure that's a good idea?"

"Absolutely. I'll stop by this evening to pick up my stuff. Tell Jock I'll see him later."

She was out the door before I could respond. I breathed deeply, relief chasing away the despair. She was going to stay on the key, at least until the murders were solved. I could live with that.

Jock came out of the bedroom, carrying a small duffel. He looked around the room. "Did I hear J.D. leave?"

"Yeah. The chief turned her loose on the murder cases. She says she doesn't need our protection anymore."

He grinned. "She never thought she needed us. I think she's going to be okay."

I pointed to the duffel. "Going somewhere?"

"I've got to go to Washington."

"What's up?"

"The director wants me up there for a briefing. Gene's murder may be part of something pretty big."

"Like what?" I asked.

"I'm not sure of the details, but Gene was doing some work for the agency. He was trying to ferret out a mole. It looks like somebody has been leaking information. We lost two field agents about three months ago."

"Lost them?"

"Dead. Their cover was apparently blown, and somebody took them out."

"This is the first you've heard about it?"

"Yeah. I knew about the agents, but something like a mole is held real tight. I'm not sure anybody other than Gene and the director were in on it. I'll know more when I get back."

"Did you check flight schedules?" I asked.

"The director is sending a plane for me. It's already on the way. It should be at Sarasota-Bradenton in about an hour. I'll be back Sunday evening."

Jock left in his rental car, and I cracked my first Miller Lite of the day. Just as I settled into my recliner with a book, my phone rang. David Parrish.

"Matt, a couple of days ago the Drug Enforcement Agency busted some guys over near Clewiston. They were living in an old house out in the cane fields. There's an airstrip about a mile from the house that we suspected was used to fly coke in from Mexico. DEA's been watching it and got a tip that a load was coming in last Tuesday night. They were there and got the pilot and the guys who were there to pick up the dope. The interrogations produced some names and the U.S. Attorney in the Southern District sent a list up to me to see if any of them were of interest to me. Guess who showed up?"

"Bagby?"

"No. Who's Bagby?"

"He's the guy who tried to take out J.D. the other night."

"Right," he said. "But no. It was Qualman."

"I'll be damned."

"Yep, and the mileage from Longboat Key to Clewiston and back is pretty much the same as the mileage that showed up on Nell Alexander's car after she was killed."

"What do you make of that?"

"I don't know, but DEA is willing to let the Longboat cops interview the guys they picked up. They're in the Hendry County jail in LaBelle."

"Okay. I'll tell J.D. Have you heard that Nell's husband, Gene, was murdered this morning?"

"No. What the hell is going on down there?"

"Beats me, but Jock just took off for D.C. for a meeting with his director. Gene was one of theirs, you know."

"Yeah. If anything comes up that might interest me, give me a holler."

"I will. Thanks for the information."

I called Bill Lester and told him what David had said, and that Jock was on his way to Washington. "Can you get somebody down to Clewiston to interview the drug guys?"

"I doubt it. We're jammed here with all these murders. Steve Carey is still on light duty so I'm shorthanded. Where are they being held?"

"The county jail in LaBelle."

"Can you get down there?"

"Sure, but the feds aren't going to let me talk to the bad guys."

"I know the agent-in-charge of the Miami DEA office. I'll call him and tell him you're our special consultant and liaison with another federal agency that's interested in this mess."

"Let me know," I said, "and tell them I might be bringing my assistant, Logan Hamilton."

The chief laughed and hung up. The law enforcement community is sometimes a small world, and a lot gets done through what amounts to a good-ole-boy network. We'd see if Bill could work some magic. He'd done it before.

I called Logan. "Want to do some sleuthing in South Florida?"

"Sure. We going to South Beach?"

"LaBelle."

"Where the hell is LaBelle?"

"It's the county seat of Hendry County. We might also get to go to Clewiston."

"Damn. Probably too good to pass up. When do we leave?"

"In the morning. I'll call you."

I went for a run on the beach. The rain had let up, but the clouds were still obscuring the sky. It was cool, but I knew I'd be sweating by the time I finished. The sand was hard packed, the legacy of the high tide kicked up by the onshore wind the night before. We'd have a little more erosion, a little more of our key taken back by the sea. Beach renourishment was an expensive fact of life for the island's taxpayers, but no one complained. The beach was too important to our tourist dollars and to our way of life.

J.D. was a problem that I had not anticipated. On a couple of levels. I hadn't heard of her a year ago and now I was having a hard time contemplating life without her. Would she leave the island once these cases were over? Would I follow her? Did I have it in me to leave the place where I'd finally found peace, where friendships abounded, where the lazy days passed without interruption? I didn't know. It was a conundrum that I hadn't seen coming before lunch that day.

I thought about the murders. They seemed disparate, unconnected, but it would be too much of a coincidence that we had three murders and four attempted murders on the key within a week. We also had four dead bad guys, but that didn't count. They were part of the murders or the attempts and they got their due. Maybe the next day would start to move back the curtain that obscured our view, to give us some inkling of why the murders were committed and if they were somehow connected to J.D. or maybe Jock.

I could always count on Logan, who had once been a combat infantryman. He and Jock were the only two people in the world in whose hands I would put my life, without reservation. It had been different back in the army. We depended on each other under difficult circumstances and part of the training had been to always cover your buddy's back. We did that without thinking about it. And over time, the bonds grew so that each soldier in the unit operated as if he was part of a family. Even if one didn't particularly like another member of the group, he would always respond as he would if his brother was in danger. I guess in a real sense, Jock and Logan were my brothers.

I sensed that J.D. was also a part of the group to whom I could trust my life, but I was starting to have doubts. If I couldn't trust her with my heart, then where was I? Okay. That sounded a little melodramatic, and the fact that she wanted her life in a different place than where I wanted it did not make her untrustworthy. She didn't owe me anything. If she couldn't continue to enjoy her life here on the key, she would move on. I couldn't hold her.

I chuckled to myself. Life sure does take some interesting turns. I'd been in love once with a pretty girl whom I'd married and then let slip out of my life because of inattention. She'd moved on and found happiness. I'd lost her through my own fault and I had not realized the full extent of what I'd had until she was gone. Would J.D.'s leaving be a repeat of that part of my life? Would I be the biggest fool in the world to refuse to give up my island and lose the girl? Would I be happy with her if I were living in Miami and watching her go out day after day to investigate homicides in some of the bleakest parts of the city, knowing that any day might be the one when she wouldn't come home? That some demented fool might blow her head off? Would I go back to the practice of law to give me something to do during the days and nights that she was prowling the streets of Miami?

No. I couldn't do that. If I followed J.D. to Miami, within a couple of years I'd be so miserable that even her love couldn't salvage me. If I were to be that miserable, her life would be miserable as well. No, I wouldn't leave the island, even for J.D. It would be her decision to make. If she wanted me, she'd have to stay. But wouldn't that scenario provide us a mirror image of what my life would be like in Miami? Would she be so miserable here that I couldn't make it work for her? Wouldn't any marriage fail simply because two people were incompatible in an environment that emotionally castrates one of the partners?

I shook my head and picked up the pace, trying to outrace the devils who were taunting me with bleak thoughts of a future without J.D. I'd weathered that kind of loss once, and I could do it again. I just didn't want to think about the pain that came with the loss.

But loss comes in many guises, and if I could have foreseen the events of the next day, I would have stayed in bed, hunkered under the sheets, seeking safe harbor.

CHAPTER FORTY-ONE

Logan was waiting for me when I pulled in front of his condo complex. At six, the morning was still dark. We drove to St. Armands Circle and grabbed some Starbucks coffee to fuel us for the trip. We drove south on I-75, crossed the wide Caloosahatchee River and took the off ramp to Highway 80. The weather had cleared and warmed. We drove east into the rising sun, the highway coursing through small river towns until we reached LaBelle. We found the jail and parked in front.

I showed my ID and told the deputy manning the booth in the reception area that Chief Lester had made arrangements for me to see Bubba Junior Groover. It turned out that he was the ringleader and neither the DEA nor Bill Lester thought the others would be of any use to us.

Logan had laughed when I told him the name of our interviewee. "There're generations of ignorant rednecks in that name. They can be some dangerous dudes."

We were asked to wait for a few minutes and were then shown to an interview room where we found Mr. Groover shackled to a chair that was bolted to the floor. He was a small man with unkempt hair hanging over his ears. He had a scar that ran diagonally from the edge of his mouth to the tip of his chin and what I guessed was a permanent scowl. His skin wore the reddish complexion that field hands in this part of the world develop before they reach their teens. It's what sailors call a blue-water tan, a mild sunburn superimposed on years' worth of deep tan. He was wearing an orange jumpsuit and cotton slippers, the kind you have to slide along the floor to keep them from falling off your feet.

"Mr. Groover," I said, as Logan and I took seats in the other two chairs in the room, "my name's Matt Royal. I'm here on behalf of the Drug Enforcement Administration." I was stretching that a bit, but I figured this was not a man who would ask a lot of questions. "Do you know that agency?"

"Yep."

"And you know that it was the DEA that arrested you."

"Yep."

"I know you've talked to some of the agents already. Do you understand that your cooperation will be taken into account at any sentencing?"

"Yep."

"Do you know Pete Qualman?"

"Yep."

"Where do you know him from?"

"We did time together."

I was relieved that his vocabulary extended beyond yep. "Where?"

"Glades."

"How long?"

"Couple of years."

"What were you in for?"

"Drugs."

"Using or selling?"

"Running."

"You working out of the same airfield where you were busted?"

"Yep."

"That wasn't real smart, was it?" I asked.

"Didn't turn out to be."

"How long have you been out?"

"'Bout two years."

"How'd you hook back up with Qualman?"

"Pete came here the day he got out. Needed work."

"What kind of work?"

"He knowed about my crew and thought I might have a place for him."

"Did you?"

"Yep."

"Doing what?"

"Mule, mostly. He'd take the stuff from the planes down to Miami to our distributor."

"How often would he make that run?"

"Two, three times a week."

"When did he leave your employ?"

"He quit 'bout two weeks ago."

"Did he say why?"

"Yep."

"What'd he say?"

"Had to go up to Sarasota. One of his buds from Glades was going to pay him a bunch of money for a job."

"Did he have a car?"

"Nope."

"How did he deliver the drugs to Miami?"

"Used mine."

"How did he get to Sarasota?"

"He said somebody was going to pick him up."

"What kind of job in Sarasota?"

"Don't know."

"You didn't ask?"

"Wasn't none of my business."

"Where do your drugs come from?" I was jumping around with my questions, trying to surprise him, catch him off guard. It was an old trial lawyers' trick. Sometimes it worked, but with a guy this dumb, I didn't think it would.

"Mexico, I think."

"You don't know?"

"I'm just the guy what gets the stuff moving."

"Who do you work for?"

"Can't help you there."

"You do know that this is the kind of information that'd do you a lot of good with a judge."

"Yep. And I'd tell you if I knowed."

"How do you get paid?"

"Money gets wired into my bank account."

I was surprised. Maybe this one wasn't as dumb as he pretended. "You have a bank account?"

"Yep. Don't everybody?"

"I guess. You don't know where the money's wired from?"

"Nope. I think those other guys from DEA was going to talk to my bank. Maybe they know."

"Qualman's dead, you know."

A momentary cloud passed across his face, perhaps a frown. "Nope. Didn't know that. How'd it happen?"

"He was shot by a government agent. Qualman was trying to kill a cop."

"Boy, that don't sound like ole Qualman," said Groover. "Must've been a lot of money involved."

"You don't think he'd shoot a cop?"

"He would if there was enough money involved. I just can't believe anybody in their right mind would give him that much money for doing anything. He wasn't the brightest-eyed beast in the gator hole."

I almost choked on that metaphor, but I soldiered on. "Where did he live when he was working for you?"

"In our bunkhouse."

"He make any friends other than your crew?"

"His girlfriend."

Ah, finally. A nugget of information. "What's her name?"

"Jenny Talbot."

"Where does she live?"

"Over near Clewiston."

"Address?"

"Don't know it. She's out in the cane fields."

"Can you give me directions?"

"Yep." He gave me a detailed route to Jenny's house.

"When did you last see Qualman?"

" 'Bout a week ago, I think."

"Can you be more specific?"

"Last Sunday. He stayed with Jenny Saturday night, and I saw him just before he left. Sunday, right after lunch."

"Did somebody bring him?"

"Nope. He was driving a BMW. Sweet ride."

I turned to Logan. "You got anything else?"

"No, Counselor. I think you just about covered it."

CHAPTER FORTY-TWO

We drove to Clewiston following Highway 80. Smoke from the stacks at the sugar refinery billowed into the sky like a beacon, drawing us forward. We stopped at a McDonald's for coffee and then followed Bubba's directions south. We made a couple of turns off county roads and found ourselves on a track that ran straight as an arrow through miles of sugarcane fields. We passed two settlements that housed the workers who cut the cane, many of them Jamaican immigrants. We pulled off the road into the yard of a single house that sat about fifty feet from the berm. It was a small, clapboard building with a tin roof showing large patches of rust. An hour had passed since we had left Bubba sitting chained to the chair in the interview room.

We parked and went to the house. I knocked on the screen door and in a few minutes it was answered by a pretty young woman wearing a T-shirt and cutoffs. She was in her late teens or early twenties. She had long blonde hair, reaching to her shoulders. It looked as if she didn't own a brush or comb. She was barefoot, her toenails covered with chipped black polish, her feet dirty.

"Can I help you?" she asked.

"Are you Jenny Talbot?"

"Who's asking?"

"My name is Matt Royal. This is Logan Hamilton. I'm a lawyer up in Longboat Key, and I need to speak with Ms. Talbot."

"That's me," she said. "Come on in."

We walked into a small room that held a threadbare sofa and two straight chairs. A small TV sat on a table across the room from the sofa, a morning show of some kind playing soundlessly.

"Have a seat," she said, pointing to the sofa. "I know who you are. Bubba called me from the jail."

I was surprised. "He did?"

"About twenty minutes ago."

"Did he tell you about Pete Qualman?"

"Yeah. That's why he called. Said Pete's dead."

"I'm sorry."

"Don't make no never mind to me," she said.

"I thought you were his girlfriend."

"Nah. We're like those people on the TV, I guess, friends with benefits."

"How so?"

"He'd come around when he got horny. Usually brought me a little gift or something. I'd haul his ashes and he'd leave. Came about twice a week."

I was surprised. "Are you a prostitute?" I asked.

I saw anger flare in her face, a tightening of the jaw, redness creeping up from her neck, a grimace. "Fuck you," she said. "I ain't no whore. I liked it when Pete come around."

I was losing her fast. "I'm sorry, Ms. Talbot. I didn't mean to offend you. Can we start over?"

She relaxed a bit, sat back in her straight chair. "Okay. What do you want?"

"I want to know about Pete," I said. "Who his friends were, why he was going to Sarasota, what kind of job he had up there, that sort of thing."

"He didn't have no friends to amount to anything. He lived down in the next settlement in a bunkhouse with some of the crew Bubba ran."

"Did he ever mention any of the crew as a friend?"

"No. I don't think he had much to do with them."

"What about the guy in Sarasota?"

"What about him?"

"Did Pete ever tell you that he was a friend, where they met, what the job was in Sarasota?"

"I know it was some guy he'd been in the lockup with over near Belle Glade."

"Glades Correctional?"

"I guess."

"Do you know the friend's name?"

"Jeff, I think."

"Last name?"

"I never heard it."

"How did Pete get here? Did somebody bring him?"

She smiled, the first sign of life I'd seen in her face other than the anger when I'd accused her of being a whore. "No. He had a sweet ride. Took me for a drive. Real leather seats and a sound system that'd knock your shoes off if you cranked it up enough."

"What kind of car?"

"I don't know. He said it was German."

"BMW?"

"Could be. I don't know nothing about cars."

"Was he planning to come back to see you?"

"I suppose. Next time he got horny."

"Did he say where he got the car?"

"Said he borrowed it."

"From whom?"

"Didn't say. I figured it was his boss's car."

"Jeff?"

"I guess."

"Do you work?" I asked.

"Sometimes I get a job waitressing. Not lately, though. Times are tough."

"Where do you get the money to live on?"

"I got a couple of kids and the state sends me a check every month."

"Where are the kids?"

"They're with my daddy. Over to Clewiston, shopping."

"Does your father live here?"

"Yeah. This is his house. Well, it belongs to the sugar company, but he works for them, so he gets the house."

"Does your mother live here, too?" I asked.

She laughed, a short, bitter-sounding bark. "She run off when I was a baby. It's just Daddy and me. Always been that way."

I paused for a moment, thinking about this young woman. I wondered what she might have become had she been born into different circumstances. She was pretty and perhaps a different upbringing would have rubbed off the rough edges. She could have been a coed up at Gainesville or Tallahassee instead of rotting in this hidden part of Florida.

We were in the middle of the state, about sixty miles either way to Ft. Myers on the west coast or Palm Beach on the east. In some reality, we were thousands of miles or years removed from the golden people that lived and played and laughed on the gilded coasts. There was surely nothing to laugh about in this blighted place.

"Do you know anybody that might help us find this Jeff?"

"Nope. Can't help you there."

I thought for a moment and looked at Logan. He caught my eye and shook his head once, quickly. I got to my feet. "Thank you, Ms. Talbot," I said. "We'll be on our way."

She stood, a flash of anger turning her face into a rictus of outrage. "You bastard," she shouted. "You think I don't know who the fuck you are? You think I'm some backwoods whore who don't know nothing? I saw it on the news. You're the bastard what killed Pete."

I didn't think now was the time to explain what happened, not that she'd believe me anyway. Logan was getting out of his seat. "Let's go, Matt," he said.

I think if I'd known what was waiting in Jenny's front yard, I would have just stayed inside. Barricaded and calling 911 for help.

CHAPTER FORTY-THREE

Logan and I walked through the door to the front porch. Two black men were standing in the front yard, spread out a little, perhaps ten feet separating them. They weren't young, probably in their forties, but they were big and muscular. They looked like men who worked the cane, worked hard getting the stalks to the trucks that hauled them to the refinery. One man held what I took to be a cane cutter, although in this day of mechanization I was sure it was obsolete, maybe an antique. It had a wooden handle about a foot and a half long with a leather strap at the end, fashioned to go around the wrist so that the instrument wouldn't slip out of the hand of its wielder. The business end had a blade set into the handle at a right angle and fastened by a screw and bolt. It was slightly curved and seemed to be sharpened on both sides. The blade terminated in a rounded point. An ominous weapon.

"Can I help you, gentlemen?" I asked, standing on the porch, Logan beside me. We'd left Jenny inside.

"Jenny called us, mon. Said narcs were coming. I guess that's you. You narcs?" His accent was Jamaican, the harshness of his tone ameliorated by the Caribbean lilt that coated his words.

"No. I'm a lawyer from Longboat Key."

I heard the screen door open and felt the presence of Jenny behind me. Before I could turn around she pushed me in the back, hard. I felt myself falling forward and put my foot out to catch myself. My momentum took me down two steps and into the yard. I caught myself before I fell and stood upright my feet planted on the dirt.

Jenny was screaming, crying, words cascading like so much water over a dam. I finally made out what she was saying. "He killed Pete, the bastard. He killed Pete."

I knew she was pointing at me, but I couldn't turn around to see. I was in a staring contest with the big man holding the sugarcane cutter. I knew Logan was also on the porch and I was sure he was on high alert.

"Did you kill him?" asked the man with the cutter.

"No," I said.

"Yes he did," screeched Jenny. "The television said it was him."

The two men had now closed ranks and were standing a foot or so apart. The second man pulled a large knife from a scabbard at his side, holding it by the hilt, bouncing it slowly in his hand, his eyes hard on me. The first man raised the cane cutter and took a step toward me. We were close, five or six feet. I took a step backward, felt my heel bounce against the first step. Out of the corner of my eye, I could see Logan standing stock-still on the porch, trying to decide what to do. I saw with some relief that he had a pistol in his hand, holding it down by his side. It was the small one he often carried in an ankle holster. I'd seen him take it off when we started into the jail that morning, but I hadn't seen him put it back on. He must have done it while I was in the McDonald's in Clewiston ordering coffee.

The man was raising the cane cutter and making a quick move toward me when I heard the shot. I watched him stagger as blood began to stain the front of his white shirt. He crumpled to the ground, dropping his weapon. I dove for it, thinking I'd get to it before the other man and maybe this mess would be over.

As I hit the ground, I heard a cry of pain from the porch. I grabbed the cane cutter and rolled to a sitting position. The man who'd held the knife had turned and was running away from us. I looked back to the porch and saw Logan moving toward Jenny. She had fallen back against the side of the house and was sinking slowly into a sitting position. The knife the second man had been holding was sticking out of her chest.

No more than a second or two had elapsed since the man came at me with the cane cutter. I picked myself up and ran for the porch. Jenny was in big trouble. The blade had sunk to the hilt into her chest. I didn't think she'd survive that kind of wound.

I pulled my phone out of a pocket and dialed 911. "I've got one man down from a gunshot, probably dead, and a woman with a large knife in her chest, critical. Can you get a location on me from the GPS on my phone?"

"I've got it. Who is calling, please?"

"Get somebody out here now."

"I need your name, sir."

"Matt Royal. We need help."

"It's on the way, Mr. Royal. Please stay on the line."

"Did you capture my phone number?"

"Yes, sir." She read it back to me.

"That's it."

"I'll need to ask you some questions, sir."

"Call me back if it's important." I hung up. I've never figured out why the 911 operators bother you with a lot of useless questions when you have a life-threatening emergency.

I looked down at Jenny. Logan was holding her hand, talking quietly to her. He looked up at me. "She's gone," he said. "Goddamnit. I just wasn't quick enough."

"You saved my life, buddy."

"Yeah, but I didn't save hers. Just as I shot the guy with the cane cutter, the other one threw the knife at you. When you hit the ground it went right over you and got Jenny in the chest."

"Nothing you could do, Logan. If you hadn't shot the guy trying to kill me, I'd be dead. Jenny called them because she thought I'd killed her boyfriend. I guess she wanted a bit of revenge, and turns out, it bit her in the ass. It wasn't your fault."

"Why the meltdown?" asked Logan. "She didn't seem to care much whether Pete was dead or alive."

"I think she was just buying time until the men she'd called got here. Didn't want us to know she cared about Pete. I guess she really did care."

"Who's going to tell her kids?"

"That'll probably fall to her father. It stinks, but what can you do."

We stood there in the stillness of the cane field, the quiet broken only by the stalks ruffling in the breeze. The sun was warm now, and bright, moving higher in the sky. It would have been a pleasant place to spend an hour or so if there weren't two dead people lying about. We'd left the bodies where they fell and were leaning against the rear quarter panel of my Explorer, waiting for the law. Logan had put his pistol on the hood of the vehicle, as far from us as possible. Unless we wanted to give up our leaning post. Which we didn't. But we didn't want to excite the officers, either.

In less time than I would have thought, I heard sirens and in a few minutes saw an ambulance and a sheriff's car bouncing down the track that led to the house. The cruiser pulled into the yard, and a deputy got out and walked toward us. The ambulance came to a stop, and the paramedics went to take a look at the bodies.

"You Matt Royal?" he asked.

"I am, Deputy."

"Could I see some ID?"

I handed him my driver's license. He looked at it carefully and handed it back to me.

"Then I guess this is Mr. Hamilton."

"Right," said Logan, handing over his driver's license.

"The sheriff told me you were okay. Part of some sort of drug task force."

"Not exactly," I said, "but the sheriff can explain it to you."

"The sheriff overheard the 911 operator calling the dispatcher. She had your name. He radioed me. He'll be along soon. He has to come all the way from LaBelle."

"Thanks, deputy," I said.

"We got forensics coming," said the deputy. "I might as well get a statement from you two while we wait for them. Is that Jenny Talbot up there on the porch?"

"Yeah," I said.

"What happened?"

I gave him the short version. I knew the statement would be very detailed. When I got to the part about the man throwing the knife into Jenny's chest, the deputy looked down, as if he'd just heard a sad story. I guess he had. The people in these parts tended to stay here their whole lives. They

knew each other and knew the families. It was a close-knit society of blue
collar people. The smartest ones found a way out of the cane business. I
suspected this deputy was one of the smart ones.

"That's a shame. She wasn't a bad kid. Worked up at Kelly's Diner for
a couple of years, but he had to let her go when she got into some kind of
drugs."

"Doesn't look like she ever had much of a chance," said Logan.

"Can't disagree with you there," said the deputy. "Her old man's full
of piss and vinegar, but he loved that girl and took good care of her after
her ma ran off. I've known him since first grade. He never made it out of
high school. Dropped out in about the ninth grade and went to work in the
cane."

"I take it he still works in the cane industry," I said.

"Yeah. He's worked himself up to some kind of supervisor over at the
refinery."

"What about Jenny's kids?" asked Logan.

"Oh, boy. They're one and three. Nobody seems to know who the
daddy is. Whoever he is, he's pretty much gone. Hell, it might have been
two different fathers. Jenny was a pretty wild little gal. She kind of spread
it around, if you know what I mean."

I nodded. I knew what he meant.

"What'll happen to the kids?" asked Logan.

"Don't know. Probably the state'll take 'em. They'll end up in the fos-
ter care system. Jenny's daddy sure can't take care of 'em. But Lord, he
does love those kids. It's gonna be tough. Lose his only child and both his
grandkids."

"Any chance of catching the guy with the knife?"

"Who knows? I hope so. He killed somebody's mom. He shouldn't
get away with that."

He pulled out a tape recorder and set it on the hood of the patrol car.
He turned it on and started the interview. We told him everything we knew
and how we came to be at that sad little house in the vast cane fields.

CHAPTER FORTY-FOUR

We spent a couple of hours at the house, giving our statements, meeting the sheriff, and telling our story again. The forensics team came, did whatever they do, and left. The ambulance had taken the bodies to the morgue to await the medical examiner. I wanted to get away from the house before Jenny's dad showed up. The sheriff would have to tell him that his daughter was dead. I didn't want to see that kind of grief, the kind that would take a strong man to his knees.

Logan and I started back to Longboat Key, stopping for take-out at a fast-food restaurant's drive-through. We ate as we drove.

"I hate shit like that," said Logan.

"You talking about the food?"

"Jenny."

"I know."

"If she hadn't called those goons."

"But she did," I said. "She wasn't the sharpest arrow in the quiver."

He gave me that look I always get when I say something he thinks is stupid. "Did the name she gave you mean anything?" he asked.

"No. I've never heard of anybody connected to these cases named Jeff. But he might be buried in that stack of papers J.D. got from Miami. If we can put somebody with that name in Glades Correctional, we may have found the first thread that'll unravel this. He may be somebody J.D. arrested."

"I don't think it's going to be that easy," he said. "It never is."

I called J.D., using the hands-free function so that Logan could listen in. I brought her up to date on what we had been doing, including the fact that we'd left two people dead in the cane field. She was quiet on the other end of the line, or whatever cell phones use to connect us.

"That's too bad, Matt," she finally said. "Poor girl. But I'm glad you're okay."

"Thanks. How're you coming along?"

"Buried in all this paper from Miami. Trying to find some kind of connection."

"Anything going on with Gene's case?"

"No. The fingerprints the forensics people found on the gun used to kill Gene aren't in the system, so we have no idea who they belong to. If we arrest somebody, we'll at least have the prints for comparison."

"Are you seeing any connection between his murder and the others?"

"Not yet. There might not be any."

"Did you check out the yard crew that was in the neighborhood?"

"Yeah. It was legit. A local company that does a lot of work on the key. They don't have any Guatemalans on the payroll."

"Did you talk to the crew members? See if they saw anybody that looked like them that didn't belong on their crew?"

"I talked to every one of them. Took me most of the evening and part of this morning. Nothing suspicious."

"You think they're telling the truth?"

"Hard to tell," she said. "None of them speaks English, so I had to use an interpreter. That makes it a bit more dicey."

"If there's a gang connection in this, the guys on the crew might be too scared to talk about it."

"Yeah. I thought of that. Not much we can do about it, though."

"Has the name Jeff popped up in all that Miami paperwork?"

"Not yet," she said. "I'm still going through it. Why?"

"Jenny, the girl who was killed, said Qualman told her he was working in Sarasota for somebody named Jeff. They met in prison at Glades Correctional."

"No last name?"

"No. Sorry."

She sighed. "I'll look for Jeff. If we can find him, we may be able to start putting these people together somehow."

"Check the sheet the super at Glades sent on Qualman. That's probably your best bet to find Jeff's last name."

"I know. I'll let you know if I find out anything. Is Jock with you?"

"No. He went to Washington yesterday. Be back tomorrow evening."

"He called me this morning. Didn't say he was out of town."

"What did he want?"

"Asked if we'd found a laptop at Gene Alexander's. He said it could be important to something he was working on."

"Was there a laptop?" I asked.

"Not that we found. I checked with the forensics folks, too. Nobody saw a laptop."

"Did he say why it was important?"

"No. And I haven't had time to call him back to let him know we didn't find anything."

"I'll call him. I need to talk to him anyway."

"Tell him I'd like to sit down with him tomorrow evening."

"Yes, ma'am." She hung up.

"She's back in full cop mode," said Logan.

"I'm glad. She needed the stimulation."

"I worry about her getting bored here on the island."

"I do too. She said as much at lunch yesterday," I said.

"This has got to be a big comedown for a Miami-Dade homicide commander."

"Assistant commander," I said.

"Well, you get my meaning."

"I do. But there's not a damn thing I can do about it."

"I wonder why that laptop seems important to Jock," Logan said.

"I'll call him when we get home. Probably not a big deal."

"I'll be off island for a week or so," Logan said.

"Where're you going? You just got back from the keys."

"Marie's got a business trip to New York City, so I thought I'd go along, and we can catch some shows, maybe run up to Nahant to see some of my family for a couple of days."

"How long will you be gone?"

"If we decide to go to Boston, we'll probably be gone the better part of two weeks," Logan said.

"The key is always a little quieter when you're out of town. Some of the bartenders who depend on you might go broke if you're gone too long."

"You'll just have to drink more. Take one for the team."

"I'll do my best," I said.

We drove on in silence, Logan fiddling with the radio, trying to find some decent music among the Saturday afternoon infomercials. I thought about the cases, the victims, J.D.'s thoughts about leaving the key, Jock's concerns about Gene Alexander's death being connected to his agency. But mostly, I thought about a pretty girl growing up in the cane fields with no hope of anything better and of her children who would never know their mom. And I thought about her father, a hard-working man who had done his best and lost everything.

CHAPTER FORTY-FIVE

Sunday was one of those days when you accomplish nothing and end up tired in the process. I was looking forward to the downtime. One of the things I enjoyed about my island was the opportunity to hide out and spend the day alone with a book. If I didn't answer the phone, no one was offended. They'd leave a message on the answering machine and get on with their day. The islanders understood the need for quiet time. As it turned out, I was tired by the time I went to bed that night, but it wasn't from reading a book. The day got a bit complicated as it wore on.

I'd called Jock after I'd gotten home the afternoon before and told him what J.D. had said. He thanked me, but said he couldn't talk about the laptop over the phone. He would fill me in when he got back to the key.

I pulled Christine Kling's latest novel from the stack of books I had set aside to read. Her character, Seychelle Sullivan, was back on her tugboat, solving another mystery. I'd heard Ms. Kling had suspended the series and was writing something else. I hoped she'd get back to Seychelle.

The outdoor temperature had moved into the seventies. The sky was clear, the sun bright, and a small breeze blew out of the south. I sat on the patio with my book until my stomach began to rumble with hunger. Some warmed-over pizza and a diet cola took care of that.

I knew J.D. would be working, trying to tie all the ends together, figure out who was trying to kill her, and why. I had thought about calling her for lunch, but finally discarded the notion. She needed some time to work and get her thoughts together. I wasn't going to be the instrument of her decision to stay on the island. That was a decision she had to make alone, to come to terms with a different existence than she'd known in Miami. If she couldn't make the transition, she'd be better off back in South Florida.

I would be worse off, but that should not be part of her equation. She had to find her own happiness, and if that cut me out, so be it.

My phone rang a couple of times, but I didn't answer. I listened to the messages left on the machine. If the calls had been important, I'd have called back immediately. Neither of them was about anything that couldn't wait until the next day. Late in the afternoon, just as the sun was beginning its daily descent into the Gulf, I heard the front door open and turned to see Jock walk in. He looked tired, stressed. I knew him better than any other person on the planet and I sensed that things hadn't gone well in D.C.

"Hi, podna," he said. "Taking a day off?"

"Yeah. Looks like you need one. Want to talk?"

He put his duffel down, went to the kitchen, and rummaged around in the refrigerator. He came out onto the patio with a cold O'Doul's and took the empty chair. "We lost another agent last week. An old friend of mine."

"Where?"

"Columbia. He was deep undercover and somebody took him out."

"Are you sure somebody figured out who he was?"

"Yeah. They carved 'CIA' in his chest."

"You're not CIA."

"No. But those people figure all American agents are CIA."

"I'm sorry, Jock."

"It's an occupational hazard. But we think somebody inside our agency had something to do with this one and the two guys who were taken out several months ago."

"The ones Gene Alexander was involved with."

"Yeah. This one, too."

"Gene was working on your friend's murder?"

"The director called him the first of this week to get him involved. He'd hit an absolute dead end on the first two murders and they called off the investigation. He said he thought Gene would be better off working than moping around thinking about Nell."

"And you think Gene's murder is connected to the investigation?"

"Looks like it."

"What was the deal with the laptop?"

"Gene was using the laptop on his end of the investigation. He could get into almost any database the agency has. He was trolling, trying to find an opening, somebody who had access who shouldn't have, or somebody communicating with the bad guys in some way."

"You think somebody killed Gene to get the laptop?"

"No. We think Gene was taken out by whoever is screwing with us. My guess is that the laptop was just there and the killer figured it might have information his bosses could use."

"Sounds like that laptop would have a lot of information in it."

"Yeah, but I doubt anybody would be able to crack the encryption. There are layers built in that would be almost impossible to break. But, the very fact that the computer was the only thing taken makes it more likely that this was a professional hit."

"Anything else point to that conclusion?"

"Gene wasn't a trained field agent. He was an analyst. Spent his whole life with computers, looking at intel, trying to stay a step or two ahead of the bad guys. Still, he would have been aware of his surroundings. I think it would have been very difficult for somebody who didn't know what they were doing to be able to slip up on him."

"Maybe Gene was asleep. We'll never know." I said.

"You're probably right."

"I talked with J.D. She wants to meet with you as soon as possible."

"Call her. We can order in pizza."

"I had pizza for lunch."

"Won't kill you to eat it again."

CHAPTER FORTY-SIX

J.D. came through the front door a couple of hours later. "I found Jeff this afternoon," she said.

"Hello to you, too, Detective," I said.

She laughed. "Sorry. This may be the break we need. I guess I'm kind of pumped."

"Happy to be back at work?" I asked.

"Bet your—well, you know what. That thing you sit on. Yes."

"Tell us about Jeff," I said.

"A man named Jeff Worthington was an inmate at Glades until a few months ago. He was doing fifteen years for manslaughter. Killed a bouncer at a club in Tampa. He did every day of the fifteen, and was released on June first. Nobody's heard from him since. He's completely off the grid."

"Why do you think he's the one?" I asked. "If he's been in prison for fifteen years, he couldn't have had anything to do with the whale tail killings twelve years ago."

"That's true, but he's the only prisoner down there named Jeff who's been released within the past year. At least the only one not accounted for. A couple of others are on parole, but they're nowhere near Sarasota and they're checking in with their parole officers regularly. And, this Jeff shared a cell with Pete Qualman for a couple of years."

"Bingo," said Jock.

"I still don't see the connection to the whale tail murders," I said.

J.D. smiled at me like she might if I were a child with little understanding of the world. "I don't either, sweetie, but we're closer than we were before you came up with Jeff's name."

"I like it when you call me 'sweetie,' " I said. "What now?"

I got the same look again. "More cross-referencing," she said. "I called Steve Carey, and he said he'd come in tomorrow and take over that job."

"So you think Jeff is in Sarasota," said Jock.

"All I've got to go on is what that poor girl down in Clewiston had to say."

"Anything new on Gene's case?" Jock asked.

"Not really. I've been through all the evidence the forensic guys turned up, but there wasn't much. Whoever the killer was, he was careful. Did you get anything in Washington?"

"Yes. But we've got a problem."

"The missing laptop?" she asked.

"That's part of it."

"What else?"

"Most of what I know is a national security problem that only the president, the director of my agency, and I know about. I can't share it."

"President of what?" she asked.

"The United States."

"Oh."

"Yeah."

"What are you telling me?" she asked.

"Nothing. That's the problem. I need to know what you know, but I can't tell you what I know."

"What are you planning to do with my information?"

"I'm hoping it'll get me closer to the killer. We're pretty sure Gene's murder is connected to something we're working on."

"And if you find the killer before I do, what then?" asked J.D.

"That's some of the stuff I can't tell you."

"Or won't."

"Gets us to the same place either way."

"You tell your president that information sharing is a two-way street."

"Not this time, J.D. I want to cooperate with you because we're friends, and you're a hell of a detective, but I can't. Not on this one. Not without your promise that the information I give you will go no further. Not even to Bill Lester. I've got the director's authorization to share my information with you, but only with the stipulation that it stays with you."

"Jock," she said, "I can't and won't work outside the department. If the chief tells me I can keep some aspects of this investigation secret, I'll do it. But not otherwise. And he's not going to agree to that. He has to answer to the town manager and, eventually, the state attorney and the press."

Jock shrugged, as if dismissing the subject. "It sounds like you don't have a whole lot to go on, anyway," he said.

"I don't. Not right now. But I will know more. And soon. I'm good at what I do."

"I know that and I need you. I'll make a call. In about half an hour, Chief Lester will give you the go-ahead." He grinned. "I look forward to working with you, Detective."

She laughed, derisively. "Right," she said. "Matt, did you order the pizza?"

I hadn't, but I picked up the phone and called Oma's.

Chief Bill Lester lived in the village a couple of blocks from my cottage. He arrived at the same time as the pizza delivery guy. He was red in the face, agitated, but he held his tongue until the pizza dude left. "Goddamnit it, Jock, do you know who I just got off the phone with?"

Jock grinned. "Yes."

"The goddamned president of the United States," said Lester, his voice loud.

"Y'all have a nice chat?" Jock asked, still grinning.

"If you call a presidential request to turn my department over to you a nice chat."

"Now, Bill," Jock said. "It wasn't that bad."

"Almost." Lester was calming down. "But the goddamned president of the United States? He said he was calling on your behalf, Jock. Can you believe that shit, Matt?"

"Sure can," I said.

J.D. sat, rooted in her chair, stunned by the chief's outburst.

Lester shook his head, turned to J.D. "He was calling about you, Detective."

"Me?" she said.

Bill nodded. "He suggested I give you the authority to work with these two jacklegs and keep it all to yourself. Take me and the whole goddamned law enforcement community out of the loop."

Her eyes narrowed. "I guess you told him you run this department," she said.

"Sure," Bill said, sarcastically. "And I didn't mention that I report to the town manager who reports to the town commission, all seven of whom are politicians. Or that I know that the U.S. Attorney and the governor, who, by the way, are members of the same party as the president, are already involved in this mess. I told him to go piss up a rope."

"What did you really say?" I asked.

"I said, 'Yes, sir,' " said Bill. "I said that a number of times. And then I called the town manager and told him what I planned to do and who had suggested it."

"And what do you plan to do?" I asked.

"Exactly what the goddamned president of the United States asked me to do. It's your show, Jock, and J.D is yours for the duration."

"Bill," I said, "I'm not sure Gene Alexander's murder is connected to the others."

"I'm not either. The president is only interested in the Alexander case, so J.D., you work them all and handle the others the same way we always do. If they turn out to be tied together, we'll talk about it and decide how to go from there."

"Just how pissed are you, Bill?" Jock asked.

"Pretty pissed. I guess a couple slices of Oma's best would probably take the edge off."

"No problem," I said.

"You got any beer?" asked the chief.

"No problem," I said.

CHAPTER FORTY-SEVEN

When the pizza and the beer and the chief were gone, Jock asked if we were up to hearing what he'd learned in Washington.

"I don't remember the president saying that Matt could hear any of this," said J.D., smiling.

"I have full discretion to tell Matt anything. Besides, he knows if he ever divulges anything, I'll kill him."

Jock was smiling as he said that, but I'm not at all sure there wasn't some sort of threat in his words. It didn't matter. I was never going to test it.

"Back in April," Jock said, "we lost two agents in Columbia. They had successfully infiltrated the guerrilla group known as FARC and were giving us a wealth of intelligence. We'd been able to take down some of their leaders and were closing in on the top dog."

"What happened?" asked J.D.

"We don't know for sure. I knew we'd lost some agents, but until yesterday I didn't know the particulars. Their bodies were dumped in front of our embassy in Bogotá. They had been tortured and then hanged with something very thin, like piano wire. It causes a painful death by choking."

"Just like Hitler," I said.

"Exactly," said Jock. "Just like Hitler did to the people involved in the July twentieth plot to kill him."

"Do you know how the guerrillas figured out who your agents were?" asked J.D.

"That's the nub of the problem," said Jock. "We think there's a leak in our system. Somebody is feeding the bad guys information. That's what

Gene Alexander was working on. Our director brought him into the investigation. Actually, the whole thing was held so closely that only the director and Gene were involved."

"Why Gene?" asked J.D.

"He was retired, out of it," said Jock. "The leaks started after he'd left the agency, so he was above suspicion. His analytical skills were about the best our agency had ever seen, so he was the logical person to bring into the loop."

"Did he find anything?" asked J.D.

"No, and we didn't lose any more agents. They thought the leaks had stopped. They figured that the leaker, whoever he was, had either quit leaking or was out of the agency. Maybe he'd had pressure put on him specifically by the FARC, or he had some philosophical identity with them. Whatever, the director gave up after a couple of months. But before he did, he had Gene set some electronic traps in the agency's computer system. If the guy showed up again, they'd get him. At least that was the plan."

"And the leaker showed up again. Recently?" asked J.D.

"We think that's what happened. We lost another agent last Sunday."

"You think it's related to the other two?" I asked.

"We think so. At least the manner of death was the same."

"Maybe the agent screwed up," said J.D.

"I don't think so," said Jock. "This agent was a friend of mine. He was about the best in the business. He had gotten himself embedded with one of the drug cartels in southern Mexico. He was born in Los Angeles, but his parents were Mexicans who came from the same area where he was working with the cartel. He fit right in."

"What was he doing?" I asked. "I mean, was he tracking the drugs into the U.S., taking out the cartel leaders, what?"

"He was trying to track the drugs back to their source. We know who the cartel leaders are, and we're trying to find where they are so that we can figure a way to take them out. We were about to put another agent in place."

"Why is your agency so interested in the drug business?" I asked.

"It's not really the drug business we're worried about. Not as such. It's the money that flows from it into terrorist groups around the world that interests us. If we can disrupt the drug flow, we make a dent in the cash flow and maybe eventually put the terrorists that depend on the money out of business."

"You've got the first two murdered agents dealing with guerrillas in Columbia and another one taking on the drug cartels in Mexico," I said. "How do you see the connection?"

"The only one that makes sense is that the same leaker is dealing with different groups. Maybe he's expanding his reach. It's probably not ideological since the Mexicans seem to believe in nothing but making money. I think FARC, even though it's involved in the drug business, actually believes in Communism. But who knows for sure?"

"Was your friend's body dropped at the embassy in Mexico City?" asked J.D.

Jock shook his head.

"Where did you find him?" I asked.

"In front of a U.S. Agency for International Development office in Flores."

"Where's that?"

"Guatemala."

CHAPTER FORTY-EIGHT

We sat in silence for a few moments, the idea of a Guatemalan connection coursing across the synapses of our brains, raising more questions than we had answers. Jock had been right. Maybe the men who tried to kill J.D. and me were really after Jock.

"Did you know about this on Friday when you said something about the Guatemalans getting you and me mixed up?" I asked.

He shook his head. "I've operated in that area of the world and I thought it reasonable that I might be a target. It made no sense to me that either you or J.D. would be in the gang's sights for some reason."

"I'm still not sure why or how they could make a mistake like that," I said.

"It actually makes some sense, now that I know what Gene was doing. Suppose they—whoever they are—knew that Gene was working on the problem of the leaker and they had somebody watching him. Maybe a loose surveillance or something. They see me with Gene, probably take a photograph and send it to the leaker. He identifies me as an agent, and thinks I'm probably here to protect Gene. It never connects with them that I came here because of Matt."

"Then how did I get in their sights?" I asked. "Or J.D.?"

"These guys aren't the smartest people on the planet," Jock said. "It may be something as simple as them finding out that I'm staying in your house and didn't realize that anybody else was here. There was a different shift watching the house, one who hadn't seen me. They saw you come and get in your car. They followed you downtown, thinking the man coming out of the house had to be me. They took their shot when you came out of the police station."

"That kind of stupidity is a little hard to believe," I said.

"Probably. But you can paint a lot of scenarios as to how they thought you were me. None of them need to make a lot of sense. Maybe you did something to piss them off. Maybe it's a big coincidence that some Guatemalan gangbangers took a shot at you at the same time we're closing in on a leaker with some sort of Guatemalan connection. Maybe the guys shooting at you aren't related in any way to Gene's death."

"So, maybe they were after me," said J.D.

"Who knows," said Jock, "but I'd like to talk to the gangbangers."

"Jock," J.D. said, "I'm not sure the Mexicans on that landscaping crew were telling me the truth about there not being a stranger along with them on Friday. You speak Spanish, don't you?"

"Yes."

"What if you talked to them?"

"I'd like that, but not at the police station. I'd want to come at them without any government connections."

"You think they'll be more likely to talk to you than if they thought you were with the police?"

"I think they'll be more likely to be scared shitless of me if they think I'm not official."

"More scared of you than of the gangbangers?" she asked.

Jock grinned. "Bet on it."

I changed the subject. "Was Gene making any progress in identifying the leaker?"

"We think so. He called the director Thursday afternoon and said he needed to see him as soon as possible. He couldn't talk about anything over the phone and was afraid to send anything over the Internet, even with the encryptions they were using."

"And they never got together," said J.D.

"No," said Jock. "When I called the director on Friday to tell him about Gene's death, he was just leaving his office to fly down here."

"Did he tell you why?" asked J.D.

"Not on the phone. He just asked me to come to Washington."

"And your interest in the laptop when you called me on Saturday was that the director thought information about the leaker might be on it," said J.D.

"Right," said Jock. "The laptop was so sensitive that the director didn't want Gene to fly to Washington. He was afraid that something might happen to the computer on the way."

"That's pretty far-fetched," I said.

Jock shrugged. "I agree, but they didn't want to take a chance on the plane crashing, the laptop getting stolen, Gene having a heart attack, anything. It was that sensitive. That's the reason the director was coming to Longboat Key to see Gene."

"Did the director have any idea what Gene had learned?"

"Nada," said Jock. "Not even an inkling."

"But somebody knew what was going on," said J.D. "We didn't think to check for bugs on his phone. Maybe people were listening to his conversations."

"Don't think so," said Jock. "Both Gene and the director were using encrypted satellite phones to communicate. Gene would never have used his home phone on something this important."

"We didn't find either a cell or a satellite phone," said J.D.

"I'm not surprised," said Jock, "but the phone wasn't particularly important. Unless somebody has the encryption code, they won't be able to use it."

"What about the missing laptop?" I asked. "Do you think somebody can break that code?"

"I don't know," said Jock, "but that's probably not important. We think Gene had somehow developed information that would give us the leaker's identity. That's probably what's in the computer. Since the leaker obviously knows who he is, that information isn't going to help him. The loss of it will certainly hurt us."

"If we found the laptop, could the director get into it?" J.D. asked.

"Sure," said Jock. "He knows the key."

"So it would seem that the best way to find the leaker is to find the laptop," said J.D.

"Yes," said Jock. "But it's probably somewhere at the bottom of the Gulf by now."

She sat quietly for a couple of beats, chewing on it. Then, "That may not be the case. That might depend on how sophisticated the hitter was."

"How so?" I asked.

"Think about it," she said. "Suppose he was just some low-level gang-banger who happened to be convenient for the leaker to hire to kill Gene. Even if he'd been told to take the computer, he might decide that he can make more money by selling it back to the leaker. Or for that matter, he might be so dumb that he'd try to pawn it. He might not have any idea how valuable it is to the leaker."

"You've got a point," said Jock, "but I was under the impression you thought the murderer was probably a professional."

"It looked that way, but I really wasn't thinking about Guatemalan gangs. I thought you were off base on that one."

Jock smiled. "Wouldn't have been the first time."

"Those gangbangers grow up killing people," she said.

"Usually in a blood bath," I said. "This one took some finesse."

"Or maybe just practice," said J.D. "What if the gang has a designated hitter, so to speak? One they use for their contract murders when they don't want it traced back to them."

"Could be," said Jock. "Can you get me the name and address of the landscaping crew chief? The shooter couldn't have gotten onto that crew without the crew chief's knowledge."

"It's in my file back at the station. I'll get it for you tomorrow."

"I'd like to go see the guy tonight," Jock said. "You up for a little action, Matt?"

I nodded. "I've got nothing else going on."

"I'll go with you," said J.D.

Jock shook his head. "J.D., this is the place where you should bow out. There're some things an honest cop shouldn't be involved in."

"I thought we were going to be a team," she said.

"We are," said Jock. "I'll give you all the information we get, but you don't need to be involved in how we get that information."

"I'm not sure I like that."

"You wouldn't like the way I work, either."

"I'm not a kid, Jock. I watched you work over a bad guy once."

"And it made you sick," I said.

She was quiet for a moment or two, chewing on her need for evidence and her gut-level hatred at the methods Jock was sometimes required to use. But she knew there was more at stake here than solving Gene's murder or the whale tail killings. I could almost see the wheels turning in her head. Finally, she raised her arms in a show of surrender. "Let's go to the station."

CHAPTER FORTY-NINE

The man standing in the doorway of the ramshackle house was big and beefy, a vision of adiposity rapidly overtaking muscularity. His long hair was tied in a ponytail, his face showing annoyance at being bothered at home. His name was Chico Suarez and he was the crew chief we'd come for.

The yard was dirt and dark, no street lights in this disheveled neighborhood in East Bradenton. A king cab pickup was parked in the yard, a van-type trailer still attached to it. The Islandwide Landscaping Service logo was on both. The sound of a Spanish-language television station blared from the living room. Jock was speaking English to the man and asked him if he was indeed the Chico Suarez who was the crew chief for Islandwide.

"Yeah," said the man. "What do you want?" His English was very good. I wondered why he'd told J.D. he only spoke Spanish.

Jock punched him in the abdomen, a quick, powerful blow to the solar plexus that brought Suarez to his knees, gasping, trying to catch his breath. Jock grabbed the ponytail and was pulling him farther into the yard, Suarez scrambling on his knees, trying to keep up, his breath ragged. Jock rolled the man onto his back, straddled him and poked a .45-caliber pistol under his chin.

"Who was the Guatemalan you let on your crew on Friday?" Jock asked.

"I don't know what you're talking about."

"I don't think this is a good time to be lying to me, amigo."

"They'll kill me."

Jock screwed the barrel of the gun further into the tissue beneath the man's chin. "If you don't start talking, I'll kill you right now," he said. "Save the gangbangers the trouble."

"No. Don't shoot. What do you want to know?"

Jock pulled the pistol back and pointed it at Suarez's face. "This better be good."

"I didn't have anything to do with it," said Suarez.

"With what?"

"The killing."

"You know about that?"

"Yes. It was on the television news. And the cops came around asking a lot of questions about it."

"How did the Guatemalan get on your crew?"

"Some guy with a bunch of tattoos came to see me early Friday morning. Told me he would be working with my crew. It was about to rain. I told him we didn't work when it was raining. He said we would work that day, and I should call my men and get them ready to go. Said he'd kill me if I didn't. He had a gun."

"Were you scheduled to work in Emerald Harbor that day?"

"Yes. We always work there on Fridays."

"But you weren't planning to go out there in the rain."

"No. We'd work Saturday if we had to. If it rained all day on Friday."

"How did the man with the tattoos know about your Friday schedule?"

"I don't know. Maybe he'd seen our truck out there on other Fridays."

"What did you do?"

"I did what he said. I called my men and went to pick them up."

"What about the tattooed guy?"

"He went with me."

"What did you tell your people about the new guy?"

"Just what I'd been told to say. That he was joining the crew."

"What happened when you got to Emerald Harbor?"

"We went to work. The tattooed guy told us to do one of the houses last. He sat in the truck until we were about finished with that house and then he went around the back of it. He came back a few minutes later and we left."

"Did you hear a pistol shot after he went to the back of the house?"

"No, but we had all the equipment going."

"All of it?"

"Yeah. Mowers and blowers and edgers. He told us to make as much noise as possible."

"You didn't find that a little odd?" asked Jock.

"Odd as hell, but what was I supposed to do? I was just hoping he wouldn't kill us all."

"Was he carrying anything when he came out of the house?"

"I didn't know then that he'd been in the house, but he was carrying a laptop. And what looked like a big cell phone."

"What did you do?"

"Nothing. We loaded up and drove back to our shop in Bradenton. We had to clean the equipment."

"What happened to your guest?"

"He called each one of us by name, told us where we lived, our addresses. Making sure we understood that he could find us. He said he'd come kill us if he heard anything about his being with us on Friday."

"And you believed him."

"He wasn't kidding."

"Did you get a name?"

"From the guy? Hell no. He didn't tell me and I wasn't about to ask."

"What do you know about the man who was killed while your crew was at his house?"

"Nothing. The cops took us in, interviewed us, and then I saw the television news. It said the man's wife was killed last week or something."

"The cops interview your whole crew?"

"Yes."

"Why did you tell the cops you didn't speak English?"

"I never said that. They interviewed me last, and I guess the officer just assumed I didn't know English because she started out giving the interpreter the questions for me to answer. I just went along with it."

"Could you identify the tattooed man if you saw him again?"

"Probably, but I'd be signing my own death warrant."

"How did you know he was Guatemalan?"

"The tattoos are very distinctive. Everybody knows who those guys are."

Jock had relaxed more as he questioned Suarez. He was standing now, and Suarez was sitting in the dirt. "Okay," Jock said. "Here's the deal. I'm not going to rat you out. What you've told me stays between you, me, and my friend here. But I'm going to need a description of this guy. Something that will tell me how to find him."

"What about the cops?"

"I'm not a cop."

"But you'll have to tell the cops who told you about the Guatemalan."

"No," Jock said, "I won't."

"Then how are you going to arrest him?"

"Do I look like a man who arrests anybody?"

"What are you going to do?"

"Let's just say that the dead man was my friend, and I'm not in the habit of letting people get away with killing my friends."

The man was quiet for a beat, trying to decide what to do. His choices were limited. If he didn't tell Jock what he wanted to know, his life was over. If he did tell Jock and the word got back to the Guatemalan, then he would die tomorrow or maybe the next day. Trust Jock or die now. The choice wasn't really that hard, and I could see in his face that Chico had made his decision. "He didn't have a right ear," he said.

"What do you mean?" asked Jock.

"His right ear was missing. Like it'd been cut off. Only I don't think so. More like he was born without it. A skin flap had been sewn over the ear hole. I don't think they would have done that if he could hear anything out of it."

"Do you know where the Guatemalans live?" Jock asked.

"I've heard they've got sort of a compound. East of here, but I've never been there."

"Do you know an address?"

"No. Never heard one."

"Okay, Chico," Jock said. "Here's what we're going to do. You keep your mouth shut about tonight and I'll do the same. Nobody has to know we've talked. I don't want the Guatemalans coming after you or your men."

"If you go after the tattooed guy, he'll know it was one of us who talked. He said he'd kill us all if one of us ever said a word."

"Trust me," said Jock. "That won't happen. If I go after him, I'll find him, and he'll never bother anybody again. Ever."

We walked down the block to Jock's rental, a nondescript Chevrolet that he'd picked up at the Tampa airport when he'd arrived in Florida. He'd used one of the many aliases he always seemed to have access to, so if for some reason our tag number was checked, it'd come back as a car rented by Mr. Hertz to somebody who didn't really exist.

"Why do you think the Guatemalan let those Mexicans live?" I asked. "Wouldn't it have been cleaner if he'd killed them?"

"Maybe not. Even if he'd been able to dump the bodies quickly, people would have missed the dead guys and questions would have been asked. I think he just figured he'd scared them shitless and they wouldn't ever mention anything to anybody. Even their best friends."

"I guess you're right. Are we going after him?" I asked.

"Does a bear shit in the woods?"

"Far as I know. What's next?"

"We need to find out where these guys live," said Jock.

"I'll call David Parrish in the morning," I said. "He'll know where they are, or he can get to somebody who does know."

"Good idea. Ready to head home?"

"Let's do it."

CHAPTER FIFTY

I called Parrish early the next morning, Monday. He made a habit of being in the office before six each day, setting an example for his employees, he said. He didn't know much about a Guatemalan gang, just that one existed. He said they were involved in the drug business and he would have an agent of the Drug Enforcement Agency get in touch with me.

Thirty minutes after I talked to Parrish, my phone rang.

"Matt," a deep southern voice said. "This is Rufus Harris."

Rufus was a DEA agent based in Orlando who tracked gangs throughout the middle district of Florida. Jock and I had worked with him before.

"Good to hear from you, Rufus," I said. "It's been a couple of years."

"Too long, Matt. I hear you and Jock are stirring things up again."

"We're being discreet."

He laughed, way down in his belly, the sound rumbling along the airways that connected us. "You guys are about as subtle as your average freight train."

I laughed. "We're trying to do better."

"The big man himself called me this morning. Told me you needed some information and I was supposed to tell you what I know. What's up?"

"We've had three murders out here on the islands in the last week. We don't know if they're connected, but one of them appears to have been committed by a Guatemalan gang member. The Sarasota cops killed two of them in a shootout at the police station last week."

"I heard about that."

"On Friday," I said, "a man named Gene Alexander, who worked for

Jock's agency, was killed here on Longboat. The director thinks his murder might be connected to something Alexander was working on for the agency."

"I take it this isn't something you want me talking about in the break room."

"No, and I wouldn't be telling you any of this if I thought you would. We're pretty sure a Guatemalan gangbanger killed Alexander."

"What led you to that conclusion?"

"Sorry, Rufus. I can't tell you."

He was quiet for a moment. "Okay. I understand. Don't like it, but if Jock's involved, I guess it has something to do with national security."

"Right. Can you tell me anything about a Guatemalan gang operating in this area?"

"They've had a presence in Tampa for the past couple of years. We think they're working with a Mexican cartel, probably as enforcers. If any of the locals working for the Mexicans get out of line, the Guatemalans take care of them."

"What about Bradenton?"

"Yeah." Rufus said, "They've sent some of their guys down there to help with the distribution."

"Do you know where they live or hang out?"

"They've got a compound out east of I-75. We've got it under loose surveillance, but that's about all we can do. We've never been able to infiltrate them. I'll e-mail you directions and a map."

"Do you know anything about one of them who doesn't have an ear?"

"No ear? Like cut off in a fight?"

"Yeah, or bit off. May be a birth defect. We don't know. That's the only description we have."

"I'll take a look at the pictures we have. I think we've caught the ones in Tampa and Bradenton on film, but new ones show up all the time. They don't seem to have any problem getting across the border."

"Thanks, Rufus. I owe you one."

"Hell, Matt. You already owe me three or four."

I laughed. "What can I say?" The phone went dead.

My week was starting out with some sizzle. I'd know in a few minutes where the gangbangers lived and might even get a picture of our buddy with one ear. Not that I thought a picture would matter a lot, since the severed ear was a pretty distinctive identifier. Still, it might help.

Jock was running on the beach. I'd begged off, planning to go later. Sometimes running helps me concentrate on things, solve puzzles, get a new direction on a case or an issue. It had always worked for me when I was practicing law. But it only worked if I was running alone. I looked at my watch. It was only a few minutes after eight. I'd do my four miles on the beach later.

Unfortunately, I didn't make it to the beach that day.

CHAPTER FIFTY-ONE

J.D. called a few minutes later. "Bagby died from an overdose," she said.

"The guy who knifed you?"

"That one."

"The lab got that done in a hurry."

"They put it at the front of the line."

"Does anyone know how the drugs got into the jail?"

"No, but it's no big secret that the jails are full of drugs," she said.

"I'm sorry. I was hoping he'd give us some information. What about talking to his lawyer? Any attorney-client privilege would have died with the client. Maybe Bagby told him something that he'd be willing to give us."

"Good idea, Matt. I'll call him. See if he'll meet with me."

"Let me know if you learn anything."

"Did you and Jock find out anything last night?"

"Yeah. The Guatemalans killed Gene Alexander."

"You're sure?"

"Pretty sure." I told her what we'd found out.

"How reliable is the information?"

"I think it's solid. Our informant wasn't holding anything back."

"How do you want to handle getting the one-eared guy?" she asked.

"Jock's out running. Probably thinking about that. I'll let you know what he decides."

"So you think we'll just do what Jock decides?" There was steel in her voice. She wasn't happy.

"I think this one is Jock's call."

"I don't have to like it." She hung up.

I put on my running clothes and headed for the beach. Jock still wasn't back, but I thought he'd probably decided to take advantage of the beautiful day and run a little farther than usual. I walked up to Broadway and turned toward the Gulf, taking my time, enjoying the warm weather. A car turned off Gulf of Mexico Drive onto Broadway and was coming toward me. It was riding low on its axles, traveling well under the speed limit of twenty miles per hour. Loud bass sounds emanated from the vehicle, so loud I thought I could feel them in my toes. As the car drew abreast of me, I saw two men in the front seat wearing the dark skin of the Central American Indian. The one on the passenger side, the one nearest me, had tattoos on his neck, visible above his collar. Bells began to ring in my head. Guatemalans? Maybe. If so, where the hell were they going?

I watched until they turned off Broadway, and then I began to run after them. They had turned onto the street that led to my house. That couldn't be a coincidence. As I rounded the corner onto my street, I saw the car parked in front of a house two doors down from mine. I stopped.

The street was deserted, no one outside. The houses on one side of the street, the side I lived on, backed up to the bay, which could be seen through the gaps between the houses. What the hell were they up to? I stood and watched for a couple of beats and pulled out my cell phone. I called J.D. "There're a couple of gangbangers parked just down from my house. Probably Guatemalans."

"Call Jock. It's his case."

I cut her off, slamming the phone shut. I was about tired of her pissy moods. I knew she was stressed. People were trying to kill her and there was apparently a Guatemalan gang trying to take out citizens on her island and a government agency that was pulling strings and screwing up her investigations. But I was getting pretty damn tired of her sarcasm.

I dialed 911 and identified myself. "There is a strange car with a couple of odd-looking people parked just down from my house. Can you send a police car to check on it?"

"How do you mean 'odd'?" she asked.

"Like they don't belong here. They're not islanders."

"I'm dispatching now."

I thanked her and hung up. Nothing gets the Longboat Key authorities' attention more quickly that a complaint about someone on the island who doesn't belong. Somebody's hackles rise, cops come, and IDs get checked. The uninvited and unwanted visitor gets the hint and leaves. It may seem a bit heavy-handed, but it makes us safer and the citizens never complain.

My phone chirped out the first bars of *The Girl from Ipanema,* J.D.'s special ring. I ignored it. It occurred to me that I'd never done that before. It took less than three minutes for the cop car to turn onto my street. I waved him down and leaned in the window.

"What've you got, Matt?" asked the officer, a man I'd known for several years.

"Not sure, Dean. There're a couple of guys in that lowrider parked up there who I think might be Guatemalan gangbangers. From the same bunch who tried to take J.D. and me out downtown last week. I didn't want to walk into some kind of trap."

"Are you armed?"

"No."

He looked at me, taking in my running shorts and T-shirt, chuckled and said, "Guess not."

"Dean," I said, "if those guys are who I think they are, you're going to need some backup out here."

He was punching data into the computer attached to his dashboard. In a moment, the screen filled with words. He looked for an instant and then said, "The car's registered to somebody named Miguel Malindez in Tampa. Mean anything to you?"

I shook my head as he keyed his microphone and called for another patrolman. He listened and said, "Rory's on her way. She'll come in from the other side and block the car."

Dean got out of the cruiser and stood talking to me, watching the lowrider. If the occupants saw us, they ignored us. In a couple of minutes, another cruiser turned the corner, coming from the opposite direction, and stopped, blocking the street.

I heard a car rounding the corner behind us, turned, and saw J.D.'s Camry coming up the street. She stopped and got out, walked over to us. "Sorry, Matt," she said. "What's going on?"

"Beats me," I said, shrugging.

"I said I'm sorry."

"I heard you," I said, my voice flat.

Dean used the microphone in the cruiser to activate the loudspeaker. "Get out of the car, hands in the air," he said, the sound reverberating about the neighborhood. I saw the curtains in a nearby house move, an anxious neighbor wondering what was going on. Nothing happened.

Dean tried again, this time in Spanish. That worked. The doors on either side of the car opened, and two small men emerged, their hands in the air. "Do you speak English?" Dean asked.

The two men shook their heads, looks of bewilderment on their faces. Dean looked at me. "I used all the Spanish I know getting them out of the car."

"What do you usually do if you can't communicate?" I asked.

"We take them to the station and put them in a holding cell until we can get a Spanish speaker to help out."

"I'd think that might raise some civil rights issues."

"We've never had a complaint," Dean said, grinning.

"What's up?" Jock said. I jumped, startled by the voice behind me. I turned to see him standing at the rear bumper of the patrol car. None of us had heard him walk up.

"You scared the shit out of me," I said.

He laughed. "Hey, J.D, Dean."

J.D. nodded.

"Jock," Dean said. "Matt thinks those guys might be Guatemalan gangbangers, but they don't speak English, so I'll have to take them in."

"Let me talk to them," said Jock.

"You speak Spanish?" asked Dean.

"Some," Jock said and walked toward the lowrider, speaking in rapid Spanish. Dean and I followed. I could see that the other cop had moved closer to the gangbangers, her pistol held casually down by her leg.

As we caught up, Jock said, "They say they were just riding around. Went to Coquina Beach and decided to see what Longboat was all about."

"Ask them what they're doing parked on this street," I said.

Jock spoke some more Spanish, then turned to me. "Says they were just enjoying the day and the view of the bay."

"Tell them I need to see some ID," said Dean. Jock translated.

They pulled out their wallets, extracted two laminated cards each, and handed them to Dean. "Driver's licenses and green cards," Dean said. "They may be fake, probably are, but I can't hold them to find out. Got to let them go. No law against looking at the bay."

"I'll bet dollars to donuts that there are weapons in that car," I said.

"I don't have probable cause to search it," said Dean.

"You can if they agree to it," I said.

"Jock," Dean said, "ask them if I can search their car."

Jock let go with the Spanish again. When he finished, the gangbangers just shook their heads. "Okay," said Dean. "Jock, tell them they can go about their business."

Jock translated and the little dark-skinned men got back in the car, cranked up the music, and drove off, the deep bass sound hanging in the still air. The female cop in the other cruiser waved, got in her car, and pulled out.

"Sorry, Matt," said Dean, "but you know the law better than I do."

I nodded. "You did the right thing. We'll have to keep our eyes open. I don't think those guys just happened to pick this street to park on."

"I don't either," said Dean as he folded himself into his car. "Take it easy, guys."

Jock, J.D., and I stood on the sidewalk and watched one of the village peacocks amble down the street. He was serene and confident that no car would dare run over him. He strutted a little, his long tail feathers dragging the road. "We should've shot the little bastards," Jock said.

"You shoot one of those birds and the cops will drag your ass to the county jail quicker than you can say 'peacock,'" I said.

"I was talking about the gangbangers."

"That wouldn't be nearly as serious. Probably treat it as an infraction or something."

"You going for a run?"

"Yes," I said.

"Keep your head down. Those guys might be back." He headed for my house, walking at a fast clip.

"Matt," said J.D, "say something."

"Okay. We have a lot to sort out, but your acting like a spoiled child isn't helping. And it's sure as hell not like you."

"You're right. I'm not sure what the problem is. I've been out of sorts lately."

"Out of sorts? You've been mean as a snake."

"Okay. Mean, I guess. Can we just start the day over? Forget my acting crazy?"

I smiled. "Sure."

"Are we okay?"

"Sure."

"I'll make this up to you."

"How?"

She gave me the big one, that smile that lights up the dark and turns her face into a vision of beauty that, like Marlowe's Helen of Troy, could launch a thousand ships. "We'll see," she said.

I nodded and headed for the beach, my heart pumping so fast it took my breath away.

CHAPTER FIFTY-TWO

The day that had started so well had taken an ominous turn. The gang-bangers in the lowrider had put a chill in my spine, an omen perhaps of a day that would get worse. The warmth of the Florida autumn should have made for a pleasant run on the beach, but I turned left at Gulf of Mexico Drive. Even in the best of weather the beaches of Longboat Key are sparsely populated. A few sun worshipers, walkers, joggers, surf fishermen, and the occasional cop on an all-terrain vehicle could usually be found, all enjoying the day in some fashion. But the beach was not a place for a man who felt hunted. It was relatively deserted.

I kept to the sidewalk, jogging at a steady pace. The two-lane Gulf of Mexico Drive was the only road that ran the ten-mile length of the island. Traffic was fairly heavy, the snowbirds slipping back to the key and starting the winter season a little early. It was a time the locals looked forward to with a kind of welcoming trepidation, enjoying the energy infused into island life by our friends from the north, but dreading the consequences. The restaurants and bars would be crowded, the traffic impossible. By Easter, when most of them left, we were happy to ease back into the quiet life of summer on the barrier islands, when the roads were clear, the restaurants and bars empty, and the locals came out like bears emerging from hibernation.

I didn't think I was in any danger. The sidewalk was full of people enjoying the weather, walking, riding bikes, and jogging. The traffic alone would be enough to scare off the predators. The gangbangers were looking for Jock, so there was no reason for me to be concerned about them. Still, the flicker of cold dread would not leave my spine.

I had run about a mile and was nearing the intersection of Gulf of

Mexico Drive and Dream Island Road when I saw the lowrider out of the corner of my eye. It was driving slowly south, coming from behind me. The left blinker winked as the driver pulled out of traffic, turning left onto Dream Island Road. He stopped, blocking the sidewalk where it crossed Dream Island. The driver's-side window slid down and I could see the dark-skinned man behind the wheel. He was staring at me. I had no place to go. An impenetrable eight-foot hedge of sea grape trees blocked me to my left. If I ran to my right, I'd be in traffic. My only recourse was to turn and run the other way. That wasn't going to happen. Never let the bastards see fear. It only encourages them. Jock had taught me that lesson.

I decided to keep running, right at the car. I'd swerve around its rear and continue. If they made any move to get out of the car, I'd run into the Cannons Marina property that took up the other side of the intersection. New boats were arrayed over the lot facing the main drag. I didn't think they'd follow. Too many people and a lot of boats to hide behind. The owner, Dave Miller, probably wouldn't like it if any of his new boats got shot up, but I figured he had insurance. And better his boats than my hide.

The car was perhaps thirty yards from me. I picked up speed, running directly at it. The driver raised his hand and pointed a finger at me. He pantomimed the pull back on the hammer and then the pull on the trigger. I was getting close and I wondered if his next move would produce a real pistol. It didn't matter. I was committed.

I was more worried about the passenger. He could easily shoot me in the back as I passed them and ran toward the marina boat lot. The more I thought about that, the more real the possibility seemed. I was seriously considering changing course and darting into traffic. I'd rather be killed by an ancient Michigander in a Chrysler than some gangbanger in a low rider.

As I was about to make my move, a car coming down Dream Island Road came to a stop at the intersection. The Mercedes SUV was between the gangbangers and me. The right side window of the Mercedes glided down and I saw the familiar face of Billy Gallagher grinning at me. Billy was from Vermont and I hadn't seen him since he'd left the island in May. "Need a lift?" he asked. He was kidding. He always told me that my exercise regimen was using up heartbeats so fast that I would very soon make a healthy-looking corpse.

I rushed his car, grabbed the door handle, swung the door open and jumped in. "Go," I said. "Quick. Get us the hell out of here."

Billy didn't quibble. He slammed down the accelerator and turned right onto Gulf of Mexico Drive. "What's up?" he asked as we headed north.

"I think those guys in that car next to you were trying to kill me."

"What's going on?"

"Nothing I can put my finger on. When did you get back?"

"Yesterday. Why would somebody be trying to kill you?"

"It's probably nothing, Billy. Sometimes my imagination gets the better of me."

"You want me to drop you at your house?"

"If you don't mind."

"You sure you're okay?"

"Yeah. Welcome back."

"Thanks. I've been here less than two days and I've had more excitement than I did all summer in Quechee. I hope you're not going to keep this up all winter."

When I walked in the door of my cottage, I heard the shower running in Jock's room. I grabbed a cold Miller Lite out of the refrigerator and sat on the patio enjoying the beer and the light breeze blowing from the north. I finished the beer and got another. I was puzzled by the events of the morning. We had all assumed that the gangbangers were after Jock, but if that were so, why were they stalking me? It didn't make much sense, but then violence seldom does.

Jock came out and took a seat. "You're back early. Short run?"

I told him about the gangbangers. "They seem to be after me. Today was some kind of warning, I guess, but why warn me if they're trying to kill you? Why not just shoot me?"

He chewed on that for a couple of beats. "They were trying to rattle you," he said, "but I don't see the connection. If the Guatemalans are involved in the leaks in my agency, why come after you? If they're somehow involved with the whale tail bunch, why kill Gene?"

"Maybe we're still dealing with only one thing. The whale tail folks may want me because they think I killed Qualman. Maybe they ran out of people and hired the gangbangers to take me out."

"What about Gene?"

"Could he have been a loose end somehow? We're pretty sure that Nell was picked at random by Qualman, but maybe Gene knew something or they thought he did, and they decided to take him out."

"Could be," said Jock. "But we still have the Guatemalan connection to the Mexican drug cartel that our people were trying to infiltrate."

"All you really have there is that one agent's body was dropped off in Guatemala and that the cartel uses the Guatemalan gangbangers for some of their work."

"Don't forget that Gene had come across something important enough for him to get the director to fly down to discuss it. And his laptop was taken by the murderer."

"That could be just a crime of opportunity," I said. "The killer saw the laptop and figured he could make a few bucks off it."

"Maybe," said Jock, "but my gut tells me there's more to this. I think it's about time to speak to the earless guy."

"How're you going to get to him without blowing Suarez's cover? If the gangbangers even suspect he or someone on his crew is talking, the whole crew will be killed."

"I've given that some thought," he said. "I wonder if David Sims would help."

Sims was a Manatee County sheriff's detective who was a friend of ours. "Probably," I said. "What do you have in mind?"

He outlined the plan. It sounded pretty good. Not great, but workable.

CHAPTER FIFTY-THREE

J.D. called mid-afternoon. "We're making progress on the Glades connections."

"What did you find?" I asked.

"Steve Carey has been working on it. He set up a computer program that will help put all the connections together."

"I didn't know he could do that."

"Me neither. I thought he spent all his time off playing golf."

"What did he come up with?" I asked.

"Maybe a lot. Maybe nothing. I've got a spreadsheet if you want to look at it."

"Sure."

"I'll come over. Is now a good time?"

The three of us, Jock, J.D., and I, were sitting at my dining room table, Steve's spreadsheet in front of us. It wasn't a spreadsheet that looked like anything I'd ever seen. It certainly wasn't something dreamed up by Microsoft. There were little boxes with names printed in them and lines running from one box to another, some lines crisscrossing others. The box in the middle had a name printed in it. Jeff Worthington.

J.D. pointed at Worthington's box. "If we start here, we see a line intersecting with Pete Qualman, the man Jock killed in the Lazy Lobster parking lot. We can also see the people he shared cells with or was close to according to the warden down there. This line runs to Fred Bagby, the man who knifed me. Worthington is the only inmate named Jeff who was connected to Bagby and Qualman at Glades. These other people were friends or cellmates of one or all of the first three. The strange thing is that not one of these people seem to have been connected to the Miami whale tail killer. The timing doesn't match. Either the men were too young at the time of the murders or they were already incarcerated."

"Did you arrest any of the men on the sheet?" asked Jock.

"Three of them. But they're all dead. Two were released and died while on parole and one died in prison. Only one of them was in for a violent crime."

"I'd think the fact that all three of them are dead would have some significance," I said.

J.D. nodded. "Normally, that would be true. But the two who died while on parole were both natural deaths. One died of cancer and the other of a gunshot to the head."

I laughed. "The last one doesn't sound very natural."

"Actually, it was. He was in prison for domestic violence. He'd put his wife in the hospital several times and on the last one he was convicted of felonious assault. Sent away for five years. When he got out, he went directly to his wife's house. She took one look at him and shot him in the forehead. The state attorney ruled it self-defense. I think of it as a natural cause. Beat on a woman long enough and she'll take you out first chance she gets."

"What about the one who died in prison?" asked Jock.

"He was up for embezzlement. Nothing violent. He stole a lot of money from some high-profile clients in Miami. I think some heavy pressure was put on the state attorney to put him away for a long time. He got twenty years."

"How long ago?" I asked.

She was quiet for a moment. "Eleven or twelve years ago, I think."

"You must have been a brand-new detective," I said.

"Not exactly. I was probably in my second year. I was still working in the fraud division, but I'd started moving into homicide. When the whale tail murders took place, I was still assigned to fraud, but was working a little in homicide, learning the ropes. That's the way I got involved in the whale tail mess, but I was pretty much on the periphery. That's the reason I don't think the murders here have anything to do with me."

I looked at the box she'd pointed to. The name typed inside was Caleb

Picket. "This Picket," I said. "Did he have any priors? Anything violent in his past?"

"No. He was part of a Miami family that had made a fortune in the cattle business back in the nineteenth century. They still own a large part of downtown Miami, but the money has been spread pretty thin over several generations. Picket was a stockbroker and money manager. He represented a lot of the old guard down there. When I busted him, the old-money people were scandalized. He'd taken them for a lot."

"Was any of the money recovered?" asked Jock.

"Not a penny. He put it away somewhere. He was living pretty good, but not that good. We found some documents on his computer that led us to believe that he was planning to disappear. I guess he hid the money so that he could get to it when he set up his new life."

"You don't see Picket as even a possibility?" I asked.

"I guess he'd be a little pissed at me, but he had no violence in his past and no connection to the whale tail bunch, so I don't think so. Have you made any progress on the gangbangers?"

I told her about my encounter with them on Gulf of Mexico Drive. "I think they may have me in their sights instead of Jock."

"That doesn't make any sense," she said.

"I agree," I said, "but what about today? They were prowling my neighborhood and then followed me and blatantly threatened me."

"This is getting a little crazy," she said.

"I think we should look more closely at Picket," Jock said. "Think Occam's razor."

J.D. frowned. "The idea that the simplest solution to a problem may be the answer and we should accept it until facts prove us wrong."

"That's it in a nutshell," said Jock.

"I've always thought that was too easy," said J.D.

"Sometimes, easy is right," I said.

"Look," said Jock, "we don't have any explanation for the fact that the same pistol used to kill two women here was used in Miami twelve years ago. And while the whale tail jewelry might be explained as a copycat, we can't explain the initials carved into the victims' necks. That information was never made public."

"And," I said, "there have been four attempts on J.D.'s life in the past week. Three of those attempts are definitely tied to the whale tail murders. I'm beginning to think that the downtown attempt by the gangbangers was really aimed at me."

"Right," said Jock. "And the connection to those three attempts are the former Glades inmate and J.D.'s only connection to them seems to be Picket."

"Okay," she said. "I'll take another look. You get anything else on the gangbangers?"

"Not yet," said Jock. "But we might have some more for you by morning."

She shook her head. "Another extra-legal operation, I guess."

"Something like that," said Jock. "I'll let you know the details tomorrow. If anything goes wrong tonight, you've got deniability."

"You guys be careful," she said. "I don't have enough friends that I can afford to lose two."

Maybe if the plan had been better she needn't have worried. Sadly, it wasn't.

CHAPTER FIFTY-FOUR

The night was dark, an overcast sky blanking out the stars and the sliver of the new moon. Jock and I were parked on the berm of a state highway that ran east from I-75. A few cars passed us, people going about their normal evening business. A compound of sorts, three double-wide house trailers arrayed in a semicircle around a dirt clearing, was on the other side of the highway. Four cars were parked in the dirt yard, the lowrider I'd seen that morning on Longboat Key among them. Pine trees and palmetto shrub closed in on three sides of the trailers. There were no outside lights, and only a few of the windows in the trailers showed any illumination. There was little movement, the occasional gangbanger walking from one trailer to the other the only sign of life.

We'd been there for fifteen minutes, sitting idly, waiting for David Sims to show up. The blue lights caught my attention, several vehicles coming from the west, their light bars stabbing the night. An unmarked cruiser and three black SUVs rolled to a stop in the clearing in front of the trailers and lit them up with their spotlights. Men in SWAT gear exited the SUVs and took up positions, squatting on one knee, their weapons trained on the trailers. Three of them ran toward the rear of the trailers, ensuring there would be nobody coming out the back windows. David Sims stood by the unmarked and used the car's P.A. system. "You in the trailers. This is the Manatee County sheriff's office. Come out with your hands in the air."

He handed the microphone to a deputy standing beside him and the man repeated the demand in Spanish. A door to one of the trailers opened and three men walked out, their hands raised. In a moment, other gangbangers came out of the other trailers. There were twelve in all, standing in a semicircle, hands in the air, light from the sheriff's vehicles splaying over them. Most were barefoot, dressed in jeans and T-shirts, tattoos showing dimly on their necks and down their arms.

The deputy with the microphone spoke again. Jock said, "He's telling them that the deputies are going to enter the trailers and if there is anybody there, they'll be shot on sight. Not a bad ploy."

"A bit illegal," I said.

"I don't think there'll be any complaints from these guys," Jock said.

Two SWAT team members searched each of the three trailers. Nobody there. A few minutes had passed, the gangbangers still in the semicircle, hands in the air. A deputy started from either end of the ragged assemblage and cuffed each man's hands behind him. Sims went from one to the other, looking them in the face, comparing what he saw to a picture he held. He got to the third man in line and waved a deputy over. The gangbanger was taken to one of the SUVs and placed in the backseat. Sims repeated the maneuver a second time and the gangbanger was placed in a different SUV. When Sims reached the next to the last man in line, he looked at his face, down at the picture, and then waved the Spanish-speaking deputy over. The man was taken to the unmarked cruiser and placed in the backseat.

"Unhook them," Sims said, pointing to the men who remained standing in the dirt yard. "Tell them to have a nice evening." He turned to his men. "Saddle up. We're heading for the barn."

In a few minutes, the SUVs drove out of the yard and headed west, back toward Bradenton. Sims was in the unmarked alone with one of the gangbangers. He gave the SUVs a head start and then pulled out of the yard. Jock started the rental and followed. After about a mile, Sims turned onto a rutted dirt road that ran into a citrus grove. It was a track used by trucks hauling the picked fruit to the packinghouses. He drove a couple of hundred yards and pulled to the side of the road and stopped. Jock parked behind him and we got out of the car.

Sims opened the right rear door of the cruiser and motioned the gangbanger out. He shook his head. Sims said, "Get the hell out of my car."

The gangbanger shook his head again. "I ain't moving," he said in lightly accented English.

I could see the right side of his head. He was definitely missing an ear. This was our guy. "We could shoot him right here," I said.

"No way," said Sims. "I'd have to clean that mess up. Just pull his ass out, and I'll put a bullet in him."

"I want to talk to him," Jock said and reached into the car, grabbed the earless guy by his arm and pulled him out of the seat. The gangbanger, his hands still cuffed behind him, hit the ground face first. Jock kicked him in the side, a kick that had it hit a football would have set new NFL records. The man screamed in pain. Jock kicked him again. Another scream.

"When an officer of the law tells you to get the hell out of his car, you move," said Jock. "Do we understand each other?"

The man on the ground nodded. He moaned a little, letting us know that he was hurt. That didn't seem to bother Jock at all. He squatted down and grabbed the man by the chin. "I'm going to be asking you some questions pretty soon," he said, "and I'm going to expect some quick answers. Are we okay on that?"

The man nodded again. Moaned a little.

"Okay," said Sims. "I'll leave him to you. Play nice now."

Jock jerked the one-eared gangbanger up by his arm and hauled him to the rental. I stayed behind to talk to Sims. "Better give me the key to the cuffs," I said.

He handed me the key. "I'm counting on you and Jock to make sure there's no blowback on this one," he said.

"No problem, David. We appreciate this. What're you going to tell your men? They saw you put this guy in your car."

"I'll just tell them that I made a mistake, and after talking to the guy, I let him out about a mile from where we found him. I don't think the gangbangers are going to be filing any complaints with Internal Affairs. Even if they do, nobody's going to believe them."

"You sure?"

"Hell, nobody in the world would believe I'd be part of this harebrained scheme you and Jock came up with." He shook his head. "I don't believe it myself."

"What about those two who went to lockup?"

"We'll hold them for a couple of hours, question them about some-thing, and cut them loose. If they ask about their one-eared buddy, we'll tell them it's none of their business."

When I got back to the car, Jock was standing beside the open rear door. The earless guy was sitting in the backseat, his hands still cuffed behind him, his face showing the pain of what were probably a few broken ribs. "You ready?" asked Jock.

"I guess," I said. I had seen Jock work with bad guys before, and it al-ways saddened me that it was necessary for him to use so much violence. I knew what it took out of him and each time he killed or beat up some-one he'd lose a little bit of himself. When it was over, he worked hard to get it out of his system, but though he always came back to being the Jock Al-gren I'd known for most of my life, he never came all the way back. Each death, each beaten adversary permanently consumed a small piece of his soul and someday there would be nothing left but the empty hulk of a man sitting idly in some bar drinking away what was left of his life. Maybe I'd be there with him, trying to push back the demons and find some surcease from the incubi that seemed to live on the edge of my consciousness, al-ways nibbling away, whispering dark promises full of dread.

We all get those sudden flashes of insight at the oddest moments. In the one that wedged itself into my brain as I stood there looking at Jock and this poor excuse of a hit man, I suddenly saw J.D. as my life preserver, my way out of the darkness. Maybe that was why I was hanging onto her, afraid to let her go. That wasn't fair. I'd have to think on that some. "Let's get this over with," I said.

Jock leaned into the car. "We can do this easy or hard," he said. "But in the end, you'll tell me what I want to know. Fair enough?"

The man nodded.

"What's your name?" Jock asked.

"Pedro Cantreras."

"Whom do you work for?"

"I'm an independent contractor."

"A hit man," said Jock.

"Yes."

"Who hired you to kill Gene Alexander?"

"Who's that?"

"The man you killed on Longboat Key on Friday."

"I didn't know his name."

"Now you do," said Jock. "Who hired you?"

"I don't know. It was all done by mail drops."

"Where do you live?"

"New Orleans."

"Is that where you made the deal?"

"Yes."

"Tell me how you arranged everything."

"The man who hired me sent a letter to a bar that holds mail for me. Told me he wanted a man killed on Longboat Key. Said he'd pay me ten thousand dollars."

"What's the name and address of the bar?"

Cantreras told him.

"And you agreed to the contract?" asked Jock.

"Yes."

"Did you save the letter from the man who hired you?"

"Yes."

"Where is it?"

"In a lockbox in a bank in New Orleans."

"How were you paid?"

"Cash. Five thousand last week and another five when the man was dead."

"Had you ever worked for the man who hired you in the past?"

"I think so. The handwriting on the letter matched."

"Do you save all the letters you get hiring you to kill people?"

"Yes. They're all in the lockbox."

"Why did you save them?"

"I figured I might need them some day."

"Like now," said Jock.

"Yes. Like now."

"Did you ever meet the man who hired you?"

"No."

"How did you get your cash?"

"In an envelope sent to the bar."

"Were you ever given a reason why your employer wanted Alexander dead?"

"No. And I didn't ask. It didn't matter."

"How did you find your target?"

"I was given detailed instructions on where he lived, and there was a picture of the man I was supposed to kill. In the envelope with the cash. I was told to make it look like a suicide."

"But no name?"

"No."

"What's your connection to the Guatemalan gangbangers?"

"I'm sort of on retainer to them. They pay me every month and sometimes they ask me to eliminate somebody."

"Is that what brought you here?"

"No. Like I said, I got a contract."

"Then why are you hanging out with the gangbangers?"

"It's a safe place to hang out until I hear back from the man in New Orleans. Or, at least, I thought it was."

"Are you sure the man who hired you is in New Orleans?"

"I think so. The letters I get from him always have a New Orleans postmark."

"Are you Guatemalan?"

"I was born there, but I came to this country when I was twelve years old."

"What happened to your ear?"

"Nothing. I was born without it."

"Were you told to get Alexander's laptop?"

"Yes."

"The satellite phone too?"

"Yes."

"What did you do with them?"

"My instructions were to give them to a man who'd meet me in Sarasota."

"And?"

"That's what I did."

"Who was this man?"

"I don't know."

"How did you handle the meet?"

"I was given a cell phone along with the money. It could only be used to call one number. I was to call that number and say simply, 'I have the merchandise.' The man would tell me where to meet him."

"Where did you meet him?"

"Downtown Sarasota. The corner of Main Street and Highway 301, the northwest corner."

"You gave him the laptop and the satellite phone?"

"Yes."

"What happened to the cell phone you'd been given?"

"I gave that to him as well."

"Describe the man you met."

"He was about five-feet-eight-inches tall, dark skin, black hair, and he spoke Spanish with a Mexican accent."

"When did you meet the man?"

"Saturday, a couple of hours after I killed the man on Longboat Key."

"Mr. Alexander," Jock said, his voice low and tight, menacing.

"What?"

"His name was Mr. Alexander and he was a patriot and a friend of mine. You speak of him with respect, you bastard."

"Yes, sir."

"Okay," said Jock. "You got anything, Matt?"

I was quiet for a minute. "I'm Matt Royal. Do you know why the gang-bangers would be after me?"

"I don't know anything about that."

"Who are the guys who drive that lowrider parked in the compound?"

"Different people use it at different times."

"Why are you still here? Why didn't you go back to New Orleans after you killed Alexander?"

"The man who hired me told me to stay in place. That he might have some more work for me in Florida."

"How was he going to get hold of you?"

"He'll send a letter to the bar in New Orleans and the bartender will forward it to me here."

I looked at Jock. "One more question," he said. "What is the bartender's name?"

"Mack Stout."

"You trust him?"

"Not really."

"Then why do you deal with him?" Jock asked,

"He's never done anything to make me not trust him. Yet."

"What's your leverage? Do you pay him?"

"Sort of. I supply him with coke."

"That can get pretty expensive," Jock said

Cantreras smiled. "I get it wholesale."

"From the Guatemalans?"

"Yes."

"What if your supply runs out? You can't get the coke for him?"

"Won't matter. He knows if he screws up, I'll kill him."

"Okay," said Jock. "Sit tight."

Cantreras laughed. "Thought I would," he said. And he moaned again.

Jock walked off a few feet and activated his cell phone. After a short conversation, he returned to the car. "Pedro," he said, "in a few minutes some men are going to come and take you away. They'll want a lot more information than you've given me, and they won't waste a lot of time getting it. If you value your skin even a little bit, you'll cooperate."

CHAPTER FIFTY-FIVE

"What now?" I asked. We had walked away from the car and were talking quietly.

"The agency guys will bleed him dry," Jock said.

"Then what?"

"I think Mr. Cantreras will disappear."

"He seemed kind of resigned to it," I said.

"These guys go through life killing people, never thinking too much about what they're doing, how the death of one effects so many others, family, friends, associates. But they also seem to have a fatalistic attitude. Death isn't a big deal. They don't expect to make it to retirement age, so they're not really surprised when somebody comes along to take them out. If it wasn't me, the gangbangers would get him sooner or later. As soon as he was a threat to them, or they didn't need him anymore, somebody would put a bullet in his head."

"I guess that's why he was talking so freely."

"Yeah. A few busted ribs let him know I was serious. He's probably already dead in his own mind. When my guys pick him up, they'll take him somewhere for a few days, give him plenty to eat, fix his ribs, and get every morsel of information he has. Then, sayonara, baby."

Jock had arranged for a retrieval team from his agency to be standing by just off the interstate ramp about five miles away. I saw headlights turn into the grove track and Jock and I pulled our pistols and took up positions that put the rental car between us and the oncoming vehicle. It stopped as soon as the headlights picked us up. A door opened and a man got out, standing beside what I could now make out as a black SUV. "Spooky place for a spook," he said.

The recognition code. "Beats Budapest," said Jock, giving the agreed response. "Who're you?"

"Jim Austin, Jock," the man said.

"Damn," said Jock, walking toward the man who was now standing in the headlights. "I told them to send me somebody competent."

"Screw you, Algren. I brought a rookie with me. I think he's minimally competent."

Jock had reached the man and they embraced. "Damn, it's good to see you, Jim," Jock said. "Last I heard you were somewhere in North Africa."

"Just got back," the man said. "I was enjoying a little down time in Tampa when the old man called and said I needed to pull your nuts out of the fire. Again."

Jock laughed. "Matt, this shadow of the man he once was, is Jim Austin. We went through training together. A long time ago. Jim, this is Matt Royal. He has clearance on everything. Directly from the old man."

I assumed the old man they were talking about was Dave Kendall, their agency director. I shook hands with Jim, and Jock went to get our prisoner. A young man, the minimally competent rookie I guessed, was standing by the passenger side of the SUV, pistol in his hand hanging down by his leg. Austin waved him over as Jock walked up with his left hand clamped around Cantreras's bicep. "I want you to meet the legend," said Austin. "Jock Algren. And this is Matt Royal."

"Glad to meet you, sir," said the rookie. "I've been hearing about you since I started my training."

"I made a lot of that stuff up," said Jock. "Looks good in the reports."

The rookie laughed and took control of Cantreras, leading him back to the SUV. Jock handed Austin the digital recorder on which he'd taped his interrogation of Cantreras.

"This all of it?" Austin asked.

"Yeah. You going to do the follow-up?"

"Probably. Somebody's coming down from D.C. to help out."

"Let me know what you find out."

"No sweat," said Austin. "Got to hit the road. Great seeing you, Jock." He nodded in my direction. "Matt."

Austin backed the vehicle between some trees, made a three-point turn, and followed the track back to the highway. Jock and I got back in the rental, and he started the same maneuver that Austin had used. He backed up into a row between the trees, dropped the gear shift into drive, and an automatic rifle let go, bullets stitching the passenger side of the car. The shooter had fired low or I would have gotten a head full of lead. Adrenalin surged and took over. We both bailed, hitting the ground, pulling our pistols. I rolled under the car and came out on the driver's side next to Jock. I thought if there were other shooters taking aim at the left side of the car, he'd have let go at the same time as the guy who fired.

"What the hell?" asked Jock, his voice low, tense.

"Got to be gangbangers," I said.

"How did they find us?"

"They probably followed your buddies in the SUV. Those things might as well have 'cops' written all over them."

The shooter let go with another burst. We heard bullets hitting metal, but none came close to us. "I hope you got the extra insurance when you rented this car," I said.

"Maybe I can get Jim Austin back here," he said, dialing his cell. He closed it. "No answer."

"Somebody's going to be circling around behind us," I said. "We can't stay here."

"I'm open to any ideas."

"Let's move back into the trees," I said. "If someone's trying to get behind us, we'll have as good a chance of seeing them as they will of seeing us."

Jock nodded and we started moving backward, crouching, scanning all around us, trying to see the gangbangers before they saw us. Another burst of fire dinged off the rental. "They're trying to keep us occupied," said Jock. "Somebody's got to be coming from the other side."

"Let's separate," I said. "Get some space between us. If they're as stupid as I think they are, they'll come straight in. Maybe we can get them in the middle."

We moved through the trees on our bellies. My eyes had adjusted to the dark, but my field of vision was very limited. The overcast sky still blocked any available light from stars and moon. The citrus trees loomed in the darkness, their trunks and low-hanging branches adding a sinister touch to the landscape. I heard another fusillade rip from the automatic rifle. No other sounds, the animals that lived in the grove scared silent by the sounds of gunfire and humans slithering through the dead leaves that covered the ground.

The trees were heavy with green fruit that would ripen and be ready for picking in the next month or so. I reached up and twisted a hard orange from its limb and tossed it to my left, the side away from Jock. I wanted to see if the movement would draw fire. It didn't. I waited a few minutes while making my way farther into the grove. I picked another orange and heaved it. The sound of the fruit hitting the limbs of the trees in the distance drew fire this time. Pistol fire. I saw the muzzle flash about twenty yards to my left.

I crawled toward the sounds of a person thrashing around in the leaves. I was quiet, barely disturbing the ground cover. Jock was silent. If I was dead, a shout from him wouldn't do any good, and if I was moving toward our shooters, any noise he made might serve as a warning to the bad guys.

I heard the sounds of footsteps on the leaves. They were close, maybe only a few feet away. I lay still, listening. More footsteps. Coming my way. I aimed my nine millimeter in front of me. Silence. A minute passed, two. Then the sound of footsteps, approaching closer. They stopped. Whoever he was, he was nervous, not sure of what awaited him. Another step, two, three. I saw a person, really just a black spot in my field of vision, a little darker than the surroundings. He moved again, took a couple of steps and stopped. He was still coming my way, slipping toward the rental. He'd have to step right over me to get there. I lay there in the leaves, stock-still, like a big cat crouched downwind of its intended prey, waiting for the moment to pounce.

The man came closer. I could see him better now. He was a small man, a large pistol in his hand, pointing toward the ground. He was taking it slow, creeping up on what he thought were two unsuspecting gringos hiding behind the car.

The little man was two steps from me when I heard the loud report of a shotgun blast coming from the direction of the rental. The man in front of me flinched and I shot him in the knee. He screamed and dropped his gun, falling to the ground, writhing in pain. I scratched around among the leaves until I touched his pistol. I threw it into the grove and stood over him, my pistol pointed at his head. I don't think he was even aware of me. He squirmed and moaned and bled.

"Jock, are you okay?" It was Jim Austin, his voice coming from near the car we'd abandoned.

"I'm fine, Jim," said Jock, shouting to be heard. "Matt?"

"I'm here, Jock. I've got one of the little bastards."

"There were only two of them," said Jim. "I'm coming toward you. Don't shoot."

I saw a flashlight coming through the trees. "Over here, Jim," I said.

Jim came into view carrying a shotgun, Jock right behind him. "What've we got here?" Jim asked.

"This one was trying to sneak up on us," I said.

Jim shined the flashlight on the little man on the ground. I recognized him. He was the one who had been driving the lowrider on Longboat Key earlier in the day. "I'll be damned," I said.

Jock took a closer look. "We know this pissant, Jim. He was threatening Matt this morning on Longboat Key. What about the one you took out?"

"My rookie's over there with the body, or what's left of it." He patted his shotgun. "This baby does a lot of damage at close range."

"Where's Cantreras?" I asked.

"He's parked out on the highway, locked up in our car."

"What brought you back here?" asked Jock.

"We saw the lowrider parked on the berm of the highway when we were leaving. Looked like gangbangers, so we decided to sneak back for a look. When I saw Jock's caller ID on my phone, I figured there must be trouble."

"Thanks for answering," Jock said, sarcastically.

"Didn't want to get into a conversation," said Jim. "By the time you called, we were parked just out on the highway and had heard the gunshots. I thought a little stealth might be in order."

Jock laughed. "Well, you pulled mine out of the fire this time for sure. The gesture is appreciated."

"Let's get an ambulance out here for this little shit," I said. "Can't leave him here to die."

Jock moved a few feet away, made a call on his cell, talked quietly for a minute, hung up, dialed again. Two short conversations. He rejoined us and said, "Let's load him into the SUV. We'll get him to Manatee Memorial and our own doc will meet us there. I don't want the law involved in this."

"How're you going to do that?" I asked. "The hospital is going to call the cops as soon as a gunshot wound shows up."

"David Sims will meet us in the emergency room," said Jock. "He'll take care of that."

"What about the stiff?" asked Jim.

"Cleanup crew's on the way from Tampa."

Jim nodded. "I'll get in touch, give them the exact location of the body. This is shaping up to be a long night."

The rookie backed the SUV down a row between the trees, and we loaded the one I'd shot into the back. He was screaming and moaning as we moved him. Cantreras sat quietly in his seat, one cuff on his right wrist and the other locked around a large U-bolt in the floorboard. Jock and I took seats next to him. He didn't even turn to look at us or react to the wounded man's screams. He was already dead, I thought, his mind closing down, oblivious to everything around him. He'd gone deep into his brain, shutting out the world, not unlike the gazelle caught in the big cat's jaws.

CHAPTER FIFTY-SIX

Jock and I were on our way to Longboat Key. It was nearing midnight. The streets were quiet and almost deserted. Bradenton isn't known for its vibrant nightlife. Jim Austin's rookie had driven us to the airport where Jock had rented another car, using yet another alias. Jim had stayed at the hospital to take care of the man I'd shot. A doctor who was somehow on the payroll of the agency would take control, patch up the knee, and order the man to be transported by his friends to Tampa General Hospital for extensive knee surgery.

"How did you pull that off at the hospital?" I asked.

"I don't know. Jim took care of that end of things."

"What are they going to do with the gangbanger I shot?"

"Probably the same thing they'll do with Cantreras. I told Jim to make sure they asked him about the Guatemalans' beef with you."

"Is he really going to the hospital?"

"Probably. They'll fix him up and keep him in isolation until he's ready to be released."

"Why only probably?"

"Somebody might want to use his bad knee in the interrogation. I don't ask a lot of questions about those things."

"Probably a good idea. What're you going to do about the rental out in that grove?"

"I'll call the rental company and tell them where to pick it up."

I laughed. "Just like that? No explanation?"

"I'll tell them it broke down."

"I take it you rented that car under a name that doesn't exist."

"Right."

"So they'll eat the damage."

"No. I bought the insurance."

"I didn't think anybody ever bought that expensive crap."

"I always do. I lose more cars than I get to turn in. Fair's fair."

"What about the lowrider the gangbangers brought to the fight?"

"Our cleanup crew will load it on a flatbed, and nobody will ever see it again."

"What now?" I asked.

"I'll hear from somebody in the agency tomorrow. They'll have sucked Cantreras dry by then, and be all over that bar and lockbox in New Orleans."

"It's a start."

"Finally."

When we turned into my street, I saw J.D.'s Camry parked in front of my house. That couldn't be good news. We pulled in behind her car and stopped. The neighborhood was quiet, no lights in any of the houses but mine. I opened the front door and found J.D. asleep on my sofa. I turned and signaled Jock to be quiet. He nodded and tiptoed into his bedroom.

I sat in the chair across from the sofa and stared at J.D. She was beautiful. It occurred to me that I'd never seen her asleep before. All that animation that made her so alive was missing. For a moment I could visualize what she must have looked like as a little girl curled up in her pajamas on her parents' sofa. Sweet and innocent and unsullied by the world of the adult.

I was staring like some dumbstruck kid when she opened her eyes. She didn't move, just looked at me for a moment. "I'm glad you're safe, Matt," she said in a quiet voice. "I was worried about you."

I didn't move. We were joined in some kind of magnetic field that kept us rooted in place, our eyes locked. "I'm glad that you worry about me," I said.

"I always do," she said, and sat up, the spell broken. She rubbed her eyes and stood. "I need to brush my teeth," she said, and walked toward the guest room.

"That's better," she said when she returned. "Did you find your guy?"

"We did." I told her about the evening, leaving out the part where Jock roughed up Cantreras.

"Will the agency share information with you?"

"They will with Jock."

"When?"

"We should know something tomorrow."

"What then?"

"I'm not sure. A lot depends on whether the agency can connect Cantreras's employer to the deaths of the agents. If not, we'll probably be on our own."

"And if they tie it in, they'll take the case away from us."

"Probably," I said. "But if they can prove to their satisfaction that Cantreras was working for someone involved in the hits on the agents, I don't think there'll be a case. Cantreras and his boss will just disappear."

"I don't like that."

"You're a cop. You're not supposed to like stuff like that. But it takes some of the bad guys off the street, and you can concentrate on the whale tails."

She sighed, sat quietly for a few beats. "The hit man was on retainer to the Guatemalan gangbangers, so it follows that the attempts on your life are tied to the hit man."

"We're not sure that the attempt at the police station downtown was aimed at me. It could have been you they were after."

"That's not very comforting," she said.

"I know, but that probably makes more sense than me being their target."

"What about the guys in the lowrider this morning?"

"Maybe they were just trying to scare me out of the babysitting business."

She made a face. "Don't be difficult, Matt."

"Sorry. I don't know what they were up to. The guy I shot was the driver this morning. Maybe Jock's people will be able to find out something."

"I've got to get to bed," she said. "Call me when you hear something tomorrow."

"Are you still working on Picket?"

"Yes. Steve Carey is supposed to have me something in the morning."

"You're welcome to stay here," I said.

"Thanks," she said, getting off the sofa, "but I need my own bed. See you tomorrow."

CHAPTER FIFTY-SEVEN

I was up early on Tuesday and ran my four miles on the beach, Jock beside me. We both carried sidearms holstered at our waists beneath our T-shirts. If anybody decided that the beach was a good place to take us out, we were prepared. As it turned out, the run was uneventful except for the chaffing of the holster on my bare skin. A small price to pay for the confidence the gun gave me.

J.D. called at midmorning. "I called Ben Flagler, the lawyer for that idiot who stabbed me. He said he couldn't talk to me because of the attorney-client privilege. Legal ethics and all. Like that really exists. Do you think you might have better luck? Lawyer-to-lawyer sort of thing?"

"I'll give it a try. The privilege died with his client. He should know that. Anything new on Picket?"

"Steve promised me something by noon."

"Good. I think I'll go see the lawyer this morning."

"His office address is a residential condo in Sarasota."

"That's odd," I said. "He must not have much of a practice."

"He's brand-new. I looked him up on the Florida Bar website. He was just admitted to the bar last week. Graduated in June from the University of North Dakota Law School."

"He shouldn't have been representing anybody on a charge as serious as the one on Bagby."

"That's what I thought," said J.D. "I checked the court file, and he was the only one who filed a notice of appearance. Maybe he was appointed."

"No judge would appoint somebody with no experience to a case like this. Maybe a misdemeanor, but not a major felony. I'll go see Mr. Flagler."

•   •   •

The condo complex where Flagler lived was on Fruitville Road, out near the interstate. It was a sprawling place that had seen better days. Paint was peeling from the sides of many of the buildings, and potholes had long since turned the interior streets into an obstacle course. A large sign near the entrance announced that anyone interested in renting should stop in at the office.

It was one of those complexes that dot the state of Florida, places that had once been homes for empty nesters downsizing now that their children were grown, and second homes for snowbirds seeking the winter sun. When the economy took a tumble, as it always seems to do in cycles that no one can predict or fully understand, the dream faded and a lot of the units never sold. The developer filed for bankruptcy and a company that buys distressed properties and rents them out acquired the complex for a lot less than it was worth. Most of the amenities promised the original buyers, such as exercise rooms, tennis courts, pools, never materialized. The few original buyers stayed on for a while, moved out, and tried to recoup their losses by renting the units or letting them go back to the lender.

It was an old story in the Sunshine State. We tend to draw dreamers, men and women seeking their fortunes, following the stories of those who had come before them and made a lot of money. They don't understand that for every person who finds the gold, fifty or a hundred find nothing but ruin. They slink back to where they came from, leaving their own broken dreams strewn among those of the people they took advantage of. Those lost dreams manifested themselves in abandoned projects and condo complexes going to the dogs. Such was the home of the young lawyer named Ben Flagler.

The parking lot was mostly empty and the few cars remaining were older and in need of repair, their bodies rusted or crumpled by some long-ago fender bender. An old dog rested under a gumbo-limbo tree that had resisted the onslaught of decay that had turned the complex into a slum festering in the autumn sun.

I parked in front of the ground-floor unit that bore the address of the lawyer I'd come to see. A new Mercedes sedan, as out of place as the town drunk at a Sunday school picnic, sat next to the spot I'd pulled into.

I stepped over a crumbling curb, walked to the door of the unit, and knocked. In a few moments the door swung open. A small man who reminded me of a ferret said, "Yes?"

"Good morning, sir," I said. "I'm looking for Mr. Flagler, the attorney."

"I'm Flagler."

He was older than I'd thought he would be, at least in his late thirties. Maybe he'd gone to law school later in life. A lot of people did that. I stuck out my hand and said, "I'm Matt Royal. I'm a lawyer on Longboat Key."

He shook my hand, and I saw a flicker of what might have been recognition move across his face, gone in an instant. "What can I do for you?" he asked.

"I'd like to talk to you about your late client, Fred Bagby."

"What's your interest in Bagby?"

"May I come in?" I asked.

"I don't think so."

"I'm working with the police," I said. "I'd like you to tell me what you know about why Bagby tried to kill a Longboat Key detective."

"You know I can't discuss my client. Attorney-client privilege."

"That privilege died with your client."

Flagler looked confused. "I don't think so."

"You haven't been a lawyer very long, Mr. Flagler, so I suppose there are things you don't know yet. But you can look it up under the ethics code. It's online. At the Florida Bar website."

"I don't need you to teach me ethics," he said in a voice that was close to a snarl.

There was something off about this guy. I couldn't quite put my finger on it, but he was home at eleven thirty on a Tuesday morning, wearing cutoffs, a T-shirt, and flip-flops. He didn't seem too sure about the ethical ramifications of his situation and he was rude. That pissed me off more than his ignorance. "I'm quite sure you've read chapter forty of Florida Statutes as it relates to the privilege," I said.

"You can put that in the bank."

Chapter forty actually dealt with juries and the ethics code was the

Florida Bar Rules of Professional Conduct. They were not part of the Florida Statutes. Anybody who had recently passed the bar exam should have known that. I was beginning to suspect that Flagler was a fraud.

"Mr. Flagler," I said. "I can assure you that you can and will talk about Bagby. He tried to kill a cop, and you've got no privilege. I can have the police out here in five minutes and drag your ass downtown. You'll be fingerprinted, your mug shot taken, and then you'll answer every question I put to you, or the judge will hold you in criminal contempt and you can sit your ass in jail until you decide to answer my questions." A lawyer would know I couldn't do any such thing, but I was pretty sure the man standing in front of me wasn't a lawyer.

"Come in, Mr. Royal," he said, and stood back to give me room to enter.

I had a sudden premonition that if I went inside I might never leave. I don't know if it was some insight or just that I'm basically a chicken. Whatever, the interior of the apartment was not exactly inviting. "No, thank you," I said. "We can talk here or down at the police station. Your choice."

He was silent for a moment. "Okay. Let me change clothes, and we'll go to the police station." He shut the door, and I heard the dead bolt snap into place.

I had not expected that. I thought the last place he'd want to be was the police station. Maybe he was who he said he was. I was thinking that we'd find out pretty soon when I heard a motorcycle engine roar to life. In a couple of seconds the bike came from behind the apartment, jumped the curb and, dodging potholes, ran toward Fruitville Road. The little man who looked like a ferret was in the saddle. He turned right on Fruitville Road before I could get to my car. He was gone, and I wasn't going to catch him in my Explorer. Crap. I hadn't seen that one coming.

CHAPTER FIFTY-EIGHT

I called J.D. and explained what happened. "Can you get a warrant to search his place? I'm sure there are fingerprints. That'll tell us who he really is."

"No judge in her right mind is going to issue a warrant on the basis of your intuition."

"It's more than intuition. This guy isn't a lawyer. How did he get into the jail, get his name on the Bar's list of lawyers? Did his notice of appearance in Bagby's case have a Bar identification number on it?"

"Yeah. He looks legit."

"Call the Bar office in Tallahassee," I said. "Tell them you want to see the paperwork he used to qualify for the Bar exam and to get sworn in. They might give it to a cop."

"I'll see what I can turn up."

"Can you run the license plate of a Mercedes parked in front of this guy's condo?" I gave her the tag number.

"Okay. What are you going to do?"

"I'll call Jock. Maybe he can get some of his people to do a forensics sweep of Flagler's apartment."

"You know whatever you find won't be admissible evidence. Not without a warrant."

"I know. But if we can figure out who this idiot is, we may be able to move up the food chain and get whoever is responsible for the murders."

"Be careful, Matt." She hung up.

I called Jock, and he said he'd get a forensics guy out of Tampa and meet me at Flagler's apartment. "It should take about an hour," he said.

"You've just got forensic teams standing by all over the world?" I asked.

"No, but we have agents who're trained in some of the forensic sciences. They aren't able to do a full work-up, but they can lift fingerprints. Do the basic stuff."

I sat in my car, listening to the radio. The news was mostly bad, troubles in the Middle East, tribal conflicts in Africa, a factory worker who killed six of his coworkers at a plant in North Carolina, a commercial for a diet supplement to help those with erectile dysfunction. The world seemed to be cracking up. I sometimes felt like the human race was circling the drain, about to consign itself to oblivion.

J.D. called back. "The car belongs to one of those fleet leasing outfits. Want to guess who this particular Mercedes was leased to?"

"A lawyer named Ben Flagler?"

"You got it."

"How did he make the payments?"

"Cash up front. He leased it for six months and paid the entire lease payment when he signed the contract."

"Didn't the leasing guys find that a bit strange?"

"They said it happens more than you'd think."

"What happens if the guy doesn't bring the car back at the end of the lease?"

"They've got insurance to cover that. They don't worry about it."

"Can you get a warrant to search the car?"

"Nope. Same problem as the condo."

"Crap."

"Hey, you're the lawyer."

"Right. I'll talk to you later."

Jock rolled up in his new rental and joined me in the Explorer. Ten minutes later a black SUV with two men in the front seats drove into the lot. Jock got out and waved them over, talked with the men for a few moments, and then led them around to the rear of the building. He came back and sat in the Explorer.

"The forensics team?" I asked.

"Well, they're what passes for one on short notice. They'll take the place apart and dust for fingerprints."

"We need to have them go over the Mercedes, too."

"You sure it belongs to Flagler?"

"Yeah. J.D. ran the tag."

"I'll get a wrecker out here and we'll haul it to Tampa," Jock said. "We'll get some of our real forensic people to go over it." He pulled out his phone and made a call, arranging for Flagler's car to be picked up.

"How did you get into the apartment?"

"Broke a window on the back door."

We sat for a while, listening to the radio. A Sarasota Police Department patrol car turned into the lot and drove slowly toward us. "I think we might have been busted," Jock said. "Wait here."

He got out of the Explorer as the cruiser came to a stop behind us, blocking my exit. Jock walked over to the police car holding an ID case in his raised hand. The cop on the passenger side motioned him over. Jock handed him the case and they talked for a minute. The cop used his cell phone to make a call, hung up, and gave the ID case back to Jock. The officers drove back out to Fruitville Road and disappeared.

Jock climbed back into the Explorer. "One of the neighbors called in what she thought was a burglary. They came to check it out. I told them we were on a national security detail and that we're the ones who broke into the place."

"Are there going to be any repercussions on this?" I asked.

"No. They accepted my credentials and called their supervisor. They're in the clear and so are we."

We sat for another thirty minutes, my stomach sending out signals that it was being starved. The two men who'd gone into the apartment came around the building. Jock got out and went to talk to them. The conversation was short, and the men got into the black SUV and left.

"They found a cell phone," said Jock, grinning.

"Flagler's?"

"Probably. One of the guys found it right next to where some ruts in the grass indicated the motorcycle was parked. It probably fell out of Flagler's pocket when he was hurrying to get away from you."

"That could be a real break," I said.

"Our techs will pull every bit of information in the phone. We'll see where that leads. But, I've got something even better."

I stared at him, waiting. He grinned. "What?" I asked.

"They found a twenty-two-caliber pistol. They'll run the ballistics in Tampa, but I'm betting it's the one used in the whale tail murders."

"J.D. isn't going to like you ruining her evidence. We don't have a warrant. The pistol can't be used."

"It won't matter. If this is the guy, he'll never go to trial."

I shrugged. I knew he was right. "Any prints?"

"A lot. They ran the best ones through the system on their portable scanner. They belong to a man named Jeff Worthington. Guess where he spent the last fifteen years?"

"Glades Correctional," I said. "He's the one J.D. came up with."

"Bingo. He got out five months ago."

"Then how did he become a lawyer named Flagler?"

"The University of North Dakota is sending me a photo of Flagler from his student ID card. Glades is sending a mug shot of Worthington. We should have them in a few minutes."

Jock's phone dinged. He opened it and fiddled with the keypad. He handed it to me. There was a picture of a handsome young man on the screen. "Is that Flagler?" Jock asked.

"Not even close."

"That's Ben Flagler, late of the University of North Dakota Law School."

The phone dinged again and Jock held up another picture, a mug shot of a man who was definitely the one who'd just ridden off on a motorcycle.

"That's the man who said he was Flagler," I said.

"Worthington took Flagler's place somehow. But why?"

"Good question. And where is the real Ben Flagler?"

Jock shook his head. "He's probably dead."

"What about his family?" I asked.

"Don't know. The agency is checking on that. A lot of manpower is coming to bear on this one."

"Have you heard anything out of New Orleans?"

"Not yet, but I'll be updated as soon as they have anything."

I called J.D. "Flagler's in the wind, but Jock's people got an ID. It's the same guy you locked onto at Glades. Jeff Worthington."

"Damn," she said. "That's got to be our guy. How the heck did he get to be a lawyer?"

"It looks like he killed a young man who'd just graduated from law school and stole his identity."

"I'll be damned. You hungry?"

"Starving."

"Why don't we meet at your house? I'll bring Steve and his paperwork and stop for sandwiches. We can eat and talk."

"I'll be there in half an hour."

CHAPTER FIFTY-NINE

We were back at my dining room table. Steve Carey was there with his laptop, his arm still in a sling. He could use both hands on the computer, but the small grimace of pain told me it cost him.

J.D. had brought sandwiches and the remains littered the table. She looked pointedly at me. "If you'd get the trash off the table we could get to work."

"Isn't that woman's work?" I asked.

She reached for her gun. "What did you say?" She was smiling. I think.

"I said I'd get right on it."

"That's what I thought," she said.

"Matt's got some kind of a death wish," Steve said.

"Nah," said Jock. "He's just not very bright."

I gathered up the lunch detritus and took it to the trash can in the kitchen.

Steve was talking when I came back. "Flagler, or actually, Worthington, may be the linchpin. He and Qualman shared a cell for a time and just before he was released in June, his cellmate was Barry Steiffel, the guy whose fingerprints were found on the boat used in the Leffis Key shooting."

"But," said J.D., "Worthington was in prison at the time of the Miami whale tail murders. He couldn't have been involved in those, and both Qualman and Steiffel were too young to have been a part of it. Plus, there's no evidence that any of them were ever in Miami."

"Look at this," Steve said, putting a page full of diagrams on the table. "We have three known participants in the attempts on J.D. Qualman from the parking lot at Lazy Lobster, Steiffel from the boat at Leffis Key, and Bagby who tried to stab her. We don't know exactly what Worthington's connection to the murders is, but he is connected to all three of the others through his time at Glades and his so-called representation of Bagby."

"But none of them could possibly have been involved in the original whale tail murders," said J.D. "And none of them would have any reason to come after me."

Steve grinned. "Look here," he said, pointing to a box in the middle of the arrangement of boxes on the paper.

J.D. frowned. "Caleb Picket?"

"Think about it," said Steve. "You arrested him, humiliated him in front of all his friends, the people he was fleecing, and ruined his life. Or at least he might see it that way."

"Okay," said J.D., "but he wasn't involved in the whale—" She stopped mid-sentence, her face going blank. I could see the idea starting to perco-late in her brain. It was coming together for her, the pieces of the puzzle starting to fall into place. Except for one.

"But he's dead," she said. "Even if he was the whale tail killer and wanted his revenge on me, he's dead."

"Maybe he's reaching out from the grave," I said.

"Don't be silly," J.D. said.

"Figuratively speaking," I said. "Maybe revenge is his legacy. He could have arranged for these guys to take care of you after he died."

"And what's in it for them?" J.D. asked. I could tell her skepticism was wavering a bit. She was trying to get her head around it.

"Picket stole a lot of money from his friends," I said, "and none of it was ever recovered. Maybe he's paying these ex-cons somehow."

"There's more," Steve said. "Our boy Worthington shared a cell with Picket for the last few years that Worthington was at Glades. Qualman and the others spent a great deal of time with Picket in the exercise yard as well. Maybe Picket was the high priest and the others were the acolytes."

Jock had been sitting quietly, listening. "Steve," he said, "any idea on how the Guatemalans fit into this?"

"That's the wild card," Steve said. "They don't make sense."

"What about Gene Alexander?" Jock asked.

"He doesn't fit either," said Steve. "Maybe the two things aren't connected."

"Then why were the gangbangers after J.D.? Or me?" I asked.

"Good question," said Jock. "Maybe my people will have some answers later today."

Just then, Jock's laptop pinged, and pages started dropping from the attached printer.

CHAPTER SIXTY

Jeff Worthington was in big trouble. He'd panicked when Royal showed up at his door, and he'd run. The controller would see this as a failure, and Jeff didn't want to think about what the consequences of that would be.

He'd stashed the bike behind his condo in case he ever needed to make a quick escape. Maybe he shouldn't have spooked so easily when Royal knocked on his door. The only concern he'd had about playing lawyer was that someday a real attorney would question him on some point of law. He hadn't really expected that to happen and certainly not this soon.

Damn Royal. If he'd only come into the apartment, he would have died there on the floor. Jeff would have used his knife and carved him up right there in the living room. No noise, no nosey neighbors wondering about a gunshot. But Royal had balked. How had he given Royal any reason not to trust him? Well, it couldn't be undone. He needed to call the controller, get out in front of the storm that he knew was coming. Maybe he could convince the controller that it wasn't his fault.

Worthington reached in his pocket for his cell phone. It was gone. He checked the other pocket, his mind sending signals of panic to his adrenal glands, flooding his system with hormones triggering his flight instincts. If he'd lost the phone, he was dead. He didn't know how to contact the controller. The number was in his phone, and he'd never bothered to memorize it.

Oh, shit, he thought. The phone. If the cops found it, they'd be able to track his calls, maybe even find the controller. God, he was a dead man.

Worthington had left the condo and run east on Fruitville Road. He had followed it blindly for twenty miles. He seemed to have ridden right out of civilization, the road running straight through flat open space. He'd pulled to the side of the road to think, to figure out what he could do to salvage his situation.

Worthington knew he was a resourceful guy, but there were limits on what he could do. He only had the money that the controller deposited in his bank account when he needed it. He couldn't even get to that account without alerting the controller and, probably now, the cops. He checked his wallet. He had a couple of hundred dollars in cash and three credit cards, two in the name of Ben Flagler and another that he'd set up right after he'd gotten out of prison. It was in the name of an inmate he'd befriended at Glades named James Barber. He'd used the card on a regular basis, paid the bills on time and developed a credit line of five thousand dollars. He could survive for a couple of months if he was careful, but after that he'd be broke.

He had no place to go. Glades Correctional Institution had been his home for the past fifteen years. Before that, he'd lived on the streets of Tampa. He knew nobody there anymore. Maybe Orlando. He'd heard that the city had a pretty large underground economy, lots of illegal aliens working construction and in the groves that had so far escaped the bulldozer. The fifty million tourists that visited every year would help him disappear into the crowds.

His heart rate was slowing as he brought his fear under control. He had to think, figure a way out of this. The name, Geoff Woodsley, skittered across his brain, almost too fast for him to catch it. He thought some more, bringing Woodsley back into focus. That was the name he'd used in Tampa before he killed the bouncer and went to jail under his own name. That was the alias he'd so painstakingly set up so that he could get into the real estate business. He laughed out loud. What a stupid idea. But it might have worked, and there would have been no prison, no deaths, no need for him to kill middle-aged women. He had never thought much about why that held such allure to him. Perhaps it was a mommy fixation. Maybe since she'd never given him any love or guidance or even a little bit of her time, maybe, just maybe, it was his sense of control that he had over the dead women that gave him such a warm feeling. The dead were at his command. They couldn't do anything, and they never complained about what he did to them.

He sat, pondering how he might reactivate the Woodsley persona. Was it possible? It had been foolproof when he set it up. Would it still work? He knew that most of the documents, like the passport and the driver's license, would be outdated, expired. But he had a valid birth certificate in Woodsley's name. He could use a cash advance on the credit card in James Barber's name to rent an apartment and get the utilities' deposit paid. He'd then have a utility bill in Woodsley's name to back up his claim of residence. The big question now was whether he could find the documents. He knew where he'd hidden them, but he didn't know if the place was still there.

If he could find the original forged documents, it might work, but how would he explain his absence since the expiration of the license and passport? He'd need the driver's license as an ID before he tried to rent an apartment. Once he had that, he could use the expired passport for a second ID. If he needed to leave the country, he would be able to renew the passport with a copy of his birth certificate and the old passport. He'd work on that, but right now he needed money. And the controller had a lot of it. The problem was, he didn't know who the controller was or where to find him. He'd think on that while he rode to Tampa, where he hoped to find the Woodsley documents.

CHAPTER SIXTY-ONE

Jock read the pages as they spewed from the printer. There were twelve of them, double-spaced. He brought them back to the table, still reading, absorbing the information. "Our guys hit the jackpot in New Orleans," he said. "They got the letters that the hit man Cantreras had saved, the ones from the man who paid him for the murders. There was one fingerprint on the inside of one of the flaps that didn't belong to Cantreras. They got a hit. It belongs to one of the big guys in a drug cartel that has been on the DEA's radar for the past year. They've found his prints at a couple of murder scenes that were definitely the result of drug deals gone bad. The prints belong to a dead guy named Raul Escondido, who was killed in a drug deal in Miami twenty years ago. He's obviously not dead, but they don't know what name he's using now. DEA thinks the guy's pretty high up in the chain of command."

"What about the bartender where Cantreras gets his messages?" I asked.

"His name's Stout," said Jock. "He was a big help. He said that he didn't know the name of the guy who hired Cantreras, but he knew he pulled a lot of weight in one of the smaller cartels that seems to be gaining ground on the big ones. Escondido and Stout had gone to high school together in Miami."

"How can Stout be sure it's the same guy?" Steve asked.

"He said Escondido came to see him about two years ago. There was no question that it was Raul. He had a scar on his neck that was pretty unusual, and he and the bartender spent a lot of time remembering old times."

"Why now?" asked J.D. "I mean, why Escondido come out of the woodwork a couple of years ago? How did he explain to the bartender that he was still alive?"

"Raul wanted something," said Jock. "He told Stout that he needed a place to drop messages and money with somebody he could trust. Stout was paid well for what he did, but he also understood that Raul would kill him if he didn't do what he was supposed to do. Raul told Stout that one of his buddies was killed in the drug deal in Miami twenty years ago, and the cops had made a mistake and identified the body as his. He thought that would be a good time to drop out of sight. Acquire a new identity."

"Anything on the phone your guys found at Flagler's condo?" I asked.

"Yeah. The phone was a burner, one of those disposable prepaid things. The only number he called was in Miami and it belongs to another burner. We followed up on the Miami end, and found the cell towers that the signals from that phone bounced off of. We can't pinpoint the phone, but if it's used again, we'll have it. The National Security Agency has its ears on it."

"You got the NSA involved?" asked Steve, his voice carrying a hint of incredulity.

"My boss did, actually, or the deputy director," said Jock. "The director's been in London for the past couple of days on some big emergency, but they're pulling in everything they can to find whoever killed Nell Alexander."

"What do you think the chances are of intercepting that phone call?" asked Steve. "It seems pretty far-fetched, if you ask me."

"Not for the NSA," Jock said. "They can track any phone call in the world if they set their minds to it. In this case, there were daily calls made between the phone in Miami and the one we found at Flagler's place. Usually late in the afternoon. Our people are thinking that the Miami connection will call this afternoon. If NSA can home in on that number, we'll have the guy on the other end."

"Then what?" I asked.

"DEA has a team standing by near the cell towers that we know were used for the calls. If NSA can pinpoint the phone's location, the team will move in."

"What is going to happen to Cantreras and the bartender?" asked J.D.

"They didn't say," said Jock, "and I didn't ask. My guess is that Stout will spend a few years in jail. Cantreras won't be so lucky. You don't kill one of ours and keep breathing."

"The law of the jungle," said J.D., a look of disgust on her face.

Jock looked at her, coldly, held her eyes for a moment and said, "That's where I live, J.D. In the jungle."

The call came in just before five. Jock moved out to the patio and talked for a few moments. He came back into the living room. "They got him."

There was a collective sigh in the room. "Who is he?" J.D. asked.

"I don't have all the details yet," said Jock, "but he's some kind of financial advisor. Has an office in one of those high-rise buildings overlooking Biscayne Bay. His name is George Perez."

"Did they find the burner phone?" I asked.

"In his pants pocket," said Jock.

"Did he have anything to say for himself?" asked J.D.

"Yeah," said Jock. "He said, 'I want a lawyer.'"

"I don't guess that's going to happen," I said.

Jock frowned. "Unfortunately, it's a DEA bust, and he'll get his lawyer. If we'd taken him down, it'd be a different story."

"His arrest may not do us any good then," I said.

"The DEA's going for a warrant. They'll take his office apart, and we'll see what they find. We should know something by morning."

"I think we need a drink," I said. "It's been a long day."

"I'll pass," said Steve. "I need to stop by the physical therapist's office before I go home. He's got some new exercises for me to start on."

I looked at J.D. She nodded. "Haye Loft?" I asked. She nodded again.

Jock said, "Why don't I leave you to it? I've got some calls to make. Call me later, and I'll meet you for dinner."

CHAPTER SIXTY-TWO

Eric Bell was behind the bar at the Haye Loft, right where he'd been for the last twenty years. He'd just opened the place and was alone, getting things ready for the crush that would come with the evening. "Hey, guys," he said. "Miller Lite and a Chardonnay?"

"That'll do," I said. "How're you doing, Eric?"

"Couldn't be better. I hear somebody's hunting you two. You okay?"

"So far," said J.D. "I've got my protector with me."

Eric laughed. "Everybody on the island thinks it's the other way around, that you're protecting Matt."

"Well," she said, "he's still breathing."

We took a table in the corner, and Eric brought our drinks over. J.D. took the first sip of her wine and sighed. "I think it's more the thought of the booze than the actual stuff. Just one sip and I'm feeling better. What do you make of all this?"

I shrugged. "Beats me. Why would a money manager be talking to a phony lawyer in Sarasota every day? I don't think it had to do with financial advice."

"This guy Perez is tied into the whale tail murders somehow. Maybe he's the one who killed those women in Miami. What I don't get, is where he's been for the past twelve years. Serial killers don't just stop for no reason."

"Good question. Maybe we'll have some answers tomorrow after the DEA goes through all his stuff."

"You know, Matt," she said, "I'm not comfortable with Jock's methods. I understand the need for agencies like his and I understand that there're times when the law stands in the way of getting information, like now. I don't always like that, but I think it's those laws that separate us from the barbarians that rule large parts of the world. The rule of law is important, and it makes us who we are as Americans. But sometimes, like now, I think Jock's way is better. If his people had taken Perez down, we'd probably be getting lots of information already."

I smiled. "You don't really believe that," I said.

She was quiet for a couple of beats, pensive. "No, I guess not, but sometimes that approach appeals to me. I get so tired of the restrictions, the way the law gets in the way of law enforcement."

"Maybe the law just keeps the cops honest," I said.

"It does. Without question. But it *is* cumbersome."

"So is democracy."

J.D. nodded. "We're a strange people. The whole human race is deluded. A large number of us are killers and thieves and even many of the good people are always just one step removed from doing something awful. Our politicians cater to those who get them elected and don't seem to have much regard for what is best for all of us. Some of them are outright crooks and a lot of them aren't very bright. We've got crooked cops, crooked lawyers, crooked everything, and we don't seem to get better as a species. The ancient Greeks and Romans and Egyptians faced the same problems we have today. Nothing ever really changes. What the hell is wrong with us?"

"If anybody ever figures out how to fix that situation," I said, "both you and I will be out of jobs."

"You're already out of a job," she said.

"Well, there's that."

She laughed. "Maybe I could just become a beach bum. Like you."

"Hey, don't joke. It's not a bad life."

We ordered another round of drinks and watched the bar begin to fill up. Jock called and suggested we meet for dinner at Mar Vista. It would be pleasant under the trees. We finished our drinks and I left some bills on the table. We waved to Eric, and J.D. and I trooped down the steep outside stairs to the parking lot and into her Camry.

As we pulled out onto Gulf of Mexico Drive, her phone rang. She pressed the Bluetooth button on the steering wheel and answered.

"J.D., it's Deanna Bichler. You got a minute?"

"Sure, but you're on my hands-free phone and I'm not alone."

"No problem. I need a favor."

"If I can help, you know I will."

"I've been retained to represent a man in Miami who's accused of trying to kill you."

"Perez?"

"Yes. You know about him?"

"Yeah. Long story. You've got to know I'm not in much of a mood to do any favors for him."

"I don't blame you, but listen to my proposition."

"Okay," said J.D. "Shoot."

"Perez is willing to make a deal. He'll tell the feds anything they want to know, including the part about trying to have you killed. I can't get to the U.S. Attorney down here until tomorrow. He's out of town or some such crap. Anyway, nobody in his office will touch this one. Apparently, it's a real hot potato."

"What can I do?" asked J.D.

"All I want is to get him into isolation tonight. He's afraid he'll be killed if he's in general population. He's on a federal hold at the Miami-Dade County jail. I was hoping you might be able to call in a favor with somebody in the jail and get Perez isolated for the night. Since you were the intended victim, I think you'd carry some weight. I'll talk to the U.S. Attorney tomorrow, and I'm sure he'll buy the deal."

"Deanna, you're asking a lot. If Perez is responsible for killing those two women here and trying to take me out, I'd rather see the bastard get shanked in jail than walk."

"J.D., I'll swear on our friendship that Perez knows he's going to spend the rest of his life in jail. All he wants in return for his testimony against some real bad people is a new identity and a prison where nobody will ever know who he is."

"Deanna, Matt Royal is in the car with me. I'd like to hear what he has to say about this. He was almost killed as well."

"Hey, Matt," Deanna said. "I'm sorry we haven't had a chance to meet under better circumstances. What do you think?"

"I think everybody would lose if Perez is killed. I'd be for isolating him, but if I were J.D., I'd want an ironclad promise from you that you won't be part of any deal that J.D. doesn't agree to."

Deanna was quiet for a moment. "Okay. I can agree to that with one caveat."

"What?" I asked.

"I have an ethical duty to Perez. I'll make him the best deal I can, and if the U.S. Attorney agrees to it, but J.D. doesn't, I'll withdraw. My guess is that in that event Perez's new lawyer would get the same deal, with or without J.D.'s approval."

"You're right," I said.

J.D. spoke up. "Look, I also have a duty, if it's in my power, to make sure that Perez gets a fair trial. I'm part of the system. I can't let the guy get killed if I can stop it. I'll make some calls and get back to you."

"Thanks, J.D., but time is running out. Perez is in an interview room now, waiting for me. I won't be able to keep him there long, and once we're finished, he's going to lockup. He's sure there's already a price on his head."

"I'll see what I can do," J.D. said, and pressed the "off" button on the Bluetooth.

"You're doing the right thing," I said.

"I know. It's not always easy, is it?"

"No," I said, "but it's always right."

CHAPTER SIXTY-THREE

The puppeteer walked the floor, pacing back and forth, rigid with anger. That fool Perez had gotten himself arrested. Had he figured out that his life was about over? He'd thought himself so clever, stashing a getaway pickup truck in North Miami. A truck. What the hell was he thinking? Did Perez know that the family was on to him? Knew about his plans for a new life? If he was planning to run, he would have to take the family's money with him. That couldn't happen. He was a dead man as soon as the family figured out where all the money was hidden. There were no second chances in this business. Even a hint of disloyalty was rewarded with a death sentence, carried out without trial, without mercy.

Had Perez arranged his arrest so that he would be safe from the family? He should have known better. He'd be dead before the night was over.

The first break came when the idiot hired a Mexican to keep the truck in running condition. He didn't know that the man he'd hired was one of theirs. The puppeteer had known about the truck within a day of the time Perez hired the driver.

The family hadn't yet figured out all the ways Perez could flee, or where all his secret bank accounts were, but they did know his escape route, or at least the first leg of it. They knew about the pickup and they'd know when Perez decided to use it. The bomb had been rigged months before. If he started it without activating the switch that disarmed the bomb, he'd be blown to hell. Only the Mexican driver knew where the switch was located. When he needed to drive the truck, he simply flipped the switch to the off position and the bomb was rendered inert.

If Perez had arranged his own arrest, it'd been done without much preparation. The family had a mole in the U.S. Attorney's office, and if any deals had been struck, or even if Perez had contacted the U.S. Attorney, the family would have been told. They had the same coverage at the state prosecutor's office, even though the state wouldn't be involved in the Perez case. Their cartel, small as it was, was of interest only to the feds.

Fuentes, the crazy don, had reacted to the news of Perez's arrest with a lot more heat than the puppeteer had expected. The don had exploded in anger. He'd trusted Perez with the family's money, with his own money, with secrets that no one else knew. Perez had been his childhood friend and now he'd turned on him. Word had already come back to them that some lawyer was trying to reach the U.S. Attorney in Miami to make a deal, to put Perez in isolation until they could work out an agreement for Perez to testify against the don. Perez had to be killed.

The don, against the advice of the puppeteer, had ordered the murder of the U.S. Attorney and sent word to the Miami-Dade jail, to inmates on their payroll, that whoever killed Perez that night would receive one million dollars upon his release from prison. The puppeteer was afraid that the murder of the U.S. Attorney would bring down the family. You didn't just go around killing government officials. The system reacted violently. If one of their own was vulnerable, all of them were. It was therefore in their interest to find and kill those who would kill them. Because of this, there had long been a truce of sorts, a tacit agreement never spoken of, between the cartels and law enforcement. Don't kill us and we won't kill you. It had worked for years, but the crazy don was now about to breach the agreement. It could bring ruin to the family.

Fuentes had decided it was necessary to kill the U.S. Attorney because he knew that none of the other people in that office would take a hot potato like Perez and give him any kind of deal. If it backfired, it was their careers. Not so for the U.S. Attorney. He was a political appointee and if he were fired, he'd go back to a very lucrative private practice. If the headman was dead, there would be weeks before any deal could be put together for Perez to testify. Cut off the snake's head and the body would be ineffective. If the don's men missed Perez in jail on the night he was arrested, it wouldn't be too big of a deal. There'd be weeks to get him before another prosecutor could be brought in to make decisions. Or so he thought.

The puppeteer hadn't agreed with the don, argued against the murder as a violation of the rules of the war against drugs. It didn't matter. The don had crossed a line that moved him from just plain crazy to absolutely insane. The puppeteer had always known it, lived with the threat inherent in the don's insanity. There had been a lot of killings that did nothing for the family's organization except instill fear in the subordinates. But the don's bloodlust had never before so threatened the cartel and the family.

By now the top federal prosecutor in South Florida was floating face down in the Miami River with a gunshot wound in the back of his head. The die was cast, the puppeteer thought, and Katie bar the door. The shit storm was about to hit them full force.

CHAPTER SIXTY-FOUR

It was a little after eight o'clock when we pulled into the Mar Vista's parking lot. J.D. was on the phone with the Miami-Dade chief of detectives, so we sat for a few minutes as she made arrangements to have Perez put in isolation. She then called Deanna Bichler to tell her that her client would be safe for the evening, that he was going to isolation.

We walked around the back of the restaurant and joined Jock at a table under the trees facing the bay. The air was cool, pleasant, infused with the smell of the sea. Electric lights that looked like tiki torches were placed among the tables. The crowd was mostly older couples, snowbirds probably.

We sat and J.D. told Jock about her conversations with Bichler and the chief of detectives. "I hope I've done the right thing," she said.

"If Perez sings," said Jock, "we might just figure out why you're a target and whether all this is connected in any way to Gene Alexander's death. But we've got a new problem, a big one."

"What?" she asked, alarmed.

"The U.S. Attorney in Miami was murdered about an hour ago."

"How?" I asked.

"Gunshot to the back of the head. An off-duty cop moonlighting as a security guard at a warehouse on the Miami River saw two men pulling a body out of the trunk of a car. He went after them and they dropped the body and took off in the car. The cop recognized the dead man as the U.S. Attorney. The place is swarming with FBI and Miami-Dade cops right now."

"This changes things," said J.D.

"Yeah," said Jock, "but I'm not sure how much. My deputy director has already called the president and he'll appoint David Parrish as the acting U.S. Attorney for the Southern District within the next hour."

"Why?" I asked.

"Because of the tie-in to Gene Alexander's death. If any of this is connected to our agency, we want to know. Perez can help us figure that out, but only if he gets the deal he wants. If Parrish is the acting U.S. Attorney, he can make the deal happen. The president has confidence in him."

"And," said J.D., "so do you. Did that have anything to do with this?"

Jock smiled. "I might have mentioned to my boss that I knew Parrish and trusted him."

"When does David take over?" I asked.

"I talked to him fifteen minutes ago. He was at Orlando Executive Airport about to board an FBI plane to take him to Miami. A federal judge is on standby to swear him in as the temporary U.S. Attorney."

"What about his job in the Middle District?" I asked.

"He'll do both, for now. As soon as the president can get a nominee for the permanent position and get it through the Senate, David will go back to Orlando."

"How long will that take?" asked J.D.

"Months," I said. "That's the reason they're sending David in. They don't want any screwups."

"Right," said Jock. "We probably won't hear anything until morning. Let's eat."

"I need to call Deanna," said J.D. "Let her know what's going on."

"I would think the DEA will be briefing her," Jock said.

"That may take a while. I'll call her." She walked down toward the bay, dialing her phone.

CHAPTER SIXTY-FIVE

W. Warren Plowden had seen a lot in his seventy years, but this evening's activities were unique. First, there was the call from the president, a totally unexpected event. He didn't like the president and hadn't voted for him. They were of different political parties, different generations, different views on how to conduct the nation's business. But when the president calls and asks a favor, it would be unconscionable to deny him if it was at all legally possible.

The favor was a fairly simple one. The president had asked that Judge Plowden go downtown to the federal courthouse and swear in David Parrish as the interim U.S. Attorney for the Southern District of Florida. It wasn't such a big deal in and of itself, but Plowden knew that David Parrish was already the sitting U.S. Attorney in the adjoining district.

Plowden had sat as a judge of the United States District Court for the Southern District of Florida for more than twenty years, and in the past year had become Chief Judge of the district. Before that, he had practiced law in Miami for twenty-five years and had the reputation as brilliant, both as a lawyer and a jurist. He was also a man who believed in the law as an instrument of good. The great body of jurisprudence built over centuries to govern the affairs of humanity was for the most part a work of brilliance. There were always little slivers of law that had not been well thought out, not tested in the crucible that was the human experience. But those occasional transgressions foisted upon the legal system were ultimately ironed out, overruled, rescinded by the lawmakers, or declared unconstitutional by the courts.

Judge Plowden had discovered this great intellectual minefield almost by accident. He'd graduated from Davidson College in North Carolina and decided to go to law school because he didn't have any plans for the next few years. He discovered his passion during those first few days of studying Real Property and Constitutional Law and other courses that would define his life. He was hooked and took to the study of law with a joy that bordered on obsession. The law was said to be a jealous mistress and Plowden had found that indeed it was. It demanded absolute fealty and devotion from those who practiced its tenets. And he had practiced law with a single-minded pursuit of justice that awed all who came into contact with him, both as a lawyer and as a judge.

Judge Plowden was saddened by the sudden death of the U.S. Attorney, a man he'd known for many years, who he'd tried cases against, and later who'd appeared before him on numerous occasions. They had been friends, at least to the extent that a judge can be friends with lawyers who appear before him. The man's death would be a great loss to South Florida.

The question that Judge Plowden was wrestling with was not whether the president had the authority to appoint an interim U.S. Attorney, he did, but whether he could appoint a man already holding the same office in another district. A quick Westlaw search gave him no answers. He could not find another instance where it had been done. The constitution was silent on the issue and the section of the U.S. code dealing with such appointments did not specifically prohibit one person being appointed in two districts at the same time. It didn't seem right to the judge, but he could find no legal prohibitions against it.

Plowden had called the president back and told him he was on his way to the courthouse. Now, as he sat on the bench, having done his duty and sworn Parrish in as the interim U.S. Attorney, Plowden peered out over the courtroom, wondering what came next. Parrish had asked him to hear a motion, a joint motion brought by the government and the defense attorney for a man the judge had never heard of, George Perez. It was a new case, one that arose from an arrest earlier in the day.

The judge fiddled with his computer keyboard, shook his head, and said, "I find no such case in the dockets, and even if there were such a case, it hasn't been assigned to me."

"Your Honor," said Parrish, "the defendant was arrested just a few hours ago, and we haven't had time to file the necessary pleadings to get the case docketed. However, this is an unusual situation, and time is of the essence."

"I'm listening, Counselor."

"As chief judge you can appoint any of the judges of this court to handle any particular case."

"I understand that," said the judge, a bit of impatience creeping into his voice.

"I'd like to move that you appoint yourself to hear this case, Your Honor. My opponent, Ms. Bichler, representing the defendant Perez, is here in the courtroom to join me in that motion. The pleadings have already been typed up, and I can sign them now that I'm sworn in. I'll file them with the court immediately. Again, with Ms. Bichler's concurrence."

"What's the rush on all this, Mr. Parrish?" asked the judge.

"Your Honor, Mr. Perez is a money launderer for a small but important drug ring operating out of Puerto Rico. He's been involved in several recent murders in the Sarasota area and has extensive knowledge of other murders and activities of the drug ring. He can give evidence against a number of people whom the government believes to be guilty of multiple crimes."

"Why can't this wait until the case runs its normal course?" asked the judge.

"Mr. Perez's life is in danger, Your Honor," said Parrish. "We're afraid that even one night in general lockup could lead to his death. We already know through an informant, that there is a one-million-dollar price on Mr. Perez's head. We also think there are other murders planned by Mr. Perez's associates. We may be able to stop them from happening if we get the information we need from Mr. Perez."

"What's your proposal?" asked the judge.

"Our joint proposal is that we reach a plea bargain that would require Mr. Perez to testify in any trial or grand jury investigation on matters of which he has knowledge. In return, you would sentence him tonight to life imprisonment under a new name. All paperwork would be under the new name and the charges would be completely different than those that bring us here today, but they would carry an equal sentence. Mr. Perez would serve his imprisonment in an institution far removed from Florida. In other words, Perez would disappear and he would serve his sentence under an alias. Nobody would know who he really is, except a few people in the Department of Justice."

The judge looked at Deanna. "Do you agree to these terms, Ms. Bichler?"

Deanna rose from her seat at counsel table. "Yes, Your Honor. My client has instructed me to accept the deal if the court authorizes it."

"This is highly unusual, but I don't think there is anything illegal about it. I do have a question, Mr. Parrish."

"Yes, sir."

"How do you guarantee that Mr. Perez will cooperate in the coming months and years?"

"He has agreed to take lie detector tests whenever the government wants. If he is caught lying, or if he refuses to testify, then the life sentence will stand, but he will be reassigned his real name and be sent to a prison in Florida."

"In other words, you'll hold a death sentence over his head. One outside the legal system, an execution by some inmate thug with a homemade knife."

"That's about the size of it, Your Honor," said Parrish.

"I won't be a part of that," said the judge. "Besides, how do you know some prisoner wherever Mr. Perez is sent won't recognize him?"

"Mr. Perez has only dealt with about three people in the organization," said Parrish. "Nobody else knows him by sight. The odds are infinitesimal that he'll be recognized."

The judge sat silently for a minute, then stood and said, "We'll be in recess for ten minutes. I have to think about this one."

The judge was back. "Mr. Parrish," he said, "does the government think Mr. Perez is a big enough fish for us to go to all this trouble?"

"Yes, sir. We think he can help us put away some major drug lords, interrupt the flow of narcotics into the country, and disrupt the money supply. We also think he may be able to give us information that will forestall at least a couple of planned murders. And we believe Mr. Perez can provide us the help we need to arrest and convict those responsible for the murder earlier this evening of the U.S. Attorney for this district."

"Very well," said the judge. "Here's what I'm willing to do. I won't sanction murder, no matter how good the cause. Therefore, I cannot agree with part of your bargain. I'm willing to go along with the name change, the new prison, all of that. Part of the deal will be that if Mr. Perez ever reneges on his part of the agreement, he will agree that the life sentence will be revoked and he will be back before this court with a plea of guilty to murder and be subject to the death sentence. The decision on whether Mr. Perez has failed to live up to his part of the agreement and whether the death sentence is warranted will be left to a judge of this court. There will be no extrajudicial punishment."

"May I confer with Ms. Bichler?" asked Parrish.

"Certainly."

Parrish and Bichler huddled in the back of the courtroom, talking in whispers. When they broke, Deanna went to her client and after a whispered conversation with him, rose and said, "The defendant will accept the plea bargain as outlined by the court."

"Mr. Parrish?" asked Judge Plowden.

Parrish rose and said, "The government will accept the plea as outlined by the court."

"Okay," said the judge. "I assume you two have worked out a plan to implement this."

Parrish was still standing. "I've talked with the head of the U.S. Bureau of Prisons and the U.S. Marshal for this district. It's going to be a bit complicated, but we think we can get it done within the next couple of days. We've arranged for Mr. Perez to be held in isolation tonight, but we'd like to get him moved first thing tomorrow. The paperwork will follow, but the marshal has assured me that they can transport him under the new name even if the paperwork isn't completed. The Bureau of Prisons will accept him from the marshal under the alias."

"Is this agreeable to your client, Ms. Bichler?"

Deanna stood. "It is, Your Honor."

"Then it is so ordered," said the judge. "Hand me the charging pleading, Mr. Parrish, and get me the other paperwork by the end of business on Thursday. You'll need to draft an order getting Mr. Perez transported tomorrow morning." He looked at his watch. "This morning now, I guess. Can you get it to me by nine a.m.?"

"Yes, sir," said Parrish. "Ms. Bichler and I will get it done tonight. Well, this morning. Thank you, Your Honor."

"Court is adjourned," said Judge Plowden. He stood, surveyed the courtroom, shook his head, and left the bench.

CHAPTER SIXTY-SIX

I was in a deep sleep, dreaming of fire alarms. They didn't stop and finally began to bring me back into the world. My phone. I looked at the clock on my bedside table. Four o'clock on a Wednesday morning. Who the hell was calling at this time of the day? It couldn't be good news. Nobody calls in the middle of the night with any news that isn't bad.

But I was wrong this time. I rolled over and answered. It was David Parrish. "You awake, Matt?"

"Barely. This better be good."

"It is. We made a deal with Perez."

"What kind of deal?"

"I'll fill you in later, but suffice it to say, he's ready to sing like the proverbial bird. Can you and Jock get down here to Miami?"

"Sure. When?"

"There'll be an FBI jet at Dolphin Aviation at the Sarasota-Bradenton airport at eight a.m. It'll bring you down and take you back."

"What about J.D.?"

"I just talked to her. She'll be at the airport."

"Okay." I closed the phone and called J.D.

She sounded wide-awake when she answered. "You going to Miami?" she asked.

"I am," I said. "You want us to pick you up?"

"Sure. What time?"

"We'll pick you up at seven. Grab some donuts at Publix, get coffee at Starbucks on the Circle, and start off our day with a wholesome breakfast."

"You're a sick person, Royal. Go back to sleep."

Not seeing any reason to disturb Jock, I set the alarm for six o'clock, and rolled over for another two hours of sleep. I'd learned the lesson in the army that you sleep when and where you can because you never know when you'll get a chance to sleep again. I could drop off in an instant and sleep as long as I'd allotted myself. I usually woke up just before the alarm went off.

I rolled Jock out at six and told him about my four a.m. conversations. He headed for his shower and I went to mine. At seven on the dot, we were parked in front of J.D.'s condo complex. She came down the elevator, got into the backseat, and we were off to the Publix Market at mid-key. I asked how many donuts we needed. Jock said he'd eat three and J.D. asked for a fruit salad. I figured a dozen donuts and the fruit would take care of us until we got to Miami. I'm a sucker for donuts.

We picked up coffee at Starbucks, and drove to the airport. The plane, a small, nondescript business jet lacking any markings that would identify it as government owned, was waiting on the ramp at Dolphin. We identified ourselves to the pilot and loaded onto the plane. We took off over the bay with a minimum of fuss and then flew southeast toward Miami.

As we reached cruising altitude, Jock's phone dinged, indicating that he had received a text message. He looked at the display for a moment and said, "The twenty-two we found at Flagler's apartment was the same one used to kill all the whale tail victims."

Uh-oh, I thought. I hadn't mentioned the pistol to J.D.

She had just taken a sip of her coffee. She put the cup on the table and looked at Jock, her face hard. "You found the gun?"

"Yes," Jock said. "Didn't Matt tell you?"

"No, he didn't. That gun was the best piece of evidence we've got and you've ruined it. No court will ever admit it into evidence."

"No judge will ever have to make that decision," said Jock, his voice low and cold as ice. He locked eyes with J.D., staring her down.

She finally looked away, picked up her coffee, and moved to a seat at the back of the plane.

Jock and I sat, our conversation limited, each of us munching on our breakfast and staring out the windows. I was worried that we were pushing J.D. farther and farther away, showing her a side of Jock's profession that she didn't want to know about. I was afraid that she would let her disdain for Jock's methods bleed into whatever relationship we may have had. I could feel her slipping away, and all I could do was watch it happen.

My thoughts turned to Perez and what he had to tell us. This could be a big break, an answer to our questions, perhaps a completion of the puzzle that had eluded us as we sought the killers and tried to discern the patterns that may or may not tie the new whale tail murders to the old and to the killing of the agents from Jock's organization. As it turned out, we got a lot of the information we wanted, but not all of it. We wouldn't know about the holes in the pattern for several days, and in the end, that lack of knowledge proved fatal.

CHAPTER SIXTY-SEVEN

David Parrish met our plane at the Opa-Locka airport. It was near mid-morning and the sun was already heating up the tarmac. A stiff wind was blowing from the south, bringing more warmth to the day. We drove out of the airport property as David explained what had transpired in court in the early hours of the morning. As soon as the locals were finished with him, Perez would be transferred to a federal prison.

"I wanted to give you guys a shot at him," said David. "I think he can help sort out who was trying to kill J.D. Jock, you can squeeze him as much as you want, but I've already been advised that your agency will be spending some time with him as well."

"Why is he so willing to talk?" I asked. "All you've got is his phone connection to Worthington."

Parrish shrugged. "The DEA folks may have suggested that they had Worthington in custody and he had implicated Perez in the murders."

"He bought that?"

"The DEA scared the hell out of him, and then they told him that a contract had been put out on him. He figured his life was over if he didn't get some protection."

"I'll be damned," said Jock.

"Yeah," said Parrish, and then swore us to secrecy about Perez's location. He drove us to a house in western Miami-Dade County, out near the Everglades, a U.S. Marshal's Service safe house, a place to hold prisoners when for some reason they could not be in jail. We were in a neighborhood of small ranch-style houses, probably built in the 1960s or '70s. The houses all seemed to be much the same, little deviation in the floor plans or the elevations. These neighborhoods had sprouted and multiplied during the boom years, and many had gone to seed in the lean years that always follow. This subdivision had only two streets that ran parallel to each other, the pavement cracked and blistered by the sun. We stopped in front of the last house on one of the streets. The houses next door and directly across the street appeared to have been abandoned. The house we were about to enter had been kept up to some degree. It would need a roof in the next couple of years and the aluminum siding needed painting, but the yard was clean and grassy and well kept. There were two small Ford automobiles parked in the driveway.

A narrow yard extended from the west side of the house to a tangled thicket of palmetto scrub that ran to the west as far as I could see. The back of the house faced north and beyond the hundred yards or so of scrub there was another neighborhood that looked as raw as the one we were standing in. The dry weather that comes to Florida in the fall had turned the palmetto bushes into fuel waiting for a fire.

We were met at the door by a young man whom David introduced as Deputy United States Marshal Bert Cheshire. "Do you have any weapons?" he asked.

Jock, J.D., and I nodded. "Please leave them with me," the young marshal said. "It's just a precaution. If somehow the prisoner were to overpower you, we wouldn't want him to have access to guns."

He led us to the back of the house and opened a door for us to enter. We found ourselves in a windowless room devoid of furniture except for several straight-back chairs arranged haphazardly. It was mid-morning and the donuts had given me a sugar high. I couldn't wait to start the questions.

A tall, slender man with a head of dark hair going to gray at the temples stood as we entered the room. I thought he looked like the actor, Ricardo Montalban. "My name is George Perez," he said. He was wearing a pair of gray pinstripe slacks, a white dress shirt open at the collar, and a pair of dress loafers that probably cost more than my car. The clothes he was wearing when he was arrested.

No one offered to shake hands. Parrish told Perez who we were and why we were there. I watched him closely as David mentioned J.D.'s name, but I didn't detect any sign of recognition.

J.D. stared hard at Perez who wouldn't meet her eyes. "Why are you trying to kill me, Perez?" she asked, her voice flat, emotionless. It was the first words that had escaped her mouth since she'd heard about Jock's people finding the pistol.

"It wasn't personal," he said, and sat in one of the chairs.

"It was personal to me," she said.

Perez smiled. "I understand from my lawyer that it was you who pulled some strings last night to keep me out of general population at the jail. Thank you for your kindness."

"My first instincts were to let you die, you cretin," she said. "Don't make me regret not going with my gut. Why were you trying to kill me?"

"I wasn't. I was just the messenger."

"For whom?" she asked.

"First," Perez said, "some ground rules."

"You don't make the rules," said Parrish, his voice low, threatening. "The rules are that you answer our questions. If not, you go back to see the judge and will probably be looking at a cell on death row."

"Okay," said Perez, "then how about some background. I'd like to put this whole thing in perspective so that Ms. Duncan doesn't think me an ogre."

"Too late," J.D. said.

Perez smiled again. "Fair enough. But I'm not a bad person."

"Mr. Perez," I said, "you've been instrumental in the killing of at least two innocent women and several attempts on Detective Duncan's life."

"That's true, Mr. Royal," he said, "but I was under duress."

I laughed. "And how about the money laundering? Were you under duress there as well?"

"Point taken," he said, "but that didn't result in any harm. The harm had already been done. I just moved money around."

"Bullshit," I said. "You made it possible for some of the world's worst thugs to ruin the lives of a lot of people, not to mention the murders your buddies commit in order to keep the money flowing."

"That's a theory, sir," he said, "but not one to which I subscribe."

I shut up then. This guy was either full of more crap than anybody I'd ever met or he was living in a dream world. Probably the latter. If any of the people involved in the drug trade had even an iota of decency, they had to manufacture a shield against their own perfidy, a safe place where they could retreat from the horrors that their actions visited upon the innocents who were destroyed by the product they pushed.

"I want to know who tried to kill me and why," said J.D. "I don't really give a damn what you think of yourself."

"In good time, Ms. Duncan," Perez said, "but first you need to know who I am."

"It's *Detective* Duncan, Perez," she said, "and I already know who you are. You're something the sewer rats dragged out of the slime."

"When I tell you my story," he said, "perhaps you'll have a higher opinion of me."

She gave it up then, sighed, and sat back in her chair. "I doubt it, but go ahead. Give us your version."

"I come from a proud family," he said. "I'm a fourth-generation Floridian."

I almost laughed. There is a conceit among many native Floridians that their peninsula pedigree means something to other people. The more generations their families have lived in Florida, the more important that seems to be. I suspect it is because there are so few natives living in the state anymore. Most of the residents are transplants from somewhere else. I never thought that one's place of birth had much importance in the grand scheme of things. Especially, if one is about to spend the rest of his life in a prison far removed from the place where he was born.

"Congratulations," said J.D., sarcastically.

It was lost on Perez. "Thank you. I tell you this because I don't want you to think I'm some Mexican here illegally. My great-grandfather emigrated from Spain where his family was part of the nobility. He came to Key West in the late 1880s and used his family money to buy a cigar factory from the Cubans who ran the industry there. There had been a strike by the workers and he got it fairly cheaply. He ran it for a few years and, seeing the handwriting on the wall, sold it within ten years for a large profit.

He came to Miami before the turn of the century and married a local girl, Mildred Hightower, from a family of cattle ranchers. They had two sons and a daughter."

Parrish interrupted. "Mr. Perez, this is very interesting, but we want to know about the murders on Longboat Key."

"I understand," said Perez. "You need to know the history so that you can understand the present. I think somebody important said that."

Parrish shook his head and signaled Perez to continue.

"One of those sons was my grandfather," said Perez, "and one of his sisters married a man named Jules Koerner. They had one daughter, Katherine Karen, who married a Miami lawyer named James Picket."

"Picket?" asked J.D., sitting up in her chair.

"You're beginning to see it, aren't you, Detective Duncan?" asked Perez.

J.D. nodded. "The Pickets had a son they named Caleb."

"Bingo," said Perez, pointing his finger at J.D. "Caleb Picket, a man you put away for twenty years for embezzlement. Only for him it was a life sentence because of the cancer."

"So Picket was what?" I asked. "Your second cousin?"

"Exactly," said Perez.

"There's more to this," said J.D.

"Much more," said Perez. "Katherine Karen, or Katie as she was known to the family, was crazy. Caleb was born when she was in her twenties. Nobody recognized the symptoms of creeping insanity. The family just thought she was a bit quirky. But after Caleb was born, she got worse. She was sneaky, and neither her husband nor anyone else in the family knew what was going on."

"What happened to her?" J.D. asked. I thought she was getting interested in this in spite of herself.

"She was torturing Caleb," Perez said. "Doing terrible things to him. When he was about eight, she tied him down, shaved his head, and cut her initials on the back of it, just above the nape of his neck."

"K.K.K.," said J.D. "Katherine Karen Koerner. I'll be damned. The same initials carved into the back of the whale tail victims."

"Yes," Perez said simply.

"How did you know about the initials?" J.D. asked. "That was pretty closely held police information."

"Caleb told me. The family knew he was the killer. But we only found out after he was charged with embezzlement and was facing a prison sentence."

"Why didn't your family say something?" asked Parrish.

"We have a reputation in Miami that we have to uphold. Four generations of successful men and women, the cream of society. We took a huge beating when Caleb was arrested for stealing all those people's money. Many of them were our friends. But the embezzlement, while bad, was just about theft. If word had ever gotten out that Caleb had killed those poor women, it would have been assumed that we have a family gene that produces crazy people."

"So, it was known that Katie had done terrible things to Caleb," I said.

"No. The family had her admitted to a hospital in Ocala under lockdown. There were some rumors about her being mentally unstable, but the family paid a couple of doctors to let slip at cocktail parties that poor Katie had developed an inoperable and fatal brain tumor and that explained some of her eccentricities. They assured everyone who asked that she was in a treatment center in Chicago and would never come home. She would die there from the tumor. If it became known that Caleb was a serial killer, all the dirt on Katie would come out."

"But Caleb's dead," said J.D. "He couldn't be the one responsible for the murders on Longboat."

"There's more to the history, Detective," said Perez. "Hear me out."

By now, I was caught up in the story, and I think everybody in the room was as well. Jock had sat quietly through the whole thing, but I knew that prodigious brain of his was soaking it all up, dissecting it, trying to make sense out of the murders on Longboat Key that in some manner had their genesis in the tortured brain of a woman named Katie.

Perez took a deep breath. "While Katie was in the hospital in Ocala, she got pregnant. The father was a Mexican peasant who worked there as an orderly. He said the sex was consensual and she confirmed it, saying that she was in love with the man. The hospital fired the Mexican, but abortion was not an option. She was pretty far along when the pregnancy was discovered. Abortion was not legal in Florida in those days, and we are a Catholic family."

"She had a little girl who was given to the father, a man we only knew as José. He disappeared with his daughter, but apparently stayed in contact with Katie. About a year after she gave birth, she disappeared too. Apparently she just walked out of the hospital one day when no one was looking. The family suspected that José had come for her."

"What happened to them?" I asked. "Does anybody know?"

"Yes," said Perez. "Caleb was ten when the little girl was born. When he was twelve, Katie's body was found over near Naples, naked and tied to a tree beside a creek that emptied into the Gulf in the Ten Thousand Islands area. She'd been shot in the back of the head with a twenty-two caliber pistol."

"Who killed her?" asked Parrish.

"Nobody knows. The killer was never found."

"Katie's death must have caused a stir in your family's social circles," said J.D.

"No. We never identified her as Katie. We wouldn't have known about her death if José hadn't told us."

"Are you sure it was her?" I asked.

"Yes," said Perez. "José had a crime-scene picture he'd somehow filched from the Collier County Sheriff's office. He brought it to us, along with his daughter whom they'd named Mariah. The picture clearly showed Katie, naked and tied to a tree."

"He brought his daughter?" asked J.D.

"Yes. The child was only about two years old, but the father wanted us to know that Katie was dead and that the child was fine. He left the picture and somehow Caleb found it. We didn't see Mariah or her father again for another eight years."

"Where did they go?" I asked, getting more and more caught up in this strange tale.

"They were migrants," said Perez, "working the fields up and down the country, never staying in one place very long."

"But they came back to see you," I said.

"Yes. When Mariah was ten, she and her father showed up at James

Picket's doorstep. Caleb was twenty that year and a student at the University of Florida up in Gainesville. José told James that he was in trouble. Somehow, he'd gotten crosswise with some very bad people who were involved in smuggling drugs. He had to run, he said, and he couldn't take Mariah with him. He was afraid that the smugglers would kill Mariah if they caught up with him. He asked James to take her in."

"James was willing to do that?" I asked. "After everything Katie had put him through?"

"He was a good man," Perez said, "and Mariah needed a home. Our family took her in and when Caleb graduated and came back to Miami, he and Mariah became inseparable. She was wild. She had very little education and Spanish was her first language. None of our family spoke it, so sometimes the communication was a little strained. But Mariah was a quick study. She'd had some schooling in the migrant camps and had a rudimentary understanding of English. She mastered it quickly and did well in school."

"What happened to José?" I asked.

"Nobody knows," said Perez. "We never heard from him again."

"Where is Mariah now?" J.D. asked.

"She got into some trouble in high school. Started hanging around with the wrong crowd. She hooked up with a Puerto Rican thug and pulled away from the family. Caleb was the only one who kept in touch. Then the thug got killed in a shoot-out with the police, and Mariah came back to the family. Well, actually, she came back to live with Caleb."

"Don't tell me there was a little incest going on there," I said.

"No, not at all," said Perez. "Caleb was gay."

"So what happened with Mariah?" asked J.D.

Perez shrugged. "Her boyfriend came back from the dead," he said. "A couple of years after she thought he'd been killed by the police, he showed back up. He had moved up in the world and now was running a fairly large drug operation. He got Caleb involved in laundering some of his money, and Caleb got greedy. He'd done well as a stockbroker and was building quite a clientele. Unfortunately, he had set up a giant Ponzi scheme using the drug dealers' money as seed. He was careful never to short the drug lords, so he was doing well with them, but all the other people, the honest ones, who invested with him, lost their shirts."

"And this is where I came in," said J.D.

"Yes," said Perez. "You busted him and he got twenty years. You also put a stop to the whale tail murders, although you didn't know it."

"Do you know what the whale tail earring was all about?" asked J.D.

Perez smiled ruefully. "The day Katie carved her initials in Caleb's head, she was wearing sterling silver earrings fashioned like a whale tail. That was the last time Caleb ever saw his mother. Until, that is, he saw the picture of her dead and tied to a tree."

"But what I don't understand," said J.D. "is who has been trying to kill me. And why replicate the whale tail murders?"

"Mariah is behind that," Perez said.

"Mariah?" asked J.D.

"Yes. She's as crazy as her mother was. Vicious and vindictive."

"What's your involvement?" I asked.

"When Caleb was arrested on the embezzlement charge, I was working in one of the large brokerage houses at its downtown Miami branch. I had a degree in finance from the University of Florida and was making a pretty good living. Caleb was out on bail and came to see me at my condo. He told me about the murders, the money laundering, and how he'd fleeced our friends. He wanted me to take over his job with Fuentes."

"Who's Fuentes?" Jock asked, speaking up for the first time.

"Arturo Fuentes is based in San Juan, Puerto Rico, and runs drugs into Florida. He was Caleb's brother-in-law. He'd come back from the dead and married Mariah."

"So you took over things from Caleb," I said.

"Yes. Caleb had stashed away ten million dollars. It was money he'd made over and above what he was doing for the druggers. The proceeds from his Ponzi scheme. He wanted me to invest that money for him and hold it until he got out of prison. He didn't expect to get twenty years. His lawyer was telling him that he'd probably have to do four or five. Nobody counted on the wrath of all the old money in Miami coming down on him. The judge gave him the full twenty with no chance of parole."

There was a knock on the door and the deputy marshal we'd met when we arrived stuck his head in the door. "Sorry, Mr. Parrish, but we have to feed the prisoner."

Parrish looked at his watch. "It's almost one," he said. "I didn't real-ize the time was getting by. We'll go get some lunch and be back in an hour."

"That'll work," said the deputy marshal. "He'll be here when you get back."

CHAPTER SIXTY-EIGHT

Parrish drove us to a small restaurant that sat on an outparcel of a tired shopping center a couple of miles from the safe house. Both establishments had seen better days, but the donuts had not held up and I was hungry. I thought nobody could really screw up a hot dog, but this place proved me wrong.

An elderly waitress brought us menus and then walked to a stool in the corner and sat down. We were the only diners in the place. The waitress was probably a retiree who couldn't make it on her Social Security check and found herself living out her days in a trailer park and taking whatever job she could get to make ends meet.

There were a lot of people like that in Florida. I wondered if she had a husband, a family. I'd never know, but I always thought about those things when I saw the old people working at menial jobs. They seemed a little sad to me, the epitome of unrealized dreams of retirement in the sunshine. They come to Florida with high hopes and then something happens. They run out of money, or their spouses die, and their children don't want to be bothered with them. They have no home to return to in the North where they'd lived their whole lives because they'd sold the house to finance their retirements. At their ages, they have no future, and hope disappears like an errant zephyr on a still day.

Reality hits them like a sledgehammer and one day they have to go back to work, waiting tables in dismal restaurants with bad food or greeting customers at Walmart. Their nights are spent in front of the TV, their sleep interrupted by dreams of happy times long gone. Maybe the melancholy that these sad oldsters induce in me is simply the fear that I'll end up in the same place someday. No spouse, no family, no money, no future.

We nibbled at our food and talked about what we'd learned. "Perez is a strange fellow," said Parrish.

"I wonder about a guy like him," J.D. said. "It seemed important for him to establish his bona fides, give us a sense that he came from a good family, whatever that is."

"I think he doesn't want to look too closely at what he is," I said. "He's caused a lot of grief and the world would probably be a little better off if he'd never been born. Is he married?"

"He was," said Parrish. "He never had any children and his wife packed it up years ago. Moved to Denver and remarried, cut all ties with the Perez family. I'm pretty sure he hasn't heard from her in years."

J.D. frowned. "I still don't know why he came after me and why he revived the whale tail killings. None of that makes sense."

"Maybe it will come together this afternoon," I said. "Jock, are you seeing any connections to the agency here?"

"Maybe. Perez said that Fuentes was killed in a drug deal and then came back to life a couple of years later. That sounds similar to what we know about Escondido. If we can tie Fuentes and Escondido together, that print we found on the flap of one of the envelopes sent to Cantreras will be a pretty good indication that it was Fuentes who ordered the hit on Gene Alexander."

"That seems like a mighty big coincidence," I said. "Fuentes is involved in trying to kill J.D. and then just happens to get involved in the killing of a man on Longboat Key who is not related in any way to the whale tail murders or the grudge against J.D."

Jock cocked his finger and pointed it at me. "Bingo, podna. That's too neat a package. We're missing something."

"Is somebody setting this whole thing up?" I asked. "Pointing the agency at Fuentes, when all he's guilty of is trying to murder J.D."

"Did you say 'all,' Matt?" J.D. asked. "*All* he's guilty of is trying to murder me? Nothing important or anything like that." She was smiling.

"You know what I mean, precious."

She rolled her eyes.

"I don't want to break this up," said Parrish, "but we've got a lot more to get out of Perez. You guys ready to start back?"

We finished our drinks and left the restaurant. I put a generous tip on the table for the waitress who probably needed the money and who was not responsible for the quality of the food.

CHAPTER SIXTY-NINE

We were back in the windowless room. Perez stood and said, "How was your lunch?"

"Sit down and tell me why Mariah wanted me dead," said J.D. She wasn't interested in pleasantries.

"Mariah is of the opinion that you knew that Caleb was the so-called whale tail killer. She was afraid that you would eventually tell somebody and word would get back to Miami and ruin the family name."

"Let's see," I said. "Your family includes one crazy woman who abused her son who became an embezzler and a serial killer. She had a daughter who married a drug lord and is crazy herself and you're a money launderer for the cartels. How much of that good name can possibly be left?"

Perez smiled. "I admit there's not much left of the family. Most of them have long since moved away from South Florida and those of us who are left are not exactly considered top drawer. But Mariah doesn't understand that. She seems consumed with the idea that the family name has to be protected. And then there was the thirty million dollars."

"What thirty million?" asked J.D.

"Well, it's not exactly thirty million," Perez said.

"Tell me about the money," said J.D., steel in her voice.

"Just before his death, when he knew he only had a few days to live, Caleb told Mariah that he had given me ten million dollars for safekeeping. He also told her the ten million had grown to thirty million."

"Had it?" J.D. asked.

"No. It was actually about five million, but I'd given Caleb reports over the years that showed the money was growing. I was afraid to tell him I'd lost a lot of it."

"What were you planning to do when he got out of prison?" asked J.D.

"Run. I've got the five million in secret bank accounts placed around the world."

"So Mariah wanted the money and you didn't have it."

"That's about the size of it."

"Why didn't you just run when Caleb died?" I asked.

"Things weren't in place yet. I thought I had twenty years, but he died years before he was supposed to be released. I had to scramble to get all the little pieces put together, get set up so that I could get the money out of the banks without any traces that would lead to me, set up my getaway house. There were just some things I hadn't done. Caleb was diagnosed with a glioblastoma about a month before his death. No chance of survival. He chose to do nothing to prolong his life by a few months. I had to stall Mariah until my plans were ready."

"How did you do that?" asked J.D.

"I knew Caleb planned to kill you when he got out of prison. He blamed you for the time he'd spent in custody. Mariah knew about his desire to take you out. She told Caleb when he was diagnosed that if he wanted you dead, he had to come up with a plan to have you killed after he died. The money was the key, so I convinced him to tell Mariah that she wouldn't get the money until you were dead. I figured that'd give me time to get the hell out of here."

"Weren't you afraid that Mariah wouldn't go along?" I asked. "That she'd just demand the money right away?"

"Sure," Perez said, "but I had a plan for that, too. By the time Mariah got you killed, I'd be gone."

"What if she decided she wanted the money without killing me?" J.D. asked.

"The only way Mariah could get the money was through me. I told her that I had it set up so that if something happened to me, the money would disappear. If I died of natural causes, the money could be retrieved by using bank codes that would be sent to her by a lawyer in another state ninety days after my death and after an autopsy had been completed by a pathologist of the lawyer's choosing. I'd hoped that she would decide that the ninety-day window was too much even if she managed to kill me and make it look like a natural death."

"She could have tortured you into telling," I said.

"I convinced her that I had a weak heart. I told her that as part of the deception so that she didn't have to worry that if I did die of natural causes the money would disappear. I thought it would also give her the idea that torture of any sort might kill me. I figured she would think she could get the money more quickly by killing Detective Duncan. I planned to be gone by the time that happened."

"So," J.D. said, "I was sort of the staked goat that would draw Mariah and give you time to get away."

"That's about it," said Perez.

"You're some piece of work, Perez," J.D. said. "I should have left you to the bastards in the jail. Tell me how you went about trying to kill me."

"Caleb had a friend, a longtime cellmate named Jeff Worthington. Caleb said he was one of the smartest men he'd ever met. He made a deal with Worthington to follow up and kill you. He told Worthington all the details of the whale tail murders. Caleb said Worthington was a natural killer. He liked the power the kill gave him. I was to fund the operation with Caleb's money and then give Worthington two million dollars when you were dead."

"Who was working with him?" asked J.D.

"He had three of his buddies from prison."

"What are their names?" J.D. asked.

"Qualman, Bagby, and Steiffel."

"Qualman and Bagby are dead," said J.D. "What happened to Steiffel?"

"He's dead too," said Perez. "Worthington killed him and dropped him in the Gulf of Mexico."

"When?"

"Right after they tried to kill you on that island just north of Longboat Key."

"Leffis Key on Anna Maria Island," J.D. said, her tone flat.

"Yes. That's it."

"Where's Worthington now?" I asked.

"I don't know," said Perez. "I was trying to reach him yesterday when the DEA showed up at my office."

"He wasn't much of a lawyer," I said.

"No, but it worked for a few days. I thought we might have to use him to get to some of our idiots if they got caught. I was pretty sure at least two or three of them would be arrested before we concluded our operation. I was just trying to cover all the bases and it worked. If we hadn't set him up as a lawyer, he wouldn't have been able to get the drugs into the jail to kill Bagby."

"What happened to the real Ben Flagler?" I asked.

"Worthington killed him. Gave the body to a gator hunter who needed some bait."

"Why the whale tail copycat?" asked J.D.

"Mariah followed through with Caleb's wishes and copied what he'd done to the women in Miami. Caleb wanted you to know that the whale tail killer was back in business and you were about to be a victim. He wanted you to live in fear for a time before you died."

"Well," said J.D., "he didn't scare me, but he managed to really piss me off."

"That wasn't the plan," said Perez, "and I didn't think the whale tail thing made a whole lot of sense. That's the reason I put a stop to it after the first two."

"Where were you going to get the two million to pay Worthington?" J.D. asked.

"I wasn't. I'd be gone before he came to collect it. I used some of the druggers' money to pay the early expenses. By the time they discovered it, I'd be long gone."

Parrish said, "With you controlling all their money, I don't understand why the cartel put a price on your head as soon as you were arrested."

Perez shrugged. "I guess they just wrote me off," he said. "They'd sacrifice the money in return for me being silenced. Purely a business decision."

"Why didn't you run before you were arrested?" asked Parrish. "You must have seen this coming."

"I thought I still had a couple of days. I would have been gone by this morning if your people hadn't arrested me yesterday."

Jock spoke up finally. "Tell me more about this guy Fuentes."

"What can I tell you?" asked Perez. "He's known as the crazy don. He's notorious for killing people in the most brutal ways. A lot of that was exaggeration."

"I've heard of him," said Jock. "Stories about the crazy don have been circulating for years. We've never had a name, just 'the crazy don.'"

"Now you have a name," said Perez. "See? I believe in living up to my end of a bargain."

"He's the one who kills his managers now and then as an object lesson," said J.D. "We always thought he was an urban legend."

"He's real," said Perez, "and he likes to torture his victims. But Mariah is the one who kills the managers. Does it for sport. Like I said, she's crazy as hell and she pretty much runs things. Fuentes is seen as the big cheese, but Mariah pulls all the strings. She's the puppeteer."

"Was Fuentes's name Escondido before he disappeared and came back from the dead?" asked Jock.

Perez looked surprised. "It was," he said. "How did you know that?"

Jock ignored the question. "Tell me about the Guatemalans," he said.

"What Guatemalans?" Perez asked.

"The ones trying to kill J.D. and Matt," Jock said.

"I don't know anything about that."

I heard a popping sound coming from the back of the house. My first thought was that someone was making popcorn, but then my brain woke up and identified the noise as gunfire. The door to our room swung open and banged against the wall. The deputy marshal named Bert was holding a pistol and beckoning us out. "Hurry," he said. "We're under assault. We need to get you out of here."

"We need our weapons," said Jock.

"They're on the table in the hall," said Bert, "help yourselves. These guys have automatic weapons."

We grabbed our pistols and ran toward the sound of gunfire. Bert stayed with Perez, put handcuffs on him and secured him to a handrail in the hall that had apparently been installed just for this purpose.

There were two other young men at the back of the house, crouched below the windows in the family room. Most of the glass panes were gone, shards littering the faded carpet. One had an M-16 rifle and the other a more modern M-4. Bullets were still coming from the rear, ricocheting about the room, embedding themselves into the walls.

"They've got us pinned down," said one of the men. "I'm Tom and this is Lloyd. We're deputy marshals."

"Anybody at the front of the house?" Jock asked.

"Bert has it," said Tom. "What about the sides of the house?" Jock asked.

"We're almost blind on the west side," said Lloyd. "Only one bedroom with a window. I checked the east side and I didn't see anybody in that house next door."

"That doesn't mean they're not there," said Jock.

"I know," said Lloyd. "How the hell did they find us?"

"I'm not real worried about that at the moment," I said. "Any idea how many of them there are?"

"Not sure," said Tom. "More than two. You can tell by the amount of fire."

Jock looked at me. "What's Special Forces doctrine for a situation like this?"

"When surrounded, attack," I said.

Tom spoke up again. "Bert called this in. We've got law enforcement on the way, but they may take a while to get out here with enough force to make a difference. The Coast Guard is getting a helicopter in the air, so we'll at least have some eyes on them soon."

"Unless that Coastie chopper is armed, it's not going to do us a whole lot of good," I said. "I don't think we can wait for a look-see from them. If we don't do something quick, we'll all going to be dead by the time the reinforcements arrive."

"Any big ideas?" asked J.D.

"Tom," I said, "do you have anything flammable here?"

"There's a five-gallon can of gasoline in the garage. We use it to fuel the lawn mower when the maintenance people come."

"How much is in it?"

"I filled it up yesterday."

"We haven't had rain in days," I said. "Those fields out there look dry as bones. The wind is blowing from the south right into the scrub. If we can set the stuff on fire, we can burn those bastards out."

"How're we going to get the gas out there?" asked J.D.

"Let me think," I said. "How far back from the house do you think the first palmettos are?"

"Probably no more than thirty feet," said J.D.

"About ten yards," I said. "I can run that in less than five seconds. Can you guys give me enough covering fire to hold them down that long?"

"Carrying the gas can?" She looked a bit incredulous.

"Yeah," I said. "Five gallons weighs less than thirty-five pounds. No big deal."

"That's a suicide mission," said J.D.

"The suicide mission is staying put in this house," I said. "How about it? Can y'all hold them for that long?"

Tom looked at J.D. "You know how to use that gun you're holding, lady?"

"I'm a police detective," J.D. said. "I was on the firing line when you were still in junior high."

"Sorry, Detective. I didn't know."

J.D. smiled at him. "It's okay, Marshal. What if we put Tom at the rear corner of the west side of the house. Think you can get there through the front door without drawing fire?"

"Yes, ma'am."

"Jock and I'll stay here and Lloyd can go to the back corner of the house on the east side. Is there a back door out of the garage?"

"Yes," said Tom. "It opens to the backyard."

"Okay," said J.D. "Tom and Lloyd can take turns with short bursts into the palmettos. Jock and I'll fire out pistols from here. That should give Matt some cover to make it to the edge of the scrub."

"Sounds like a plan," I said. "Let's do it."

But, as with many plans, we'd made a slight miscalculation. And that proved deadly.

CHAPTER SEVENTY

I was standing behind the door that led from the garage to the backyard. Gunshots were coming from the scrub, sporadically, but often. They sounded closer, as if the men had moved up, getting into position for a full-out assault on the house.

I'd found a screwdriver on what served as a workbench in the garage and had that in my right hand, holding the handle of the gas can with my left. I opened the door a crack and called as loud as I could, "Lloyd, count down from five."

I heard him begin the count and I stabbed the bottom of the gas can with the screwdriver, making a hole large enough for the gas to pour out. Lloyd's count ended and he fired a short burst into the scrub. As soon as he let up, I heard Tom firing from the other end of the house. Jock and J.D. also began firing.

I headed toward the palmettos at a dead run, or at least as fast as I could go while holding the can and bending over at a forty-five-degree angle. I reached the scrub and dove to a stop at the edge, the gas can beside me. I began to crawl along the edge of the scrub, emptying the can as I moved along. The firing from the house continued. Nothing was coming from the scrub. I guessed that maybe fifteen seconds had elapsed since I'd left the cover of the garage. The can was empty. It was time to go back.

I waved toward the house, signaling my intention to make my way back. The bursts of fire from the house started up again, and I began to run, full tilt this time, not worrying about being seen. I could make the house in under three seconds, and if one of the bad guys raised his head and took a shot, he'd have to be awfully good or very lucky to get me.

I made it to the door and fell into the garage. The firing stopped. It was quiet for a few moments and then I heard more gunshots coming from the palmettos. I pulled out a book of matches I'd found in the kitchen, lit one, and then set the whole book on fire. I threw it onto the gas trail I'd left as I ran for the scrub. It flared up immediately and began its run toward the palmetto thicket. When the flame reached the pools of gasoline I'd left, they exploded into a wall of fire. I could hear the crackle and pop of the dry palmetto bushes catching fire and adding to the growing conflagration. The wind was still blowing from the south hard enough to push the fire rapidly north as it gathered more and more fuel from the bushes. Smoke was beginning to rise, and I could hear scurrying out in the scrub, animals and, I hoped, men running from the inferno. Screams started drifting toward us, horrible screams of men who couldn't move fast enough to outrun the flames. Somehow, I knew I'd hear those sounds in dark dreams for a long time.

I went back into the house in time to hear Perez scream. "No, Arturo, I've told them nothing."

A loud cry in Spanish came from the hall. "*Bastardo.*" Then three gunshots. I rushed to the hall to find Jock ahead of me. A man was standing over Perez, a pistol in his hand. Perez had a hole in the middle of his forehead, two others in his chest. Jock grabbed the man's arm and in a deft move twisted it making the man drop his weapon. Jock continued to bring the man's arm around his back and pushed up until I heard a pop from the region of the man's shoulder. He screamed and Jock pushed him to the floor, his knee on the man's chest, his right forearm pressing down on the man's throat.

The man struggled and Jock pushed harder on his throat, choking off the man's breath. He was gasping for breath and Jock said, "Be still and I'll let you breathe." The man dropped his arms and lay quietly, his ragged breathing the only sound coming from him.

"Mr. Escondido, I presume," said Jock. "Or do you prefer Fuentes?"

The man didn't move, made no attempt to speak.

"I want you to understand something, Mr. Fuentes," Jock said. "You're responsible for the death of a friend of mine. I haven't got much time here and I don't care how or when you die. But, I promise you, you're going to die hard if you don't start talking to me."

The man swallowed and ran his tongue over his lips. "Who are you?" he asked.

"My name isn't important. The man you had killed was named Gene Alexander. My friend. I want to know why."

"I don't know anything about this."

Jock bore down with his forearm. "Don't lie to me," he said.

"I'm not," the man squeezed out, barely able to talk.

Jock let off the pressure. "You're lying."

"No," the man said. "I know my wife was trying to have the detective killed. I don't know anything about this man named Alexander."

"Your wife, Mariah," Jock said.

Fuentes nodded.

Jock looked back at me and stood up, leaving Fuentes on the floor. By now J.D. and the deputy marshal named Bert had joined us, both holding their pistols down beside their legs, pointed at the floor, ready if needed, but not threatening. The other two deputy marshals had fanned out around the house making sure there were no more ambushes in the making.

"How did you get involved with the Guatemalans?" Jock asked.

"I've used them from time to time in my business," he said, "but not lately."

"What about a hit man named Pedro Cantreras?" Jock asked.

"I know him, but I haven't had anything to do with him in many months."

"You didn't hire him to kill Gene Alexander?"

"No. I swear."

"Did you have the Guatemalans try to kill Detective Duncan or Mr. Royal?"

"No. I haven't had anything to do with the Guatemalans in months. They proved less than trustworthy. I had no plans to ever use them again."

I was wondering how Fuentes had gotten into the house. Bert was at the front and would have seen him coming. Or should have. Unless he had moved to the back to help out there. And where the hell was the cavalry? Some sort of law enforcement should have been here by now.

"Where can we find your wife?" Jock asked.

Before he could answer, a gun roared in the narrow space of the hall-way. In a split second that seemed to last an eternity I saw red blossom on Fuentes's shirt, turned to see Bert holding his pistol and moving it away from Fuentes and toward the next closest person: me. I didn't have time to react. I'd holstered my pistol during Jock's interrogation of Fuentes. J.D. hadn't. Another explosion of gunfire and Bert dropped his gun. Blood appeared on his chest, but he was still breathing as he hit the floor.

I used my foot to push the pistol away from Bert. I kneeled beside him. He looked at me with fear in his eyes, a fear that was quickly turning to resignation as he accepted the fact that he was dying.

"Why, Bert?" I asked.

His lips turned up in a grimace. "Money," he said. "Lots of money."

"Then why kill your boss?" I asked.

"He's not my boss," he said.

"I don't understand," I said.

"Mariah paid me." He coughed once, twice, and then he slipped into oblivion.

The other deputies, Tom and Lloyd, came running into the narrow hallway, weapons drawn. "What the hell?" asked Tom. "Bert?"

"He's dead," I said.

David Parrish, who had stood quietly during the entire time we'd been in the hall, began to explain the situation to the stunned deputy U.S. mar-shals.

Jock looked at me and said, "Who the hell hired the Guatemalans?"

The answers would change our view of the world we thought we understood and make us question the dimensions of the good-evil dichotomy.

CHAPTER SEVENTY-ONE

"This thing won't be over until we find Mariah," J.D. said over a drink at Tiny's. It was late and we'd had a full day. Teams from the marshal's office, the FBI, DEA, and Miami-Dade Police Department had swarmed over the little house full of death. They found five bodies burned in the scrub that had gone up with such speed and ferocity that the men hadn't been able to escape. Their car was found on a street in the neighboring subdivision on the other side of the palmetto field.

We'd all given detailed statements to representatives of the various agencies, and the FBI plane flew us home. It was nearing ten in the evening and we were winding down at a corner high-top table in what the owner Susie Vaught called the best little bar in paradise.

"I'm sorry I had to shoot that young marshal. I know it was the right thing to do, but it's going to stay with me for a while."

"Probably forever," said Jock. "And that's what makes you one of the good guys."

"I barbequed five guys this afternoon," I said, "and I don't feel any remorse whatsoever."

"You will, podna," said Jock. "I know you too well."

"Yeah," said J.D. "You still dream about enemy soldiers you killed."

"How do we go about finding Mariah?" I asked.

"The same way we find any murderer," said J.D. "We just keep on plugging."

"Did you believe Fuentes when he said he didn't know anything about the gangbangers?" I asked Jock.

"Yeah. I think he was telling the truth. Since Perez was the handler for the operation against J.D., and he didn't know anything about the Guatemalans, I doubt that Fuentes did either."

"Mariah must be the one behind the Guatemalans," I said. "But I don't get the connection to Gene."

"Maybe," J.D. said, "Mariah was protecting her mole in Jock's agency."

"I don't think the Fuentes cartel is big enough to worry about that sort of thing," Jock said.

"Suppose," I said, "that Fuentes was moving in on some of the bigger guys. He'd sure have a leg up if he knew the inner workings of the big cartels. He could find out a lot from the agents who had infiltrated the major groups."

"True," Jock said, "but if Mariah was after information for Fuentes, why kill the agents?"

J.D. said, "Maybe Fuentes had inside information from the mole as to who these agents were and where they would be at a certain time. He could have had the agents kidnapped, tortured, and wrung dry of information, and then have them killed and dumped. Your agency would think they had been killed by the cartels they had infiltrated."

"That's a pretty good hypothesis," said Jock.

"I don't understand why Mariah hired Bert," I said. "If she were going to have Perez killed, that'd make some sense. But Bert could have taken Perez out at any time after he got to the safe house."

"Maybe," said J.D., "Mariah had Bert as a safety valve of sorts. Let Fuentes exact his revenge on Perez, but have somebody in place in case Fuentes ran into trouble. She might not have trusted him to keep his mouth shut."

"That has a certain twisted logic to it," I said. "Perez seemed to be of the opinion that Mariah ran things and that Fuentes was just the figurehead. Maybe she always considered her husband expendable."

"I'm not going to feel safe until we get all of this wrapped up," said J.D. "I'd also like to find that cretin Flagler or Worthington or whatever his name is."

"He'll turn up somewhere," Jock said.

"If we find him, that pistol could have put him on death row," said J.D.

"Now we'll never be able to use it as evidence. Jock, did you even think about that when you turned it over to your people?"

"I thought about it," said Jock. "But we were never going to be able to get a warrant to search that apartment on what we had. No warrant, no gun in evidence."

J.D. sat quietly, chewing her bottom lip. "Okay," she said finally. "You've got a good point. But we still can't do anything without the pistol."

"I can," said Jock.

"That's what I'm afraid of," said J.D. "I'm beat, guys. Time to turn in."

We paid the tab, said goodnight to Susie, and went out into the night. We drove J.D. back to her condo, and Jock and I headed for my cottage and a good night's sleep.

CHAPTER SEVENTY-TWO

I slept like a rock and didn't get out of bed until a little after seven on Thursday morning. Jock had left the house. Out for his morning run, I assumed. I made coffee and popped a pastry into the microwave. Not much of a breakfast, but I was still tired from the day before. If I'd dreamed during the night, I didn't remember it, but as I watched the coffee drip, somewhere in the far distant reaches of my mind, I heard the faint screams of men being roasted in a palmetto patch. I shook my head to clear the image and took my coffee and pastry to the patio. Maybe the morning newspaper would take my mind off the events of the previous day.

I thought about calling J.D. The mere sound of her voice would brighten up the gloom that surrounded me. Then I thought better of it. She'd had a bad day as well and would need a little time to bounce back. Knowing J.D., I was sure she'd gone back to work. That was the way she handled bad moods and rare fits of depression. She simply worked at her job and stuffed the bad feelings back in the part of her mind that she could seal off.

The first bars of *The Girl from Ipanema* jangled me out of my reverie. J.D. was on the phone. "We got Worthington," she said. "He's in jail in Tampa."

"How?"

"A Tampa PD officer found him in an abandoned building early this morning. It seems he had lived there a long time ago when the building was part of a public housing project. It was owned by the county and had been abandoned a couple of years ago."

"Was he living there?"

"No. He was searching for some papers he'd hidden there before he went to prison."

"I doubt they would be there if he left them that long ago. He's been in jail for the past fifteen years."

"He found them. He'd apparently placed them in a hole in the wall of the bedroom and then plastered it over. He said he'd put them there for safekeeping."

"What were the papers?"

"Documents, actually. There was a driver's license and a passport in the name of Geoff Woodsley. They had pictures that were probably of Worthington the way he looked before he went to prison."

"The names are similar enough," I said. "Makes it easier for him. How did Tampa PD get to you?"

"Once we figured out Flagler's real name, Bill Lester put out a bulletin to all police agencies that we were interested in Worthington for the murders on Longboat and Anna Maria. When the fingerprints came back, Tampa called us."

"That's good news. Things are starting to fall into place."

"I'm going up to Tampa to interview him. You and Jock want to go?"

"Jock's out running. I'll call him on his cell and let you know if he wants to go with you. I think I'll sit this one out."

"I'm surprised at you," she said.

"I'm tired of these assholes," I said. "I'll let you handle this one. I'll call Jock."

I called Jock and told him that J.D. was on her way to interview Worthington and she wanted to know if he wanted to join her.

"Can't do it, podna," he said. "I'm on my way to the airport to meet Dave Kendall. He's back from London and he's flying here. Said it was very important that we meet as soon as possible. Tell J.D. to be sure and follow up on the Guatemalan connection."

I called J.D. She told me she'd come by when she got back from Tampa and fill us in on what Worthington had to say. I decided to jog the beach.

My mind wandered back over the past few days as I jogged on the hard sand just above the surf. Things were coming to an end, and I marveled at the parts that fate and stupidity play in the biggest events of life. Two crazy people, Caleb and Mariah, had decided that J.D. had to die, but in the process they would take down other people whose only involvement was the happenstance of being in the wrong place at the wrong time. Nell Alexander and the prostitute from East Bradenton had been killed on a whim, picked out of the great mass of people simply because they were available when the killer needed a victim.

Fuentes was a murderer, but at least most of his kills made sense in a twisted way. He was running a business, moving and selling illegal drugs, and when somebody got in the way he had to be taken out. It was just business as usual in the dark underworld of the druggers. But in the recent murders, he'd been following his wife's orders and even though he knew they made no sense, he went along because of either his love, or more probably, his fear. Now he was dead at the hands of his wife's hireling.

Perez went along with the plan. He'd been stealing from the people for whom he had worked for years, and they were people who would think nothing of killing him if they found out about his scheme. He was taking care of his retirement plans and didn't let a little thing like murder bother him. He may have been the worst of the bunch. He set up the murders out of sheer greed. And now he was dead at the hands of the man he'd duped, his old pal Fuentes.

The three men involved directly in the murders of Nell Alexander and the prostitute and the knifing of J.D. were dead, two of them at the hands of Worthington, their buddy from the years spent in prison. Their deaths seemed fitting to me. Live by the sword, as the man said, and die by the sword.

Worthington was in jail in Tampa and would probably spend the rest of his life in prison. Perhaps his death would be hastened by the state at the end of a needle filled with the drugs used for executions. He deserved whatever he got.

Mariah was still out there somewhere. We had to assume that she would continue with her quest to kill J.D. Crazy people just don't think rationally. That's the reason they're crazy, I guess. The fact that her husband was dead and her drug business was crumbling around her wouldn't be reason to give up her plans. She'd carry on until she was in jail or dead.

The Guatemalans were a puzzle. Maybe the mole in Jock's agency had been responsible for pointing Cantreras at Gene Alexander and the fact that we found Fuentes's fingerprint on the flap of an envelope that Cantreras had saved, didn't exclude the possibility that other people used the same drop for contacting the hit man. Fuentes swore that he hadn't set up the hit on Gene, and I tended to believe him. He was too scared at the moment to lie to us. Some of the most ruthless men are cowards at heart and will do anything to escape the pain that they'd so gleefully visited on others.

So, we needed to run down the Guatemalan connection. I was pretty sure Mariah had set that up on her own. She would have known how to contact the Guatemalan gangbangers and Cantreras. I still couldn't see any reason she would have wanted Gene Alexander dead unless she was afraid he knew something about the killers or the reason for the murders. The mind of a crazy woman was beyond my ability to fathom, so we might never know, even if we eventually found her.

I wondered why the director wanted to see Jock so urgently. It was likely a problem out there in the world somewhere, some threat to the homeland that would take Jock back into the shadowy world of terrorists and assassins.

By the time I finished my run on the beach, my mind was as tired as my legs. Too much thinking can do that. I'd learned years ago when I practiced law that exercise would loosen up the parts of my brain that I used for problem solving and solutions would come to me. When it didn't work, when I finished the run as perplexed as when I started, my brain wanted to shut down, think of pleasant things or nothing at all.

I decided I'd do just that. Go home, crack a beer, and think about nothing at all. I couldn't have contemplated the news Jock would bring back from his conference with the director, news that would change my view of the world in which Jock lived, that world I had been on the periphery of for so many years. News that would seal J.D.'s decision on moving back to Miami.

CHAPTER SEVENTY-THREE

Jock's cell phone wrenched him out of a deep sleep. He was instantly awake, a habit honed by his many years of clandestine operations in some of the world's most dangerous places. The caller ID was blocked. He glanced at his bedside clock. Six o'clock. He answered on the second ring. It was his agency's director, Dave Kendall.

"Jock," he said, "I'm boarding a plane at Reagan Airport as we speak. I'm flying down to Sarasota to meet you. Can you be at Dolphin Aviation by eight?"

"I'll be there. What's up, Dave?"

"I'll tell you when I see you." The call ended.

Jock dragged himself out of bed, took a quick shower, dressed, and left Matt's cottage. He stopped at the 24-hour Starbucks on St. Armands Circle, ordered a large vanilla latte, a pastry, a *Wall Street Journal,* and a *New York Times* and took them outside to one of the cement tables that lined the sidewalk.

He lingered over his coffee, the espresso giving him the jolt of caffeine he needed. He scanned the papers, looking for some clue as to what part of the world he might be headed. He hadn't been unduly alarmed by the director's call. It wasn't the first time, and it certainly wouldn't be the last. Jock knew he was the go-to guy when the director needed an immediate response to a problem, and often the director would meet him somewhere to deliver the orders and documents or weapons that Jock would need.

Nothing jumped off the pages of the newspapers. Not that he'd really expected it to, but sometimes he could discern inklings of issues that he might be called on to address. He finished his coffee and went back into the shop. He dropped the used cup and napkins in the wastebasket and put the papers in the community rack for other people to read. By the time he pulled into the parking lot at Dolphin Aviation, Dave's jet was being waved to a parking spot on the tarmac.

Jock watched as the door of the plane opened and the stairs unfolded. He walked toward them and met the pilot coming down, the copilot right behind him. "Hey, Jock," the pilot said, "The boss is waiting for you. Mark and I are going for coffee."

Jock climbed aboard the aircraft and found the director sitting in a chair with a table in front of it. A coffeepot and cups sat on the table. Nothing else. No documents, no weapons.

"Good morning, Jock," the director said. "I hope I didn't roll you out too early."

"No problem, Dave. Good to see you. I could have come to D.C., you know."

Jock took the seat across the table from the director and poured himself a cup of coffee, took a sip. It was bitter, as if it'd been in the pot too long.

The director laughed. "Bad coffee is the government's biggest failure."

Jock smiled. "Well," he said, "it's certainly *one* of them. What's up, Dave? You didn't come down here to pass the time of day."

"No, I didn't, Jock. How long have we known each other? Twenty years?"

"That's about right."

"Have I ever withheld any information from you that I thought was pertinent to your assignment?"

"Not that I'm aware of."

"I've been a bit out of the loop for the past few days," said the director, "but my deputy brought me up to date last night."

Jock said, "Then you know everything I do."

"I haven't been honest with you, Jock. I'm sorry, and now I need to bring you up to date."

Jock was taken aback. This was not what he'd expected. His relationship with the director went back to when he was recruited into the agency.

Dave Kendall had been a middle-aged, middle-level agent then, and he was responsible for Jock's joining the agency. Dave had been in Jock's chain of command and as he rose to director, Jock always reported to Dave. In the five years that Dave had been director, Jock had reported directly to him and gotten his assignments directly from him. Jock had never been given any reason to distrust his friend and boss.

"Tell me about it, Dave."

Dave had a rueful look on his face and there was a hesitancy in his demeanor, as if he was about to deliver terrible news. He took a deep breath, let it out, and said, "I killed Gene Alexander."

"What?" asked Jock, Dave's statement hit him like a shock wave, bringing disbelief and pain. "You killed one of our own people?"

"I didn't actually kill him, but I ordered it done. Gene was the mole."

"That can't be true," said Jock. "Tell me you're kidding."

"I wish I was. In all my forty years with this agency, this was the toughest call I ever made."

"Did you have Nell killed, too?"

"No. That was one of those terrible coincidences that happens sometimes. Her murder was random."

"Tell me about Gene," said Jock.

"As you know, Gene was working with me on trying to ferret out the mole who was responsible for the deaths of our agents a few months back. He hit a dead end and we called off the investigation. But we left some traps in the computer system that would lead us to the mole if he ever started working again. Gene knew about the traps, but he didn't know about all of them. That was my decision and the tech who set it up was one of my best and totally trustworthy. Plus, he didn't know Gene."

"And you got him?"

"Yes. After the last agent was killed a couple of weeks ago, the tech and I started our damage assessment. It took a few days, but we finally figured out that Gene was the one passing out the information to the cartels. He was responsible for the death of three of our agents. That couldn't go unanswered."

"Why would Gene do something like that?"

"We think it was all about money. We were able to find some bank accounts hidden away in the Cayman Islands that belonged to him. There was a lot more money in there than he ever earned."

"I don't understand," said Jock. "Money never seemed to mean much to Gene."

"I don't think it did. But something changed. I think I know what it was."

"What?"

"His autopsy showed that he had advanced prostate cancer. He only had a few months to live. My theory is that when he found out about the cancer, he blamed the government."

"That doesn't make sense," Jock said.

"Think about it. Are you familiar with how the Veterans Afffairs is handling some of these cancers in men who served in Vietnam?"

"No."

"The docs finally determined that the medical evidence linking Agent Orange to certain cancers was so overwhelming that the VA had to do something. They came up with a matrix that essentially said if a person was in certain parts of Vietnam for a certain amount of time during a certain period of time and that person developed any one of several forms of cancer, then he or she would be entitled to benefits. In other words, the government was accepting the fact that the Agent Orange it spread over large parts of Vietnam was a carcinogen."

"Do you know when Gene was diagnosed?"

"Yes. We found the medical records in his house. It was about three months before our first agents disappeared."

"I still don't understand the money part."

"Gene was sixty years old. Nell was fifty-five. They had plans for a life together in Florida that would last twenty or thirty years. The cancer was going to put a quick end to that. I think he wanted Nell to have lots of money, sort of compensation for having to go through the rest of her life without him. I think he was just taking care of his family."

"At a great loss to other men's families."

"That's why he had to go," said Dave. "You don't kill our agents and walk away. Even if you just have a few months to live. And he could have done a lot of damage in a few months."

"Would you have had him killed if Nell was still alive?"

Dave shook his head. "I just don't know, Jock. Goddamnit, I just don't know."

The look of pain that spread across Dave's face told Jock how much the order to take Gene out had cost him. It was an unpleasant part of the director's life, the ordering of the death of anyone, but Jock was pretty sure Dave had never had to order the death of one of his own.

"When did you find out that Gene was selling information?"

"We didn't know for sure until last Wednesday. We suspected it, but couldn't nail it down until Wednesday evening. When you called me the Saturday before and told me about Nell's death, I thought it might be the cartels trying to put pressure on Gene. After you killed the murderer on Sunday night, that began to seem a little far-fetched to me."

"How did you do it?" asked Jock.

"I was aware of Cantreras and the fact that the cartels used him to kill their enemies. I knew how he was contacted. I thought we could use the same system without bothering with the middleman. In other words, I knew how the contacts were made and we simply followed the system. Cantreras thought he was dealing with Fuentes or one of the other cartel people. I told him to make Gene's death look like a suicide."

"That didn't work," said Jock.

"Yeah. I was hoping that if it appeared to be a suicide, it would be chalked up to his grief over Nell's death. I didn't want the police to begin looking into it."

"Was that your man Cantreras gave the laptop and satellite phone to?"

"Yes."

"Then why bring me to Washington last weekend over the laptop?"

"The man I had pick up the computer from Cantreras didn't turn up in Tampa when he was supposed to on Friday night. I needed you to find that laptop. You were doing a good job of finding people and I didn't want to stop you. I figured if you found Cantreras, you'd find the laptop."

"And why didn't you tell me about Gene?"

"I'm sorry, Jock. I knew you and Gene had a history. I was afraid your sense of loyalty to him might make you less inclined to help with the laptop. I was afraid you'd be so pissed, you'd quit the agency. And then I had an emergency in London and had to let my deputy take the lead on what was going on down here. If I'd been in D.C., I might have been able to keep you from getting involved in all the crap since Monday."

"Then why tell me now?"

"Last night, I read the statements you gave to the federal people after the mess yesterday. I knew you were not going to give up on the connection between the whale tail murders and Gene's. I wanted you to be satisfied that the one who ordered Gene's death wasn't still at large."

Jock was quiet for a moment. "So the laptop is still missing?"

"No. It turned up Sunday afternoon."

"How?"

"The agent I sent to retrieve the laptop got his signals crossed. He thought he was supposed to deliver the damn thing to me in D.C. He couldn't get a flight out of Sarasota until Saturday, and when he got to Washington, he went home and turned off his phones. We finally found him Sunday afternoon and dragged his ass in. He said he didn't understand that there was any urgency in getting the laptop back to the agency."

"Come on, Dave. That sounds like the Keystone Kops."

"I'll admit it wasn't our finest hour."

"And the guy who had the laptop?"

"He's no longer with the agency."

"That's it? You just fired him?"

Dave laughed. "I wanted to have him executed," he said, "but our lawyers kept telling me some crap about due process."

"Why didn't you tell me you'd found the laptop when I called on Sunday afternoon?"

"You told me you were moving on Cantreras. I figured I'd let events take their course. I wanted him and we'd lost him. I knew if you got him, I'd have my crack at him."

"But he was your man."

"No. He was just a contract killer I hired because I could never ask one of our agents to take out one of our own."

"Why do you want him now?"

"I thought he might have some information about the money flowing from the cartels to the terrorists. I told him to stay in the Sarasota area on the pretense that I might have more work for him. I thought he'd be easier to find that way. And he was expendable. I didn't want his actions to ever be traced back to the agency."

"Did he know anything about the money trail?"

"No, as it turned out."

"Where is he now?"

"Where he can never do harm to anyone else."

Jock knew not to follow up on that. Cantreras was either in some supermax prison or a grave. It didn't really make any difference to Jock, and he didn't have the need to know.

"Were you responsible for the Guatemalan gangbangers trying to kill Matt and J.D.?"

"No. I think that was some sort of coincidence."

"Dave," Jock said, "you and I have known each other a long time, and I've put my life in your hands time after time. I trust you implicitly, but there sure are a lot of coincidences popping up here."

"Jock, listen to me. You know that the agency never, ever messes with our people's family members. Never, not even once in all the years I've been with this agency."

"I know that, Dave. But still—"

"Don't you think I know Matt is your family? I've given him complete clearance to know everything you know. I did that years ago so that he would have the resources to pull you back from the brink when you finish a mission. To see you through the cleansing times."

"Why am I not surprised that you know about that?"

"Not from Matt. I have to know everything about my agents. I've known for years about the times Matt has had to bring you back from the edge of insanity. If you didn't have that need, I don't know that I would have trusted you with the missions I've sent you on over the years. If you didn't need to get past what you do for your country, you'd just be your garden-variety sociopath. I don't want that kind of person within ten miles of this agency. No. I'd never put Matt in danger. And before you ask, I know Matt is close to J.D. and that makes her family too."

"I believe you, Dave. I'm just sick about Gene."

"I am too. I'm thinking it's time for me to retire. My job just dictated that I kill a friend of many years standing. I won't be able to do that again."

Jock left him then, sitting alone on the plane, staring into a cup of coffee and probably into his future, trying to divine whether he would ever be able to wash Gene's bloodstains from his mind.

CHAPTER SEVENTY-FOUR

I got back from my run on the beach, took a shower, and realized I had nothing to do. The high that I'd been on for days was ebbing away, and I knew depression would follow if I didn't find something to keep me busy. The only downside to living on an island and not having a regular job was the ennui that hovered just over the horizon. Too much downtime brought it on, and the only way to beat it back into oblivion was to get busy with something.

J.D. was suffering from the same feeling of lassitude that can overtake the unwary. She had a job, but after the fast pace of Miami she was bored. Chasing car burglars on Longboat Key did not seem as interesting as chasing killers in Miami.

I picked up a book I hadn't read and tried to lose myself in the story. It wasn't working. My mind kept wandering back to the guys burning to death in the palmetto scrub. I'd made a mistake by not going to Tampa with J.D. I might not have been much use, but at least I would have been kept busy.

Jock called at noon. "Long meeting," I said.

"Not really. I've been sitting on the beach at Lido drinking coffee and doing some thinking. Is J.D. back from Tampa?"

"Don't know. I haven't heard from her."

"I need to talk to you both. At the same time. Can we get together this afternoon?"

"I don't see why not. What's up?"

"I'll tell you when I see you."

"Are you off on another assignment?"

"No. Dave just needed to tell me some things that I want to bring you and J.D. in on."

"I'll call her cell and get back to you," I said.

"Thanks, podna."

I called J.D. She was on her way back to the key. "I'm in downtown Bradenton. I should be on the island in about thirty minutes. The traffic is getting worse."

"Any luck with Worthington?" I asked.

"No. He lawyered up. Not saying a word."

"Can you come by the house?" I asked. "Jock needs to talk to both of us."

"I'll be there. Have you guys had lunch?"

"No."

"I'll stop by José's and bring some Cuban sandwiches."

I called Jock and he said he'd be at my house within the hour.

When Jock arrived, J.D. and I were setting out the sandwiches and drinks on the dining room table. He looked troubled. "You okay, Jock?" I asked.

"No. Something's come up that you two need to know about. J.D., do I still have your word that nothing goes any further than this room?"

"Unless it has to do with my cases."

"This does. It'll solve one of your cases, but I can't tell you without your promise of confidentiality."

"Here we go again, Jock," she said. "You're putting me in a tough spot."

"This is nothing, J.D. It gets worse."

"Give me a hint," she said.

"I can solve a murder for you, but you won't be able to do anything about it. You won't be able to arrest the murderer. On the other hand, if you spend years and lots of resources on finding out who the murderer is, you still won't be able to do anything about it."

"That sounds very mysterious. Why won't I be able to bring the murderer in? Is he dead?"

"No, he's not dead. But trust me on this, J.D. I give you my word that what I'm telling you is the truth. Your investigation might as well stop right here. It's not going anywhere. All you can do is turn over rocks that are better left in place."

"I don't get this, Jock," she said. "Are you telling me that if I don't quit, I'll find out stuff I don't want to know?"

"I'm telling you it's an issue of national security. If I tell you, you'll know stuff you'd rather not know, but at least, with your promise of secrecy, the information will not endanger good people who are trying to protect this country."

She was quiet for a moment, a pensive look on her face. "I need to talk to the chief," she said, finally. "I'll be right back."

J.D. went out to the patio and closed the sliding glass door. I watched her pull out her cell phone, tap in a number, and engage somebody in conversation. It looked to me as if a heated discussion was taking place, but I could have been wrong. In a few minutes, she closed the phone and returned to the dining room, sat, took a bite of a sandwich, a swallow of her Diet Coke, and said, "I've cleared it with the chief. You have my word. Nothing goes out of this room."

"Not even to the chief?" Jock asked.

"Not even."

"What did Bill say?" I asked.

"He said he didn't want to be hearing from the president again, and if we couldn't ever arrest the murderer, it wouldn't make much difference what Jock told me. At least we'd be able to close the case."

"There is a way to do that," said Jock. "This is about the Gene Alexander murder."

"I figured as much," said J.D.

"We know that Cantreras killed him. You can file a report that all evidence leads to that conclusion, but that Cantreras has disappeared."

"You're sure he murdered Gene?" asked J.D.

"I'm certain."

"What if he turns up, arrested for some other reason, somewhere else? All I have is your word that he's the killer. That's good enough for me, but it's not evidence."

"Cantreras will never show up anywhere," said Jock. "I promise."

"Okay," said J.D.

"Cantreras killed Gene Alexander," Jock said, "but he did it on orders from my agency. Director Dave Kendall, to be specific."

"Christ," I said, letting out a breath I didn't know I'd been holding in.

"My God," said J.D. "And he's supposed to just get away with that?"

"It had to be done," said Jock. "The mole Dave and Gene had been looking for turned out to be Gene."

"Why didn't you just arrest him?" asked J.D., her voice a little high, incredulous.

"It doesn't work that way," said Jock.

"Why not?" asked J.D. "This is still America."

"There have to be sacrifices for the greater good," said Jock.

"Don't give me that crap," said J.D. "That's the same excuse every tyrant since the beginning of time has used."

"We're not tyrants, J.D." said Jock, a note of sadness creeping into his voice. "We're trying to hold the tyrants at bay."

"By using their tactics," said J.D. "Where's the morality in that?"

"There's no morality in these situations," said Jock. "There's just necessity."

"How about expedience?" she asked.

"That, too," said Jock. "I can't excuse what we do. I can only hope that it's right under the circumstances."

J.D. frowned. "If you base morality on circumstances, you really don't have a moral code. If it's subject to change from time to time, it's nothing."

"Sometimes," said Jock, "the immoral thing is the right thing to do."

"That's pure sophistry," said J.D. "Situational ethics."

"How about the three agents whose deaths Gene was responsible for?" asked Jock, a little more heatedly. "What about their families?"

"They're not the issue here," J.D. said. "The murder of Gene Alexander is."

"I'm sick about this, J.D.," said Jock, "and so is the director. Gene was a friend, a man I trusted with my life. I'm sick that he turned out to be a snake. I'm sick that three of our agents died horrible deaths because of him, and I'm sick that I have to live with the memory of the men I've killed. But I have always operated with a higher goal in mind, the security of our country."

"I'm sorry, Jock," J.D. said. "I know you are a moral man. I didn't mean to imply that you weren't. I'm glad we have people like you, and I guess in some ways, I'm one of you. I killed a man yesterday. It had to be done to protect people I care about, you and Matt. But that rationale doesn't take away the fact that I killed a man, not for the first time, and that I'll have to live with that. But what I did wasn't murder."

"What would you call it?" asked Jock.

"Self-defense."

"But you killed Bert because he was about to shoot me, not you."

"He would've gotten around to me."

"But you shot him to keep me alive," said Jock. "How is that different from Dave having Gene killed to protect the lives of our agents?"

She was quiet for a moment or two, mulling over Jock's points. "I didn't just decree Bert's death," she said. "I acted in the emergency situation that he created. How does your director have the right to make the decision as to who dies?"

"An executive order from the president."

"That might make it legal," said J.D., "and that's questionable, but that doesn't make it right."

"We're back at the beginning of the argument, J.D. This isn't getting us anywhere. Dave had to order Gene's death. It was the only way to ensure that our agents wouldn't be killed."

"So Dave just utters a fatal decree," she said, "and Gene dies."

"Let me tell you everything Dave Kendall told me this morning," said Jock.

When Jock finished, there was quiet in the room. It had been a sordid story, a story of life and duty and tragedy and despair and, finally, treachery, torture, and murder.

"God, Jock," said J.D. "how do you do it?"

Jock shook his head and said nothing. Our sandwiches had grown cold during Jock's recitation, but I didn't think any of us had an appetite after what we'd heard.

"What now?" I asked. "We know everything except where Mariah is. We have to find her before this thing is over."

"We keep looking," said J.D. as she got up from the table. "I've got to write a report." She turned and walked out the front door.

CHAPTER SEVENTY-FIVE

Jock got a call from Dave Kendall late that afternoon and left immediately for Tampa. He would spend the night in an airport hotel and leave early the next morning for Houston. He had a new assignment. "Back to the jungle, podna," he said as he hugged me goodbye. "See you soon."

"Be careful, Jock," I said. "Come back whole."

My day had started with a feeling of lassitude and was ending in agitation. I took a beer to the patio and sat quietly, watching the darkness unfold and slowly work its way over the key. I was worried about Jock. Gene's death, or at least the necessity of it as decreed by an agency to which he had given his life, had rattled him in a way I had not seen before. I worried he might lose focus, and I knew that even a small amount of distraction could prove fatal in the violent environment in which he worked.

J.D.'s reaction to Jock's disclosure that the order for Gene's murder had come from an arm of her own government was one of disgust. I knew her well, and I knew that she would understand the necessity of the director's actions, but she would never be able to reconcile them with her innate sense of justice. She had left the turmoil of Miami for the relative peace of Longboat Key and found herself enmeshed in the actions of a governmental agency that seemed unbounded by the normal rules of civilized behavior. At least in Miami, there had been an order of sorts in the discord created by the criminal elements. Their actions didn't always make sense, but at least she knew that at the root of whatever evil they perpetrated on the city, there was always money. There was a certain symmetry to criminality that was absent in the world of the terrorist who killed merely for the shock murder always generated.

I was not unaware that when J.D. left, she hadn't muttered the usual pleasantries. No promise to "see you later" or "I'll call" or even a "good-bye." She was angry at the uselessness of the murders on Longboat, at the sheer lunacy of the attempts on her life, at Jock and everything he represented, and maybe even at me for being Jock's friend.

I'd have to give her time to wind down, see if she'd call me or stop by. If I didn't hear from her soon, I'd call her. Probably the next day. If that was too soon, the hell with it. I went for another beer and thought some more.

There was nothing I could do if she chose to leave the island. That would be her decision, and I'd have to live with the emptiness, kiss a phase of my life goodbye, and move on. Not a pleasant thought, but I knew I'd survive and I knew I'd always wonder about the what-ifs. Over the years of the future, thoughts of J.D. would bring smiles and some pain, but the pain would diminish over time, leaving only the good memories. It was the way of human nature. Perhaps it was time for me to tell her that I loved her. If she left, at least she'd take that knowledge with her.

The evening wore on, and I thought myself through an entire six-pack and went to bed without reaching any conclusions, other than I'd probably have a headache in the morning.

CHAPTER SEVENTY-SIX

I awoke a little before eight the next morning, Friday. I showered, shaved, dressed, and drove to the Blue Dolphin. I sat at the end of the counter and read the morning newspaper. I finished off three eggs, bacon, grits, toast, two cups of coffee, and two Tylenol. I was starting to feel a little better. Damn beer.

I walked to my car and called J.D. I didn't like the way she'd left my house the day before. I'd square it with her somehow. The phone rang twice and a computer-generated voice said, "I'm sorry, but that number has been disconnected at the customer's request."

I looked at my phone. I'd used the speed dial feature. J.D.'s number was two, right after the number one with the preprogrammed voice mail. I tried again. Got the same message.

I drove the block to the police station, parked, and went into the reception area. Iva was behind the desk. "Morning, Matt," she said.

"Good morning, beautiful," I said, sounding a lot more cheerful than I felt. "Is J.D. in?"

"No, but the chief wants to see you. Said if you dropped by to send you back."

She buzzed me through the door leading to the back of the station. I walked down the corridor and stopped at Chief Bill Lester's office. He looked up and said, "Come on in, Matt."

"What's up, Bill?"

"J.D.'s gone."

"Gone?"

"Afraid so."

"What do you mean, gone?"

"She left the police department and the island." He handed me an envelope. "She said to give you this. Said you'd be here as soon as you realized her phone was no longer working."

I was stunned. J.D. gone? "Gone where? When?"

"She left last night after she turned in all the paperwork from the murders. Came by my house to turn in her resignation. I talked her out of that. Told her she could have a leave of absence, but only until the end of the year."

"Where did she go, Bill?"

"I don't know. She wouldn't say. Said she had a lot of thinking to do about her future. Maybe she said something in the letter."

"She brought this to your house?"

"No. As she was leaving my house, she said she was going to write you a note and leave it on my desk last night. I found it when I came in this morning."

I looked at the envelope. My name was written across the front of it in her neat and very recognizable handwriting, each cursive letter perfectly formed. Above my name were block letters spelling out "PERSONAL."

"Did she give you any reason for leaving, Bill?"

"Nothing, other than that she had to do some thinking."

"She's had a bad time of it the last couple of weeks," I said. "And Mariah Fuentes is still out there, probably still trying to kill J.D."

"Mariah didn't run her off. She's got more guts than that."

"I know. Maybe too much in the way of guts. But these last two weeks have taken their toll."

"Did she say anything to you?" Bill asked. "Anything that would lead you to believe she would just up and leave?"

"Nothing. I know she's been a little bored lately and had even been thinking about going back to Miami. But I thought she just had a little case of island fever and she'd get over it."

"Apparently, she didn't."

"You've got a small force, Bill. How are you going to handle her absence?"

"I'm going to use Steve Carey as our 'sort of' detective and Bob Snead said he'd come in if I needed help on the patrol side." Snead had recently retired from the force and lived in the village.

"Matt, I know she's a lot more than just a friend to you. But give her some space. Don't go looking for her."

"I won't try to find her, but if you hear from her, tell her I'd appreciate a phone call."

"I'll do it, Matt. Call me if you need somebody to drink beer with."

I nodded, and left the station.

I drove to Coquina Beach at the southern tip of Anna Maria Island. I sat on the sand and watched the sea wash shyly onto the beach, little ripples of turquoise water that was the Gulf of Mexico's idea of surf. I felt very alone. My lawyer brain told me that I had to talk to J.D., argue with her, point out the weaknesses in her resolve to leave, if that's what it was. I would tell her more about my feelings for her, bare my shriveled soul, even beg her to stay.

But the more rational side of my brain told me that was a fool's errand. J.D. had to work it out for herself. If she were to stay on the island, it had to be her decision. If she wanted me in her life as more than a friend, she had to make that choice. My life was on Longboat Key. She would only become part of that life if she were ready to commit to living on the island.

I wasn't making a choice between J.D. and Longboat Key. And I didn't think J.D. should try to make a decision between me and Miami. Love of a good woman was part of life, but so were so many other parts to it. If I chose to leave my life on Longboat and try to build another one solely on love, I would fail and the love would die.

I pulled the letter out of my pocket, read the envelope again, put it on my lap, and watched the sea. The beach was filling with families spending the day together, children romping in the surf, dads cooking on grills, moms calling to the children to stay in the shallows.

I thought about the elderly waitress in the dim little restaurant near the safe house in Miami and wondered what she was doing. Life could turn into a lonely existence without warning. One day you are surrounded by the people you love and the next day they're gone.

I mentally kicked myself. I'm not above self-pity, but that is one of several of my traits that I despise. I opened the letter. It was in her handwriting and as I read, I could hear her voice.

Dear Matt,

Please try not to be angry with me. I know I'm running away and I know that I'm causing you some pain by doing so. But, I'm leaving because I'm afraid I'll cause you more pain by staying.

I tendered my resignation to Bill Lester earlier this evening, and he asked why I wanted to leave. All I could tell him was that I needed to do some thinking about where my life is headed. He suggested that I use some vacation time and the sick leave I'm entitled to from the stabbing and he would grant me a leave of absence for the rest of the time. He gave me until the end of this year to make a decision as to whether I wanted to keep my job. So I have a deadline, and that's good. It does tend to focus one's thoughts.

I'm not sure where I'm going, but I have some money saved and I'll be able to take care of myself for the time I have, and then some. Please don't try to find me. Give me the gift of time to sort all this out.

I love you, Matt. There, I've said it. Does that change things for us? It shouldn't. I have to make my decisions on the terms I set, and the question of whether your feelings are as deep as mine isn't a part of the equation. But, my feelings for you, well, they color everything, don't they?

I am deeply troubled by Jock's disclosures of earlier today. It upsets my entire belief system about justice and what I do every day when I put on the badge. Jock is your family, and if our relationship ripens, he will become part of my family. I'm not sure how I'm going to handle that. I'm trying to convince myself that Jock's a soldier, doing what soldiers do, and there is honor in that. I think that is probably what he is, an honorable soldier doing his duty, and I'll either come to accept it or I won't.

I would never ask you to make a choice between Jock and me. If I cannot put his profession aside and love him for the gentle man I know him to be, then I will choose neither of you. I will simply slip quietly out of your life. Please don't ever tell Jock what I've said here, because if he knew my ambiguous state of mind about him, and if he thought you loved me, he would separate from both of us. I do not want that.

There are other issues that I wrestle with. You and I have discussed my thoughts of leaving lovely Longboat Key. I would never ask you to go with me, so I know that if I want you, I'll have to stay. I also know that if I can't be happy on Longboat, I'll make your life miserable. So I have to work all that out.

And once my way is clear and my decisions made, I may find that you don't want me, and that will break my heart. But, at least, I'll know that I did my best, made my decisions, and professed my love for you. I can live with the rest of it, good or bad.

Stay safe, Matthew, and remember that whatever happens,

I love you,
J.D.

CHAPTER SEVENTY-SEVEN

As November slipped into history, the key settled back into its languid rhythms. I was unsettled, spending too much time at Tiny's and the other bars on the island. Logan was back on Longboat and spent a lot of time with me, leaving Marie to fend for herself as he made sure I wasn't drinking more than was good for me.

Jeff Worthington was released from the Hillsborough County jail on a five-hundred-dollar bond the day after his arrest. Without either the murder weapon or the testimony of Perez, the prosecutors could not prove that he'd been involved in any of the murders. He could only be charged with the unauthorized practice of law, a misdemeanor.

Worthington did not show up for his first court appearance a week after his release, and the bond was forfeited. Nobody had heard from him since. He was gone, and the state would not spend any money looking for a man charged only with a misdemeanor.

Jock made a quick appearance during the first week of December, stayed three days, and went back to the wars. On his first day, he sat me down in my living room and said, "What's going on, podna? Where's J.D.?"

I told him about her leaving, about the decisions she was trying to make. I didn't tell him about the letter. And I didn't tell him she had written that she loved me. I knew I was acting a bit like a lovesick high school kid and I was afraid if I gave any of it away to Jock or Logan, they'd think I'd slipped a gear.

"Are you in touch with her?" asked Jock.

"No. She asked me to stay clear."

"I'd like her to know that Mariah Fuentes is no longer a threat."

I was surprised. "Somebody found her?"

"I did."

"Where?"

"She was in Mexico, living with one of the jefes of a drug cartel."

"What happened?"

"She and I had a conversation," Jock said.

"And?"

"She was the one who sent the Guatemalan gangbangers after you and J.D. She said it was to teach Mr. Worthington a lesson. He wasn't moving fast enough for her. She thought if she had the gangbangers kill you, Worthington would get the message and take J.D. out. She figured that J.D. would be well guarded after the other attempts on her life and that you'd be an easy target and a grand object lesson for Worthington. One that would let him know that she had other assets and a long reach. Your death was supposed to convince Worthington that he had to move quickly on J.D. Mariah was crazy and none of what she did was the least bit rational."

"Was?"

"She died," Jock said simply.

I wasn't going to ask how. "Did you ever figure out who was paying Gene Alexander for the information he was peddling?"

"Yes. They died, too."

"You?"

"No. Dave sent some of our other guys after them. I got a chance to talk to Mariah, but that was my only involvement."

"So, you're okay?"

"I'm fine, Matt. Dave has me doing some analyst work, shuffling paper. I think he's afraid I'm not yet ready to go back to the field."

"What do you think?"

"I think Dave's right. Maybe it's time for me to give it up."

"Retire?"

"I don't know. I don't think I could be a beach bum just yet. I may see if Dave will let me continue with the paperwork. Stay out of the field."

"I'm glad to hear that. You're getting a little long in the tooth to be a field agent."

Jock was quiet for a beat. Then he smiled. "Screw you, podna."

"With Mariah out of the picture," I said, "I guess Worthington is the only one left. I wonder if he has the balls to take another swing at J.D."

"He won't," said Jock.

"Why do you say that?"

"The day I left here, I went to Tampa and took care of him."

"Took care of him?" I asked.

"Yes. Dave told me on the phone that he was being released that evening. I met him when he came out of the jail."

"And what do you mean, you took care of him?"

"He won't ever bother J.D. again. Or anyone else. Ever."

I let it go then.

CHAPTER SEVENTY-EIGHT

The Christmas season in Florida is a bit strange, a paradox of traditions bred in the cold north juxtaposed against the reality of life in the sun. The temperature hovered in the high sixties and low seventies. People were on the beaches working on their tans, and congratulating themselves for being wealthy enough to spend their winter in the sunshine. The condos and homes along Gulf of Mexico Drive were displays of tasteful Christmas lighting, créches and foam reindeer and Santas, their sleighs resting on green grass spread beneath palm trees. The air-conditioned bars were full of people drinking hot toddies or whatever it was they drank in the cold nights of the season back where they came from. A shopping mall on the mainland had fake snow as part of a display so that the kids could play in it and pretend they were at the North Pole.

I loved it. The air itself carried a hint of joie de vivre. Happiness permeated our lives and filtered down even to me, pushing away the dark mood I'd been in since J.D. left. I hadn't heard from her, and I assumed that I probably wouldn't. Her deadline, New Year's Eve, was a week away, and I'd been half expecting to hear from Bill Lester that he'd received her letter of resignation in the mail.

It was Christmas Eve and Logan had been busy planning his annual Christmas dinner. He invited all the singles and those couples who had no family to his home for a noontime feast, all sumptuously catered by a Sarasota restaurant.

Susie Vaught had decided to keep Tiny's open that evening until the usual closing time, which was whenever everybody finally went home. She and her husband, Captain Dave, would be at Logan's for dinner the next day.

It was nearing eight in the evening, and I was about to leave the house and join Logan and Marie and some other friends at Tiny's. My doorbell rang, probably a neighbor wanting a ride, too lazy or too tipsy to walk the four blocks to the little bar. Just part of island living, I thought as I went to the door.

The most beautiful woman I'd ever seen was standing on my stoop. Her dark hair fell to her shoulders, framing the lovely face that graced my dreams. Her lips parted in a smile so big and dazzling that I stepped back. Her emerald eyes danced with mischievous glee at the surprise she saw on my face. "Hello, Matt," J.D. said. "Remember me?"

I was dumbstruck. I didn't know how to respond, so I stood there like some schoolboy, mute with surprise. Finally, I found my voice. "You do look a little familiar," I said, "but I can't quite place you. Do come in."

She came through the door, and I closed it. I stood there, facing her, not sure what to do. She opened her arms, and I stepped into them and held her, drinking in her scent, my nose buried in her hair. "God, I've missed you," I said.

She pushed me back a little, put her hands on my cheeks, and pulled my face down to hers. Her lips brushed mine, and she pulled back again, looking at me as if trying to memorize my face. She closed her eyes and put her lips to mine, not moving, just touching for a long moment, and then she opened her lips and I felt her tongue against mine.

I drew back and looked at her, absorbing her smile, her eyes, the look of sweet contentment that had settled on her face, and I knew that my dreams of her were finally becoming reality.

She disengaged herself, patted me on the chest, and said, "Let's talk."

"We can talk in bed," I offered.

"Matt, I love you and I love this island and I want to live here forever and I want to tell you about the past six weeks. I want to tell you about how I came to understand Jock and appreciate what he does, and how much I missed you, and—"

I put my finger against her lips, hushing her, stopping the torrent of words "You've already said everything I need to know."

"But there's a lot I want to tell you."

"I love you, J.D.," I said. "We can make a life together. Here on the key. That's all I need to know for now. We've got the rest of our lives to talk."

She kissed me again, her hand at the back of my head, her other arm encircling me, pulling me close. The kiss was deeper this time, more passionate, and as it lingered, as we stood there in my living room welded together, I knew that my life was about to change, profoundly, irrevocably, and forever. And that made me a very happy man.